Life is Pants

A novel about life, not pants...

Ella Sherbet

✑

Kelly Walker
Editor

Gina Adams
Illustrator

© Copyright 2005 Ella Sherbet.
All rights reserved. No part of this publication may be reproduced, stored in a retrieval system, or transmitted, in any form or by any means, electronic, mechanical, photocopying, recording, or otherwise, without the written prior permission of the author.

Note for Librarians: A cataloguing record for this book is available from Library and Archives Canada at www.collectionscanada.ca/amicus/index-e.html
ISBN 1-4120-5570-9

PUBLISHING™

Offices in Canada, USA, Ireland and UK
This book was published *on-demand* in cooperation with Trafford Publishing. On-demand publishing is a unique process and service of making a book available for retail sale to the public taking advantage of on-demand manufacturing and Internet marketing. On-demand publishing includes promotions, retail sales, manufacturing, order fulfilment, accounting and collecting royalties on behalf of the author.

Book sales for North America and international:
Trafford Publishing, 6E–2333 Government St.,
Victoria, BC V8T 4P4 CANADA
phone 250 383 6864 (toll-free 1 888 232 4444)
fax 250 383 6804; email to orders@trafford.com
Book sales in Europe:
Trafford Publishing (UK) Limited, 9 Park End Street, 2nd Floor
Oxford, UK OX1 1HH UNITED KINGDOM
phone 44 (0)1865 722 113 (local rate 0845 230 9601)
facsimile 44 (0)1865 722 868; info.uk@trafford.com
Order online at:
trafford.com/05-0468

10 9 8 7 6 5 4 3

About the Author...

Ella Sherbet was raised in poverty and remains in poverty. She had an unhappy childhood, teenage years, twenties, and is still unhappy.

Ella is very modest about her achievements (with good reason). Although she showed signs of excellence at an early age, winning the egg and spoon race on her school sports day at the tender age of eight, sadly she has been unable to sustain such memorable achievements and has done nothing of note since.

Ella worked hard in her attempt to gain a first-class honours degree (not in English, as you'll soon find out), going so far as to offer to sleep with her year tutor to achieve this. Unfortunately she failed to make the grade (he turned her down).

Ella has been sacked from every job she has ever had, fallen out with most people she's ever met, and been useless at everything she's turned her hand to. Ella is currently unemployed (correction, unemployable).

Ella has been having counselling for most of her life, and very recently made some headway identifying a suitable career path, pinpointing the need to work in solitary confinement. She is now studying to become a Beekeeper.

This is Ella's first (and probably last) novel. It has been highly acclaimed (by her best mate who called it 'a work of fart' and who owes her fifty quid and a family-size pack of Maltesers).

Wise sayings...

'[I love men] even though they're lying, cheating scumbags.'
Gwyneth Paltrow, perceptive skinny actress

'I say to all women who are in turmoil about their weight, life is short and it's here to be lived.'
Kate Winslet, perceptive sometimes skinny actress

'Women are cursed, and men are the proof.'
'The fastest way to a man's heart is through his chest.'
Roseanne Barr, perceptive not-so-skinny actress

'Never eat more than you can lift.'
Miss Piggy, perceptive porky actress

'A Mars a day helps give you a fat arse.'
Me, perceptive, chubby and unemployed

Chapter 1

January, England
(f'ing freezing as usual)

Maybe it's because I'm a Londoner that I can't wait to leave for the exotic shores of South East Asia (sounds romantic, doesn't it!). So I'm off, to Hong Kong to be exact, former Empire of Queen Betty Windsor and home to English ladies in wide-brimmed straw hats carrying dainty parasols, and gentlemen in jaunty panamas and cream suits being ferried around bustling incense-smelling streets in rickshaws, off to afternoon green tea.

OK, so I've watched too many movies and have absolutely no idea what to expect. But I particularly like the thought of becoming waif-like from lack of food (I hate Chinese food with a vengeance, plus I'm a strict vegetarian) and having a natural tan all year round to replace the streaky orange zebra look I've mastered through years of self-tanning. No more freezing winters wrapped in sensible woollies resembling a wobbling Weeble. Yeah-hey! I'm saying goodbye to pasty flab and hello sunshine!

'Hi, Emily! We made it!'

That's my friend Clare, or 'Golf Ball Cheeks' as my worse half, James, calls her. I don't know if I'll miss hearing about her boyfriend Keith's refusal to say goodbye to his student days and finally get a job. She's got a point—he's thirty-three and has never left the education system. (I thought guys with names like Keith left school at sixteen to vandalise cars and breed spotty children?) Clare's not a happy bunny.

'What a day!' she grumbles. 'Keith scraped the car so I've had all that to deal with. He says he was tired and the lamp-post just came out of nowhere. I don't know what made him tired, seeing as he's on half-term and doing sweet FA all day.'

'I thought he was going to get a holiday job,' I say.

Clare puffs out her cheeks. Christ, I see what James means and try not to giggle.

'Keith! Ha! Nooooo! Says he hasn't got time to work with all the studying he's got to fit in. Like how many cans of beer can be humanly consumed in a day, or whether he can learn a week's football results by heart!'

I don't know how she puts up with him. As I see it, he has no redeeming qualities and an amazing amount of body hair (should I suggest he find a holiday job in a zoo in the ape pen?). They've recently got engaged and I can just imagine the vicar cocking up the wedding vows: 'Do you, Chewbacca, take Gerbil Face to be your lawfully wedded wife?' I dread to think what their kids will look like but then they could always find work in the Hammer Horror industry.

'Emily! Emily!'

'Emily, yoo-hoo!'

Ah! The Gloria Gaynor fan club has arrived: Mary, Mandy and Cheryl. Thankfully, they're not wearing their matching 'I Will Survive, You Wanker' T-shirts tonight and look like three relatively normal late twenty-/early thirty-somethings on the pull. (We sometimes refer to ourselves as 'The Jinxsters'—our relationships are jinxed so we're spinsters!)

'I'm gonna really miss ya, girl!' says Cheryl, pulling me towards her for a hug against her enormous breasts. (Strange, but true, her surname is Teets, so she's affectionately known to all as 'Tits'.) Whoa! Enough perfume on to trigger an asthma attack!

'Andy couldn't make it,' shouts Mandy over IT-Club's music which is getting into party mode. 'He's still in a big huff with me for getting preggers.'

As long as I've known Mandy she's wanted kids, and after six years of dating Andy (good looking but suffering from that exclusively male complaint 'commitophobia') and turning the big 3-0, she 'forgot' to take her pill for several months and hey presto. They both still live at home with their parents, can you believe. Andy's devastated at having to do the right thing and set up home with Mandy, leaving mummy and daddy behind. My heart bleeds.

Personally, I couldn't wait to leave home the moment I turned eighteen. In fact, my suitcases were packed and I was ready to go six years earlier but unfortunately it was against the law to leave aged twelve. I appealed to my parents to put me up for adoption (with good reason, but only my shrink gets to hear about that) or send me to an orphanage—preferably Annie's, because I knew all the songs—but, sadly, I had no option but to stay put.

Mary I love to bits. She's a truly great friend and a real laugh. It's rather ironic that her strict Catholic parents named her after the Virgin Mary, as she's a real slapper, I mean 'free spirit'. (Anyway, how could a virgin have got pregnant? It sounds really unlikely to me. Interestingly, though, I recently read in 'All Woman' magazine that there's a chance of getting pregnant through anal sex—so that must have been it then! The Virgin Mary liked it up the arse! I didn't say that! Don't send me to hell God—only ribbing! What am I like?) Mary just loves comparing the size of men's dicks—how weird is that? Seriously, she could write a book entitled 'Global Survey of Male Members'. She's got a great figure so is always surrounded by men, even though her face is somewhat 'plain', let's say. James says of her: 'Body like Baywatch, face like Crimewatch'. A bit mean, perhaps, but an accurate description.

My God, so this is my leaving party. I can't believe it! I'm not one to venture beyond Zone Two on the Tube, let alone half way around the world. I'm petrified of flying—it runs in the family. My parents told me at an early age that it's genetic and a sensible fear to have. So to date holidays for us have been to lovely English seaside towns like Blackpool, Clacton-on-Sea and Great Yarmouth, where you grapple to hold the windbreaker down as gusts sweep across the beach, blowing sand into all your crevices (saucy!), while you munch on hard-boiled eggs covered in sand and candy rock which no one really likes. I've had Anglesey and Cornwall on my must-travel-to list for years, but they've always seemed so far away.

Amazing then to think I'm now going to be living in a country that's pretty much as far away from Zone Two as it gets—no less than a thirteen-hour flight away. Yikes! I've been sweating about it for the last four months, suffering sleepless nights and horrific nightmares. Picture the scene: I'm on an aeroplane that crashes—into a mountain, the sea or my ex-boyfriend's house (preferably the latter). Or else the plane blows up, gets taken hostage, the engines fail, or I get sucked through the toilet bowl as I flush it. Miraculously, I'm often the only survivor out of hundreds of passengers, but then very unfortunately I land in shark-infested waters, so have to battle for my life once again, this time against Jaws himself. My saving grace is that he backs off when I communicate to him that I'm vegetarian and therefore pose no threat to him or any other creature, alive or dead (it's a mutual respect thing). So there you have it: my two biggest fears in one go. And it could happen (didn't I read in the newspapers recently that it did? Eek!).

Last week in desperation I went to my doctor to get some medication to calm my nerves for the flight, but the silly cow wouldn't give me anything except the advice, 'Meditate and inhale chamomile aromatherapy oil'. After all the contributions I've made to the NHS this is all I'm entitled to? The advice of a sadistic hippie?!

I try another doctor (male this time, so eyelash-fluttering goes down a treat) who takes pity on me and prescribes a huge bottle of Valium (great!). James, naughty sausage that he is, has persuaded me to let him have a couple for him and the lads to get happy on later. I think this is acceptable considering this may be our last night alive before being blown to smithereens (an early explosion might prove merciful in the end, since we'd only be flying around for hours knowing the plane could not land as the computer had gone potty, and then be left writing letters bidding farewell to our loved ones. I wouldn't have many to write). So I figure we may as well spend our last night on a high note.

Isn't that my pint-sized mate Sandie up there on the podium, moving like a Morris dancer on ecstasy? (Real name: Sandie Beech—no joke, hippie parents.) Good job she chose to sing for a living, although you'd think she might have opted for folk music with a name like that. Instead she went for R&B, belting it out at those classic R&B venues, you know, weddings, anniversaries, Bar mitzvahs. I look again. Yes, it definitely is her! Oh, and with that stunning, willowy Karen Mulder look-alike, Fern, model-cum-serial celebrity shagger. I wave frantically at them, but they're too busy to respond, trying (and succeeding admirably) to look hip and stroppy at the same time in order to please the adoring and visibly dribbling male crowd forming at their feet.

I note that hoards of James's friends have turned up while most of mine haven't. I'll never hear the end of it from James—how popular he is and how popular I'm not (opposites attract, blah, blah, blah). He doesn't understand that girls are smashing to each other until there's a bloke on the scene and then suddenly friends get put to one side.

Take my good pal Katie Thorn-Smythe (yes, really). She's besotted with her fiancé Timothy Cox (who won't allow us to call him Tim, or even Tiny Tim, strangely enough). She blew me out this evening with, 'He's been working really hard lately so we're going to have a quiet night in.' We chicks understand this. Once you've got a man under your belt (in your pants more like!) you don't need your friends. But if, God forbid, Timothy was flying on business and his plane's engine got tangled with a goose and plummeted out of the sky and they couldn't even send back any body parts, then we'd be one hundred percent there for each other and best buddies again.

On the other hand, if James was flying on business and

the pilot landed the plane on a motorway thinking it was the airport landing strip, leaving James's spine broken in several places and confining him to a wheelchair, also taking away the use of his pint-holding arm and forcing him to eat through a straw and to wear sanitary towels due to loss of bowel control, his mates down the pub would say, 'Bloody awful. I'd much rather be dead. I'm not going to visit him as I don't think he could handle it,' meaning, of course, that said mates couldn't handle it.

Even so, I'm really pissed off at the no-show from three in particular of my best friends. No doubt Tracey is getting it on with some DJ in another club (only DJs acceptable to our Trace), DeanO—fab guy who swings both ways, mainly to the right—is cooking coq-au-vin (ooh, err!) for his boyfriend Calvin, and Jane is at home crying over her latest love-rat.

I party like a wild thing and have 'Sex on the Beach' four times (gives me a sore head rather than a sore pussy, though!). Surely a mega late night will mean I'll sleep like a baby on the flight.

As it turns out, I somehow manage to OD on the Valium as, due to my nerves, I keep popping the pills to ensure I've taken enough of them to work. Consequently I spend most of the flight puking up in the aeroplane toilet bowl (but rather fortunately am not sucked through it).

Chapter 2

February, Hong Kong
(would you believe it, it's flipping cold!)

We land at Hong Kong's Chek Lap Kok Airport. I've been bracing myself for the notorious experience of weaving in and out of mountains for our landing, but a stewardess, noticing I've turned deathly pale, reassures me that that was the old airport route. Phew! James is hacked off with me for 'making myself sick' when he'd wanted us to join the mile-high club (actually he's already a gold member, but wanted me to do it so he'd gain extra points). I tell him 'next time', but he's none too happy. I reason with him that the flight was full so it was unlikely it'd have come off (quite literally), but I think he liked the idea of an audience anyway.

The new airport looks like something out of Star Wars—a cavernous space, all pristine white, metal and glass. Aren't airports usually noisy at five in the afternoon? You can't hear a pin drop—spooky! I start sweating while we wait in the immigration queue, as I mustn't tell them I'm going to be living here with my boyfriend and looking for a job, but instead that I'm here for a long holiday (just with an amazing amount of luggage).

The immigration official ahead looks stern in his official little cubicle and I don't think fluttering my eyelashes will work. James goes through ahead of me. The lucky bastard has already landed a job and got his visa sorted out. I, on the other hand, feel uncomfortably hot... Christ, am I blushing? I never normally blush, but I can feel the heat rising to my face. I'm praying they won't frog-march me into an interrogation room and make me take a lie-detector test. Don't people get thrown into prison over here for the slightest reason, never to be seen again?

'What is reason for coming in Hong Kong?' the Charlie Chan look-alike questions me in a staccato voice. I want to say, 'Oh, my gorgeous boyfriend and his big dick, of course!' but don't imagine that would go down too well.

'Work... time off work... holidays... vacation... ' Oh God, I've blown it. I'm going to be thrown into prison and get head lice and dirt under my fingernails.

'Enjoy your vacation,' the very nice immigration man says. I give him a winning smile and scarper.

At baggage reclaim my suitcase comes down the chute with a thump. What on earth have they done to it? I look in disbelief at my once beautiful case—naturally picked for its elegance rather than durability—now with its front and back pockets ripped off and black oil streaked across it. James sees my tears welling up and attempts to comfort me as only he knows how.

'Ha ha! You'll look like a real traveller now!'

Hmm.

I try to think positively and thank God I can't afford the Louis Vuitton luggage that the likes of Posh and Becks seem to carry, as I'd surely be in hysterics by now and end up in hospital with head lice and dirt under my fingernails.

We have an unbelievable amount of luggage piled high on two trolleys as James's bloody new company would only pay to ship the belongings of a wife, not a girlfriend. Pu-lease! Am I wearing a crinoline? What century do they think this is? If we were a gay couple, on the other hand, they would have paid (apparently so PC but no doubt afraid of being sued in some pansy court in Europe). I was so infuriated at this injustice that, for a millisecond, I considered a sex change before quickly realising that this was perhaps not the greatest of solutions; I don't really want any more body hair as I have to use a combine harvester on my bikini line as it is.

So I ended up having to wear at least a third of my clothes on the flight and consequently looked like your typical 'all I do is eat fried chicken and raspberry jelly doughnuts all day' American. The obese get-up did, however, provide excellent protection against the drinks trolley which the flipping stewardess banged into me four times (no doubt done deliberately as I have acne-free skin and clearly don't use a bottle of foundation with every make-up application. It must be an expensive business for her; no wonder rumour has it they sell sexual favours on board as well as aftershave and ciggies).

We had been somewhat sneaky at Heathrow Airport, breezily checking in our luggage, all weighing in right on our measly 22kg allowance (so no excess baggage charge due, yeah-hey!), while hidden just around the corner was James's mate Dave, happily minding another huge stack of our belongings and puffing on a joint. When the stewards swiftly shooed everyone onto the plane to get going, we, rather cunningly, made sure we were the last to board, making out our four large sports bags contained magazines and boiled sweets rather than 80kg of my essentials. (Well, I need all my favourite products in case I can't buy them in Hong Kong, and of course this includes a shoe collection to rival Imelda Marcos's, raggedy old teddy bears dating back to my childhood and such like. 'Hoarding rubbish' James calls it.)

All this means that our bags are incredibly heavy and I can barely move under the strain (is this like moon-walking, I wonder, or the complete opposite?). So much for all my weight-lifting at the gym, although I did only go bi-monthly and preferred to chat to whoever would listen rather than pump iron (yawn, yawn), even if it meant talking to myself (hands-free mobiles are a God-send, incidentally, as now this behaviour can fall under the guise of sanity). Then again, after seeing the purple burn marks which James and I end up with across both shoulders from the bags' straps, we might seriously contemplate entering the Iron Man competition next year, as lifting a car should be somewhere in the region of the load we shifted today.

Wowzers! We're in Hong Kong! We're in Hong Kong! We take the Airport Express rail-link to the city centre. A Government committee must have spent many weeks agonising over a suitable name for such a grand city and ended up calling it... 'Central'. Nought out of ten for effort, guys.

I can't believe the train. It arrives and departs exactly on time, is amazingly fast, scrupulously clean and even pleasant-smelling. There are no yobs in sight who try to scare (or scar) you, and staff aplenty. In fact the total opposite of the Tube. It feels like we're being whisked away on the Star Trek Enterprise, whizzing through long tunnels before entering Central Station.

The station looks like something out of Star Wars—a cavernous space, all pristine white, metal and glass. Aren't stations usually noisy at six in the evening? You can't hear a pin drop—spooky! This whole experience is becoming a little surreal—perhaps our plane did crash after all, and James and I are now actually dead, being transported to heaven...

Nope, it would appear not. We emerge from the station to the noise of furiously hooting red and white taxis on streets reeking of carbon monoxide. And there I'd been worrying that Hong Kong was just a quiet, cavernous space, all pristine white, metal and glass. In fact, it resembles Canary Wharf slightly with its tall, modern, bland office buildings disappearing up into the sky... hey, isn't this sky supposed to be blue rather than this shade of London-grey?

Ouch! A Chinese woman bumps into me with such force she nearly knocks me unconscious.

'Why don't you look where you're going!' I mutter under my breath.

'Welcome to Hong Kong!' laughs James, hailing a taxi. I notice he's flapping his hand in a rather peculiar fashion, much like he's patting a dog on the head.

'What's with the hand?' I ask.

'Everyone else is doing it like this,' he points out.

I look along the street and see several Chinese people waving their hands in this bizarre manner.

'I think they're doing Tai-Chi, James,' I say.

But it transpires that this hand-patting is in fact the far less relaxing pursuit of taxi-hailing. We manage to attract a taxi driver's attention after only a few minutes—not bad, considering in London you usually end up walking six miles home without spotting an empty cab. The taxi screeches to a halt beside us. As I reach for the handle the door opens automatically. Wow! How cool is that!

While the taxi may be hi-tech, the driving ability certainly isn't. Our driver seems to have missed his lessons on gears (we spend the entire journey in first), braking (we either bomb it along or sit at a complete standstill), and road etiquette (he's oblivious to other drivers, including those of dangerously large vehicles). James is instructing him from the back seat.

'Easy on the brakes, fella! Go on, be brave, move into second gear, you can do it! Whoa! Not a good idea to undercut a bus. Do you really have a driving licence, my man?' We both discreetly look at the driver's photo ID card on the dashboard and then at the driver—amazingly it is him and he is licensed. (Perhaps someone should tell Geri Halliwell to take her test in Hong Kong as I hear she's failed it about a dozen times back home. Back home... this is home now!)

We pull into the driveway of a building so tall I hurt my neck looking up to the top of it. Robinson Road Residence on Robinson Road—maybe I could get a job here thinking up better names for the buildings, like 'Breakneck Heights Residence'?. The taxi door opens before I reach for the handle (still cool) and the boot lid flips up automatically. Before I can say 'Robinson Road Residence' a porter gathers up all our luggage and whisks it away through a lobby that looks like something out of Star Wars—a cavernous space, all pristine white, metal and glass. Aren't lobbies usually noisy at six-thirty in the evening? You can't hear a pin drop—spooky! You'd think the porter worked for the royal family, dressed as he is in his smart navy blue uniform complete with tassels and shiny gold buttons, peaked hat and white gloves.

'Good evening to Wobinson Woad Wesidence. My name Sunny,' he introduces himself. Not the easiest of addresses to pronounce, poor guy.

We're staying with James's old school friend Peter until we find our own apartment. Full name: Peter Victor Croft, affectionately known by all as 'PVC' (whatever were his parents thinking or doing, when they named him?!).

The porter loiters for a tip and James sniggers, 'I'll give you a tip, fella: don't eat yellow snow.' This is one of James's favourite sayings and I've heard it a million times before in taxis and restaurants. Trust me to have a tight-arse boyfriend (but he does have a very cute tight arse).

Robinson Road Residence has fifty floors and a 'podium' (I've read Asians are big fans of these).

'How unsavoury to have strippers in a nice block like this,' I observe scathingly.

'It's a swimming pool area for the residents, you idiot!' laughs James.

Fortunately, although we're on the 37th floor, the lift is fast. Peter flings open his front door.

'Welcome to PVC's brothel!' he greets us.

James and I giggle (little did I know he was only half joking) and Peter sweeps us in. He's not what I expected, and is wearing nothing but puffy, bright orange tie-dyed trousers with the crotch hanging to his knees. You'd guess he was a Buddhist monk rather than a mergers and acquisitions lawyer.

The apartment reminds me of Katie and Timothy's pad in Canary Wharf—wooden floors throughout, functional Ikea-style furniture and top of the range mod cons. While Katie and Timothy overlook the River Thames, Peter has panoramic views of Hong Kong's famous mountains and harbour. James and I simultaneously drop our bags to look out and take it all in.

'I rarely look at the view,' chuckles Peter. 'I'm usually too busy pleasuring some wench in the bedroom. Mergers expert that I am.'

Right on cue a young girl (is she legal? She only looks

about fourteen!) joins us in the lounge.

'Heerlo, I'm Shandy,' she says.

Shandy is unbelievably skinny (to give you an idea, I was about her size aged seven), with legs the circumference of my wrist and a waist so tiny I can't see how she can have any internal organs. She's wearing little more than a skimpy black lacy bra top, tight hipster bootleg jeans with ripped knees (didn't rips disappear twelve-odd years ago along with Bros?), and red patent high heels (definitely 'shag me' footwear, but I guess the shiny surface saves on mirrors).

James and I make our introductions. Shandy ignores us (what a slut!—dear me, I mustn't be so quick to judge!), instead snogging Peter passionately (yuck, I can see their tongues slobbering around, and it goes on and on). The atmosphere gets rather awkward, to say the least. 'Helloooo! You're not actually alone! Your guests have just arrived from half way around the world!' I want to say but don't. Thankfully, Peter starts coughing and spluttering (probably some nasty STD) so the kissing ends. Shandy excitedly proclaims to Peter, 'I love you!' Peter responds casually, 'That's nice.'

Shandy turns to me.

'Ahh, you so beautiful,' she tells me.

I'm beginning to really like Shandy and think we may hit it off after all.

'You look just like Barbie doll!'

Hmm, isn't Barbie platinum blonde, blue-eyed, tall as a giraffe and busty? I'm the absolute total opposite. In fact, I couldn't be more different.

'Yes, yes, yes you dooo. Ahhh, she look like Barbie, Barrrrbiiiee.'

Oh well, I'd rather that comparison than the other ones I get now and again—Sarah Brightman (bulging eyes) or Liza Minnelli (in her young, slim 'Cabaret' years I hope!). James often says I look just like Audrey Hepburn (no wonder I love him) but as he's got extremely poor eyesight and is colour-blind I don't take this compliment too seriously.

Our bedroom has no curtains and looks directly into the

neighbour's lounge. I see a Chinese lady and gentleman watching TV looking straight at me. They're so close I can describe them to a T. Hmm, while having an audience during sex appeals to James, it's a total turn-off for me and I'm already getting mildly paranoid about how we'll manage to retain a modicum of privacy without curtains.

Peter calls out, 'Why don't we go grab some dinner, guys?'

I'll think about those curtains tomorrow... or maybe later tonight.

'Loads of restaurants to choose from,' Peter continues. 'Chinese—no, really!—Indian, Italian, French, Greek, Spanish, Mexican—you name it. So what do you fancy?'

'Italian,' I say.

'Tapas,' shouts James.

'Tapas it is then,' says Peter. I guess Shandy has no say in the matter either. No such thing as women's rights here, I figure. Maybe Shandy's vocabulary is limited to, 'You look like Barbie doll', or, like Barbie, she doesn't eat in order to stay pencil-lead thin. Whatever the reason for her non-participation, I'm out-voted. I imagine tapas tasting of Chinese food. A horrible thought indeed.

As we walk down the hill that leads to all the restaurants I wonder whether I'll ever wear high-heeled shoes again as the gradient is incredibly steep and I'd inevitably slip over (soft landing, though, with the size of my arse). We reach an area called SoHo, of all things (apparently the name stands for 'South of Hollywood Road'), which boasts row after row of restaurants. Glancing at a few of the menus gracing the walls, I can see Hong Kong's SoHo certainly has the exorbitant prices in common with the London equivalent, and judging by the way Shandy's dressed, its fair share of Soho-style whores strutting around, too.

We end up in a place called 'Havana'. Our table is tiny, I mean 'intimate', and the lighting dingy, correction, 'romantic'. We order a selection of starters and main courses and, thankfully, there seem to be a few vegetarian options, despite the waitress not having a clue. James and Peter start gassing about football (didn't take them long), while I try to make small talk with Shandy.

'What line of work are you in, Shandy?' Good opening gambit.

'Me helper,' she tells me.

'In a hospital or nursing home?' I ask.

'No, I work for my boss.'

Right. Change of subject methinks. 'Are you from Hong Kong?'

'No, Philippines. Very beautiful. You must go there. Go to Philippines. When will you go there? Soon?'

Mercifully the food arrives, putting an end to our painfully inane conversation, but then, annoyingly, the starters arrive at exactly the same time as the main course.

'Asian moment!' quips Peter.

Before I can say, 'Wobinson Woad Wesidence', everyone's tucking into my vegetarian dishes. Why do meat-eaters always bloody do this? Invariably I end up with a measly portion (good for my diet, though, I suppose). James rescues a few dishes for me, as on occasion, he's amazingly considerate.

The food is slightly cold but tasty enough. I note from the menu the soft drinks cost as much as a dish. Outrageous! Shandy isn't much of a talker and I'm now at a loss as to what to say to her. James and Peter are too busy discussing David Beckham's amazing tackle (I bet Posh would agree!) to notice that Shandy and I are sitting in silence.

Just to prove me wrong, James turns to us and asks, 'How are you girls getting on?'

'Ahh, she looks just like Barbie!' Shandy shouts.

This is going to be a long night.

Jet-lag. Fifty-six sheep, fifty-seven sheep. Bloody jet-lag. Two thousand and ten sheep, two thousand and eleven sheep.

'James, are you asleep?' I whisper.

'No I'm bloody not,' he groans, 'and I have to start work tomorrow—unlike you.'

We're holding hands lying in bed. I snuggle closer to him, breathing into his ear, 'I truly, madly, deeply love you, James.' Very original stuff, I know.

'That's nice,' James chuckles softly.

Hmm, I can see Peter's going to be a bad influence.

The lack of curtains means we can see that the neighbours are no longer watching TV and luckily have not got their binoculars out to get a close-up of James and me in bed. The coloured lights from the office buildings and harbour shimmer, reassuringly reminding me of London.

'Seeing as we can't sleep,' James whispers, 'we might as well have a shag.' Who said romance is dead?

He's a fantastic kisser (except when he's been eating those bloody Scotch eggs that he can't seem to get enough of. One of my motivations for coming to Hong Kong included saying goodbye to those revoltingly smelly things). James tweaks my nipples which are already erect and calling, 'Suckle me, baby!' He raises my silk nightie (well, that polyester material that looks like silk) over my head and says, 'Open wide, sexy girl!' (I swear he was a debonair gynaecologist in a past life) as he gets his nose down into my wet pussy (hopefully tasting of honey rather than fish paste) and starts eating me alive. His head bobs up and down, showing no signs of pausing for breath (excellent training for underwater swimming). Mmm, absolute bliss! I languidly stretch out my arms above my head and sigh in pleasure. Pure ecstasy. I can't wait to return the favour and clamp my lips around his deliciously thick cock.

Suddenly, I think I see movement in the Chinese couple's lounge.

'James, stop! Hey, stop! Next door are watching us!'

James gets up, totally nude with an enormous erection, and peers through the window.

'They'll see you!' I warn him.

'So let them!' is his reply. 'Anyway, I can't see anyone, darling.'

'You may not see them—especially with you being virtually blind without your contact lenses in, I want to add—but they can see you!'

The prospect of some hot sex disappears along with my pert nipples (why can't they stay like that all the time rather than becoming unattractive big pink blobs?). James huffs, clearly put out by the lost moment.

'I'm sorry, but I feel really uncomfortable without curtains,' I reason.

'Well bloody do something about it because we haven't had sex for two days!' James snaps.

I'm beginning to regret being a conscientious objector during my school Home Economics lessons, and start thinking about makeshift drapes. I discover that thinking of curtains is far more effective than counting sheep, as I quickly fall into what turns out to be a fitful sleep.

James is snoring like a dying walrus so I assume he's asleep, or pretending to be Darth Vader. The neon red digits of the clock say 6:02 a.m. (Why is it that when you sleep soundly the night goes by in a flash, yet when you can't drift off it seems like an eternity?) I creep out of bed to go and pee.

Peter's bedroom door is wide open and I can't help but notice him and Shandy totally naked and shagging for England (Hong Kong!). Christ alive, how embarrassing! I flee to the bathroom, praying they didn't see me. Fancy leaving their door wide open like that!

Crikey O'Riley, I've never seen anyone shagging (live that is. James owns the world's largest collection of porno movies). Tell a lie, I once glimpsed my parents at it when I was nine years old. I'd deliberately hidden in their wardrobe to observe through the crack of the door (viewing other cracks!) what caused all those strange grunting, clanging and whipping noises I often heard through my bedroom wall. I chickened out of seeing it through, though, and thankfully my parents where so surprised when I jumped out of their wardrobe that they were too lost for words to tell me off—for a change.

I try to pee silently and for one of the first times in my life do not flush the toilet, not wanting to alert them to my presence (yuck, think of the germs!). As a hygiene obsessive, I draw the line at not washing my hands and rinse them as thoroughly as I can under a quiet trickle of water. I make a mental note to buy a new block of soap the next day as this one looks very used indeed, and keep washing for thirty long seconds (did you know anything less than this and you may as well not bother at all?).

I tiptoe back to the safety of James's arms, convinced Peter caught a glimpse of me walking past. Sleep finally hits me like a tonne of bricks just before the alarm goes off (typical). Poor James looks knackered, and sadly not from a passionate night with me. Peter, on the other hand, is as bright as a button.

'First day at work, mate,' he says, addressing James. 'Are you scared shitless?'

'A bit nervous, mate, but nothing I can't handle. Once I win over the secretaries with my dazzling blue eyes I'll be a big hit.' And he's right. James is very cute-looking—tall, well built, with natural blond hair and ice blue eyes, a combination I imagine the Chinese secretaries will find rather unique and attractive.

'Well, you've got three minutes before the shuttle bus leaves, mate.'

James gives me a quick kiss on the lips, grabs his briefcase and charges out.

Alone with Peter I start to feel awkward. 'What time do you leave for work, Peter?' I ask, hoping it's not too obvious I hope it's soon.

'Whenever I feel like it. Help yourself to breakfast. There's not much in the fridge. I can never be bothered to go to the supermarket.'

I go back to bed for a while and wake up to an empty apartment (good!). I waddle into the kitchen, still sleepy, only to jump out of my skin, startled by the girl cleaning the floor.

'Heerlo, I'm Jodie, Peter's helper.'

Ahh, so that's what Shandy does for a living, she's a maid, I mean 'domestic helper'!

'He says leave your washing and ironing and I will do it for you, too.'

Is she for real? Or an angel of mercy sent down from heaven to wash and iron James's dirty pants, thus putting me out of my misery? I give her a few items and cringe seeing James's poo-stained pants (of course, my panties have no such thing, hee hee hee!) and sincerely hope she's seen worse. I try to make light conversation but Jodie looks at me as though I'm mad. I realize it's probably not the done thing to get matey with your maid.

I gaze out of the lounge window taking in the picturesque harbour and mountain views again, but this time in daylight. I'm feeling strangely scared of venturing out alone, thinking I may get lost and end up being kidnapped by Triads who decapitate me when they realize my parents aren't at all bothered about their ransom demand, telling them, 'Bugger off, you're blocking our phone line!'. Believe me, my parents wouldn't give a monkey's arse. They tell my three sisters, Emma, Elizabeth and Eve and me (collectively known as 'The Four Es'—a bit spooky as the bus we caught to school was the E4) that they never wanted children in the first place and still don't. It always seemed strange to us, then, why they had not just one but four kids if we were so bloody unwanted, particularly as my stupid cow of a mother is a frigging family planning doctor!

I bravely venture into the Robinson Road Residence gym for a quick workout—always a good way to dispel angst and unhappy memories. Despite the block being a bit posh, the gym's equipment could easily feature in a museum. I've never seen such antiquated facilities. They even predate the exercise bike my parents had at the foot of their bed in the 1970s which of course they never bloody used as my mother has an arse the size of Scotland and no doubt it would have been painful (or erotic?) for her to straddle the saddle, and my father is built like a prize whippet, so doesn't think he needs to exercise. Instead, they stubbed their toes on it on a daily basis, cursing each other and arguing ferociously (there was a World War III, you know. It was in my house. I lived through it and it was particularly nasty).

I park my none too perky butt (actually, it's very perky but as a recovering anorexic I see instead something like Sporty Spice when she stopped being sporty and became sedentary) on a reclining exercise bicycle, the ones you get in hospitals for people learning to walk again or recovering from heart attacks. Always take it easy when warming up, I recall my Personal Trainer saying (our partnership was a short-lived affair, but then one session did cost the same as a weekly food shop for a family of five).

A middle-aged lady who looks like the Asian equivalent of Jane Fonda sits down on the bike next to mine. She's wearing a canary-yellow thong leotard with matching headband, shiny black tights and flashy gold 'DKNY' trainers. It's uncanny how much she resembles a bumblebee. I wonder whether she's a friendly one or does she have a sting in her tail? I don't know where a tail would fit—she's so thin she must have to run around in the shower to get wet.

'Hiii there, I'm Crystal!' she trills brightly in a strong American accent.

'Nice to meet you. I'm Emily,' I reply. You've got to make an effort. 'I moved here yesterday.'

'Oh greeaattt, we can be gym buddies!'

Ahh, how lovely and friendly; have I made my first pal in Hong Kong?

'My husband travels a lot so I use the gym most days.'

Fantastic! I'm going to get sooo fit with Crystal!

'I wish I had abs like yours,' I sigh, admiring Crystal's amazingly flat six-pack stomach.

'Gee, thank you, Emily! Well, it took some help from my surgeon.'

'Oh!' squeaks out of me. I've never met anyone who's had plastic surgery, although it has to be said that we Brits don't talk about such things so openly and probably wouldn't admit to having had it.

'He's simply fantastic,' Crystal goes on. 'My husband bought me the liposuction for my last birthday. I had my eyes lifted and arms tucked for Christmas.'

Maybe socks, jellied fruit sweets and a couple of satsumas from Santa aren't so bad after all?

'Isn't it painful?' I can't help but ask.

'Nah, no worse than going to the dentist really. They knock you out, work their magic, and you wake up a little sore and bruised, that's all. Have you had any work done?'

I look at Crystal in horror. 'No, I'm only twenty-eight,' I stammer.

Crystal rolls her eyes. 'You're never too young to start, you know. Hey, my parents paid for my nose to be reshaped and breast implants for my eighteenth birthday.'

If I were Crystal I would dread Christmas and birthdays. I'm scared of general anaesthetic (what if you don't wake up?!), let alone scalpels (all that blood!) and I can't imagine having an operation for vanity's sake. A life-saving op at a stretch, perhaps. In fact, if I were Crystal I'd convert to Judaism to escape Christmas and, like Joan Collins, stop having birthdays.

After half an hour of listening to Crystal's detailed explanation as to why she decided not to make her waist smaller by removing a couple of her ribs like Cher, I try to change the subject.

'Are you originally from the States?'

'Nah, the Philippines. But I hardly know the place now. I love California too much to want to be anywhere else. I'm only here because of my husband's job, but I've told him I miss home so much I want to go back.'

'Can't he get a job in California?' I ask.

'Sure, easily, but taking the transfer really increased his package. His company pays all his tax, and for our apartment, utilities, car and chauffeur, maids, home-leave flights, rest and relaxation holidays—you name it. So I've told him he can't go back for many years. I'm hoping he'll let me live in California for most of the year and I'll just come out here to visit him. He knows it's making me real unhappy here.'

'Why don't you like it?' I enquire, hoping I won't end up feeling the same way.

'It's not California!' Crystal snaps. Hmm.

My butt is sore from the reclining exercise bike and my ears are sore from Crystal. Jodie is still cleaning the flat when I get back and I feel really guilty lazily sitting on the sofa watching TV while she's vigorously polishing the wooden floor around my feet. (Does the Queen ever feel like this, I wonder, cuddling her Corgis while one of her maids wipes up the doggie poop from the marble and gold gilt floor?)

I flick through the English-speaking channels—CNN, BBC World, Pearl, ATV World, ESPN Sports, Star Sports, sports, sports and more sports (well, it is a boy's flat). I can see I'm going to get very up to date on current affairs at this rate. Perhaps I'll end up as a contestant on a game show, winning loads of money owing to my exceptionally broad knowledge of world events. Not much on the news today, though. No news might be good news, but it won't help me as a contestant.

Pearl is showing a repeat of 'Mork and Mindy'. Spooky. I clearly remember watching this episode over fifteen years ago! It's still just as crap as it was then, and Robin Williams is as hyperactive as ever (perhaps he drinks too much orange squash?). I'm amazed the live studio audience howls with laughter, as I haven't so much as cracked a smile. Booooring!

So that leaves... sports. Football, football, more bloody football and some weird-looking men with thick-set glasses and an abundance of facial hair using a broom to sweep discs along an ice rink (they call that a sport? It looks so easy even I could do it and I'm the world's worst sports person!) I wonder whether these guys help out with the housework or leave that to their wives, preferring to sweep ice rinks rather than kitchen floors? Saaadd and booooring!

I admire the stunning harbour and mountainous landscape once again. I'll never get bored of this view! Do I dare go out and explore Hong Kong on my own? Nope, I'll wait for James to come home because the Triads may well be waiting out there for someone exactly like me, although, that said, it would spice up the news a bit on CNN and BBC World.

It's still only Day One in Hong Kong and I'm feeling a bit low and lost. I can't believe I miss my friends already, even the ones that didn't make it to my leaving do. I don't miss my sisters yet, though. I switch on Peter's computer and after twenty minutes of fiddling around I'm finally online. I hate the fuss of writing letters so emails are a total God-

Life is Pants

send in my opinion.

From:	emilygreenhk@hotmail.com
To:	hicks16@hotmail.com, katiets@abbotts-dury.com, janeheffer@yahoo.com,sandiebeech@yahoo.com, fernrocks@yahoo.com,deano@btinternet.com, mandyandandy@yahoo.com, teets@hotmail.com, mary1972@hotmail.com, clare_adair@btinternet.com
Subject:	Hallooo from Hong Kong!

Hi guys!

Miss you already!

What a journey! I nearly didn't make it here. I let James take charge of the tickets (so he'd feel manly, blah, blah, blah). Never again! We got to Stansted Airport on time but the f*cking idiot thought 17.40 was 7.40 p.m.! Men, eh? Good for nothing, apart from the occasional shag. So GBP1,300 quid down the toilet. The trolley dollies (I've got a hunch they're actually drag queens with all that make-up plastered on) reminded us our tickets were non-transferable and non-refundable. Mean minxes or what!

You know I'm scared of flying, well I told James this was an omen and I wasn't meant to go to Hong Kong with him. He went totally ballistic in this huge queue of passengers, bit me hard on the cheek (looks like a weird love bite now!) and said he'd kill me if I didn't go... so here I am! We ended up bolting down to Heathrow in the commuter traffic and jumping on board an expensive flight with BA (still chicken-crate class, though). What a frigging nightmare!

But I'm here now and the sun is shining, though it's colder than I expected—I assumed it was always hot and balmy in Hong Kong so only bought skimpy tops and shorts with me. You'd think it was the Antarctic, though, as the local Chinese are dressed in fur coats and snow boots. They look totally ridiculous—I must scan a photo to you. Apparently it's a fashion thing as this is the only time of year it's remotely possible to wear the latest winter ranges. Weirrrddd! Anyway, I haven't seen much yet as am cooped up in James's mate Peter's apartment fighting terrible jet-lag. It's on the 37th floor, way up in the smog and I've discovered I suffer from vertigo (you guys know I'm dizzy enough as it is!).

Let me know all your gossip.

Love n Hugs

Emily x

From: mary1972@hotmail.com
To: emilygreenhk@hotmail.com
Subject: R U MAD GIRLIE?

Nooo... you trusted him with the tickets? But he's a MANNNNNN! What were you thinking of?!

...and you don't need men for shagging as vibrators do the job just as well, if not better. So enlighten me, girl, what do we need them for?

Cheery bye for now

Mare :)

From: teets@hotmail.com
To: emilygreenhk@hotmail.com
Cc: mary1972@hotmail.com, mandyandandy@hotmail.com
Subject: how true...

Hey dolls, this is so true...

Man: 'Let's try changing positions tonight.'

Woman: 'Sure—you do the ironing and I'll slob out on the sofa drinking beer while burping and farting.'

Loads n toads

Tits xox

From: mandyandandy@hotmail.com
To: emilygreenhk@hotmail.com, mary1972@hotmail.com, teets@hotmail.com
Subject: how true...

Christ, lucky Andy didn't read this one before me!! But yeah, very true, very, very true.

I'm sure Andy censors my emails so be careful what you send, as I don't want him offended. I could do without his strops.

Tar very much

Mandy

From: teets@hotmail.com
To: emilygreenhk@hotmail.com, mary1972@hotmail.com, mandyandandy@hotmail.com
Subject: how true...

That joke was about Andy!!!

Better set up your own email account as there's plenty more where that came from!

Heeheehee!

Tits xox

From: mandyandandy@hotmail.com
To: emilygreenhk@hotmail.com, mary1972@hotmail.com, teets@hotmail.com
Subject: ENOUGH how true...

very funny, very very funny, hahaha

From: deano@btinternet.com
To: emilygreenhk@hotmail.com
Subject: London Life

Hello darling!

Nice to hear from you so soon.

Hope you and the hunky James are settling in well.

Big news from my end... I've had to ask Calvin to move out as he was getting way too serious too soon. Also, he kept telling me off for leaving my laundry all around the apartment and even called it a pigsty—bloody cheek! So I sent him packing back to his grotty little bed-sit in totally not trendy Tooting! No more Shad Thames living for him, little weasel!

Do you think I was a little hasty? He only moved in 9 days ago.

Oops, running late for work again as always.

The man of your dreams...

DeanO—n big sloppy kiss!

From: emilygreenhk@hotmail.com
To: deano@btinternet.com
Subject: London Life

I don't understand you, DeanO! You've been telling me for over a year you can't find a guy who wants commitment, only quick shags, and then you find a sweet guy and boot him out after a week! Calvin's right—you are a bit of a slob even if your pad is on snooty Shad Thames. Hope this helps, sweetie!

Emily x

From: deano@btinternet.com
To: emilygreenhk@hotmail.com
Subject: we kissed and made up...

I've just asked Calvin to move in again and I apologised and said going forward I'd treat him like a queen (pun intended!).

You're so much cheaper than a shrink.

LOL

DeanO—n very big sloppy kiss!

Time flies even when you're not having fun. The last couple of days have flown by but dragged by, if you know what I mean (maybe not, I don't have a clue what I mean myself half the time). CNN and BBC World are sooo repetitive I continually get a sense of déjà vu. I guess you're not supposed to watch it eight hours straight, but still.

I've been to the gym a couple of times with Crystal (what a good girl I am), and eaten out every night with James

Life is Pants

(what a bad girl I am). He's in my bad books after forgetting to tell me most Hong Kongers work Saturday mornings (slave labour or what!), so today I'm counting down the hours until he's all mine. As I have time to kill I take extra care doing my make-up (minimalist, I mean 'natural') and choosing an outfit (slob-out gear, I mean 'comfort-wear'). Four minutes later I still have two hours to kill until I meet James.

After a right old carry-on trying to buy tickets from reception for the Robinson Road Residence shuttle bus (you'd think I intended to take it hostage or something), I'm on my way to an area called 'Admiralty'. As we drive along twisting roads I expect to see Buddhist temples burning incense and people riding in rickshaws. Instead I see hundreds of modern apartment blocks, lots of them painted pale pink for some reason (must be good Feng Shui, but they look very phallic to me, ooh err!), chauffeur-driven Rolls Royces (James always jeers, 'Big car, small cock!' and says he imagines it is 'particularly appropriate in Asia'—he can be a racist little bugger at times!), and numerous street cleaners (how civilized! I know I'm going to just love Hong Kong!).

Admiralty is not what I envisioned at all—there's no fleet of ships in its harbour nor Lord Nelson look-alikes in sight, just a couple of huge malls swarming with shoppers. I follow the crowds up an escalator leading into the Queensway Plaza Shopping Mall. There's a pungent, sickly sweet smell in the air that gets stronger and stronger until I reach a counter of what look like traditional Chinese sweets. The sweetness is so intense I feel rather queasy and have to hold my breath until I can move away from the smell. Hopefully the experience will put me off chocolate and other sweet temptations for life.

The shop windows display some really strange fashions. Oddly, frumpy beige polyester blouses finished off with ivory lace and bows, teamed with long brown corduroy skirts covered in tassels, seem to be all the rage. It occurs to me that if they won't take on someone new to name their buildings, then maybe I could become a fashion designer out here. I can't draw or sew to save my life (oh if only I hadn't been such a right-on feminist in art and textiles class!) but what I do know is that beige and cream lace with bows is simply not hip. Will this mean that every time I need to buy something new to wear I'll have to fly home to trawl Oxford Street?

I've still got a bit of time to kill so decide to try on a plain linen suit (white, no lace). I spot one in a shop called (no, surely not! Is this a joke?) 'Wanko'. I can't help but laugh out loud. Locals walk past and stare at me like I'm some sort of lunatic. Wanko. The name suggests vibrators, dongs, blow-up dolls and PVC French maids' outfits but certainly not linen suits. Shouldn't someone enlighten them about this cock-up? (Pun intended.) I decide against trying the suit on. It's one thing work colleagues thinking you're a wanker. It's quite another having it written on your clothes' label.

I'm still in fits of hysterics when James arrives, who's pleased to see me looking so happy to see him. He's already heard of the Wanko chain of ladieswear, but unfortunately this logically leads onto the subject of his favourite hobby. He tells me he's had to have three 'BTWs' (Boys' Toilets' Wanks) this morning, all because we didn't have sex last night. Hmm, obviously he's been working hard this Saturday morning. As we queue for cinema tickets at the UA Cinema, Pacific Place, he begs me to give him a blowjob during the movie (men, eh!). So I agree (I've heard they're good for defining cheekbones; another non-surgical beauty tip I should pass on to Crystal).

James pigs out at the pick-n-mix sweets counter while I buy a bottle of Evian water. Why is it that he (lucky bastard) can eat as much junk food as his heart desires and not get fat, while I (poor cow) only have to look at sweets to pile on the pounds? It's so unfair! If there is a God he/she obviously doesn't like women, cursing us with bloody periods and insatiable chocolate addictions.

The cinema is very cold and very dark. The usherette seems too shy to lead the way with her torch so we feel our way to our seats as best we can. We find our row and clamber past people merrily stuffing their faces with toffee-flavoured popcorn. I discover, to my pleasure, that the armrests lift up so James and I can have a cuddle (and the rest!). Nice. There's quite a big audience here to see the latest Hollywood action movie starring that actor with thighs so big I imagine they could strangle someone (they actually proceed to do so throughout the movie and I sense another career opportunity for me as screenplay writer or casting director).

It's incredibly noisy in here, more like a football stadium than a cinema. Despite the adverts repeatedly requesting that mobile phones are switched off, there's a whole orchestra of ringing. To add to that, after sitting here for a while it's worse than very cold, it's fucking freezing. The woman in front of us puts on two sweaters, and the one next to me is already wearing a fur coat (so this is why they need them in Hong Kong!). James and I, obviously not dressed for the Antarctic, are soon covered in goose pimples. We're holding each other tightly, not for love but for life-giving body heat, as though we're stranded in a wind-beaten tent in the South Pole fighting off the onset of hypothermia. I slip my arms up James's sleeves as a sort of hand-muff; he sticks his head under my thin sweater and peeks his eyes over the top like a baby kangaroo. We might be a sight but next time I'll know to bring my quilt and furry earmuffs. (They should bloody well give out blankets in here, the way they do on aircrafts, together with the pick-n-mix.) On the upside, my body is probably working overtime in its efforts to keep warm by eating up my fat reserves.

An American female voice, which resonates throughout the auditorium (could it be Crystal?) pipes up, 'Shut the fuck up!' She's addressing an incredibly annoying group of Chinese people who chat away as though they're in Starbucks rather than half way through a film. Mobiles continue to sound every couple of seconds and when a phone rings loudly in front of us, James—not to be outdone by the American—barks, 'Turn it off!' Astonishingly, the owner simply proceeds to answer the call and chat away (as you do in a cinema). With my blood now beginning to boil

I can see myself being incarcerated for the murder I will be driven to commit. It looks like James will beat me to it, however, as he leans over to the woman talking and shouts into her ear, 'Oi, turn that fucking phone off! We're trying to watch the movie, you idiot!' And just like a football stadium, others join in, backing James up. I'm ducking down further in my seat expecting a punch-up any minute, but instead the woman at last caves in to public pressure and ends her conversation.

Unfortunately, my heated rage has not prevented me from turning into a human icicle. My bum's gone so cold I wonder if I've lost it to frostbite (yippee! Must tell Crystal—it'll save her husband a fortune!). The movie (such Hollywood dross I've already forgotten its name) is mercifully over. Time to thaw out (wow, my goose bumps are the size of nipples!). What I need is to go home and have a long hot bath.

That'll be a Chinese-sized bath. To the English, this is more like a kitchen sink; perhaps to Americans it's rather more like a finger bowl. It reminds me of when I was four years old and used to sit in the kitchen sink. Quite why, I don't know, but I'm sitting in a kitchen sink for most of my childhood photos. (Did I become a cleaning obsessive at an early age?)

I get in and my knees are under my chin, the water only covering half of me. I try to manoeuvre myself around to wash off my soapy bits properly but it's an ordeal. I give up and empty the sink, I mean 'bath', and have a shower instead. James steps in to join me and we soap each other's naughty parts, giggling like children. Despite three BTWs this morning James is ready for action. We throw our towels around us and stumble with longing in our loins to our bedroom. I notice the Chinese couple next door watching TV.

'James,' I whisper as he gently kisses my neck, 'we can't do this. They can see us!'

'Oh boy!' snaps James irritably. 'Why haven't you put up some bloody curtains? You've had all week to sort this out. Bloody hell, Emily!'

He storms out of the bedroom in a huff.

Oh bugger! He's right. I should have dealt with the curtains issue by now. I try to attach a sheet by wrapping it around the window frames but it falls down after thirty seconds. I seek out James to enlist his help but he's watching the sports channel and drinking a big bottle of Heineken. I snuggle up to him.

'I'm sorry,' I say tenderly. 'I really wanted to make love to you, darling.'

Silence is not always golden. I turn to the Internet for some company instead.

From:	emilygreenhk@hotmail.com
To:	hicks16@hotmail.com, katiets@abbottsdury.com, janeheffer@yahoo.com, sandiebeech@yahoo.com, fernrocks@yahoo.com, deano@btinternet.com, mandyandandy@yahoo.com, teets@hotmail.com, mary1972@hotmail.com, clare_adair@btinternet.com, clare_adair@btinternet.com
Subject:	Hong Kong Pooey

Well all, 'Hong Kong' may mean 'Fragrant Harbour' in Chinese, but the name really should be updated to something more appropriate instead... like 'Filthy Stinking Harbour'. I thought London was dirty with terrible smog but this place is something else—after just a week I'm sure I've developed asthma as sometimes I can hardly breathe.

As you well know, I haven't eaten Chinese food since walking in on that waiter in London's very own China Town peeing over a lettuce in the kitchen sink (Tits' birthday bash, remember?). I can't walk down a street here without feeling like I'm going to gag as there's always an overpowering smell of boiled eggs and oily noodles which seem to be sold on every single frigging street corner in Hong Kong! I'm fast discovering there isn't anything the Chinese won't eat after James's company took us out for 'Dim Sum' last night—does chicken's feet, shark's fin and sheep's eyeballs sound yummy to you?! (No wonder they're all so skinny here!) I kid you not, though, they seriously looovvvve this food here. A soup was served that looked like someone had scraped a shovel along a beach and thrown the contents into a pot—sand, shells, seaweed, odd-looking shrimp, baby octopus, other unidentifiable gunk (old Wellington boot, bicycle wheel, flip-flop). Scrummy.

Luckily, my being vegetarian saved me from this fate worse than death and I ended up with a limp salad (I couldn't tell if it came with pee dressing) while I watched James try to impress his colleagues without puking up. Actually he did rather well, but then he does eat anything (and anyone, but we're in HKG now so hopefully no more temptation to stray). James says it's traditional for the Chinese staff to subject an expatriate to Dim Sum for a laugh, and that no one likes it really and that they all have a sneaky Big Mac afterwards. Crafty buggers. Well, they won't get me!

Big news. I found a Pizza Hut today—eureka!—so I won't starve after all. But then I won't lose weight either. Oh well, you can't have it all.

Keep me posted on the gossip. A lot can happen in a week.

Love n Hugs

Emily x

From: teets@hotmail.com
To: emilygreenhk@hotmail.com, mary1972@hotmail.com, mandyandandy@hotmail.com
Subject: pizza the action!

Wow, you have Pizza Hut out there! That's all right isn't it mate. Means I can come and visit you.

From: katiets@abbotts-dury.com
To: emilygreenhk@hotmail.com
Subject: Hello Emily

Hello Emily

How are you? Well and happy I hope.

Thank you for your emails. Sorry I didn't reply sooner but Timothy has injured his groin playing rugby and it's a real worry for us with the wedding being only 82 days away.

How exciting to be so far away from home in Hong Kong! Although the meal of chicken's feet sounds horrendous.

Do you miss good old Blighty yet? Early days still, I figure.

Chin up.

Best wishes

Katie

I really didn't expect to miss home so soon. I suddenly realize what a big step I've taken moving so far away from everybody and everything I know. Perhaps I didn't think hard enough about leaving home and instead got too excited and simply went with the flow. It's dawning on me that this isn't a long holiday but a new life.

I feel a cop-out already. I can't go home after a week—I'd look a right baby and everyone would laugh at me! Stiff upper lip needed. I locate James (what a surprise, still lolling on the sofa watching football) and snuggle up to him. It's just him and me stranded on this God-forsaken island (yes, I can be a bit dramatic at times).

Just the two of us. Hmm, maybe things aren't so bad. James kisses me passionately and suddenly I don't miss home. He deftly undoes the hooks of my bra and stokes my breasts tenderly. I feel the heat rising in both of us... yeah-hey, the moment has returned!

The front door bursts open (alas, the Law of Sod prevails). It's Peter, holding hands with a lady (although judging by her hemline she's no lady) and it isn't Shandy.

'Oops! Carry on, carry on, don't let us stop you lovebirds!' laughs Peter, who then plonks his bony butt down next to us on the sofa. He pulls the anonymous lady down to sit on his knee and kisses her. 'Oh, how rude of me!' he says. 'By the way, this is Cindy.'

I look like Barbie more than Cindy looks like Sindy. She's about 4ft 8ins with the figure of a nine year old (even smaller breasts than mine if that's possible)—child-woman not

Sindy-woman. I think she's Filipino but am not sure. Peter obviously has a female fan club, although I'm at a loss as to what it is about him they're attracted to. He seems pretty juvenile to me so far and is nothing to look at—just skin and bone with a huge honker (maybe that's it—he can satisfy women with his nose as well as his tool, giving triple penetration!).

'Hey, mate,' Peter turns to James, 'I've organised a welcome party for you tonight. Anyone who's anyone will be there. Down at Yeltsin's Pub in Lan Kwai Fong.'

James is the world's biggest party animal. 'Excellent! Thanks, mate.' He nudges me. 'Great opportunity to network, Emily.'

Fine, I think, as long as it's not with the likes of Shandy or Cindy.

'What time does it kick off, mate?' asks James. What is it with all this mate business? I've never heard James say 'mate' so many times in his life.

'About nine, mate. I'll sort you guys out with some Charlie, no problemo.'

James and I enjoy the occasional bag of coke but I'm determined to stop this habit, not because it kills brain cells and leads to memory loss but for vanity's sake—I don't want my nose falling apart like that pretty girl with the whiney voice from EastEnders. No thank you. I like my pert little nose (a friend once described it as 'regal', how lovely!) and really don't want the Michael Jackson look either if I can help it.

I make a big effort tonight to look my best and make an impact, choosing my slinky red top, trendy black (mini not micro) skirt and knee-high suede (simply a by-product of meat and no point letting it go to waste once the carnivores have had their fill) black boots which always make me feel like 'sex on legs' and leave men begging for mercy (slight exaggeration, perhaps, but they do turn James on big time). I can always tell when I look good as James is all over me like a rash, like now, kissing me, hugging me close and stroking my hair. The extra effort is certainly worth it!

'Do you know you're gorgeous?' he whispers in my ear before pushing me onto the bed and jumping on top of me. As his weight lands, the bed creeks ominously and then drops down a few inches.

'Oh Christ,' grins James, 'we've broken the bloody bed!'

We laugh until the tears run down our faces. I'm sure my mascara has run and no doubt I now resemble Alice Cooper somewhat.

'Oi, are you two rabbits ready to go?' Peter shouts.

James pulls me up off the bed and it creeks again.

'Let's get out of here before we do any more damage!' he smiles, patting my bum lovingly.

Yeltsin's Pub has a few token pictures on the walls. These depict anonymous landscapes rather than well-known alkies (Boris himself?) or members of the KGB, and lamely pretend to be of the English countryside rather than Lan Kwai Fong. The smell of beer is no different from that of any pub I've ever set foot in. The barmaids are all local girls and are probably forced to wear those micro dresses with 'Carlsberg' emblazed over their flat chests.

'What are you having, mate?' Peter pats James on the shoulder.

'It's got to be Guinness, mate!' James asserts.

'Vodka Cranberry please, Peter,' I chip in. 'Thanks.'

'Cranberry juice, eh? Good for vaginas,' quips Peter. 'Women's infections, pussy plague, yuck!'

James cuts him off. 'Yeah, that's enough information thanks, Peter. Don't confuse Emily with all your whores, err, girlfriends.'

He is a love, stepping in when I just stand there flabbergasted, unable to articulate any kind of response. I can hear shouts of, 'Fight, fight, fight' in my head but Peter seems happy enough with James's slip of the tongue.

'Mmm, yes, mate, we all love w-h-o-r-e-s!'

What on earth do all these women see in him?!

The pub is packed. I'm already standing under James's armpit (thankfully smelling sexy and manly), but still get jostled by other customers. Beer's being sloshed everywhere and the floor is fast becoming a skating rink. I'm amazed and (sorry if this is politically incorrect, folks) very pleased to see it's full of Westerners. It really feels like I'm in a pub back home and it crosses my mind that everything's going to work out fine for me in Hong Kong. Peter's introducing us to so many people that I can't keep up with all the names, and the faces are becoming a bit of a blur (or is that my Vodka Cranberry kicking in?). Oh well, everyone else seems to be drinking for England, I mean Hong Kong! And loads of strangers are offering to buy me drinks just because I'm with Peter. Cool! (At this rate, though, I'll have liver failure within a month.)

What the...! Hmm. I only have to turn my back for half a second and James is being chatted up by a pretty bleached blonde (thankfully with tree-trunk thighs). He senses my watching him.

'Hey Emily, meet Melody,' he says, the picture of innocence.

'Hi Melody,' I respond, faking interest, while Melody gives me the once-over. I imagine I'm in a golden bubble (my Reiki therapist says it wards off negative energy from other people. Probably total bollocks but worth a try). 'You can't touch me in my golden bubble, mammoth-thighed Melody! And yes, hon, he's all mine!' I think, but don't say.

Melody in turn gives me an airy, 'Oh, hiii...' and drifts off into the crowd, looking for her next victim, no doubt.

'Find your own man,' I mutter. James starts laughing gleefully.

'You're so possessive, darling. I love it!' He's such an overgrown schoolboy sometimes.

Peter strolls over to us, happily arm-in-arm with another lady—a Westerner this time. He smiles.

'Emily, meet Deanna, my wife.'

I lift my jaw up from the floor. I know I look shocked but am too shocked to cover it up.

'Oh, soon to be my ex-wife, I should say!' laughs Peter.

I look at Deanna who looks so normal, so girl-next-door.

'It's true,' she says wistfully, looking up at Peter. He kisses her full on the lips.

'You're fantastic, darling!' he tells her.

Deanna beams a huge, toothy Julia Roberts smile at him. I'm totally confused.

'Hey, let me introduce you to the girls!' Deanna drawls.

'Where are you from, Deanna?' I ask, trying to sound normal.

'New York, New York. And Peter tells me you're from London, right?' As she asks the question, Deanna's big green eyes almost pop out of her head, making her look just like Marty Fieldman.

'Yeah. First time living away from home.' What a complete baby I sound.

'Don't worry, Emily, you'll soon settle in. It's a great place, one big party!'

It turns out 'the girls' could justifiably be called 'The Gestapo' as they fire twenty questions at me from all angles.

'How old are you?' (I want to say 'younger than you, sister!' but instead squeak up, 'Twenty-eight.');

'What job do you do?'(could I get away with saying 'Supermodel' rather than 'Office Manager'?);

'How long have you been going out with James?' ('Two years.' I don't add, 'But it seems like twenty.');

'What form of birth control do you use?' (I'd like to say 'up the bum no babies is my favourite,' but instead I confirm 'the Pill').

Once that interrogation is over (phew!) they throw another twenty fast ones at me, this time about James (oh no!). I get the impression James is going down a storm with the female population here. I make him out to be low paid and impotent to put them off flirting with him.

Heather, another American, with an unruly mop of bright ginger hair, lowers her voice, 'You know, Emily, the guys in this town aren't interested in Western women. They all end up going for the Asian girls as they're really subservient and take loads of shit without complaining.'

'Hey, Heather,' Deanna interrupts, 'Emily's just arrived. Don't put her off!' She turns to me and says under her breath, 'It's true, though, honey, so keep an eye on your man.'

Bloody hell. Maybe I should go super-glue myself onto his arm right this minute. I'll be buying him a chastity belt at this rate and storing the key in a bank vault.

I glance over at James and see Melody is in deep conversation with him. Crikey, it didn't take her long to hone in on him again. Little does she know, James isn't into blondes... hmm, here's a thought: shall I sidle over and let Melody know one of his favourite sayings is 'Never trust a woman with thighs bigger than your own'? That should put her right!

Fortunately the night passes quickly. So much for networking—I've only learnt interrogation skills tonight. James is totally unsympathetic to my plight.

'They were only being friendly, darling.'

Who needs friends like that, I think, but know better than to say it.

'Well they were too friendly!' I huff.

'Emily!' James snaps. 'Don't talk rubbish! How can you complain that they were being too friendly?'

'They were too much, that's all.' I correct my words but it's too late.

'Well I think you're being downright bloody stupid. They even invited you on a girls' night out next week, which is very nice of them, seeing as they don't know you from Adam. I hope you're going to go.'

Oh great, I'll start preparing my twenty answers now.

Why are weekends always over so quickly when the rest of the week seems so long? I miss James terribly when he goes to work. The fun stops when he's not around—what a sad case I am! I love him to bits and he's such a laugh to be with. Tonight I'm meeting the Gestapo Girls from the party for some indescribable fun, no doubt. We're meeting in a bar in Lan Kwai Fong—surely this isn't the only watering hole in town?

I have a whole day to think about what I'm going to wear. Boring! CNN then? Boring! Instead I flick through the jobs section from Saturday's edition of the 'South China Morning Post' and this week's 'HK Magazine'. I see no adverts wanting Office Managers (yeah, yeah, I order the paperclips. Actually, offices run like clockwork because of people like me, but don't get me started on the subject).

There are a million ads wanting 'NETs'. What are they? Oh, got it: not granny curtain makers but Native English Teachers. Nope, doesn't appeal to me at all, not one itty little bit. I've no patience with children (James is quite enough for me, thank you) and hate the thought of noses being picked and bogies the size of sprouts being flicked around the classroom with rulers. Well, that's what we all did, right?

The remaining few ads are for Western girls with big boobs for bra-fitting work. No hope there—my cherry cakes were made without baking powder. I wouldn't mind a size 34B, what with my paltry 34A! (Surely a travesty of justice as my mum and three sisters are all D cups. What the hell went wrong with me?) And there's one ad asking for Westerners for 'Adult Chat Lines'. Now the Samaritans is one thing but I'm not so sure about telephone sex (although I guess it would all be over in seconds! Men are so gross!). Maybe the Gestapo Girls will know of some jobs going... pretty, pretty please!

I arrive fifteen minutes late because I couldn't decide on what to wear (I lost track of the time watching CNN in the end). The girls are seated in a circle, beer in one hand, fag in the other. Not much in common so far I think. I drink the occasional fancy cocktail—more than the taste I love their luminous colours, bright umbrellas, limp, definitely recycled slice of pineapple, and sugary artificial red cherry—the ones your mother wouldn't let you have as a kid because they rot your teeth. I don't smoke; in fact, I can't bear the smell of it. Did you know smoking is dangerous for your health? Not many people seem to.

'Hi, Deanna,' I squeak nervously.

Deanna flicks her lank, mousy fringe out of her massive eyes. 'Oh hi, Emily, glad you could make it! Hey, you guys, this is Emily, new in town with her boyfriend James. They're staying with Peter until she's got a job. Rather them than me!'

Lots of cursory 'hi's from the group follow. I pull up a chair but the magic circle doesn't open up for me; do I need a password? Just before I try 'Abracadabra' Deanna comes to the rescue.

'Hey, shuffle up, guys, let Emily in!'

The girls spend the next hour agreeing they're all desperately trying to give up smoking (they've discovered it can kill you—no way!) while puffing away on their cigarettes. This is a truly bizarre conversation. I want to chip in, 'If you want to stop so badly then why are you all chain-smoking?' but obviously don't. I can't be labelled 'Miss Congeniality NOT' after only a week!

An hour and a half of this inane chatter passes and I'm bored stiff. I attempt to strike up a conversation with a frosty Swiss girl to my left named Sonja, who is clearly more interested in discussing how she lacks the willpower to stop her disgusting habit, but she at least makes an effort by smoking 'Marlboro Lights'. I turn to my right, hoping Tabitha—not a cat but a stick-insect, I mean 'immaculate blonde from the Kent borders'- is up for a change of topic, but she's marvelling at how cigarettes keep her weight down (she'll get even thinner when her cancer-riddled body is in a coffin).

I discreetly make my excuses and leave. Deanna's sweet to me but probably senses I'm too much of a squeaky clean Sandy—I don't drink, I don't smoke (I just do dope, ooh!)—to join the smoky Pink Ladies. Again, so much for networking. All I've done is passively smoke sixty-plus fags (I often ponder I'd simply die if I end up getting cancer and a smoker friend doesn't!).

James isn't going to be at all impressed with my coming home so early. I need to kill some time. I think about the Triads but they might at least know of some job opportunities (albeit illegal ones but then I am getting desperate now) and they probably don't chain-smoke (I figure they wouldn't karate kick very well with a hacking smoker's cough, aiming to screech 'Aieeyaaa!' but coughing up white globules of phlegm instead). So I pluck up the courage to take a little wander through the streets, veering off from

Lan Kwai Fong.

I remember James telling me, at least thirty times, if I get lost to simply make my way back to 'The Escalator' which would carry me home to Robinson Road. I climb some worn stone steps onto Hollywood Road. Sadly, no sign of Tom Cruise or Meg Ryan but, to make up for that, lots of interesting tiny antiques shops and galleries.

I peer through the windows. If I had money to burn I wouldn't buy any of this stuff. It reminds me of the bric-a-brac cluttering my parents' tiny semi-detached house in leafy Wimbledon during the 1970s. Dainty porcelain tea sets with blue and white dragons 'hand-painted' (i.e. resembling the artwork of a four year old) and with handles so small you can't clasp them properly so end up with hot tea in your lap. Crap only useful in a dolls house or for the vertically-challenged.

It appears that my opinion isn't shared by a party of German tourists (wearing fawn shorts, long white socks, brown open-toed sandals, and sporting tight perms like Kevin Keegan in his heyday, I guess they have to be). They're talking excitedly while madly purchasing loads of these tacky tea sets as if they're going out of fashion—which they are. But I won't enlighten them out of respect for Granddad Tommy, who badly broke his arm in World War II (actually in a fight with his friend Ernie in a pub brawl in Hackney, but I like to think it was with Jerry). I move along and see countless busy-looking porcelain vases and gaudy black lacquered chests. Each to their own, as they say, but I prefer the Swedish minimalist look (OK, Ikea) to local 'Chopsticks' restaurant decor.

I leave the shop and realize at this point I'm lost. Well and truly lost. I can't see The Escalator anywhere. My heart is pounding. I ask a Chinese shop assistant, 'Which way do I go to get onto The Escalator?' She replies, 'Sooorrryyy ahh.'

I try the shop next door but the chap there doesn't even respond, and instead starts picking his nose—nice and helpful, thanks! I try to engage my brain (it's been a long time) and retrace my steps. Come on, Emily (I give myself a pep talk)—if a couple of children like Hansel and Gretl can do it then so can you. Thankfully I can suddenly see in the distance the outline of The Escalator high above street level and I make for it like a lifeboat.

There now, that wasn't too bad! My first excursion on my own, and everything's fine and dandy. Just one thing—where the hell am I now? I spot a Western lady and ask her how to get to Robinson Road. Ah, no problem, I just overshot The Escalator, that's all. Panic over. Christ, is it left or right? I turn left, which looks unfamiliar, then double back and turn right, which also looks unfamiliar. I finally reach Robinson Road Residence. It's such a huge and striking building I can't understand how I hadn't spotted it earlier.

'Where the hell have you been?' James barks as I unlock the front door.

'Drinks with the girls,' I respond gingerly.

'Deanna called Peter over an hour ago to say you were on your way home. I was getting really worried!' Poor James.

'I'm having an affair,' I jest, but James isn't in a jokey mood. 'I did a bit of window-shopping and got lost, that's all. No big deal, I'm home now. How was work?'

Changing the subject fails to change James's foul mood, so I leave him to calm down on the sofa watching 'The Migration Patterns of Salmon' on the National Geographic channel. I tidy up our bedroom, which is already scrupulously neat. The Chinese couple from next door are watching TV. As usual they're seated at opposite ends of their sofa. No chance of me catching a bit of Asian-style rumpy-pumpy with them! I return to James for a cuddle to find Peter talking animatedly.

'She had big tits for an Asian bird, at least a 32E, maybe bigger. Huge nipples—it felt like I was sucking on a young boy's cock!'

James tilts back his head and roars with laughter. Funny that. I happen to think Peter's conversation is offensive and totally gross.

Rather than listen to Peter's account of what he pulled on Sunday afternoon, I turn to the Internet for some sane company. My Inbox shows I've received an email from Nora (do I know a Nora? No, only Nora Batty off the TV), one from Bernard (who the hell's Bernard? Bernard Manning? The saintly dog?) and another from my sister Elizabeth. Have I been forgotten by all at home so soon?

> From: Nora@natural_remedies.com
> To: emilygreenhk@hotmail.com
> Subject: IMPORTANT Information You Requested
>
> WANT TO ADD 4 INCHES TO THE SIZE OF YOUR PENIS OVERNIGHT?
>
> WE HAVE THE ANSWER FOR GIVING YOU A HUGE THICK PENIS. 100% SATISFACTION GUARANTEED OR YOUR MONEY BACK. DON'T DELAY, REQUEST OUR FREE IN-FORMATION PACK TODAY!

Weird or what! I consider sending a response saying, 'I'm a WOMAN. And plan to stay this way!' but don't waste my time. I hate this junk mail—where, oh where do they get my email address?

> From: Bernard@picsbiz.com
> To: emilygreenhk@hotmail.com
> Subject: I've been trying to reach you...
>
> HOT, HOT, HOT. Asian babes spread ALL their holes just for YOU. Come take a look, CUM NOW!
>
> Click here for the ULTIMATE fucking frenzy!

Weird or what! I consider sending a response saying, 'I'm a WOMAN. And this doesn't turn me on, you pervert!' but don't waste my time. I hate this junk mail—where, oh where do they get my email address? I'm actually looking forward to reading my sister's email now!

Elizabeth is third in the pecking order of the four of us. As the eldest it was ALWAYS, without exception, my fault if anything went wrong. I could be a hundred miles away from Wimbledon yet still the blame would fall squarely on my shoulders. I've never forgiven her for scratching 'Mum's a breeding cow' on the bathroom wall during one of her many tantrums. I, of course, received the smack for it despite Elizabeth owning up that it was her handiwork and not mine. My mother was livid for weeks as she had only just had the bathroom redecorated and her new wallpaper was now tarnished. It didn't make any difference to her that her appalling taste for elaborate paisley designs meant you'd have to study the wallpaper hard for several days with a powerful magnifying glass to notice Elizabeth's profound addition.

Bloody Elizabeth, always getting me into trouble. I don't like to say this, as I know it sounds mean, but I never liked her. She looks like sweetness personified (a bit like Britney Spears without the fake boobs and dark roots) but is truly the daughter of Satan. Constantly up to no good, waltzing around oblivious to the consequences of her actions. Popular with the boys (she inherited my share of the boobs, lucky bitch) and teachers' pet (plagiarised all my bloody homework), and in my mother's eyes she can do no wrong.

My sister Emma is only a year older than Elizabeth (my mother let it slip recently, 'I didn't think I could get pregnant so quickly.' Pu-lease! And this coming from a family planning doctor! Emma and Elizabeth are like two peas in a pod and spent our entire childhood conspiring how to get up to mischief while not getting into trouble (perhaps they'll become politicians if they ever grow up).

Eve, on the other hand, is much younger than the three of us, a whopping twelve years younger than me. My mother refers to her as 'the fluke', yet another shining example of the wonders of birth control. As the baby of the family, Eve's spoilt rotten, gets away with murder, and is a total wet. My mother mollycoddles her like she's retarded or something. I'd put money on it she'll never leave home and will end up an old maid or marrying the boy next door (eighty-three-year-old Wilfred).

Being the eldest totally sucks. If I ever have children I'll never inflict this on them, and instead will somehow bypass having an eldest child (send me your suggestions on a postcard). My father stays the hell away from all of us, saying he only likes male company. He's permanently holed up in our loft playing with his train set (no, he didn't grow out of them by the age of nine like the rest of his peers) and talks to himself all day long rather than to five hormonal women (most men would surely envy him). He's like a fugitive up there, although he looks more like Woody Allen than Harrison Ford, and has justifiably fought off the high competition in our area to earn the reputation of 'The Local Nutter'. Yes, my father is a barking mad hermit. Super, eh?

From: ElizabethGreen@hotmail.com
To: emilygreenhk@hotmail.com
Subject: Hi

Hi Emily

Mum wants me to tell you that she's had to throw out your box of shoes as the utility room was flooded last week as stupid Eve left the sink on in there and it overflowed big time. They've gone all mouldy. I guess you probably don't need them any more anyway as you're probably walking around in flip-flops all day now!

Bye

Elizabeth

P.S.—I've borrowed the CDs you left here. Okay?

I'm fucking fuming. This is so typical of Elizabeth. Selfish bloody cow, aaarrrgghhh! I could kill her! I'd boxed up my CD collection and stored it in the utility room with the rest of my stuff that was too expensive to ship over to Hong Kong (my lifetime's collection of useless junk that I couldn't bear to bin). My shoes alone (those I left behind!) would have sunk the ship so I nobly diverted another Titanic-style disaster by dumping several pairs in my parents' utility room (they could just about open the door when I left!).

And now she's helping herself to my CDs. She drives me mad. As for my shoes, well frankly, I'm in deep mourning. They weren't cheap—if I totted up the figures they probably cost the same as a deposit on a penthouse in Belgravia (OK, I exaggerate a wee bit—perhaps more studio flat in Dagenham). Plus, I spent so much time in the sales rooting out good buys that we're probably talking somewhere in the region of five precious years' worth of haggling and bargain hunting.

I can only describe it as a tragedy of great magnitude (shall I inform CNN?). Thinking about it, I might just as well have given all my belongings to Oxfam. At least some poor woman in deepest, darkest Africa could now be wearing pink satin sling-back heels from Pied A Terre, listening to the Bee Gees while wasting away from starvation (effortlessly achieving the waif-model look I spend good money aspiring to). If I was back home I'd hold a burial service in loving memory of those shoes that have served me so valiantly, but since I'm in Hong Kong I'll simply start dressing in black in loving remembrance.

I'm depressed, and in retrospect should have watched 'The Migration Patterns of Salmon' with James (or would I be even more depressed by now?). I retreat to the lounge only to hear Peter saying excitedly, 'Eh mate, look at the udder on that!'

I note we've moved on from salmon to cattle.

Err, not exactly. I discover a porno movie is actually on the TV starring a frizzy-haired black woman with collagen-enhanced lips and melons the size of pumpkins—enormous and vile. The stretch marks are so prominent it looks like she's had a zebra crossing tattooed across her boobs. I think about how my bust looks nice and shapely in comparison and this cheers me up no end.

'Having fun boys?' I ask them sarcastically. Judging by Peter's huge erection (right now about the length of the Leaning Tower of Pisa) he's certainly enjoying the movie. Fortunately for James his groin is at rest—I'd be mightily worried if he was getting turned on by this freak.

James looks rather sheepish. 'Erm, Peter got this movie on his business trip to Amsterdam,' he stammers.

Well that's OK then! Yes, Peter certainly acts more like a seedy low-life pimp than a high-flying solicitor.

Peter laughs. 'That's what business trips are for, mate! I really shat myself going through customs, though. You see, my friend Thea asked me to buy her a couple of tubs

Life is Pants

of baby milk powder as apparently it's much cheaper in Europe than here. So if they'd opened my bags they'd have found this substance that looks very much like cocaine and a stack of extremely filthy illegal porn. I tell you, I was sweating like a paedophile in Mothercare!'

Once again Peter shocks me more than I think possible. I need to get a job very soon and we need to move into our own place fast. I don't want James to be corrupted like this.

Deanna sweetly invites me out for lunch at 'Post 97' in Lan Kwai Fong and kindly picks up the tab. She wants a shopping buddy and we traipse around the malls in Central for what seems like an eternity. Deanna spends money like water and buys an ill-fitting see-through white blouse (what can I say?) and pointed shoes that pinch her toes (and that's just in the shop! What will they be like when she does the road test?).

Ahh, Marks & Spencers, home from home. It is so reassuring to be amongst the familiar shop fittings and uninspiring clothes. I see a top I like, probably twice the price I'd pay back home, and ask the shop assistant if they have it in my size. Her badge reveals her name is Cherries (someone should tell her it's spelt 'Cherry' or 'Cherrie' or even 'Cherie').

'You try this one on instead!' Cherries whines.

'But it's not my size,' I reply, looking at the label of the one she's thrust into my arms. In fact, it's two sizes too small. How weird! Cherries isn't put off, however.

'You try in orange colour instead!'

'But I want blue. I don't suit orange.'

Cherries can't understand why I don't want to try on something in the wrong size and the wrong colour. They may be more attentive than English shop assistants here but are they more of a help? Deanna finds the bewildered expression on my face highly amusing.

The days aren't dragging by so much at the moment. My feverish attempt to send out my CV—at least a hundred times—has netted me a grand total of three job interviews and these are only with poxy recruitment agencies rather than prospective employers. I'm on my way to one of them now at 'Hutchinson House', which Peter tells me is between Central and Admiralty.

The taxi driver drops me outside Hutchinson House although it seems to be actually called 'Bank of America Tower'. How can one office block have two names? Strange and confusing for a poor soul like me just trying to get to an interview on time. A strong smell of polish and depressed workers wafts through the dark interior. It's all a bit unnerving. Thankfully the security guard on reception seems to know where I'm going, even if I don't, and instructs me to take the lift to the 22nd floor.

The lift is packed and stops at every flaming floor, where more and more people try to cram in. I recall the 'how many people can fit into a telephone box' competition that formed part of my study relief at Uni and which was tremendous fun. This, however, is not.

'Why don't you stand on my head?' I feel like suggesting to the idiotic new arrivals. I guess I could, as they probably wouldn't understand anyway, but I hold my tongue. After all, I'm the visitor here. The lift has a small silver sign stating that the maximum capacity is twelve people. I can count at least twenty-three. They clearly haven't seen those movies in which a packed lift, unable to take the weight, terrifyingly plummets to the basement killing all passengers instantly.

Fortunately, I now have a few seconds in which to ponder the inevitable and save my miserable life by timing a flying somersault to coincide with the moment of impact. Since I was never very good at gymnastics I also check out the ceiling to see if there's an escape route in the event of such a catastrophe. At the very least I'll try to make a run for it rather than just pick my nose, which is all this lot seem to be thinking about. Then again, I do have the advantage of having been in the Brownies and our motto 'Always be prepared' had a profound influence on me from a tender age.

Yucky yoodles! Did that guy behind me really let out a deafeningly loud burp? Bloody hell, that's utterly disgusting! So why am I the only one looking appalled? James warned me this is the norm—that the Chinese think nothing of burping, spitting, gobbing and farting in public (Gazza might be in his element here). But it's simply uncivilized! Hark at me, being so self-righteous, but I can't help it. It's totally gross and it really stinks, too. I hold my breath and gulp for air as I get out on the 22nd floor.

I'm sure I've turned blue, so let's hope it doesn't put the interviewer off her stride. She is called Agnes (so that name didn't die out with the Victorian chambermaids!) Woo (she should marry a Mr Wee to call herself 'Woo Wee'—cool!). The receptionist at Hong Kong Recruit speaks very poor English and I hope Agnes knows I've arrived. I wait for ages, twenty-eight minutes and forty-six flipping seconds, before Agnes finally appears.

'Green, this is Agnes,' says the receptionist.

'Emily,' I say authoritatively, trying to make a formidable impression, and shaking Agnes's limp, sweaty hand.

Agnes, confidently modelling Wanko apparel, shows me that there is indeed a market for bland, beige clothing here. She offers no apology for keeping me waiting and so needs to start earning some brownie points fast.

'You are from Australia,' she begins.

'No, England,' I respond, trying not to sound indignant. No criminals deported in my family that I know of.

'Ahh, England. I have been there to Scotland.'

I consider enlightening Agnes that Scotland is in Scotland not England, but can't be bothered, responding instead, 'Right.'

'It raining all the time,' Agnes chatters while it's on the tip of my tongue to say, 'Well it is Scotland, what do you expect?' Thankfully the laboured small talk ends there.

'You look for secretarial job.' Agnes clearly hasn't read my CV.

'No, I'm an Office Manager. But I guess I could consider secretarial work, too.'

'Have you had any interviews with companies in Hong Kong?'

'No,' I reply, but Agnes persists.

'What companies have you seen advertising?'

She's obviously fishing for leads with no interest in me. I realize I'm wasting my time here. Once she establishes I don't have any leads the interview is over. As suspected, I never hear from her again.

Fortunately, my spirits are lifted the next day when I meet the smooth and petit (is a four foot nothing man defined as 'petit'?) Angus Turner of 'Direct Search'. A little smarmy for my liking (I think he'd like to search my knickers and borrow my heels) but he seems well connected and confident that he can place me with a good company. He goes through my CV in great detail, annoyingly showing more interest in my crummy student jobs that the seven years' experience I have under my belt working for blue chip companies.

After just over an hour he pats his stomach. 'Let's finish talking through your options over lunch, Emily.'

Wow, that was very smooth indeed. I bet he times all his interviews with non-married female candidates with boyfriends (still classed as 'single' for some reason) just before lunch. Seeing as I have nothing else to do today (or the rest of the year if I'm honest), I agree.

His secretary is hovering right outside his glass office door, but Angus presses his intercom to communicate with her.

'Fanny, book my usual table at The Grand Hyatt, the brassiere not the restaurant!'

No 'please', no 'thank you', I note. But, Christ, 'Fanny'! What a fantastically lucky name to be landed with. British definition: vagina; American: bottom. Either way, destined to be a laughing stock if ever you set foot outside of Hong Kong. Not only that, it's just a bloody awful sounding name—ridiculous and old-fashioned. If I was forced to choose, it would have to be Agnes, any day of the week.

The Grand Hyatt is a sophisticated hotel, and the brasserie is tastefully decorated, with spectacular views across the city and harbour. Directing me to my seat, Angus's hand lingers on my shoulder a little too long for my liking. Fortunately for me the tables are wide, creating some distance between us. Phew!

He proceeds to bore me stiff for the next two hours (doesn't this hotshot have any work to do? Does he really think I'd be interested in him?). He talks about his penthouse in exclusive Shoulson Hill and tells me it's the most expensive area in Hong Kong to live in (bully for him, eh? Being so short it must have floor-to-ceiling windows so he can see out). He talks about his Lamborghini (I can hear James—'Big car, small cock') and about his maids (precisely why does he need two?).

He literally drones on and on and on. I try hard not to glaze over. If I could, I might consider slipping into a peaceful coma right now to escape his drivel. But at least the food's good, delicious even, particularly the 'Devil's Chocolate Cake' (I wouldn't mind going to hell if this is what's on offer; heaven probably only has prunes and lentils on the menu).

Just before I really do slip into a self-induced coma, Angus pays the bill and we leave. I remember my manners (yes, I do have some, despite going to a crappy Comprehensive).

'Thanks so much for lunch, Angus.'

'My pleasure. We must do it again soon,' he purrs like the cat who got the cream (how misguided he is!), while I give him a small, fake 'I don't think so, Shorty Pants!' kind of smile, chuckling to myself about the fact that at least he gets to look at Fanny all day!

I make my way to my third interview—this one in Causeway Bay. I decide to be brave and take the MTR 'Tube' there. Thankfully the carriage isn't packed and I find a seat opposite a pleasant-looking young businesswoman. She's obviously got a bit of money as she's nicely turned out, wearing a very smart, navy blue pinstriped suit with matching shoes and handbag. Sitting there I wonder whether—coincidence being what it is—we end up being friends one day.

Blimey! The woman's just dropped her guts big time! I can't believe someone who looks like such a lady farts like such a pig. I stare at her incredulously. She in turn looks blankly at me. Christ alive, she doesn't even know she's done anything embarrassing! (Maybe I should advertise Etiquette lessons rather than English lessons?) I get up and move further down the carriage in protest. What's the hell's going on today? Why have people got so much wind in this town? Must be all the muck they consume. Yucky yoodles! I exit the carriage swiftly and find I have a blue oxygen-starved face for the second time that day.

My mind's taken off the farting business executive when I realize the station has approximately two million exit options. Now, think, think, think: which one did Kevin McCann, the interviewer, say I should take? A1. No, E1. No, it was definitely A1. I think. I end up trekking from A1 to E1 but, luckily for me, I'm not running late so this detour is acceptable, even though I'd rather be mooching around shops than a station.

I'm relieved that Kevin's office is right by the station as Causeway Bay is chock-a-block with bland buildings and shopping malls and I know I'd get very lost here. Like Angus, Kevin is about knee-high to a grasshopper (why are these recruitment guys all so short?). He's tubby, too, with reddish, tight curly hair and a friendly lopsided grin.

'Let's get out of the office and go for a coffee,' he suggests in a soft, lilting voice.

Here we go again.

We end up in Starbucks (they're everywhere in Hong Kong) and he slurps his frothy cappuccino while I sip my hot chocolate (perhaps not the wisest of choices after the Devil's Chocolate Cake. I've had so much sweet food today I'm running the risk of becoming diabetic!). Kevin doesn't want to talk about my CV. He wants to talk about how hard it is to find a Western girlfriend in Hong Kong. I'm not kidding you.

'It was so easy living in Kilburn. I used to hang out in a couple of the pubs there and always met someone to chat up,' he laments while I think, but don't say, 'Yeah, Kilburn has a reputation for being full of Irish prostitutes, Kevin, so it was probably them you were chatting up.'

How is it I have become Kevin's confidante in such a

short space of time? I don't know this guy from Adam.

'I moved here six months ago and there's been absolutely no one,' he continues. Hmm, that's a little more information than I need, although I imagine with his unfortunate looks and tedious verbal diarrhoea he experiences frequent periods of celibacy. Unless the Kilburn street-walkers gave him one on the house out of pity—a selfless act of charity to ensure a place in heaven (no, noo, noo, no—as much as I'd like to keep him quiet that's simply not an option for me!).

'I like Western girls.'

How refreshing Kevin is.

'This lot out here just want your money, status and a Western passport.'

How perceptive Kevin is.

'Are you happy with your boyfriend?'

How misguided Kevin is. If he were the last man on earth and I the last woman he still wouldn't have a hope in hell.

'Amazingly happy,' I wickedly ham it up. 'We're talking about getting engaged,' I add for good measure. Well, we have talked about it and James said absolutely no way (he doesn't believe in marriage, particularly not to me), but I don't need to let Kevin in on this. I attempt to steer the conversation towards my CV and prospective jobs.

'Oh, that's the other thing making my life a misery,' Kevin rambles on. He's beginning to make my life a misery. 'Work is slow, there's not much recruitment being done at the moment. Hong Kong's been in recession since the Brits handed it back to China. Not good, not good.'

Fuck. This is really not good news at all. I make my excuses, saying I have another interview to go to, and Kevin reluctantly gets up to leave.

'Oh and Emily, let me know of any companies you come across that are recruiting!' Kevin pipes up hopefully, as I turn towards the entrance of the MTR.

I nod and smile sweetly, thinking, 'Yeah right, twitface.'

James is pleased I've made a bit of headway on the job-front but displeased to hear about two of the seven dwarfs—'Shorty Pants' and 'Misery Guts'—trying to make a move on me. He pulls me down onto the bed for a long steamy kiss. Hmm, wonderful! Our tongues dance in tandem, stirring our desire to make love, and someone knocks on our door.

'Oh bloody hell!' curses James.

It's Shandy.

'Heerlo, James. Please you help me. Peter say I can do my washing here but I can't open the machine door.'

James and I reluctantly traipse into the kitchen to find Shandy tugging at the handle of the dishwasher which is mid-cycle. Christ, and this girl is a maid for a living? Surely one of the prerequisites for the job is the ability to recognize a washing machine when it's staring you in the face?! (Perhaps she really is an escort girl as I first imagined and the maid thing is all a cover-up.) We point out her error and Shandy finds it hysterical.

'Sooo sooorrryyy, sooo sooorrryyy, James!' she giggles, fluttering her eyelashes and looking demented. Dippy cow.

Oh great, now Peter's arrived back—definitely the end of our shag that never began. James and I haven't made love for the entire month we've been in Hong Kong—not good at all. I'm going to be as tight as a virgin when we eventually do it.

'Fancy coming to a party tonight, mate?' Peter chirps.

'What, on a Wednesday night?' James queries.

'Yeah, mate. It's party night every night in Hong Kong. Shazza and Damian are leaving Honkers for Rotherham, God help them, so they're having a farewell do at Dolce Vita in Lan Kwai Fong.'

Here we go again. James can't resist a party. He looks over at me sheepishly. I know exactly what he's going to say: 'Let's just go for one, shall we? It'll be fun.'

Right on cue. 'Erm, Emily, let's just go for one, shall we, it'll be fun.'

I no longer bother to say anything to the contrary, as it only ends up with James calling me boring and a hermit just like my old man, which starts an almighty row. I just can't be fagged, so I respond unenthusiastically, 'Yeah, why not?'

Same old Lan Kwai Fong, same old people. I haven't met one person yet who I'd like to make friends with. I'm not even fussy, that's the scary thing. I have zero in common with or interest in the Shandys and Deannas and Sonjas and Crystals of this world. My tummy lurches. Suddenly I feel really lonely and homesick. I wish Mary and Teets and Clare and the all gang were here.

Dolce Vita is a trendy little bar in the heart of Lan Kwai Fong. It looks like something out of Star Wars—a cavernous space, all pristine white, metal and glass. And boy is it noisy in here! It sounds more like an airport terminal or a railway station than a bar.

'What do you want?' James screeches over the din.

'A Slow Comfortable Screw would be nice,' I shout back.

'Yeah,' James laughs, 'I could use one of those, too. My gentleman hasn't been this out of action since I was eleven!'

We sip our drinks (they're too expensive to slurp down) and spot a Chinese guy dressed as Elvis Presley in a sparkly white suit with huge collars. Peter comes over and laughs.

'That's Melvis,' he informs us. 'Hong Kong's answer to Elvis. He's a scream. Hey Melvis! Play us 'Tie a Yellow Ribbon Round an Old Oak Tree'!'

Melvis, the 'King of Lan Kwai Fong', happily obliges, making us all snigger at his efforts. Definitely great entertainment for fifty pence and the best laugh I've had in a while.

'Melvis competes all around the world in Elvis lookalike and sound-alike competitions,' Peter quips, 'even if he keeps coming last!'

Melvis walks down the road singing, 'Lub me wender, lub me woo...'

I nurse my drink, looking around the room, and feel a tap on the shoulder.

'Err, hello there. I'm Pippa,' a nervous sounding English woman introduces herself to me. She looks a bit like Princess Diana, but prettier, and happy rather than sad-looking. For some unknown reason, I'm instantly at ease with her.

'Oh I do hate all this relentless boozing in Lan Kwai Fong,' says Pippa. 'It's so incredibly boring! I just want to stay at home and watch 'ER' but Rupe insisted I join him here. He loves a party. Makes him think he's still a youngster.'

Ah, so we're kindred spirits.

'Oh, he's having a whale of a time in Honkers,' Pippa continues. 'He's either drinking or dragon boat racing, sometimes both at the same time. Whatever you do, don't let anyone talk you into joining a dragon boat racing team. You get calloused hands that no manicurist can deal with, and Rupe's aged ten years with all the sun exposure. Plus it's jolly hard sweaty work. Take up shopping instead!'

Pippa and I spend the next three hours talking solidly. I learn that she was a nurse before marrying Rupert, a doctor (now how Mills & Boon is that!). She's such good company I could talk to her all night but her husband's flying out on business early the next morning so they say their goodbyes and leave. Before she goes, we swap numbers.

'It was super to meet you, Emily. Please do call me as I'd love us to be friends. Bye!'

Super, indeed—I've made my first friend! I'm sooooo happy! I wander over to James who puts his arm around me. He's laughing at what a guy called Gideon is saying (my giddy aunt, what kind of name is that?) in very plummy vowels.

'Another time, chaps,' I hear Gideon say, 'I went to Bangkok on a rugger tour and my team mate Harry thought he'd pulled a stunner in this decidedly seedy strip bar. The next morning at brekkie he came down with a huge smile on his face and confided in us that he'd gone all the way and that she'd strangely insisted on keeping all her clothes on, and, get this, having anal sex only! Whally! You should have seen his face when we told him she was obviously a lady-boy... a he not a she! Harry puked up his breakfast. He hadn't even used a rubber Johnny. What a complete whally.'

Dear God in heaven, is this really true?!

'An easy mistake to make, though, lads,' chimes in Peter. 'And some of them look darn hot.'

This sets Gideon off.

'You're wrong there, Peter. You can easily pick out the lady-boys as they have narrow arses, high calf muscles, big hands and feet, and make much more of an effort than women to look glamorous—you can spot them a mile off.'

'Well I hear they give the best blowjobs,' Peter quips, 'as they really know what men like. Whenever I go to Phuket I see loads of old boys from Europe, usually the Crouts, dirty buggers—quite literally—hanging around with the most amazingly good-looking lady-boys.' He raises his pint glass, giggling, 'Bottoms up, lads!'

Peter sounds like the voice of experience, but let's not go there. I'm feeling queasy already.

Chapter 3

March
Big Jobs

Angus 'Shorty Pants' Turner has lined me up an interview with a firm of solicitors. Kevin 'Misery Guts' McCann has arranged an interview for me, too, with a telecoms company. Maybe these guys are not so bad after all?

I desperately want a job. Apart from going stir-crazy having so much time on my hands, I want James and I to have some privacy (and sex!). Peter's been very kind putting us up for so long and I don't mean to sound ungrateful, but I just can't put up with him much longer. Life has become one endless party for James and at this rate he'll be joining Alcoholics Anonymous a couple of months down the line. I get the impression Peter would love James to be single so he could be his constant drinking companion in hedonistic Lan Kwai Fong and whore-infested Wanchai, and that I'm just an obstacle to his little fantasy. I'm sure he's subtly trying to get me to run home to London. I'll give you a classic example.

Even though his bedroom has its own large en-suite bathroom he strangely uses our designated guest bathroom and never ever flushes the toilet. I nearly gagged the first time I walked into our bathroom after he'd emptied his bowels in there. The putrid stench alone practically knocked me out and the sight of his fermenting big brown log (a sinker not a floater, so not a healthy plop to boot—no

Life is Pants

surprise there) had me evacuating the apartment, gasping for air. I'm distressed to learn Peter never washes his hands afterwards either (yucky yoodles!) and then goes and helps himself to the food I've bought for James and me. I still can't fathom how he attracts women—a lot of women at that. Please God, help me out here! Find me a job!

I haven't worn any of my work suits for over a month now and I'm shocked to find the waistbands feel very tight indeed. I guess the cloth must have shrunk on the plane, as eating out every night and an addiction to Devil's Chocolate Cake could have nothing to do with it. For the record, supermarkets are expensive here and the produce goes off really quickly so it actually works out cheaper to eat out or order in, which is absolutely fine by me. I must get into going to the gym again, though. I'm becoming lazy, frighteningly lazy, but then I do have the excuse that I've been avoiding Crystal who's permanently glued to the stepper machine (her blow by blow accounts of her brother-in-law's penile implants were starting to do my head in). Ah ha! Just maybe I'll get away with not exercising for a bit longer as I manage, thankfully, to do up my skirt, even if it is cutting into my waist. I could always leave the zip only half done up, I suppose (passing out from severe abdominal restriction won't land me a job, will it?).

My first interview is in 'Jardine House' in Central, an unusual edifice with hundreds of small 'porthole' windows. (Peter enlightened me that Hong Kongers refer to it as the 'House of a Thousand Arseholes' but I don't think I'll ask the taxi driver to take me there). It looks like something out of Star Wars—a cavernous space, all pristine white, metal and glass. Aren't offices usually noisy at nine in the morning? You can't hear a pin drop—spooky!

The receptionist at HK-APTC Telecom Corporation Inc offers me a tea or coffee (sadly not Devil's Chocolate Cake) while I wait for Mrs Lam. I become mesmerised, watching spectacularly coloured fish dart about in an enormous tank, bright blues and fluorescent yellows, large, small, thin, fat, stripy and polka-dotted. How they put the dear but dull British goldfish to shame!

I'm startled out of my newly discovered fascination with aquatic life when the receptionist comes over to show me into Mrs Lam's office. I tell myself to get a grip and prepare to impress with my astounding skills-set.

'Hello, Emily? I'm Angel, Angel Lam.' (Let's hope she is an angel and gives me this job!) She's a tiny woman with sleek black hair and pretty, delicate features set in smooth porcelain skin—a real live little China doll. Were it not for the horrendous fawn dress covered in lace and twee little bows, and the long pointed brown shoes that have to be size elevens, she'd look stunning. We make chit-chat for a while before cutting to the chase.

'My department has undergone many changes in the past year,' says Angel. 'I'm re-structuring my team now and looking for someone who will be both our Office Manager and my Personal Assistant.'

Hmm, two jobs for the price of one I think but, remembering Peter's particularly smelly turd this morning, don't say.

'I work very long hours,' Angel goes on, 'from 8 a.m. to at least 9 p.m., so the person who gets this job will have to do the same.'

What a dream job this is starting to sound!

'Ideally, I need someone who speaks good English and Cantonese.'

Does that rule me out? Can I learn Cantonese in a weekend? Unlikely, seeing the good that five years' of French lessons did me—I don't remember a word. Actually, that's a lie, I do recall some really useful stuff like 'bonjour' (hello), 'jambon et fromage' (although as a veggie I obviously don't eat ham and the cheese has to be rennet-free), 'merde' (shit), 'merdique' (shitty), 'putain' (fuck), 'sucer' (suck), 'salope' (slapper), pute (whore), and, best of all, 'morpions' (genital crabs). Everything else I've forgotten. So, realistically, I don't think I'd pick up Cantonese very quickly. Bugger!

Fortunately, seeing the downcast expression on my face, Angel (little 'Lam' that she is) adds, 'But Cantonese isn't essential for the role.'

Is it in the bag then?

No. And the past hour's efforts to sell myself have been a complete waste of time. Angel ends the interview only to inform me, 'In truth I don't think I have the budget to recruit this role right now, but you have some very good ideas.'

What the hell does that mean? A total flipping brush-off! And what a ridiculous name Angel is—does she know she sounds like a Miami porn star? I should have pointed it out before I left.

The lift is full as I get in. Why does it smell of rotting cabbage in here? Please, please, don't break down! I don't think I'd survive for too long as I'm already turning blue in an attempt not to inhale. I pray that no one farts or burps and that the lift will open any second to save me from imminent suffocation.

When it stops I'm hyperventilating and force my way out. Have I just experienced my first panic attack? Or was it just my lungs crying out from oxygen deprivation?

I spot a telephone on the ground floor reception and call Kevin McCrap to tell him what a miserable interview I've had.

'Kevin, it's Emily.'

Before I can launch into my sad tale he begins in hushed tones, 'Emily love, I'll call you back in a mo, I've got to smooth things over with my girlfriend after last night.'

Ah, what a professional our Kevin is! And he told me he didn't have a girlfriend! He must have met her only a couple of days ago and already she's his 'girlfriend'? Blokes! All of them sad and bad—except for my James, of course.

I try to focus on my second interview of the day and to hold out hope that this company has the budget to hire someone. Me! The firm is called 'Edwards Hathaway Woodbridge Wing Wong'—Christ, what a mouthful! I'm meeting the Head of Personnel, Gilly Shaw-Cross, then one of the senior solicitors, Alan Armstrong Jenkins. Oh my, do I need a double-barrelled name to put me in the running? My mother was so relieved to get married and rid of her maiden name it seems silly for me to take it on. 'Emily Hoare-Green'. It does have a certain ring to it (an underage porn star perhaps?!) and Alan Armstrong Jenkins may like it. Hmm, food for thought.

Gilly proves to be your typical Head of Personnel: post menopausal, divorced (acrimonious), cats (replacing the men in her life), table for one (when she does venture out), busy shiny suits (Dynasty style), singles' holidays to luxurious spas (screaming at the staff in between meditation sessions), vibrator (on its last legs)... yes, you know the sort. Oh, and bitter, too. Full of regrets and envious of all pretty young things with boyfriends.

'So Emily, let me get this right,' she begins. 'You resigned from your last job in London as your boyfriend's company transferred him here to Hong Kong? I hope he's worth it!'

Here we go sister.

'Actually,' I say, 'I always wanted to live and work in Asia so I saw this as an opportunity for me rather than him.'

Nice one! Round two.

'Humph,' Gilly seems lost for words. I imagine this rarely happens. 'Well, Emily, I'm glad you're here as we need someone like you.'

There is a God! And I want to give him a big kiss!

'I find Westerners have much more initiative and the role on offer certainly needs a self-starter. Not wanting to jump the gun, I should tell you that as we're hiring you in Hong Kong you'd be on a local package. A fair package, mind you, just missing a few of the bells and whistles expats expect.'

The bells and whistles turn out to be minor elements, like a housing allowance (boo hoo), home-leave flights (I'll never see my family again—I think I can live with that) and an inferior local medical plan (must recap on the Green Cross Code).

Gilly pulls a tight smile. 'Now, time for you to meet Alan Armstrong Jenkins. A word of warning: he likes to be dominated.'

What?! I didn't realize this place doubled up as an S&M parlour! If I'd known, I'd have worn my black fake leather skirt (which always guarantees great head from James) instead of my pretty lime green suit! (I own about half a million cute, snazzy suits of every colour imaginable. Unlike most office workers whose wardrobes tend to be inspired by funeral homes, I like to brighten up the place like a rainbow.)

Alan Armstrong Jenkins seems rather proud of himself, strutting over to me like a peacock to give me a firm, sweaty handshake. He's nothing to look at (in fact he resembles Ken Dodd, all buck teeth and bulging eyes) and is definitely somewhat lacking in the personality department (he'd make John Major seem riveting). As he gets closer and I get a good look at him, my jaw momentarily drops (Crikey, the man looks nine months' pregnant!) but then I reason it's more likely to be a beer gut, as science has only come so far.

Alan's face is flushed red, probably not so much the result of healthy, outdoor living but of his laboured breathing and daily steak, chips and sticky toffee pudding business lunches. All that money and he won't live to enjoy it (I'm sure his wife will, but no doubt she's earned it).

'Well, well, well,' Alan booms, despite the fact that I'm right beside him. 'Welcome to Honkers Kongkers, missy!'

'Missy'? No one's ever called me 'missy' before. Alan's been watching too many movies set in Rednecksville, Texas, or maybe Essex.

'An impressive CV, Emily,' he enthuses. 'Good, good, good. Gilly tells me you're available immediately. Excellent, excellent, excellent.'

Why does he keep repeating his words three times over? Is this how he justifies charging clients such extortionate fees? He gives them more words for their money?

'And where are you originally from, Emily? I suspect there's Italian blood in you, what with your hot-blooded Latino colouring?'

Oh yikes, is he getting saucy with me? 'Wimbledon actually, Alan,' I respond weakly.

'Ha, so I'm mistaken, you're a Womble not a Señorita!'

Oh God, what drivel. He does appear a bit nervous, though, so perhaps he's not being this ridiculous intentionally.

'Marvellous, marvellous, marvellous. Would you be able to start on Monday? Gilly will courier the paperwork to you this afternoon.'

'I love you, Alan, I love you, Alan, I love you, Alan!' I think, but can hardly say.

I find a telephone in Edwards Hathaway Woodbridge Wing Wong's rather austere foyer, which looks like something out of Star Wars—a cavernous space, all pristine white, metal and glass. Aren't solicitors' offices usually noisy all hours of the day? You can't hear a pin drop—spooky!

'James, it's me. I've got a job! That firm of solicitors wants me!'

'Excellent news, baby! I'm really happy for you. It sounds great. You'd better start looking for an apartment for us then.'

Thank fuck for that—we're finally getting our own place, just me and my man. James is actually really pleased to be leaving Peter's pad. As much as he revels in the on-tap laddish company, he confides in me that he thinks it's a security risk to stay there.

'Do you remember that girl he brought home one night who looked like a prostitute?' he asks.

I have a think, but there have been so many and they all looked like prostitutes to me.

'You know, the chain-smoking one in the very little black dress?'

Oh yes, she entered and left the apartment in a puff of white smoke.

'She nicked his passport!'

'Jesus!' I respond, gob-smacked. 'That's terrible!'

'The funny thing is,' James chuckles, 'she stole his TV remote control as well!'

'What! Why?' I'm amazed at this.

'I guess she thought it was something else. Anyway, he was really pissed off, more about the TV remote than his passport, but he let on that this sort of thing happens all the time.'

'You'd think he'd stop picking up those sorts of girls.'

James laughs. 'No chance, they're just too easy!'

Maybe, but at a price!

James has got it into his head that he wants us to live in a 'Serviced Apartment' for our first year while we settle down. He says it will make things easier for us and that I (note, not him) won't have to worry about cleaning and ironing and all that sort of bollocks. That sounds more than fine by me. I need to focus my energies on making the right impression in my new job. I scan a free local magazine and estate agents' flyers given out on The Escalator and find the addresses of four such blocks of apartments in the posh Mid-Levels area where, apparently, all the expatriates live. A Western 'commune'.

James says he wants to celebrate my success by buying me a ticket to the 'Hong Kong Rugby Sevens'—not that I have any particular interest in going. I realize he needs an excuse to go, since the tickets are pricey and it's a three-day event. I play along with it and attend just on the Saturday.

Hong Kong Stadium is huge and completely packed. James tells me we're down the fun end, although Deanna's warned me it's the rowdy end. (I know who I believe!) True to form, the infamous South stand is mobbed with lads and ladettes intent on drinking as many jugs of warm beer as humanly possible. The chatter is deafening and we just about manage to find seats. No one seems to be paying much attention to the rugby, although I quite like looking at the fit bodies on display and all their bottom clutching action. Peter drunkenly starts hurling verbal abuse at the Hong Kong Royal Yacht Club's box, despite being a corporate member himself.

A lot of people are in fancy dress, funny wigs and elaborate face paints. One group of women are dressed as the 'Pink Ladies' from Grease in hot pink jackets, black leggings and hair scraped back in girlish ponytails. There's a group of men in 'Reservoir Dogs' suits, looking cool in shades and black and white, and another kitted out as doctors, complete with stethoscopes. James and Peter look relatively normal for a change, wearing just the bog standard England shirts to tie in nicely with their rendition of

'Sweet Chariot' which they sing (shout) until their voices go. I wear a red and white T-shirt from French Connection which reads 'Show Me Your Tackle'. This seems very fitting and does go down rather well with the blokes who are sober enough to make out the words. One lad is kind enough to streak across the pitch and actually show his to the crowd (though Peter's binoculars reveal it isn't very impressive and resembles a shrivelled up slug).

Unfortunately, tackle exposure becomes a bit of a theme as the afternoon wears on, when men dispense with urinals and piss directly into their empty beer jugs. This is going on all around me, and just as I am thinking it couldn't get any worse, a fat Geordie guy decides it would be great fun to throw his jug of piss all over the crowd in front of him. I duck to miss the spray of golden pee. James and Peter think this is highly amusing, but seeing my mortified expression, James, with a touch of chivalry, shouts, 'Oi, there's ladies here!' Consequently, more pee is flung in our direction and Deanna gets soaked. Fortunately (or unfortunately) she's too pissed to understand what's going on. I'm not pissed enough to put up with this disgusting behaviour and make to leave. I hear James shouting, 'Party pooper!' at me as I go.

The following week I pick up a free magazine called 'BC Mag' to find a couple of pages dedicated to photos of the Hong Kong Rugby Sevens' crowds. I scroll down the pictures, giggling at the Pink Ladies who look a bit worse for wear with smudged mascara and squewiff ponytails. I spot James, Peter and Deanna. Deanna's asleep in her seat with her mouth wide open, probably unconscious. Peter just looks like his usual drunken self, while James is smiling broadly with his arm around a pretty Filipino girl who's looking up at him with starry eyes.

Chapter 4

April
Home Smelly Home

Work, work, work, flat hunting, work, work, work, flat hunting—you get the idea. There's little to choose from in our price range, as the rents here are truly extortionate. (I've read that Hong Kong is the most expensive place in the world to live—fan dabby bloody dosy!) For the same money in London we could get a big flat in a decent area with great views—that's how expensive we're talking. Here, we have a choice of 'cosy' (i.e. tiny) studio apartments with or without 'balcony' (i.e. flowerbox). All the apartments on offer have horrible 1980s-style black plastic furniture, tacky Chinese bird motif wallpaper—possibly the most vile I've ever clapped eyes on—and threadbare carpets in a speckled grey colour that doesn't show up the dirt but just looks dirty.

I'd much rather move into an unfurnished flat and make it our own, but every time I suggest this to James he balks at the prospect of going to Ikea. To him, this would be a fate worse than death, what with the hoards trapped in a maze leading directly to the checkout, with no escape route in sight. So I'll just have to get used to slightly 'time warped' surroundings.

We end up choosing a seven hundred square foot one-bedroom flat with a balcony big enough for a table, chairs and barbecue. I don't feel particularly excited about securing the apartment, which is a bit odd considering I'm so desperate to get out of Peter's pad. But it'll do, I guess. James tries his best to negotiate the price down but the Chinese managing agent is stubborn and all our pleading efforts and cries of poverty don't get us very far. Not even my sweetest smile does the trick (damn, am I losing my touch?). We do, however, persuade them pick up the electricity bill, which is a bit of a bonus (and I can keep my vibrator on charge without worry).

In between emptying out boxes and suitcases and trying to squash everything into insufficient cupboard space, I have the delightful task of applying for my Hong Kong identity card. Sounds simple. It isn't. I end up spending nearly a whole day at Immigration Tower in Wanchai, being shunted around from department to department along with hundreds of other poor buggers.

The whole exercise is carried out with military precision. You queue in Zone One to get the paperwork, Zone Two to get it signed off, Zone Three for fingerprinting, Zone Four for photographing. I think of Hugh Grant when the LAPD caught him with that hooker who looked like a transvestite with balloon lips, and begin to empathise. I haven't even committed a crime. Yet. I feel like murdering the guy who takes my mugshot when he pushes me and shouts, 'Back on the wall, now!' Little Hitler. He's obviously feeling powerful. This really is too much of an ordeal and quite frankly one I could not go through again in this lifetime. I'll just have to make sure I never lose the bloody thing. Then again, looking at the highly unflattering picture maybe I should re-do it.

I end up spending my first week in the apartment cleaning it from top to bottom. So much for having a cleaner; the place is absolutely filthy. Every cupboard is covered in a layer of thick black dust and stubborn grime and it transpires that the grey kitchen units are in fact white. All my nails have broken from so much scrubbing. Oh, woe is me! The life of a skivvy!

When I finish the place looks a million times better and I forget the hardships undergone. Even the 'cleaner' who comes into our apartment every morning (incidentally using one cloth on the entire building's kitchen sinks, surfaces and toilets—aaarrgghhh!) looks really pleased with my efforts. Do I really have to teach the cleaner how to clean?

James and I have a tiff over his smelly sports kits. While I've no complaints about his athletic physique (how could I?) his natural talent in football, rugby, tennis, squash, badminton, Eton fives, pool, golf, scuba diving and ten-pin bowling (the list goes on) has its drawbacks. For one, he has a different bloody kit for every bloody sport and they are beginning to take over the entire flat. And he has the cheek to complain about all my shoes! At least they don't smell like a musty old locker room!

James convinces me it's easier in an apartment this size to get the launderette to do all our washing. Big mistake. When I get our sack of clothing back I find my pale yellow 'Paul Smith' T-shirt now grey and shrunken to a child's size (it would fit the local girls, though), three of James's socks missing and an inherited 'Gay Pride' T-shirt in their place. Oh, and my lovely white gym bottoms are now missing all their funky buttons. I try them on and they slide down to the floor, rendered useless. Just fabulous. All our clothes ruined. Why on earth do I listen to James? From now on, I do our washing (what am I saying?!).

From: emilygreenhk@hotmail.com
To: hicks16@hotmail.com, katiets@abbottsdury.com, janeheffer@yahoo.com, sandiebeech@yahoo.com, fernrocks@yahoo.com, deano@btinternet.com, mandyandandy@yahoo.com, teets@hotmail.com, mary1979@hotmail.com, clare_adair@btinternet.com
Subject: New address…

Well, old friends, apologies for the mass email. Time to catch up with you all.

Finally, we have our own pad. Yippee! It's roomy enough to swing a kitten in, fab!

Apartment 34A (yes, by sad coincidence, the same as

my pathetic bra size!)

Staunton Street Mansions

12 Staunton Street

Mid-Levels

Hong Kong SAR

Tel/Fax: +852 2869-0202 (don't forget, we're 7 hours ahead of you!!!)

Let me know if you want to come and stay, and when, as we're now ready for bookings! Very comfy sofa-bed if you're under 5ft 1ins. If you're taller you're in for a bit of neck ache, but don't be put off by this as you'll be getting sooo trollied every night in Lan Kwai Fong (our West End boozing area equivalent) you won't even notice!

Life in Hong Kong is buzzing. It really is a bizarre mixture of old and new, oriental and modern. The area I live in reminds me of Covent Garden, crazy but true! I don't know why, as it's really nothing like it—except for the prices! Actually, you'd better start saving for the trip pronto as it's a lot more expensive out here. Luckily my new job demands I work 24 hours a day 7 days a week so no time for spending money, hahaha aaaaaahhhhhh! Although I have to say (so far) the job is good—the people are a lot more chilled out here, expats united on a jolly. Tally ho!

It's a huge hassle moving overseas, I don't know if I'd do it again. I've been living out of a suitcase these past couple of months as I've only just received my shipment (James's company wouldn't pay to transport my stuff over here so I had to arrange it myself). But James and I are very happy together (hopefully not famous last words!). We don't see that much of each other (the secret of every successful relationship?), as we're so hectic doing our own thing.

I've joined a gym as I've exploded into pre-weight loss Vanessa Phelps dimensions (it doesn't take long to get out of shape). The gyms here are a bit archaic—and it's back to Jane Fonda style aerobic workouts, tedious stuff that doesn't help fighting the flab. Fortunately, there are quite a few tasty chaps to ogle to pass the time. Eight

Western men to one Western woman out here, yippee! So best get your bags packed fast, girls, hahaha! Plus (and this is a big plus) the locals are so short you feel like a supermodel! Move over, Giselle! Bugger off, Heidi!

Bad points so far include being ill every other week (apparently all new expats suffer like this until they get used to the pollution, heat, humidity, water, food, extortionate prices, etc). The restaurants are lovely but the supermarkets dire. The produce is rank (my cooking was always bad but not this bad!). Over there you walk into Tesco smelling freshly-baked bread and aromatic coffee; here you walk in to the stench of rotting fruit and veg and God only knows what else. I nearly bought some yoghurt yesterday but the sell-by date was six weeks ago! Yuck! Plus the cheese section is covered in loads of green mould! Gross. In the UK these 'super' markets would be instantly shut down. So clearly restaurants do very good business here.

Also, all the bugs out here (affectionately known as 'mozzies') love me—I'm being eaten alive and now look like a leper (not kidding). I've been told to eat loads of Marmite to ward them off—I've never eaten so much of the stuff in my life, but to no avail. I'm covered from head to foot in mosquito repellent, but the little buggers still manage to attack the postage stamp area that I miss.

The worst thing by far, though, is missing my pals...

Anyway, enough of my ramblings.

Keep me posted with all your news.

Take care

Love n Hugs

Emily x (ouch, was that another friendly mozzie, feasting on my knee? oh good...)

Three days later and no one's replied. Maybe the latest instalment of life in Honkers Kongkers will get a response!

From: emilygreenhk@hotmail.com

To: hicks16@hotmail.com, katiets@abbotts-dury.com, janeheffer@yahoo.com, sandie-beech@yahoo.com, fernrocks@yahoo.com, deano@btinternet.com, mandyandandy@yahoo.com, teets@hotmail.com, mary1979@hotmail.com, clare_adair@btinternet.com

Subject: WE'RE UNDER ATTACK!

Oh my God, I've had my first huge, fat, shiny black (calm down, Mary!) cockroach experience and it nearly gave me a heart attack, no lie. Alert the authorities, we're under attack! I've just discovered there are bloody MILLIONS of them out here. It's like a horror movie—I can hear that deep-voiced American actor who does the voiceovers for all the cinema trailers (don't you often think it's strange the same guy gets all the work? He must be minted):

'They holidayed in the Costa del Sol in winter, but came to Hong Kong in summer—sniffing out feeeaaarrrrrr. Hunting down the most terrified woman on the planet… Emily Green. Turning her life into a living hell!'

I swear they know I'm scared of them. I was walking along our road yesterday and got chased by several big black and brown ones (Mary I told you to stop getting worked up!). I ran for my life, screaming at the top of my lungs while the locals just sat on the pavement and watched in amusement. I made it to my apartment, plonked myself down on the sofa only to discover a whopping king-sized cockroach sitting right beside me! Probably the biggest ever seen by human eyes! He then spent the evening sitting comfortably on the sofa watching 'Sex and the City' while I hovered between kitchen and lounge with my heart beating like a drum (a huge African tribal one), not knowing how to handle the situation. I was so frozen to the spot I couldn't even spray the repellent. My heart was palpitating so hard I thought the end was nigh.

Luckily Prince Charming came home from work and zapped the bugger with the spray. It took ages to die. All that was left was his shell. So Mary, men do have their uses!

> There's also a lizard in our kitchen. I was cooking (overcooking) some pasta when it ran across the wall. I screamed at the top of my lungs and ran out into the lounge, flapping about. I told James there was a huge lizard and, my hero, he checked it out. He called me an idiot saying it was just a tiny gecko, good for eating spiders, and completely harmless.
>
> I'm thinking of coming home. How can I live like this?
>
> Thanking you all in advance for your kind prayers.
>
> LOL
>
> Emily :(
>
>
> From: mary1972@hotmail.com
> To: emilygreenhk@hotmail.com
> Subject: bloody hell
>
> I don't like the sound of that, not one itty little bit. Yeah, maybe men do have their uses after all!
>
> Rather you than me, matey.
>
> Praying hard to exorcise the critters from your flat. Perhaps I'll drop the Pope a line on your behalf!
>
> Miss ya!
>
> Mare

Good old Mary. Nobody else has bloody answered my emails. Have I really been forgotten so soon? I miss them all big time but evidently they don't miss me back. I guess they're jealous I've moved to 'exotic' Hong Kong while they carry on with their mundane little lives back home. I don't mean that. I just yearn to hear from them, to catch the news, laugh at the gossip, that's all.

It's so strange, feeling so out of it, when I used to be in the heart of the group. I don't know if Mare's on one of her downers (always over a moron, I mean a man), or if Cheryl's putting the weight back on that she recently lost through 'Slimming World' (she really believes 'a Mars a day helps you work, rest, and play'). I don't know the latest developments on our favourite soaps—which actor's being given the heave-ho, off you go, never to work again on EastEnders. I don't even know what the headlines of the Daily Mail are (probably something on Yobbie Williams). I know nothing. It truly is just James and me, stranded together on the other side of the world. At least working crazy hours doesn't leave you with much time to be homesick.

My boss Alan Armstrong Jenkins has lost his Personal Assistant. Quite how one loses a PA is beyond me but my suggestion of filing a missing person's report with the police didn't go down too well. How, you might ask, did Carmen Ip get lost? On her way to work? In some dark recess of the office block? In an alien abduction? Or did Ms Ip lose it with Alan and his incessant verbal diarrhoea? Hmm, methinks the latter is most likely.

So, not only am I Office Manager and General Dogsbody to Gilly Shaw-Cross, but I am now Alan's flipping PA as well. To look at the bright side, the days—and evenings—go quickly and most of the solicitors here are male (yeah-hey!). In fact, even the women here act like men (deep voices, cropped hair and trouser suits, but thankfully no crotch rubbing).

Alan's Number Two is a bit of a dish—Byron Baddcock. What a name... what a man! He's tall, dark, handsome and exceedingly nice to boot. Unlike the majority of good-looking guys who know it and revel in it, Byron's just an exceptionally lovely person—possibly because he's married (alas! Should I add 'only kidding'?). On my first day he bought me a 'sunshine smoothie' from the scrummy 'Mix Juice Bar' next door to the HSBC HQ building, and introduced himself. I wouldn't have minded if he'd added the date rape drug! (I know, I know, what a dreadful thing for me to say.)

Alan's Number Three, on the other hand, Rick Lyons, has already established himself as a complete tosspot in my books. Like Byron, he comes up to me on my first day, but instead of a welcome, says, 'I hope you're not going to prove to be as useless as the last girl,' and with that he's gone. Hmm, nice to meet you, too, Rick (the dick). Despite having a protruding potbelly and wobbly arse he swaggers around the office as though he's God's gift.

My predecessor Nikki Jayne Barton (note how to cheat with a double-barrelled name) was certainly a messy pup, although Rick's description of 'useless' seems somewhat harsh. Luckily, it doesn't take me long to get things in order. Being a Virgo has its advantages—'excessively neat and tidy' really means 'terribly well organised and efficient'. (Not that I believe in star signs. OK, just a little bit, but only when my horoscope says negative things. The good things never seem to happen.)

I'm happy enough at work, all in all. My desk is next to a window (in London I couldn't even see a window which definitely sent me a bit ga ga) and it looks on to a row of swanky designer shops that the likes of me will never set foot in. Not that I want a fur coat or anything. People can be such animals!

Alan startles me.

'Well, well, well, Emily, how's my report going? Got to grips with PowerPoint yet? I can't fathom it out for the life of me.'

He's leaning so close to me I can smell his lunch (steak—cooked rare and bloody, potato croquettes, mushroom sauce, English mustard, and a glass of dry white wine?).

'I'll email it to you in the next ten minutes, Alan,' I promise.

'Excellent, excellent, excellent,' Alan enthuses as he wanders off.

It's actually quite interesting stuff: a presentation he's going to give at Hong Kong University on Edwards Hathaway Woodbridge Wing Wong's graduate entry requirements and trainee programme. It looks like the intake will have a ball—there are more social events lined up than work! Welcome drinks, welcome luncheon, welcome ball, and that's just for starters. Then there are junk trips on the company cruiser, weekly cocktails at the Ritz Carlton Hotel and the graduates' global annual get-together (wow, in Paris this year! In my next life I know what I'm coming back as!). In return, all they have to do is rotate through the different departments, i.e. six months in corporate law, six months in entertainment law and so on, getting a feel for what they'd like to do when they grow up. There are only eight places available at our Hong Kong office so it's no wonder the competition is so stiff.

Thankfully, Alan likes the fancy clip-art and noises I've attached to his presentation to make it a bit more ear-and-eye-catching. I thought my end result was slightly OTT but I remember how boring these things were as a student and that a few pictures and funny tunes could hold my attention for longer than the usual three seconds (there again, I did do a History of Art rather than a Law degree, so a slightly different crowd with very different brain cells—think Prince William, brightest on the outside). What the heck, though, I should use my artistic skills whenever an opportunity arises so that my education is not completed wasted!

'Marvellous, marvellous, marvellous!' Alan's very impressed with my display of creativity. 'Much, much, much better than my presentation last year. Done on cue cards, but Nikki put them in the wrong order so I ended up speaking a lot of gobbledygook.'

'No change there!' I want to retort but don't.

'I'll need you to be with me in case there are any problems with the laptop. It gets the better of me sometimes.'

So, Alan's none too confident about his computer skills. It'll be good for me to get out of the office for a change.

HKU is a bland, modern building that makes the hallowed turf of Oxford and Cambridge seem even more sacred. Alan and I are shown into a state-of-the-art room, and instruct the technician to set up the presentation. The room fills up quickly and quietly (not like my fellow students who sounded like the charge of the Light Brigade) and we're actually ready to start on time (but then this lot obviously didn't take the time to finish their spliffs).

As much as Alan's an irritation to work for, I've got to hand it to him, he's really good at public speaking. Supremely confident (or is it arrogance?), taking all the students' diverse questions completely in his stride. Impressive stuff indeed. Afterwards, Alan thanks me profusely for making it so hi-tech and for a second or two I consider him to be a very nice man.

Back at home, the evening is no different from most. Now that we've got our own place, James and I are back to having loads of sex every night (it is a cheap source of entertainment!). We fancied the pants off each other from the moment we met. One glance between us and I'm dripping wet and he's got an almighty hard-on. Any time, any place, which used to be particularly annoying when we went to his mum and dad's in Chigwell for Sunday lunch. Consequently, I'm permanently saddle-sore and walk with bowlegs much of the time. We just can't get enough of each other. We kiss deeply, clinging to one another, praying it will never end. We linger over oral sex, him licking me to oblivion, me sucking him until his balls are ready to burst. Moving in harmony to the rhythm of primal desire. My wet juices running down my thighs, his sweat sexily dripping into my arse crack. My nearing the clouds, his cry as his hot white cum splatters over my back (and in my bloody hair!). Apart from cystitis, the main drawback of so much bonking is that it gives us a huge appetite. We end up famished and go out to eat (he hates to cook and wash up as much as I do). Unfortunately, our bedroom workout doesn't stop me piling on the pounds afterwards and it is no wonder my skirts are feeling so tight.

When James told me Pizza Express was opening here I nearly cried from sheer joy. Mmm, a slice of home! Just what the doctor ordered. We go on opening night, probably asking for trouble, but our taste buds are insisting on it. Ah, the aroma! So what if a quarter of a pizza costs the same as a whole McDonalds Happy Meal—I HAVE TO HAVE ONE! And some of those scrummy dough balls smothered in garlic butter. And some of that divine chocolate fudge cake accompanied by a scoop of vanilla ice cream with a single strawberry on top (the healthy part). Absolute heaven on earth. The service is a little slow (teething problems, to be expected) and portions a bit on the small side, but then Asians don't eat humungous Western-sized portions and it is Pizza Express so can get away with pretty much anything. It's strange, though, how you can eat a three-course meal there, go home and within an hour feel hungry enough for another one. I know, I know, I should live in America.

We arrive back at our luxuriously decked out apartment (plastic furniture, lino wallpaper and polyester curtains) to find the night porter in the lobby in the midst of a screaming match with his wife. The porter looks tame enough—a small, grey-haired old man, permanently in ancient slippers which are held together with tape. His dumpy young wife, who must be at least half his age, is clearly giving as good as she gets, screaming at him in an eardrum bursting high-pitched shrill. Their eight or so children, ranging from newborn to the high teens, are all present and watch their parents expressionlessly while lolling on the yellow lobby sofas.

'Quiet!' James shouts. 'This isn't the place for your argument!'

They take no notice.

We can still hear them once we're inside our apartment so James leans out of the window and yells, 'Oi, QUIET! Idiot chunksters!'

It turns out we're not the only ones objecting to their heated domestic, as we can see a police car slowly pulling up with neon blue lights flashing hypnotically. Our porter, his wife and the kids spill out onto the road, although the arrival of the two wee policemen fails to calm things down. If anything, the porter is getting angrier, raising his voice all the more and flinging his arms around wildly. I wish I knew what they're arguing about. We're watching from our window and can see other residents and neighbours doing the same. Well, it beats watching another repeat of a repeat of 'Friends'.

The policemen are so docile out here that they just stand doing nothing. They look uncomfortable.

'Come on, do something!' James calls out to them.

The police look up at us and then speak into their walkie-talkies.

'Christ, it's a good job they're not working the Brixton

beat!' I pipe up. 'They'd be eaten alive!'

After about half an hour our porter is bundled into the back of the police car and they drive off. The entertainment is over so we close the curtains and get back to 'Friends'.

The next morning as James and I leave for work, 'Cellotape Slippers' as we now refer to him, is back on reception duty. He's in a cheerful mood and flashes us a grin, displaying brown and yellow teeth. We put his mood swings down to seemingly working a twenty-four hour seven-day week, only to go home to a huge brood of demanding children. What a life!

The months are whooshing by at work. I'm just plodding along doing my job, but Alan thinks I'm the best thing since sliced bread. He gave me the most wonderful probation report after three months, ticking all the 'Excellent' boxes, much to Gilly's chagrin. I was thrilled with it but she waved it off, saying, 'Alan should have discussed this with me first. We never give anyone 100% excellent.' So instead of being pleased about what an asset I was to the firm, my report put her in an almighty strop with me. It seems these frazzled women in Human Remains, I mean Resources, always need something to complain about.

Nonetheless, Alan is so taken with my office management skills he encourages one of the other partners, Morag Po, to use me (as if I haven't got enough work to do!). Morag was raised in Scotland and it's a little weird hearing a Chinese woman speak with a heavy Scottish accent. Our geographical connection fails to warm me to her, however, and it turns out she is a right unsmiling hard-nut (I guess she's sacrificed a lot to make it to partner level). She has zero people-management skills and constantly snaps at her staff and flies off the handle at the slightest provocation. Unsurprisingly, no one who works for her can stand her.

'Emily,' she says to me one day, 'I need you to write a report for me. Titus Wong is looking to outsource our payroll function and wants to know the pros and cons.'

So what Morag really means is that old Titus, her boss, wants her to write this report and she's passing the buck to me.

Since I know jack shit about this subject I ask Morag, 'Isn't this Gilly's jurisdiction?'

'She says she doesn't have the time to do it,' Morag replies.

Well neither do I! I ask Morag to elaborate on what she wants me to cover. I should have known better, as she just snaps back at me.

'Just see what you can come up with!'

Hmm, with so little to go on, bugger all I suspect! This really isn't in my job description.

We chill out that evening, playing cards round James's pal Tony's apartment. He lives on Discovery Bay, a small island off the coast of Hong Kong—only a twenty-minute ferry ride from Central. Discovery Bay is otherwise known as 'Delivery Bay' as it's absolutely teeming with young families. In fact, they're so kids-orientated here that they've banned cars and drive around in daft golf buggies that move at about half a mile an hour. The women are permanently pregnant. It's like some reproductive disease has hit the island, leaving everyone breeding like rabbits. I take the precaution of avoiding the tap water.

Tony has a pretty, petite 'mumsy' wife called Rebecca who wears a floral pinafore like those you see on 'Ma' and 'Grandma Walton'. Her excuse for having five children under the age of five is the Catholic faith (the Pope has a lot to answer for!). Poor Rebecca looks knackered, despite having two live-in Filipino maids to help her. She yawns throughout our card game but still manages to bloody win.

Tony, on the other hand, isn't Catholic and didn't want five children (nor four, nor three for the matter). James mentioned to me on the ferry that Tony had told him, 'I only dare to fuck my wife up the arse these days as I don't want any more kids.' (Lucky old Tony, 'king of the arse bandits'. I can't quite imagine Rebecca agreeing to the dry route, looking like a picture of innocence in her virginal outfit.)

Every ten minutes one of the kids comes out of their bedroom, needing a pee or poo. Rebecca jumps up and down doing the toilet runs. Tony shakes his head in despair.

'Fuck, I need a fag!' Rebecca says suddenly and lights up

a cigarette, drawing on it heavily. (Shame we didn't bring her some hash instead of white wine to take her mind off things!)

'Tony,' she then says, 'have you noticed the layer of dirt on top of the fridge?'

'I can't say I have, my love.' Tony answers sarcastically.

Rebecca sits down again at the table in a huff. 'Bloody maids! They pretend to clean. It drives me mad!'

I nod sympathetically, since the cleaner at our serviced apartments is certainly no cleaner.

Rebecca leans forward, adding in a low voice, 'God only knows what they get up to all day. I once knew a woman...'

Tony cuts in, 'Oh, don't tell them that story, honey, it'll put them off kids for life!'

'Do tell!' I encourage Rebecca—anything to put me off breeding the wee buggers.

'Well, I won't mention any names, and this will leave you sick to your stomachs. This woman, who is a friend of a friend, moved to Singapore with her husband and their two boys, fourteen and twelve. You know the Singapore authorities are so anal? Well, they test all the foreign maids for HIV on a regular basis. One day her maid comes home and says she's tested positive for HIV and has been told by the authorities to go back to her home country. Anyway, the family really like her so fight for her to stay in Singapore. When this fails, they try to organise healthcare in Canada, but can't arrange this. Anyway, they see her off at the airport and she turns to her boss, this woman, and says, "I'm very sorry to have to tell you this," and the woman instantly says, "Please don't tell me you've been sleeping with my husband!" And the maid says, "No, but I've slept with your two boys." Aged twelve and fourteen, for God's sake—both of them HIV positive! Poor little children.'

James and I have turned pale. How awful. How utterly sickening. I do hope it's not a true story, but in this day and age anything's possible.

Tony tries to break the morbid silence with, 'Anyone up for group sex?'

We laugh, welcoming the change of subject. James

winks at me.

'He was joking, James!' I point out.

James and Tony roar with laughter and Rebecca and I roll our eyes at each other. Still playing cards, we up the stakes. Rebecca takes the lot. Just as well we are still only playing with cents and pennies. I wonder if James and I will ever end up living on Discovery Bay. I would resemble Ma Walton surrounded by angelic children with blonde ringlets and blue button eyes without a maid in sight. Just me—supermum—taking everything in my stride. Dream on!

We enjoy the evening, although it's certainly been an education on the necessity of contraception. We say our goodbyes, meaning to come back soon, but it doesn't happen. It turns out that whenever we make arrangements to meet them one of their kids falls sick or some other such drama kicks off. Ah, the joys of parenthood...

The odious Rick Lyons has a very annoying habit of coming and sitting on my desk when he wants to talk to me. In fact he doesn't sit, he half lies down, so we end up being nose distance apart. He just moves my pens and papers aside and lolls onto my desk. Today he's telling me how his only child, Cymbeline (well she would have a name like that. Cymbals for short, perhaps?), is higher than top of her class (how can that be? Obviously she hasn't inherited his mathematical mind). It's all Cymbeline this, Cymbeline that—as if I give a monkey's arse! He shows me a picture of her—she's a plain mousy child of about four, wearing a peculiar suit and tie. She's really just missing the executive briefcase. Very sad.

He then shows me a picture of Cymbeline's birth, exiting her mother's cavernous fanny. She's blue, covered in blood, white waxy muck and poo—yuck! What a complete weirdo Rick is! Like a God-send, Byron passes by.

'Oh you're not showing that gruesome photograph to Emily are you, Rick? He's shown it to the entire management committee, Emily, and we've all commented on how grotesque it is, and why anyone in their right mind would want to frame it for their desk. It's enough to put you off roast beef sandwiches for life!'

I'm in love with Byron Baddcock, but alas, he's very happily married with two children, Charlie and Chloe, with number three on the way. And his wife is, apparently, really beautiful (ex-model) and really nice (does a lot of charity work). A fucking saint no less. Bugger.

'Did Rick tell you about the placenta?' Byron adds.

I look to Rick blankly, who chuckles smugly.

'Yes, yes, I ate it. There you have it. It's well known they're absolutely packed with nutrients. It went down very well with a dash of soy sauce. Absolutely delicious!'

Somehow I know he's not joking and try not to gag.

I'm dreaming of Byron having an identical twin who falls madly in love with me, when Morag storms over to my desk. What now?

In her loudest voice she snaps, 'Emily, I am very unhappy about this report you wrote for me. It's not at all what I wanted.'

Seeing as she wouldn't tell me what she bloody wanted, what a nerve! I want to respond, 'I don't have psychic skills, Morag!' but don't.

She continues, 'I'm most disappointed with this and have told Alan you can't write reports.'

What! I'm now fuming and want to tell her, 'No, I can't write reports on subjects I know nothing about and with no background information to go on!' But I remain silent, becoming aware that other people in the office are ear-wigging.

'I can't believe I have to teach you how to write a report, Emily!' the old bat goes on. 'Once you've got all the details together that I asked for, send me what you have and I'll show you how it should be written.'

She steams off into her office. What a silly bitch! I thank God it's time for lunch—time to escape!

I'm not one for variety. It may well be the spice of life but I'm quite happy eating my jacket potato with grated cheese and spring onions every day for lunch. My philosophy when it comes to eating is, why try something else when you've found a winner? I go to a chain of sandwich shops called

'Oscar's Super Sarnies'. They're OK. 'Super' is pushing it a bit, but 'Oscar's OK Sarnies' doesn't have quite the same pulling power.

So I eat the same old thing nearly five days a week. For three months now, Monday to Friday, I've been served by Winky (!) who is assigned to the spuds counter. Despite my smiling and saying, 'Lay Ho?'('How are you?'—how many people even bother to be friendly?) she always treats me like she's never clapped eyes on me before. It's very strange—perhaps she has the memory of a goldfish? But surely even goldfish have some powers of recollection? I try to be tolerant of Winky, after all, we do speak different languages, but it's really proving difficult not to lose my rag with her.

'A take-away jacket potato with grated cheese and spring onions, please,' I say brightly.

'Eat-in jacket potato with cheese—is that grated?' Winky responds.

'Yes, grated, but take-away, please.'

'With margarine, bacon bits and no spring onions?'

Stay calm, Emily. 'No, grated cheese and spring onions.'

'Take-away?'

'Yes, thank you.'

'With bacon bits?'

Is she taking the piss? Every flipping day we go through this ritual of crazy confusion. I WANT TO TAKE AWAY A JACKET POTATO WITH GRATED CHEESE AND SPRING ONIONS—that's it! Simple! Nothing else! Zip! Often she adds bacon bits in error and we have to start again. And she annoyingly thinks three strands of grated cheese should suffice despite my telling her otherwise every flaming visit (the Chinese don't eat much in the way of dairy products, you see, they're anti-mucus, although they think nothing of gobbing phlegm all over the pavement). I very rarely say this about anybody, but Winky truly ain't up to the job.

I'm eating my jacket potato at my desk, reading 'The Mirror' online about Lesley Ash's horrendous (but hilarious) collagen implants which have earned her the nickname 'Trout Pout', and about the 'Bennifer' saga (I have classy taste). Poor Ben Affleck, though I have to say I think the name the press has given him does suit him. Will he, won't he, marry Jennifer López? Does anyone give a shit? All I want to know is how come she's got such a big backside when she has her own Personal Trainer and Nutritionist.

I'm thinking about J-Lo's arse when (speaking of arses) Morag approaches my desk.

'Emily!' she snaps.

Christ, can't she see I'm eating my lunch?

'Have you re-done that report for me yet?'

What? In the last ten minutes! I'm getting so pissed off with this. 'Morag, you said you'd write the report,' I remind her.

'No, I didn't. I gave it to you to write. Anyway, I need to see whether you can actually write a report.' With that, she returns to her office and slams the door shut.

This woman is awful. My jacket potato is now cold and anyway I've lost my appetite. I think of Morag's bulging eyes and general all-round unattractiveness, and wonder how she's managed to peg herself one of the Executive Partners as her husband. Not that he's anything to write home about, if I'm honest. Josh Adamson is British but lacks the sense of humour most Brits are born with and, like his wife, he's unsmiling and downright ugly so doesn't in fact have many (any?) endearing qualities. No wonder Morag's miserable. I feel better knowing she has to sleep in the same bed as him every night.

The next morning Morag comes over to my desk... smiling!

'How are you, Emily?' she enquires, beaming at me.

I stare in bewildered silence, wondering why this sudden change of demeanour. She lingers at my desk, smiles again (a whole year's worth in one minute) and leaves. Whatever's got into her? Maybe she avoided getting laid last night.

Shivers are running down my spine from the gross thought of sex with Josh, when Alan strolls over. He asks me to take the minutes of their monthly global telephone call, starting in a few moments. The delicious Byron, the odious Rick and the jolly, permanently flushed Hamish McIntyre are all present. This call is notorious for going on for hours, with people nipping out for a four-course meal only to return to find it still labouring on the same point and not a lot being decided. The only upside is that we get pots of English Breakfast tea, Colombian coffee, Perrier water and McVities dark chocolate digestive biscuits (a good pretext for any meeting!).

There are technical difficulties, as always, trying to join the conference call, so we chat away while an IT guy rummages around connecting cables. Byron turns to Hamish.

'Did you hear about the shark attack last night?' he asks.

'What happened?' I butt in, genuinely curious.

'Someone was fatally wounded by a Tiger Shark in Repulse Bay.'

I look horrified but Byron dismisses it.

'Oh this happens every year, Emily. The Government puts out half a million adverts about not swimming outside of the shark nets, especially early in the morning or late at night when the blighters are hungry, but every year some moron ignores this.'

'Well,' Rick interjects, 'as you know, I live in Deep Water Bay and I go swimming outside of the shark nets—in fact I was swimming last night when that chap must have been eaten! Ha, can't catch me!'

I have visions of a massive, mean-looking shark with huge gnashers spotting Rick's fleshy potbelly and thinking his Christmas and birthday had come at once. That would keep any animal well fed for several months! Trust bloody Rick Lyons to get away with swimming in shark-infested waters. It's true what they say: only the good die young.

Byron and Hamish clearly don't believe Rick.

'Rick,' Hamish begins incredulously, 'you don't seriously swim outside of the shark nets?'

Rick smiles smugly. 'All the time, and it's very refreshing indeed. Anyway, according to the newspapers it's only gay hairdressers that the sharks go for.'

'Well,' Byron chips in, 'if the sharks don't kill you the toxins will. People who swim in the seas around Hong Kong glow in the dark!'

All the while I sit there, fantasizing about Rick being consumed by a shark.

Hamish turns even pinker than usual, chuckling, 'Rick, is it true your new secretary's called "Fanny Chew"?'

Rick smiles and nods.

Byron guffaws, 'That's not as bad as my previous one, "Fanny Pong", believe it or not!'

We all laugh except for Alan, who shakes his head in hopelessness at our lack of professionalism. I daren't mention James's favourite Chinese names, 'Suk Mi Kok' and 'Lik Mi Balls'. Byron's on a roll and riffles through the company's internal telephone directory on the hunt for more ludicrous-sounding names.

'How about "Fuch" or "Kunt" as a surname?' he asks. 'Sexy stuff!'

The call connects. Byron sits back in his chair and shuts his eyes, apparently asleep. Hamish tries to get me to play noughts and crosses with him. Alan is working his way through the twenty or so biscuits, licking off the chocolate intently before demolishing the digestive. Rick is writing down copious notes (well he bloody would) and I'm trying to write down copious notes but getting distracted by glimpses of Byron's sleek chest through his shirt buttons. The nasally twang from Randy Mann (say no more) in our New York office addresses Byron.

'What do you suggest?' Randy puts to him.

Byron opens his eyes, leans forward and impressively discusses his thoughts and some technical details before closing his eyes and nodding off again. He's my dream man (sorry James!).

Randy clearly likes the sound of his own voice and waffles on for an eternity. Alan, having consumed the equivalent of two family-sized packs of biscuits, decides to crack open a bottle of Perrier. The bottle explodes like champagne, miraculously missing everyone except Rick, who now looks like he's wet himself. Byron and Hamish roar with laughter (posh sounding 'hoare-hoare-hoare'), I'm crying with girlish giggles and Alan doesn't know where to put himself. Rick thinks it's far from funny.

'OK, OK, just a bit of water,' he says standing up.

We laugh even harder as he's absolutely saturated in it.

'He's pissed himself!' I pipe up, getting rather excitable.

Alan tuts and Bryon and Hamish snigger like naughty schoolboys. I can just about hear Randy in the background saying, 'Hey, guys, share the joke with us!' but Byron puts us onto silent mode for the laughter to continue in private.

I return to my desk and have a sneaky look at my Hotmail account. I always clear the junk mail first and savour my real mail afterwards.

From: CurtMogoo@hotstuff.com
To: emilygreenhk@hotmail.com
Subject: HUMONGOUS RODS IN TINY SLITS

Yuck, I don't open that one.

From: Peepo@nastygirls.net
To: emilygreenhk@hotmail.com
Subject: Flash your rack!

Not today, thank you! I don't think my colleagues would appreciate it (or have magnifying glasses handy).

From: TravisBongo@xyz.com
To: emilygreenhk@hotmail.com
Subject: ARE YOU THIRSTY FOR CUM?

Nope, but I'd love a Diet Coke! Another one to delete.

From: James1969@yahoo.com
To: emilygreenhk@hotmail.com
Subject: kidz

A husband and wife decided they needed to use a code to indicate that they wanted to have sex without letting their children in on it. They decided on the word 'Typewriter'.

One day the husband told his five-year-old daughter, 'Go tell your mummy that daddy needs to type a letter.' The child told her mother what her dad had said, and her mum responded, 'Tell your daddy that he can't type a letter right now because there is a red ribbon in the typewriter.' The child went back to tell her father what her mum had said.

A few days later, the mum told her daughter, 'Tell your daddy that he can type that letter now.' The child told her father, returned to her mother and announced, 'Daddy said never mind with the typewriter, he already wrote the letter by hand.'

Bloke joke!

From: mary1972@hotmail.com
To: hicks16@hotmail.com, katiets@abbottsdury.com, janeheffer@yahoo.com, sandiebeech@yahoo.com, fernrocks@yahoo.com, deano@btinternet.com, mandyandandy@yahoo.com, teets@hotmail.com, emilygreenhk@hotmail.com, mary1972@hotmail.com, clare_adair@btinternet.com
Subject: One for the Girls!

Question: What's the difference between men and cheese?
Answer: Cheese matures.

Hee hee hee! Want another?!

Question: What does PMS stand for?
Possible Answers:
Psychotic Mood Shift
Perpetual Munching Spree
Puffy Mid-Section
People Make me Sick
Provide Me with Sweets
Pardon My Sobbing
Pimples May Surface
Pass My Sweatpants
Pissy Mood Syndrome
Plainly Men Suck
Potential Murder Suspect
Pass My Shotgun

Love it!

Mare :)

Chick joke!

From: deano@btinternet.com
To: emilygreenhk@hotmail.com
Subject: sounds like a true story...

Hi Emily!

You'll like this...

A Londoner parks his brand spanking new Porsche in front of his office to show off to his colleagues. As he's getting out of the car a truck comes speeding along too close to the kerb and takes the door off before speeding away. More than a little distraught, the Londoner grabs his mobile and dials 999. Ten minutes later the police arrive. Before the policeman has a chance to ask any questions, the Londoner starts screaming hysterically, 'My Porsche, my beautiful silver Porsche is ruined. No matter how long at the panel beaters, it'll simply never be the same again!' After the Londoner finally finishes his rant, the policeman shakes his head in disgust. 'I can't believe how materialistic you bloody Londoners are!' he says. 'You lot are so focused on your possessions that you don't notice anything else in your life.' 'How can you say such a thing at a time like this?' snaps the Londoner. The policeman replies, 'Didn't you realize that your right arm was torn off when the truck hit you?' The Londoner looks down in absolute horror... 'F*CKING HELL!!!!' he screams...'Where's my Rolex???'

Good one!

Take care, peeps!

DeanO

I really like this last one. I see Byron and beckon him over to get him to read DeanO's email. He leans over me to look at the screen and roars with laughter. Boy he smells good—though I bet he'd smell good after a hard workout at the gym without deodorant.

'Excellent joke, Emily! You've got a great sense of humour.'

Byron saunters off while my heart is in my mouth. He is just too delicious for words. I know he's married, I know I'm just fantasizing, but he puts a spring in my step. I start humming to myself. I get in the lift to go for lunch and spontaneously make up a little song: 'He makes my heart go flutter. He makes my body shudder.' I get into the swing, my voice getting louder: 'My limbs go moist...' and the lift door opens, revealing two open-mouthed Western businessmen who gawp at me. 'Oh Christ, oh Christ!' I sing softly.

The next morning I work really hard (only taking a ten-minute 'mental health' break every five minutes instead of every three) to produce a PowerPoint presentation for Alan and Rick. For once I don't feel particularly peckish at lunchtime and instead feel clammy and tired. Come the afternoon I'm really out of sorts, sweaty and faint. Alan walks past my desk to find me with my forehead in my hands and my eyes closed.

'Late night on the tiles, Emily?' Alan asks.

I look up at him.

'Oh, you don't look too good!' he comments.

'Thanks, Alan,' I manage to whisper. 'Would you mind if I go home early to rest?'

'Go ahead, Emily.'

I walk home at a snail's pace, my legs feeling more like lead weights than usual. I really don't feel well at all. I phone James at work and ask him to buy me some provisions since I'm too sick to get them myself.

I reel off my list: 'Aspirin, orange juice, Wotsits and the largest Toblerone you can find.'

'Hmm,' James responds sceptically. 'You're not so sick to stay off the chocolate!'

I have a sleepless night, tossing and turning. The alarms trill (we have three since we're not early birds and have a tendency to ignore the first two and fall back to sleep) and James dresses for work.

'Come on, sleepyhead, time for work.' He shakes me gently.

'I'm taking the day off, I really don't feel well,' I groan.

James tutts. 'Come on, slacker, duty calls, you should at least make an effort.'

'I can't get out of bed, let alone go into work!' I respond irritably.

'Suit yourself,' he says, giving me a wet peck on the cheek and leaving.

I try to sleep but have terrible cramps. Going to the toilet proves to be a major operation as I'm bent double in pain and can't straighten up fully. I must have overdone it on the onions yesterday. Shouldn't have eaten the entire Toblerone either (it was supposed to tide my chocolate fixes over for the entire month rather than one evening). The telephone rings. It's Gilly from work.

'Emily, I have Rick on my back.'

Yuck, what a hideous image!

'He's jumping up and down for a PowerPoint presentation you were meant to give him today and is most disappointed that you left early yesterday!'

'I'm really sorry, Gilly, I've got a bad fever and cramps and feel too ill to come in. If I just felt poorly I'd be there but I feel terrible,' I croak.

Gilly huffs, saying reluctantly, 'Well, get well soon. I'll tell Rick you're sick.'

The receiver clicks and the line goes dead. Bloody hell, talk about unsympathetic.

By three in the afternoon I'm perspiring so heavily the bedclothes are soaked. (I've never had this result in the gym—must remember to eat more onions!) The cramps get so bad I'm moaning aloud and want to scream. I phone James at work.

'James, I'm sorry, but please come home now and take me to the doctor,' I plead.

'Christ, can't you get yourself there, Emily!' shouts James. 'Just get a taxi.'

'Please, James, I can't even get out of bed. Please!'

'OK, I'm on my way,' he sighs.

Thank God! I lie in bed waiting for James, feeling like I'm going to die. Twenty minutes later he arrives, totally pissed off with me.

'Why aren't you dressed yet?' he barks. 'Come on, I've got to get back to work!'

'I can't!' I start crying.

'Oh for God's sake!' James hauls me up roughly and I let out a scream, bent over double. 'Are you due your period?' he asks innocently.

'Since when have I had a period like this!' I ask him. Men are so clueless.

Somehow I manage to get into a taxi and to the doctor's surgery. The haughty receptionist turns me away as there are no appointments free and tells me to come back in two days' time. James looks enquiringly at me.

'I have to see someone!' I gasp.

The receptionist insists I can't. Luckily a doctor passes by and overhears the exchange. He says I have a right to be seen and just to sit down in the waiting room. It's too painful to sit so I lie across a sofa, much to the receptionist's annoyance.

An hour passes and I can feel myself slipping in and out of sleep (or is it consciousness?). The same doctor walks out of his office again and looks at me. I'm as white as a sheet and very sweaty. He gets another doctor to see me. I shuffle into his office and lie down on the examination table. He presses my lower tummy and I spontaneously let out a scream. He does it again. (Why does he do that? I think the first scream revealed enough!) He starts to get panicky and gets a nurse to quickly take a sample of my blood. I hate needles! I try to get up.

'It's OK, I don't need one!' I plead unconvincingly. But I'm now writhing on the table in agony and James is finally looking concerned.

'As I thought!' Doctor Claude Liu says. 'Acute appendicitis. You need to get to the hospital immediately as I believe it's about to burst. It'll be quicker to take a taxi than wait for an ambulance.'

Oh no! I'm the world's biggest wimp—this can't be happening to me! James looks equally petrified and virtually carries me to a taxi.

'I think he may have got it wrong,' I tell him. 'I think

you're right, it's period pains. Take me home instead.'

'You're joking, aren't you?' says James. 'You could die! I'm afraid you've got no choice, my darling.'

My condition plus our urgent cry of 'To the Matilda Hospital, fast as you can!' and the taxi driver has put two and two together.

'You having a baby?' he asks, concerned.

Bloody cheek! Do I look that fat! This makes me feel even worse and I let out a loud, anguished groan. The driver puts his foot down and we hurtle up the Peak at a death-defying speed. What will kill me first—my appendix bursting or this lunatic's driving?

We're greeted at the hospital by a very business-like anaesthetist. No time for a second opinion. He ignores me as I tell him as brightly as I am able, 'I'm feeling a lot better now. I think I'll just go home.'

There's no time either for me to come to terms with the fact that I'm going to have an operation. I'm not even sure it is my appendix. A nurse gathers up my hair into a blue showercap (do I really have to wear that unattractive thing?) and I draw the line at taking my knickers off under my white gown.

'Just do what they say!' James orders.

Before I know it, I'm being whisked into the operating theatre. No opportunity to write on my chest in lipstick: 'Appendicitis' (well, you do read of people going in for a hernia and coming out with a sex change). Bugger, no chance to write a note to the doctor either, asking for a bit of fat removal from my tummy while he's at it. This is all too fast!

James waves goodbye and suddenly I realize this may be the last time I see him (maybe no bad thing? No, surely I don't mean that?!). I start blubbing like a three year old, wailing hysterically to the doctor and nurses, 'I don't want to die! I don't want to die!' The surgeon (I pray that he's washed his hands!) tells me to count to ten. I start counting, still sniffling, 'One, two, thr...' and darkness engulfs me.

When I come to, I find a glass jar holding a long pink appendix (I assume it's not a little willy!) being waved in my face by my surgeon, and I vaguely hear him mumbling on about what a long appendix I have (I had). I feel myself going cross-eyed in horror and pass out again.

I wake up to find myself alone in a dimly-lit private room. Intrepidly, I lift up my gown to see the extent of my war wound, only to discover an enormous white plaster covering the area—and that I have no knickers on! Oh my God, did they have me totally starkers on the operating table? Did they all have a good laugh at my racing stripe bikini line? Bloody hell, and it was well due a trim! I'm mortified. How dare they rob me of my dignity! My skin crawls just thinking of all the perverse things they could have got up to without my knowledge (yeah, I know, I've got a dirty mind). I've probably got my own website on the Internet by now!

A friendly Ozzie nurse pops in to give me an injection for pain relief. I tell her not to worry as I don't feel any pain but am briskly told that's because I'm still benefiting from pain relief. God I hate injections! James is nowhere to be seen—bastard! He turns up sheepishly the next morning saying he wasn't allowed to see me after the operation—a likely story. He didn't think to buy me a magazine or to bring my bedside book from home. He offers me a packet of polo mints instead. Fantastic.

A huge basket of exotic fruit arrives.

'Read out the card, James!' I ask excitedly.

'"Dear Emily, get better very soon. Thinking of you. All the best, Byron".'

I blush.

Five minutes later a beautiful bouquet of exotic flowers arrives. James reads out the card: 'Get well soon Emily, from Rick Lyons.' Ha! Creep with a guilty conscience. Nice, though.

Hang on a minute, fruit, flowers—whatever happened to good old-fashioned chocolates? What can you do with fruit and flowers, for crying out loud, apart from just sit and watch them rot?

Just then the nice Ozzie nurse comes back and changes the plaster covering my wound. She rips it off in one smooth move—fuck that hurt! They should have given me a general anaesthetic to cope with that level of pain; it was worse than the bloody operation! The nasty Ozzie nurse presses a new plaster on—bitch.

I stay longer in the hospital than the doctor predicted—not because of my medical condition but because I like the food so much. Not like the old inedible NHS offerings, but cooked by The Ritz Hotel no less. A good chance to stuff myself silly on five-star grub! Every time James visits he orders a four-course meal, too. We don't realize meals aren't covered on my medical insurance until I check out and am given an almighty bill. Whoops!

After five days of bingeing I'm sent home to an empty fridge. Bugger, I've gained six pounds! Don't most people lose weight staying in hospital? The doctor has signed me off work for three weeks—not much fun, though, hobbling around holding onto my wound like the stitches will split if I let go. James suggests I get a temporary Amah (maid) in to help with the cooking and household chores. Whoopee!

Whoopsey more like. Jeabey, a stout middle-aged lady from the Philippines, makes my cooking taste like Delia Smith's. She prepares a salad for me (takes her over an hour) and it's crunchy for all the wrong reasons (it hasn't been washed properly and is full of grit and dirt). Her 'dressing' consists of excessive acidic lemon juice and black pepper, and it's all enough to put me off salads for life—not that I was a huge fan in the first place, despite being a veggie.

Also, not only does she take hours to clean our miniscule apartment (she reminds me of the Butterfly McQueen character in 'Gone with the Wind'—how would she cope with a big expat family, for crying out loud?) but she does the cleaning while singing—badly. Unbelievably badly, in fact. She puts my singing voice on a par with Celine Dion's. I can't bear it. I'm doubled up in pain, not from my operation but from her warbling and I'm often on the verge of screaming out at the top of my lungs, 'Have mercy on me, Jeabey, and stop singing, for the love of God!' I eventually beg James for us to do without a maid, and by the end of

Life is Pants

my sick leave I'm actually looking forward to going back to work and putting the horrendous experience that was Jeabey far behind me.

I spend one morning back at work and revise my opinion. There's piles and piles of work waiting for me—no one's covered any of it while I've been away. It'll make the time pass quickly at least.

Thank fuck it's Friday! James (looking supremely sexy!) and I hook up for a bit of nosh with Peter at 'Caramba!', a Mexican restaurant in SoHo. We dig into a big bowl of nachos smothered with melted cheese, refried beans, guacamole, salsa and sour cream—delicious. James eats so quickly it's always a race to get your fair share.

His mobile rings, set to its funny rave tune, and everyone glances over our way. I follow the gist of the conversation and gather that our cable company needs to replace our existing box with a new digital one.

'No you can't come and do it now,' James booms, 'as I'm not at home... No, I'm in a restaurant... No I can't leave!'

I look at my watch—it's 9 p.m.

'Jesus, he wanted to come round now to install this new system—on a Friday night!' says James angrily.

His mobile goes off again. 'Yes? No, I just spoke to one of your colleagues. I'm not home tonight so you can't come round. No, I'm not in. Call back tomorrow!'

How bizarre! Don't these idiots ever rest?

The mobile goes off yet again. 'Yes! Tomorrow? Yes, you can come round tomorrow morning. No, I can't do four o'clock as I'm out then. In the morning is OK. No, I can't do three o'clock. How about the morning? No, I'm not in during the afternoon. No, I can't do one-thirty!' James is clearly fuming; he has a blue vein popping up on his forehead. 'Christ, these chunksters really can't take no for an answer!'

'I know what you mean, mate. The Asian girls all want my stupendous cock and it's hard to say no,' laments Peter.

James and I walk home, side-stepping the perpetually dripping air cons which protrude from most buildings.

They're supposed to be illegal but nothing ever gets done about them. Getting hit by one is pretty much like having a hair wash, so one of the things you soon master in Hong Kong is how to dodge the dripping water. James chats as we walk.

'It's all well and good Peter getting laid easily, but it all ends in tears.'

'For the girl?' I jest.

'A lot of them steal from him. He's just had some money pinched that he left out for the Amah—over two months' pay he owed her! Plus she took his credit card and front door keys!'

'Jeez,' I mumble. Let that be a lesson to you, James, I think, but don't voice.

James and I are going to spend Saturday night in Macau, an island just off Hong Kong, once colonised by the Portuguese. I'm meeting James at lunchtime after he's finished work. Hoping for a sexy weekend, I cover myself from head to foot in hair removal cream, leaving my skin silky smooth (well that's the result described on the box—I'd call it a bit tight, red and itchy). I pull out all the stops and bleach my 'moustache' (oh, the joys of being a hairy brunette!). Ever since Bradley Matthews took the piss out of me at school in front of the whole class shouting, 'Oi, everyone, Emily's got a moustache! Are you growing a beard next, Emily? Look at her hairy legs an' all!' I've kept a watchful check on it. I'm careful not to leave the bleach on for too long—I've learnt from painful experience that a red moustache is more eye-catching than a brown one. To complete the hairless look, I use James's nose hair-clippers to prune my love hedge. James insists on a clear landing strip when he goes down on me, and goes bonkers if he finds the slightest strand (even though he doesn't reciprocate this and I always end up having to floss my teeth after going down on him). There, as naked as the day I was born, if not more so!

We catch the ferry from the Shun Tak Centre (I'd have arrived earlier if I'd known how many shops there were!) and it bumps along for an hour. James orders sweet and sour pork noodles and a Tiger beer. The stench from the fast food, together with that from the heavily utilised toilets next to our seats leaves me quite nauseous. I can't wait for the journey to be over. I've made an effort to look chic, wearing a funky floral print sleeveless dress and pretty but painful cerise shoes with a little heel. As we exit the ferry and walk down the steep ramp, I lose my balance and teeter ungracefully, full speed to the bottom. James shakes his head believing this to be downright hilarious. Great. You try to look elegant and cool and just get laughed at. Next time I won't bother and simply stick to my comfortable boyish combat trousers and well-worn trainers.

We're accosted by tour guides as we leave the Macau ferry terminal. A small man with a thin black moustache (a bit like mine before I bleached it) implores us to use his services.

'Five hundred dollars, I take you all the best places.'

That would make a change!

'Four hundred—what you say?'

'No,' says James, walking on swiftly.

'Three hundred—what you say?'

'Bugger off!' James barks.

The guy gives up, just as another ten or so guides descend. Luckily, one look at James's formidable size and they stop hassling us, unlike the poor elderly couple behind who give in rather than risk abduction or heart attacks. We jump into a taxi and steam toward our hotel.

The hotel bellboy who meets our taxi wearing an old-fashioned uniform with white gloves promptly shows us to our room. I try to wrestle my luggage away from him, as carrying it for five seconds means he'll expect a decent tip. He waits in vain as he'll get nothing from us tight arses.

James pipes up as always, 'I'll give you a tip—you won't get a tip from us!'

Nicely put, I know, but I don't believe in tipping either; no one ever tipped me when I waitressed as a poor student, so tit for tat! Then again, I was a crap waitress, always cocking-up orders and spilling drinks.

As soon as the door slams shut, we make the most of the king-sized bed and James fucks me hard, slapping his big cum-filled balls noisily against my perfectly mown lawn (and getting more fun out of the noise than the screwing!) before I've even had a chance to go and pee. Hmm, it seems to make it more intense dying for a pee! James does have a gorgeous body, muscled from years of playing so much sport, smooth golden skin and movie star looks—in my eyes anyway. He bangs his cock hard into my pussy, making me beg for more. I feel terrible for suddenly imagining it's Byron getting his end away with me. But then I'm sure James is imagining Jordan rather than me (there's no accounting for taste). We both have huge orgasms before passing out, exhausted, and ready to sleep. The crisp white sheets are now crumpled and covered with sticky cum (I must get room service to change them before tonight).

Macau is famous for its nightlife—mainly the casinos. Betting is banned in Hong Kong, with the exception of horse-racing for some reason. So lots of Hong Kongers hit Macau purely for the gambling and not for its charming Portuguese-inspired architecture. As with everything that's against the law, people simply become all the more mad for it.

James and I visit the famous Lisboa Hotel, housing one of the most well-known casinos in town. The building is shaped somewhat like the Leaning Tower of Pisa and is covered in thousands of fairy lights and gigantic chandeliers. It is quite dazzlingly tacky. A mini Las Vegas, you might say. James and I have no intention of gambling a buck, so he orders a beer (as usual) while I have a lime soda (I would have iced water but no free drinks allowed). We observe the locals crazily gambling away their life's savings. Cries of joy and cries of woe—haven't they heard the saying, 'The house always wins'? We notice scantily-clad barmaids serving drinks, karaoke rooms full of locals happily singing away, and giant TV screens with young, doe-eyed, semi-naked girls dancing seductively. It doesn't feel glamorous or sexy, just seedy.

We take a stroll outside the front of the hotel to get a breath of fresh air and notice several blonde streetwalkers touting for punters.

'We should take one of them back to our hotel and get her to lick out your lovely pussy!' James suggests half-jokingly.

Hmm, she'd probably do a better job than you, I think of teasing him. But the idea of some STD-riddled streetwalker doesn't turn me on, funnily enough. We keep walking and notice several bars advertising 'erotic dancing'. James breaks the silence.

'Shall we take a look and see what all the fuss is about?'

I look up and see neon lights advertising 'Canadian Dancing Girls'. Why Canadian? Do they strip off their lumberjack shirts while smothering themselves in 'Ben & Jerry's Ice Cream' or something? I feel like a right prude saying no, but I have zero inclination to watch other women take off their clothes—I get to see that in the gym changing rooms and it's not pretty.

The next day we make the most of our complimentary continental breakfast, stuffing ourselves silly so we won't have to buy lunch later (result!), sneakily taking away some pieces of fruit that may well end up in the bin, for all our healthy intentions.

Macau has some beautiful buildings and with the sunny weather we could well be in Portugal. No good-looking men here, though. I have a guide-book and lead us to St. Paul's ruins. Only the attractive façade is left and I peer up through the cracks in the structure, imagining how the church used to look. James has found a postcard shop and is looking at a card which reads 'Bottoms up from Macau', picturing three girls' bottoms facing the camera in scanty, bright red g-strings. Nothing like a bit of culture.

Much to James's annoyance, I try to fit in as many sites as possible. We're like chalk and cheese in this respect. He's happy enough to sit in a bar all day, claiming to be 'soaking up the atmosphere', while I want to cover as much as humanly possible. I always laugh at Chevy Chase in 'National Lampoon's Day Out' as I'm so like him—he and his family arrive at the Grand Canyon, stand on the edge for half a second, then go back to their car and drive off. James laments that my motto is 'Been there, seen it, done it', and that travel for me is just one long check-list to be quickly ticked off before I die. He does have a point. To date, we've done the Pyramids, the Acropolis, Disney World, the Inca Trail, the Blackpool Illuminations, the Grand Canyon and the Cadbury's Factory—what's next? I must save a few places for my retirement (and remember to add the moon to my list).

James surprises me that evening with a lovely meal at the exclusive Felix restaurant in The Peninsula Hotel in Tsim Sha Tsui. It's best known for its urinals (strange but true) as the toilets' windows overlook the harbour towards Central. Guys have the pleasurable sensation of peeing over the spectacular views. The service is slick, the food a work of art, the bill—huge! Oh well, you only live once! We go Dutch so it doesn't seem quite so bad and this way could probably afford to do this once every couple of... years!

Actually, as long as I don't frequent the likes of this place too often I should be able to start saving some money soon. I'm only just breaking even now after our relocation and set-up costs—it's an expensive business moving countries! I don't know what I'll be saving up for, though. Liposuction? A white wedding in the Maldives? Probably my pension, as I can be sensible (and dull!) at times. It feels good, though, to be finally getting on top of things and settled.

The week whizzes by. Suddenly it's Saturday morning again and James is at work, the poor sod. I've set the morning aside to take a look at the Aberdeen Marina Club, since Alan mentioned the company had a spare debenture membership there, which I could use. The club has a reputation for being one of the best in Hong Kong, and a lot of expatriates join for a bit of R&R. I'm running a bit late but manage to jump on a light bus straight away.

These light buses are a God-send. There are millions of them for starters, so you can generally catch one quickly, and the drivers always go at the speed of light so you reach your destination in record time. My bus driver today looks about a hundred and should probably have retired forty years ago. He leans forward, squinting through the window—hmm, not a comforting sight.

It transpires that this guy clearly wanted to be a racing driver in his youth (if racing driving existed then). We all cling onto the rails in front of our seats, holding on for dear life, and I make a mental note to buy a gum shield for all future bus rides. An old lady clambers on, and before she has a chance to sit down the bus lurches full speed ahead. She grabs my ponytail and keeps hold of it to stop herself from falling. If she doesn't pull out all my hair, then the stress of the journey will see to it that I have none left by the time I get off.

Red lights are apparently a signal to put your foot down. Zebra crossings, simply nice patterns on the roads. Pedestrians are to get out of the way or risk collision and possible death. Kerbs are to be mounted. Only prospective passengers can stop a bus but there are no bus stops—they just wave a hand and the driver will slam on the brakes, wherever (imagine this in London!). Another passenger alights. A centimetre on and again we lurch to a halt for someone else. Nevertheless, the time wasted stop-starting is easily made up by the breakneck speed. (I wonder if this is what it feels like to be in a rocket launching into orbit, and realize I can use this experience as preparation for my eventual trip to the moon.)

I feel rather queasy from the sharp braking and speeding around corners on two wheels, and marvel at how the bus doesn't topple over or fly off the mountainside road into the valley below. I guess this man must be a good driver, despite appearances (or perhaps someone's looking down on us in mercy). Meatloaf's 'Like a Bat Out of Hell' would be a fitting accompaniment as we travel along but instead the driver chooses a Chinese version of 'Rainy Days and Mondays'. Unlike the soothing, velvety tones of Karen Carpenter (who would probably turn in her grave if she could hear this rubbish), the Cantonese trills and warbles are unbelievably grating. It's total carnage and is doing my head in. Fortunately, I reach my destination alive and without having thrown up. I shout 'Lido m-goy!' to the driver and he makes an emergency stop, nearly causing me to fly headlong through the windscreen. On the upside, I'm on time and it only cost thirty pence.

The Aberdeen Marina Club looks very grand from the outside. Immaculately coiffured tai-tai's (loaded local ladies) draw up in large chauffeur-driven Mercedes with smoky windows. One of them tries to smile at me but is too botoxed up to manage it by the look of her.

I'm shown around by Mrs Kellis Tsang. I'm not feeling too good this morning (the bus tied my intestines in a bow) so don't act terribly enthusiastic, even though the club is truly wonderful, although perhaps a bit posh for the likes of me! Beautiful decor, lovely restaurants, a fantasy pool area complete with palm trees, and wonderful views over a Monte Carlo-like marina, where expensive-looking boats (are they mini cruise liners?) are moored.

They have loads of sports facilities and even a bowling alley. Embarrassingly, as we walk past the gymnasium room I suddenly get the uncontrollable urge to poo. And I absolutely have to go NOW! I politely ask Kellis where the very nearest toilet is and she points to the gymnasium. I bolt for it and lock myself in the single toilet cubicle as quickly as possible before splurging my guts out. The consistency of my poo is far from normal, particularly soft, bright orange in colour and horrendously smelly. There's no air-spray so I can only pity the next person to pay a visit.

I flush the toilet and it makes a clanging sound. I try again, getting a little worried, but there's no sign of any flushing action. I then notice there's no water in the toilet bowl and that the waste pipe at the back of it has been disconnected—holy shit! Someone is obviously working on it and it's out of bloody order! I wash my hands before scarpering. Stupidly, there's no 'out of order' notice on the door, so I feel somewhat excused, but I have visions of a poor workman on a measly salary having to clean up my disgusting turd. I get out of the gymnasium as fast as I can, not wishing to identify myself to this unlucky person. Kellis asks if everything's all right and I say fine, feeling my cheeks burning pink.

Kellis shows me the gym and coffee shop. I notice there

are no people using the equipment but a number of ladies sipping hot chocolate, nibbling on croissants, exercising their jaws. They're all very smartly attired considering where they are. I overhear an American Chinese woman with a thin mouth set in a miserable pout bitching about her husband.

'Linton never stops working. He even gets phone calls from his London office in the evening which drives me so crazy!'

Doesn't she realize Linton's busting his balls to pay for her membership to this exclusive club and the like? It must be a hard life having it so easy. I catch her eye and she looks down her nose at me. No one's smiling and not a single person looks happy. What is it with these affluent ladies of leisure? I certainly wouldn't mind swapping places.

We pass beautiful tennis courts where podgy women clad in designer outfits play pathetic patter ball. With the amount of time and money they no doubt invest in this hobby they should be as good as Martina Navratilova—but aren't even close.

Kellis leads me back to reception. On the way we pass the gym again and I can't help but look through the window to see if there's some workman lying down who's passed out from the stench. There isn't, but there are about thirty golden-haired children of about five or six running around having fun. I feel really bad and just hope the poor wee mites stay out of the toilet. I don't want to take their innocence away. I thank Kellis for the tour and tell her I'll get my company to organise the membership. I just hope the toilet episode doesn't bar me.

That afternoon my tummy feels almost back to normal so James suggests we take a 'gentle stroll' around the Peak. He doesn't realize it's a two-hour hike, much of it uphill. Bless him—just what I need after having my energy zapped with a dodgy tummy. We trudge onwards and upwards as the quaint Peak tram passes by, crammed with tourists who look at us—no doubt wondering why we are walking when we could have taken the wee tram.

It's August—monsoon season. The clear blue sky is misleading today as suddenly the heavens open and torrential rain falls. We're stuck on a hiking path with no cover in sight and so our only option is to continue our 'leisurely stroll'. We start running, as if that's going to help. Turns out there's over an hour of the hike to go. Within minutes we're totally and utterly drenched. Saturated. The rain is beating down so hard a river seems to be flowing from the sky. The paths are slippery and dangerous and my lovely new trainers squelch with every step.

I start to see the funny side, behaving like a kid let loose to go and get muddy. I'm laughing as we run and James is clearly relieved that I've taken this attitude rather than giving him a grilling. After all, map reading and weather forecasts are his duties! We're so soaked that two taxi drivers refuse our fare. But you always come across one greedy bugger who can't turn down a dollar, thank God! We create puddles on the taxi's floor, holding hands and grinning from ear to ear.

Smoochie Sundays, that's what I live for. No alarms, no appointments. Just cuddling up to James and snogging. We read the newspaper (well he does, I just read the kids' comics section) and take a leisurely shower together. It's not quite like in the movies—the shower isn't powerful enough to wet the both of us so he soaps my bits and as I rinse off the suds I lather his tackle (wonderful!).

As usual we end up bonking our brains out. James is an assured lover, capable of swiftly moving through the entire Kamasutra in around half an hour. He uses his tongue, fingers and cock to great effect, making my body shake with longing, his tongue flickering languidly over my pert nipples, before nudging his rock hard rod into my mouth and then entering me, deftly changing positions and creating new sensations for my welcoming pussy. He's incredibly sexy and every cell in my body lusts for his big hard cock inside me. He was always keen for me to experience the pleasures of anal sex ('back-door entry' as he calls it), although he's got such a big chopper it seemed a scary prospect. 'A ring for a ring,' I would half joke. He got his ring—I didn't get mine. It was rather sexy once you broke through the pain barrier (I left teeth marks on the bed post!) although I'm not so keen on the toilet antics afterwards (the felch splurge, with an accompanying orchestra of sounds), or the feeling of it all hanging out, if you know what I mean. He's taken my anal virginity! Dirty bugger! Maybe he should write a follow-up to 'The Joy of Sex' entitled 'The Pleasure and Pain of Anal Sex'.

Later that day we decide to go and explore the infamous Mongkok market on Kowloon side. I've heard it's the place to go to find really cheap fake designer handbags so I'm pretty excited, and have plenty of cash on me ready to buy Louis Vuitton rip-offs.

The market is packed. A Chinese man treads on the back of my heel (ouch! I hate that!), overtaking me, only to slow down to a snail's pace. I take vengeance and step on his heel, and he turns round and apologises profusely, 'Sorry ah!'

James is accosted by a wiry man who's selling fake designer belts. He tries a few on and is so impressed with them ('Calvin Klein'!) that he ends up buying three off him. James is chuffed with his purchases and the little man keeps following us, not realising he's already sold James a life time's supply of belts.

I, big spender, purchase a pair of wellies (just like the ones the street cleaners wear) which reach halfway up my calves and come in a fetching maroon colour. I'll be darned if I let my leather shoes get ruined by the monsoon rains heading our way! James can't believe I've bought them.

'You're not seriously going to wear those?' he says.

'Maybe,' I respond, as James tuts at my compulsive spending. 'I was in the Brownies, you know. "Always be prepared" remains my motto!'

'Yeess,' James sounds unconvinced (with good reason, as I end up wearing them only once after Rick Lyons mercilessly takes the piss out of them in the office).

I stop at a stall selling handbags but they look really fake and tacky (a fake shouldn't look like a fake!). The woman running the stall jumps up from her chair and gives me the hard-sell.

'You want a handbags? Ahh, so nice! You like?' She thrusts into my hands a horrible black plastic bag with a huge metal label which has 'George Armani' etched into it. Well, I wouldn't know an Armani bag from my arse, but I do know his name is Georgio not George.

'You buy? You buy now, I give good discount.'

I don't think so!

The woman seems really put out by my lack of enthusiasm and starts tugging on my arm.

'You like?'

'No thank you!' I tell her, trying to walk off, but she holds my arm in a vice-like grip. James comes to my rescue and leads me away.

While I've been dealing with psycho bag lady he's bought himself a cigarette lighter (not that he smokes) picturing a girl owning mammoth breasts in a tiny bikini.

'Watch this,' he tells me. 'It's wicked!' He holds the lighter upside down and the girl's bikini comes off to reveal her birthday suit. Hmm, very sophisticated, James. But then boys will be boys! He is ecstatic about his find and at least I now know where to come for his Christmas presents.

A young man comes up to me with his eyes darting left, right and centre. He seems a little shifty, to say the least, and I loop my arm through James's.

'You look for designer handbag?' he asks in a low voice.

'Yeess?' I answer tentatively.

'Follow me, I show you best quality.' I look at James who doesn't seem frightened by this guy. I guess at twice his height James sees nothing to worry about.

The man, who tells us he's called Wengee, leads us to a rickety old apartment block. We climb up two flights of stairs (filthy dirty, yuck!) before reaching an apartment with about half a million locks on the door. I look at James who simply shrugs his shoulders—he's probably hoping it's the set of a seedy porno movie! The door opens to reveal, not Ron Jeremy and Tiffany Minx going for it, but hundreds of fake designer handbags, wallets and watches. Everything smells of leather (look, it's just a bloody by-product which will fizzle out when the rest of the world comes to its senses and goes veggie and they start to design decent plastic shoes and handbags). Thankfully, the labels are spelt correctly.

The shop sparkles and gleams—it's quite simply Aladdin's bloody cave. I can feel my heart beating faster, sheer adrenalin to part with my hard-earned cash. I feel the soft leather insides of an Yves Saint Laurent rucksack and wonder if I'm having a mini orgasm. A soft Gucci evening bag and I'm having a full one. A Louis Vuitton handbag like Sarah Jessica Parker's and it's a multiple orgasm. James shakes his head.

'You chicks are all the same,' he laughs.

While I'm facing the impossible task of choosing which one to buy, James is eyeing up an impressive fake Rolex. It's totally ostentatious and even looks big on his wrist. He barters the price down to a ridiculously low level and buys it. I just can't choose so end up buying seven handbags, justifying to myself that seven of these babies cost less than one real one. I've just bought a ten-year supply in ten minutes at bargain prices and if you consider future inflation, I've been a very canny shopper indeed!

James escorts me out of the building, despite my protesting that I want to look at the matching purses. We fight our way through the heaving market crowds, with James navigating us into a quiet back street, somehow knowing the direction to the MTR. Even on a virtually empty pavement like this the locals manage to walk bang into you. It never ceases to amaze me how uncoordinated they are as a race (their athletics performance at the Olympics means I can say this!), bumping into you for no good reason, tripping up over nothing. The only form of self-defence against this annoying national characteristic is to walk with your elbows stuck out—then, miraculously, they see you and avoid the collision course. James uses elbows effectively and if he's carrying one of his heavy sports bags (which is most days!) he makes sure to wallop them with this, too, nearly knocking them unconscious.

We return to Central and witness the thousands of Filipino maids congregated on their only day off. The poor souls have nowhere else to go to, so sit on concrete walkways chatting ten to the dozen to make up for a whole week's worth of gossip. They always smile, which is nice, particularly as they don't seem to have much to smile about. I read in the newspapers how some of them are beaten by their bosses, and left with burns from hot irons thrown at their backs. Some fall out of the apartment windows while cleaning them, resulting in terrible injuries or even death. Most of them are made to sleep in the kitchen's utility room under the dripping washing. It's terribly sad. But still they smile warmly. One of them—I'm not sure if it's a boy or a girl—plays a guitar and sings about the joys of Christianity. You wouldn't think they'd have any faith at all with the miserable lives they lead. They have nothing, but look amazingly happy. James and I walk by to the sound of our favourite worst song, 'Kum-By-Ah My Lord'. I'm so lucky.

Alan's on holiday, I mean a 'business trip' this week. He's gone to Singapore on a two-day seminar but for some reason is staying a whole week. Could it be the prestigious golf tournament that coincides with his trip, which he's been dying to attend? Anyway, at least it gives me a bit of time to put my feet up for a well-earned rest and clear my Hotmail inbox! Fat chance. Turns out Morag has another flipping project for me and I have to pull out all the stops to get it finished in time for Alan's return.

Incidentally, if you want to ensure confidentiality, never, ever, speak to the Human Resources department as you may as well advertise your issue on national radio. Gilly's told half the office 'in confidence' about Rick diddling his expenses. Rick's in hot water (hee hee!) as, not content with being paid a quarter of a million pounds a year, he's got Cymbeline's school to invoice the firm for extra-curricular activities such as, get this, 'Advanced Examination Preparation', 'Netball Team Subs and Uniform', 'Trip to Shanghai' and 'Visit to the Hong Kong Stock Exchange'. She's only flipping four! On top of that, he managed to get the school to reimburse an 'overpayment mistake' to him personally—crook! Hawk-eyed Gilly checked the invoice and quite rightly requested that Rick be dismissed on the basis of 'gross misconduct'. But somehow Rick (jammy bastard) gets away with no more than a feeble slap on the hand and is told by the partners not to do it again. Gilly's furious; her authority undermined. Rick pathetically blamed the school for the 'error' and the partners chose to give him the benefit of the doubt. Only he could get away with fraud. At least the office had a laugh at his expense (or the firm's!).

James and I are really going for it with the weekend trips away and we're on a last minute trip to Beijing at a bargain price. As soon as we set foot in the dingy hotel we understand why the price was too good to be true—it was too good to be true! Since we're only here for two days we hire a driver to take us to all the tourist sites. The obvious starting point is the Great Wall of China.

We drive through majestic tree-lined boulevards and feel like we're in Paris, of all places. The weather is simply perfect—warm with expansive clear blue skies—and the city quite beautiful. Most people seem to ride ancient bicycles; they're a healthy lot! It's quite a journey to the Great Wall and we nearly have two car crashes on our way there, both of which could have been fatal. The first occurs when a battered old car cuts us up and our driver avoids collision only by almost driving into a large ditch at full pelt. Then our driver fails to see a massive pile of rubble looming ahead on one of the dual carriageways(!) and almost careers straight into it. As James and I get out of the car, luckily having reached our destination in one piece, we're shaking—and not from excitement!

The first thing we see at the Great Wall is an enormous car park with spaces for about fifty million coaches—most of them filled. The second thing is the 'Golden Arches', AKA McDonalds. (Isn't it heart-warming to know McDonalds is more eye-catching than the Great Wall of China?) Despite our disappointment at how touristy the whole operation is we have tremendous fun. A cable car takes you up (we didn't consider the walking option an option!) and once there, you find local people on top of the wall dressed in traditional, colourful outfits, madly banging drums and trying to sell exceptionally large knives. You have to ask, what kind of sad twit would want to buy one of these huge swords? Would you even get it through the airport control? James starts negotiating for one of the more lethal looking knives, answering my question.

I wander along the wall which, it has to be said, is so much more impressive than Hadrian's Wall which is just your bog standard farmer's wall. This is elaborate and pretty... and it goes on for flipping miles! It's also mind-boggling to think that this is the only man-made structure visible from space (if you don't count my Wonderbra). I look behind me to discover James pretending to thrust his sword into my back. Beyond him, the wall snakes up the mountains. I try to focus on the spectacular views over Mongolia rather than on James, who's now trying to sever my head from my body.

We walk and walk until we remember we have to walk back again, at which stage we make an abrupt U-turn. To our delight, we find we don't have to walk down the mountain back to the car park—there's a toboggan run which you can slide down sitting on some kind of metal baking tray with a brake! This proves to be the highlight of the day; whooshing down the side of a mountain at breakneck speed has got to be the greatest fun to be had anywhere in the world! I have the foresight to let James go first, knowing he'll be trying to break the sound barrier, and God help anyone who happens to be in his way.

It's nice when you get to that stage in a relationship when you know someone in and out. As predicted, James hurtles himself down the mountain, despite the cries of the poor operator ('Slow down, ahh!'). I'm merrily waltzing down at my own pace, appreciating the beautiful green trees and yellow and mauve flowers. I can see James up ahead out of control, screaming at the Western guy in front of him, 'Go faster, you wanker!' (remind me if I ever have a son to strangle him at birth). James has picked a fight with a German—never a good opponent. The man gives as good as he gets—and rightly so—making me titter with laughter when he calls James a 'Redneck!' I slow down so as not to shunt James up the arse (although I'm very tempted to do so).

The German (quite handsome, but German) is telling James, 'Stop being a fucking arsehole!'

I couldn't have put it better myself.

'Fuck off, Kraut!' is the best James can do.

Eventually, once about ten people have come to a standstill behind me, the German moves off back down the hill with James about an inch behind him.

'Keep your distance. It's dangerous!' he shouts at James.

'Go faster then!' retorts James.

Boy, oh boy.

The ride comes to an end. I can see the German waiting for James at the bottom with a group of well-built men. Hmm, this looks interesting. I speed down to the bottom and put myself between James and the others.

'No fighting!' I say with as much authority as I can muster, and thankfully the Germans walk away.

James on the other hand is waving his fists at them shouting, 'Pussies!'

And that's how the war was won.

Our driver, patiently waiting for us where he said he'd be, takes us to the 'Old Summer Palace'. I'm rather taken with its French architecture, gardens and lake, which are truly exquisite. James is rather more delighted by the Wall's Ice Cream on sale. We sit on an old wooden bench overlooking the sizeable lake, watching the crowds sailing past happily on colourful pagodas. The view is breathtaking and it quickly lodges itself in my mind as one of my favourite places (narrowly beating Woolworth's Pick-n-Mix sweets section). I don't want to leave when the glorious sun starts to set, but James pretends there's a legendary ghost residing here so I leave pronto.

We decide to give our weary feet a break by having a reflexology treatment in a massage salon next to our hotel. It's not very clean and I make a mental note for us to wash our feet afterwards. The women assigned look at us like we're a complete novelty and giggle girlishly every time I make eye contact with them. When James takes his socks off the women gasp loudly—not due to the smell (which makes me gag rather than gasp) but the colossal size of his feet. The therapist beckons over the receptionist to have a look and there's much oohing and ahhing before they finally massage our tired tootsies.

The foot massage is only moderately enjoyable as it's so very painful. The therapists not only use their hands but also wooden sticks to really get to the point! My frequent 'ouches' are a source of great amusement to my therapist who, every now and then, burps loudly and then yawns, revealing her tonsils. I wonder if there is no such thing as service standards here and in fact am pleased when the session finally comes to an end. She wipes the excess cream off my feet using a towel which resembles a piece of curtain that's never been washed, and I graciously tip her—God knows why. This evokes a sudden appreciation of the importance of customer care as we are given an extra ten-minute neck and shoulder massage, and a boiled sweet to boot (like the ones my gran kept in her handbag for years, covered in hairs and gunk).

We eat out that night in a trendy expat area. I convince James to try the Mexican restaurant, and the food is unexpectedly good. James loves the succulent salsa burger, all the more so for being denied a McDonalds at the Great Wall. You know, I could live in this charming city. A Chinese youth enters the restaurant selling fake DVDs for fifty pence each, including movies yet to be released. Result! James and I spend about half an hour sifting through three million DVDs and feel we're onto such a bargain that we buy a hundred and sixty-two of them, cutting out trips to the cinema for the next five years. (To our great annoyance we later discover that most of them are missing the last fifteen minutes. So consequently we've now seen a lot of films we don't know the ending to. Bollocks!).

We spend our last few hours in Beijing walking (only because the taxi can't go in) around Ditan Park and visiting ABT—yet another temple. The locals here frequently stop in their tracks, staring at James and me—not in a horrible way, mind, more like we're film stars (at least that's what

I hope—in my opinion James looks a bit Steve McQueenish and I'm a bit Natalie Woodish, although perhaps on a very bad day for the both of them). They even want to have their photograph taken with us! It feels great—anyone for an autograph?

On Monday at work I'm totally knackered. Alan stops by my desk to talk enthusiastically about how good the Singapore Golf Tournament was (surely he means how beneficial the seminar was?). I tell him how much I liked the Aberdeen Marina Club.

'Good, good, good,' he replies. 'Yes, go ahead and have the membership. We've been paying for it for nearly a year with no one making use of it. You may as well get some enjoyment out of it.'

'Thanks a lot, Alan. It all looked super!' I say.

I complete the joining form (three frigging pages, they want my life story!) and return it to Po Lam (a lovely lady I sometimes have lunch with), Gilly's Dogsbody, I mean 'Assistant', in Personnel. About five minutes later, Po Lam phones me (despite sitting in the adjacent office) to pass on the message that Gilly wants to see me urgently. Hmm, I wonder why? Gilly's not one for exchanging pleasantries.

'Emily, what's all this about you getting a club membership?' she barks, true to form.

'Alan told me I could join the Aberdeen Marina Club...'

Gilly cuts me off.

'Alan has no right to tell you that. He should have consulted me first. We only offer club memberships to staff at manager level.'

Well, I could name several secretaries who've wangled club memberships from their bosses.

'Alan thought it would be OK,' I tell her, 'since no one's used the membership for nearly a year and the company still has to pay for it every month.'

'That's not the point!' Gilly snaps, getting ridiculously worked up. 'I don't think it's appropriate. You've obviously put Alan under pressure to agree to this, Emily, which I don't look upon very kindly.'

'That's really not the case, Gilly. I'd really love to join, as it'd help me make some friends here. I'm actually finding it difficult to meet people. I'm happy to pay the monthly fee.'

'Humph, no Emily, it's the principle of the matter. You've manipulated the situation and put me in a very difficult position. I will hold an emergency meeting with Alan to discuss where we go from here. I hope you realize this is a serious issue.'

I can't believe Gilly has made this into such a big deal, a complete mountain out of a molehill. I just hope Alan stands up to her for a bloody change and sticks up for me.

He doesn't, bloody wimp. Gilly calls me into her office to do what she does best: stab people in the back.

'Emily, I'm afraid I have some bad news for you. We're terminating your employment with us.'

Bad news! This is tragic news!

'Why?' I whisper in complete shock, feeling the colour drain away from my face.

'We feel the loss of trust means the relationship between us has irreversibly broken down.'

'But why?' I plead, totally confused.

Gilly ignores my question. 'You will be paid your one month's notice period and won't be required to work it, so long as you sign here.'

She hands me a termination letter. My heart is beating fast and I feel faint. I can't help myself and start crying. Gilly stares at me expressionlessly.

'I'm sure you'll find another job in no time at all, Emily. Now, if you'll excuse me, I have another meeting to attend. Please sign the document and I'll show you out.'

Gilly showing me out of my own office!

'I'd like to say goodbye to a few people,' I choke back the tears.

'No, that's inappropriate,' she replies, standing up and opening her office door. One of the secretaries is on the other side of it with my handbag, jacket and a small cardboard box full of my things. Tears are now streaming down my face. Dear Jesus, this is the most awful and humiliating day of my life. Why is this happening to me? What have I done wrong? Surely I don't deserve this unfair treatment!

Gilly briskly walks me along the corridor for all my colleagues to see me crying, and then into the lift lobby. Dead man walking. She abruptly takes my security pass from me and makes sure I get into the lift.

I phone James from a 'Pacific Coffee', speaking to him in a low voice.

'James! It's me!'

'Hello me,' he jests.

'James, Gilly's sacked me!' I start to cry, despite the queue of customers waiting nearby for their mochas.

'What? Why?' James sounds stunned.

'I don't really know,' I sob.

'Oh baby, come to my office and we'll talk about it over lunch.'

I catch the Star Ferry over to Tsim Sha Tsui, Kowloon side, in a zombified state. I just can't believe I've been sacked! The boat lurches across the harbour and the strong smell of fuel lingers in my nostrils. I feel sick with the shock of it all.

James greets me at the ferry terminal with a bear hug.

'Don't worry, baby,' he whispers in my ear, 'you'll find something else soon.'

I've lost my appetite (for once) and watch James demolish enough Tapas for a party of four. Not even the chocolate brownie he downs in two bites tempts me. I'm well and truly depressed.

Chapter 5

November
Time Flies Even When You're Not Having Fun

Staying in bed late every morning sounds great in theory but it's awful to have nothing to get up for. I've sent my CV to a million companies over the last two months and not a single interview. Not even a response—how bloody rude! I'm useless. No one wants me. Angus Turner refuses to take my calls—bastard! Even James is getting a bit worried about having to pay my share of the rent and I sense he's pissed off with it despite my telling him I'm now applying for everything and anything. Some days I stay in my nightie all day long and can't even be bothered to shower. My hair looks greasy and I'm getting fatter by the day as only chocolate makes me happy these days.

James suggests I go home to the UK for a month and come back refreshed and ready to go for it on the job front. It's a great idea and I book a flight for two days later.

> From: emilygreenhk@hotmail.com
> To: hicks16@hotmail.com, katiets@abbottsdury.com, janeheffer@yahoo.com, sandiebeech@yahoo.com, fernrocks@yahoo.com, deano@btinternet.com, mandyandandy@yahoo.com, teets@hotmail.com, mary1979@hotmail.com, clare_adair@btin-

ternet.com
Subject: I'm coming home!

Hi all

I'm coming home! For two weeks. Can't wait to catch up with you all.

I'm having a drinks bash this Saturday night...

7.30pm @ Browns (bar/restaurant), St. Martin's Lane, near Covent Garden. Starting with drinks, ending in the gutter!

I don't have a mobile but I'll be arriving on the 20th, staying with my parents for a bit initially. So you can reach me there or leave a message.

See you very soon!

Miss you!

LOL

Emily x

Fern immediately fires back a response.

From: fernrocks@yahoo.com
To: emilygreenhk@hotmail.com
Subject: I'm coming home!

Emily

I'm afraid I won't be able to make your drinks bash as I will be shagging at the Southampton Boat Show for the weekend.

Orlando (you may have seen him, he's the drummer for the band 'Int It') is starting legal proceedings to get his ex-wife out of their house and to agree a settlement. The bitch is entitled to fifty percent of everything so he's hoping she's not expecting that! His solicitor has advised him to make sure she doesn't think he's seeing someone else, so she's not so harsh on him when demanding her portion of the assets. Therefore, since I'm not seeing much of him at the moment, if I get the opportunity to spend the whole weekend with him then I jump at it. She knows he goes to the Boat Show every year so won't be suspicious.

I will endeavour to meet up with you next time.

Fern xxx

I can't believe she's not coming just because of a flipping shag! Next time? I probably won't be back for another couple of years! Christ, Fern goes through men like I go through tights! This guy won't last five minutes—especially if he's stripped of his assets! I can't believe she's not making the effort to see me. This is just great.

I'm so depressed I'm not even scared about the flight or travelling alone; crashing would be a merciful end for me. The plane is pretty empty and I get to share a row of four seats with one man. We try to sleep spread across two seats each, which proves to be backbreaking and terribly uncomfortable. The little local guy honks a bit (seafood noodles by the smell of things) and burps and farts intermittently throughout the thirteen-hour flight. I walk along the aisle to see if there are other seats available, but all the passengers are stretched out asleep. I sleep fitfully next to Mr Smelly and wake up after a few hours to find that Mr Now Incredibly Smelly has his feet resting on my legs. Yuck! I lift them up to remove them, waking him in the process. He looks a bit peeved, bloody idiot. This is the flight from hell.

A bleary-eyed Elizabeth meets me at Heathrow Airport at five in the morning. She doesn't look too happy about it.

'Alright?' she mumbles sleepily when she sees me. We don't hug as she's charging to the car park. 'Christ, the parking is so expensive!' she curses. 'I'll need an overdraft after this trip!'

'Don't worry, I'll cover your parking and petrol,' I reassure her. 'Thanks so much for coming to get me.'

'Yeah, mum insisted. There is a national coach, you know.'

I feel butterflies in my stomach as Elizabeth pulls into our driveway. Home.

Mum opens the front door, looks at me and says, 'I don't like your hair like that.'

Is that all she can say after not seeing me for nearly a

year? Nope.

'It looks very flat, dreadful—whatever have you done to it?'

I just look at her.

'Funny, we all thought you'd lose weight in Hong Kong. Just goes to show!'

I realize now why I haven't missed her that much: all she does is criticise me. If I wasn't so beat I'd go straight back to Heathrow and jump on the first available plane back to Hong Kong (even with Groupa Guaranteed Death Airlines!).

I sit at the kitchen table reading 'The Mirror' and looking at the photos of Robbie Williams bonking Rod Stewart's ex-Mrs. Where's he hiding his tackle? I wonder. My dad walks past me to sit at the other end of the table. He starts to read a mail-order catalogue for garden ornaments.

'Pass the butter please, Emma,' he says to me.

Christ, I really do come from a family of nutcases.

'Here you go, dad,' I say.

He looks up at me, startled.

'Ah, Emily?' He smiles, nods, and puts his head back in his catalogue.

Am I too old to be adopted?

None of my family gives two hoots about me. No one asks about me, James, Hong Kong—zip. It's like I never left and I'm being ignored as usual in favour of the Brookside omnibus or the task of selecting horrendous garden ornaments. Emma is aloof, Elizabeth stroppy and Eve tearful for some unknown reason. I decide to cut down on my time spent with the family and add a few more days on to staying at Mary's place—if she'll have me. My mother arranges a half-hearted farewell Sunday lunch in my honour.

'Do you still eat chicken?' she asks me.

'Not for the last twenty-two years, mum,' I respond flatly.

'What about chicken nuggets?'

I don't rise to her stupidity.

Finally, the whole family is united round the table for the first time during my trip—if not ever. How very civilized!

Seemingly, my dad has really calmed down these days. When we were kids he used to rant and rave, shouting at us every five minutes, 'You're all useless! Fucking useless!' but now he keeps quiet, reading mail-order magazines I can't believe anyone would buy anything from. Throughout my childhood he'd act depressed and sulk. He didn't speak to Emma for two years as she accidentally broke his beetle-shaped shoe-horn. During that time we had to endure him ridiculously asking my mother, who dutifully played along, 'Wife, ask Emma to pass the gravy boat,' and Emma responding, 'Mum, please tell dad to get it himself.'

Eve's all red-eyed.

'What's the matter with you?' my mother snaps.

'I'm pregnant!' Eve wails.

Shocked silence hits us. My mother drops her serving spoon which clatters into the gravy boat, splattering brown spots over her cream shirt. My father picks up the 'Sunday Observer' and starts reading. My mother screams, 'Pregnant!' and Eve starts to cry loudly.

Elizabeth pipes up, 'Glad to hear you're not a virgin like I thought!' and Emma laughs hysterically.

'What will everyone think?' my mother says to herself quietly.

'Is that all you're worried about?' Eve cuts in. 'What the bloody neighbours will think?'

'What will the whole flipping village think!' my mother screams.

'Who gives a shit!' shouts Elizabeth. 'All the pop stars are unmarried mothers these days.'

'Yeah,' adds Emma, 'all the magazines say a baby is the latest must-have accessory.'

'You're sure you're pregnant?' my mother asks Eve.

'Any chance of getting lunch served?' dad calmly enquires.

'Oh fuck off!' mother shouts at him.

Dad starts to help himself to food and I follow suit.

'Have you seen any ornaments you want for the garden, dad?' I ask, trying to change the subject.

'There's a rather nice stone hedgehog,' dad says.

'Eve's pregnant!' mother screams.

'Well, what do you expect me to do about it?' dad shouts back, still reading his newspaper. 'You're the family planning doctor!'

'What will everyone think?' mother repeats, biting her nails.

'They won't use you for family planning advice ever again!' laughs Elizabeth.

I casually raise the big question: 'Whose is it, Eve?' and Eve starts to cry again.

'Who is the father?' mother asks sternly.

Eve shrugs. 'Either Rod,' [recent ex-boyfriend] 'or Jez.'

'Who the hell is Jez?' mother shrieks.

Eve looks up. 'I don't really know him that well.'

'Well, you know him well enough to screw him!' mother yells. 'And what kind of silly name is "Jez"?'

'It's short for "Jeremy",' advises Emma.

'"Jerry" is short for "Jeremy", not "Jez"!' mother insists.

'It's Jeremy Rosevere,' Eve whimpers.

'Not that short, posh twit with the ginger hair?' Elizabeth asks incredulously.

Eve cries harder.

'God, get it aborted!' Elizabeth says in all seriousness, 'He's a right nutter!'

'Should fit in well with our genes,' I pipe up.

'How many months are you?' asks mother, attempting to sound calmer but failing.

'Seven.'

'Seven months!' mother screams back, turning pink-cheeked.

'So that's why you've been wearing baggy jumpers all the time!' chips in Elizabeth.

'Wife, pass the gravy boat, please,' dad asks.

'Oh fuck off, you prick!' is mother's reply.

There's a knock on the door.

'I'll get it!' says Emma, jumping up. It's very unlike her to volunteer to do anything.

It's Carol, our next-door-neighbour and, by happy coincidence, the village gossip. Emma can't resist it.

'Eve's pregnant!'

Carol looks delighted and hugs Eve.

'Oh, what a clever girl!'

What's so clever about getting pregnant by accident, I don't know, but my mother chimes in, 'We're all so proud and I can't wait to be a...' she falters, '...a grandmother!' There. She even manages to plaster a false smile on her face.

Carol's flapping jaw will mean the whole village will know before Jez does.

I leave the mad house for the mad city. London is grey, dirty and full of good-looking men. I've never come across so many veiled beggars in my life—or is it a fashion statement? I'd been looking forward to trawling up and down Oxford Street buying up the place, but the latest fashion isn't actually fluorescent stilettos and polka-dot tights but wearing your rucksack on your front to stop the contents being nicked! Crikey, seems you can't even walk through England's finest shopping precinct these days without taking paranoid precautions! I follow suit but it's rather off-putting.

Everything seems to have become much more expensive since I left, too. Who needs non-descript handbags when you can buy fabulous fakes! I must say, the general public is looking remarkably well dressed these days. Gone are the dodgy perms and shell suits—instead everyone looks like Geri Halliwell or Victoria Beckham, with multi-coloured highlights and designer togs.

I meet Sandie for a bite to eat during her lunchbreak, going for a tasty crepe at 'Café Creperie' in St. Christopher's Place behind Selfridges. She's looking funkier than ever, wearing an attractive Native Indian-style dress, flip-flops and big feathers as earrings—cool! If she gets a headdress she'll look just like Pocahontas! I'm so out of touch and must go shopping!

Sandie hates her job (currently working as a receptionist for a snobby 'nail spa'), hates her love life (non-existent) and hates her house (her parents' place). She also hates having given up smoking and one-night stands last month. She tries to convince herself, I mean me, asserting, 'I am

reformed! I'm gonna wait for someone spesh—or speshish.'
Poor Sandie, clearly delusional. At least I'm not the only one with a shit life.

I walk all the way down to Embankment Station and buy a ticket for the Tube to get to Mary's pad near Aldgate. Three pounds forty for a couple of stops? That can't be right. I approach the ticket counter.

'Excuse me, I think I've been overcharged. I'm only going a couple of stops.'

A man with terrible acne and greasy hair squints at my ticket. 'Nah, it's right, love.'

My jaw hits the floor. 'You are joking. Just for two stops?!'

I leave the counter muttering that I could travel the length and breadth of Hong Kong for this amount. How do people manage to live in this town? A few weeks of wining and dining and I'll have run up a bill matching the national debt of an Eastern European country! I catch a glimpse of 'The Evening Standard's' headline: 'A Nation Living on Credit Cards'. I guess there's my answer.

My drinks bash is disappointing, to say the least. Despite a hoard of chums promising they'd be there only five turn up: Mary, Clare, Cheryl, Tracey and DeanO. Sandie left a message: 'Got laid last night, so sorry but staying in tonight.' Cheers, Sandie! Nice one. Jane doesn't materialise—no doubt at home crying over some love-rat.

'Browns' is packed as always with trendy professionals all booted and suited. It's tastefully decorated and in a hip location, making it a long-standing hit. They make delicious cocktails, too, and before I know it I'm giggling like a silly schoolgirl. DeanO, I discover, has a new boyfriend, Trey (actually Trevor, but he insists on 'Trey'). So DeanO's all loved up and he and Trey can't keep their hands off each other. They go to the toilets together on a very regular basis—must be all the booze!

I giggle as I overhear Mary telling Cheryl, 'He drops his dirty laundry on my bedroom floor and as if by magic it's washed and ironed by muggins here! That's it, he's chucked.'

Cheryl responds thoughtfully, 'Aren't you going to wait until after your birthday and at least get a pressie for your efforts?'

'From him!' Mary snorts. 'No way, he's tighter than a gnat's chuff.' She's always coming out with little gems like that.

We finish up just after midnight—a very tame affair really. Everyone's keen to get home. Great, I've been away for a year and they don't want to party the night away with me. I guess people carry on with their lives and I don't fit in any more.

I realize that as much as I've missed home I have no inclination to stay here for good. I don't feel that close to my family and friends now and the hamster wheel spins at too fast a pace here. There's also an undercurrent of violence. You can't jog in a park for fear of being raped and stabbed, or even walk anywhere at all during the evening for fear of being mugged or worse. And despite not watching EastEnders for over a year I haven't missed much. It's all very depressing. All this, combined with the relentless rain and biting wind during this so-called 'summer', and quite frankly you can keep it! I have seen the light, and it's in the form of a red lantern. I can't wait to get back home. Wow, Hong Kong is home now!

From: emilygreenhk@hotmail.com
To: hicks16@hotmail.com, katiets@abbottsdury.com, janeheffer@yahoo.com, sandiebeech@yahoo.com, fernrocks@yahoo.com, deano@btinternet.com, mandyandandy@yahoo.com, teets@hotmail.com, mary1979@hotmail.com, clare_adair@btinternet.com

Subject: All dressed up and nowhere to go...

Hi-dee-hi!

Bessie Bunter here! How is it possible to put on sooo much weight after only a few weeks of bingeing on all my favourite foods in the UK? Does it have something to do with my eating enough to feed an African tribe for a year?

Had a fab time back in Blighty and it was excellent catching up with you all!

I've hardly got any work on at the moment so am lounging by the pool feeling sorry for myself (not really, just lounging by the pool). Cellulite doesn't look too good with my itsy-bitsy bikini so strict diet has already started. Three weeks of eating cardboard, I mean rice cakes, and I've put on 3 pounds and 2% body fat—think I'll stick to pizza and chips after all.

Still searching for a job, but alas nothing on the horizon. I'm looking throughout the region too, but nothing around. I applied for a job in the newspaper the other day and the search firm called me up for a preliminary interview. I got suited and booted up (an ordeal in this sweltering heat, believe me!) and the first thing the recruitment lady said to me was 'This job isn't actually located in Hong Kong'. I said 'Oh' thinking it was in Singapore, Japan etc. But no. Kuwait! My jaw hit the table. Kuwait!!! She asked me 'Would this be a problem?' I responded (somewhat pissed off at this point) 'Do you really think a young female, unmarried, British, with a Jewish surname would go down well in Kuwait?' She waffled on about the high salary and extensive benefits—benefits include a coffin I assume? I said there was also the rather significant issue to consider re. a certain cowboy, I mean President, Billy the Kid, I mean George 'Dumbo' Bush, kicking off a nuclear war with Iraq. But all she said was 'Really? I don't think it's that bad.' Christ alive, doesn't she watch or read the news! She ended the interview saying perhaps I'd like to take a 'look-see' trip to Kuwait—'It's just like Texas I hear' (more like the bloody Gaza Strip! What planet is this woman on?).

So things are looking up for me. Kuwait does have one plus point—I'd have to wear a Yashmak (a black tent so no flesh exposed) which would mean I could stop my diet. Who cares about cellulite out there? Must be great for stopping wrinkles too I imagine. But I can't think of any other plus points (I have actually spent time mulling this over). Does anyone know if they swim in pools in their Yashmaks? What about running on a treadmill? I have grave safety concerns about accepting this job.

Can things get any worse? You bet!

Let me know all your gossip!

Love n Hugs

Emily x (soon to be known as Fatima?)

I'm sooo bored. There's only so much lounging around by the pool one can do, believe it or not. I have the bright idea of researching my family tree on the web. I phone my dad to gather some of the surnames in the family. He's about as much use as a chocolate teapot, and can't even remember his mother's maiden name.

'I shouldn't bother if I were you, Emily, I'm sure you won't find anything of interest.'

Crikey, could you be any more pessimistic?

'You'll find we've either come from workhouse or madhouse stock.'

Hmm, likely, but not a foregone conclusion. I keep being told I have a regal nose—surely that must mean something? That maybe there's blue blood coursing through my veins? I speak to my Aunt Sylvia instead who is the font of all knowledge (trivia only) and she sends me on my path of discovery. However, the deeper I get into this ancestry malarkey the more frustrated I become. I have to pay to access this link, pay for that information—I may as well pay a professional to do it and at least get it right! My 'free' hobby ends up becoming very expensive, but I wait for the results with baited breath.

Oh joy, Christmas again. 'Christmas time, mistletoe and wine, we're so pissed all of the time...' (Well, that's my version!) It feels like a miserable Christmas, being out of work and James so obviously disappointed with my being out of work. He's gone all distant on me recently and I feel bad for him. I ate my Galaxy advent calendar by 3rd December so feel that Christmas really should have been and gone by now. No bad thing to be ahead of schedule, though. Every year I vow to eat my advent calendar in date order and every year temptation overpowers me. It drives James mad; he can't understand why anything naughty in the apartment doesn't last for more than twenty-four hours. I figure it's good-going if it lasts more than twenty-four minutes!

I feel no excitement this year. I don't notice the gaudy Christmas decorations in the shop windows. Or the enormous tree in Statue Square, twinkling with hundreds of fairy lights. I can't even be bothered to put up our plastic Christmas tree and Woolworth's value-pack baubles and tinsel. I'm a sorry case. I don't have the money or the inclination to treat James, either. He's beginning to feel like a fair-weather friend. I feel crappy. Instead, I half-heartedly trudge along The Lanes in Central. These are crowded alleyways with market stalls selling everything your budget desires. I buy him a fake Versace tie that looks really real and it even comes with a proper box and labels. Only a fiver, too. Bargain. And I pick up a fake Gucci briefcase for only a tenner. That's him done.

We spend Christmas Day at home. In keeping with my childhood tradition, I wake up at six in the morning wanting to open all my pressies. James groans as I bounce on the bed, clutching all the gifts and squealing in excitement. James opens his presents while still half asleep. He grunts when he sees the ones from me. I pretend that I've spent a fortune and that they're the real McCoy.

'Oh, you shouldn't have done, darling!' exclaims James in a gruff voice, not meaning a word of it.

He in turn gives me a fake cashmere Burberry scarf with a hole in it. Hmm, that would never pass for the real thing. But I remind myself that it's the thought that's supposed to count.

We snuggle up under the duvet and make slow, sleepy love. He kisses me tenderly and goes down on my pussy for ages (bravo boyo!). We slip into our familiar repertoire, moving effortlessly into our favourite positions—after mutual head, 69, missionary, on top, then doggie, then chocolate-dip route—ending in an explosion of cum, this time up my nostrils.

'Bulls-eye!' chuckles James.

It's true—the best things in life are free! I do love the silly sod, even though he's hard work most of the time. James props himself up on one elbow and grins.

'Are you free this afternoon?' he asks.

'Of course!' I say. 'What else do I have on on Christmas Day?' Berk.

He leans over me and from under my pillow pulls out an envelope.

'Get your passport, babe!' he smiles.

I tear open the envelope and find, to my great delight, that my beloved has bought us a long weekend in Cebu, the Philippines. I scream with joy and hug him tight. I'm now sorry I didn't buy him the real thing and feel tremendously guilty. I promise to myself to be great fun during this trip and forget about my job worries. I'll be his dream girl and take plenty of sexy underwear and do lots of shagging.

We quickly throw clothes into suitcases and bolt off to the airport. I can't believe he's done something so wonderful! I'm ecstatic. We're acting like a couple of excitable kids, larking around. I buzz the air-hostess before take-off just to say, 'Are we nearly there yet?' in typical childlike fashion. James guffaws with laughter and sticks a fluorescent pink sticker on his forehead which reads 'Wake me for meals'. We hold hands during the entire flight and can't stop grinning at each other. We're off to the flashy Shangri-La Hotel on the exclusive Mactan Island—it doesn't get much better than this!

It's the most beautiful hotel I've ever set foot in. Lush green gardens, immaculately tended, with real live parrots, flamingos and peacocks (only the ones with the pretty blue tails) adorning the lawn. We're allocated a lovely room with a king-size bed (yeah-hey!), and it overlooks a couple of lagoon-like swimming pools. James and I run around our room, jumping on the bed and squealing with joy. Not bothering to unpack, we just dig out our swimsuits and run down to the hotel's private beach. The sand is pristine white and the sky and sea clear blue (just like the brochure adverts that are normally digitally altered to look that good). Magical! A smiling waiter wearing matching Hawaiian shirt and shorts comes over and I order a Virgin Colada. James has a pint (no change there). This is the life!

We splash around in the sea, donning goggles to see the

colourful array of tropical fish. James chases them, trying, and failing, to catch one. I spot a yellow and black striped sea snake and bolt back to the shore. James follows me, presuming I must have seen something at least the size of a Great White to bring on such a frantic yet dazzling display of Olympic-speed front crawl. We flop onto our loungers, giggling like two year olds.

Christ, this bikini feels unusually tight on me. I have to lie down fully stretched out to flatten out my layers of flab or else I fear Greenpeace might turn up and try to roll me back into the sea! I'm not the only one who can pinch more than a yard I notice, as two middle-aged men walk the length of the beach with bigger breasts than mine! Bastards! We fall asleep in the three o'clock sun—without applying a drop of suntan lotion.

A waitress wakes me up to tell me to be careful not to burn as the sun is very powerful. Just a couple of hours too late, love! James and I are both lobster red and rather sore. Bugger! Here on in we're identifiable to the other guests as the idiots who got sunburnt on their first day, but then we're just your typical Brits! Oh well, at least people back home will actually know we were lucky enough to go on holiday somewhere sunny, rather than stuck in cloudy Hong Kong all Christmas.

That evening we dine in the hotel's seafront restaurant. It's a big wooden hut with an extensive seafood buffet. As I don't eat the stuff I end up being a good girl and just have a big salad (plus a slab of chocolate cake). Everyone's looking happy—it's truly wonderful. A group of jolly musicians work their way round the tables singing romantic ballads. Somehow they manage to plaster big smiles on their faces throughout the songs. James sees them heading our way.

'Oh no!' he cringes. 'Don't come to us!' He's such a romantic.

They start singing 'Tonight I Celebrate My Love for You' and James gets up and leaves for another helping from the buffet. Obviously the lyrics mean nothing to him. I sit there on my own, blushing like a geek. Thankfully they move away to torture the couple next to us who had been bickering earlier, but they return to sing 'I Just Called To Say I Love You' as soon as James returns. Ha!

James plays up to the romance of the evening.

'Did I tell you about Scarface's flopsy?' he asks.

He means Simon's Filipino partner (and yes, he's got a tiny scar on his neck from shaving). I can tell he's going to reveal something shocking.

'He just divorced her, right?' I respond, not really caring either way.

'No, that one's history. He's been seeing two of them. One claimed she was pregnant by him and he told her to fuck off. Then she came round to his pad wielding a knife at him! The police came and everything.'

I can't keep up with these guys and their flopsy-hopping.

'And now,' James continues, 'he's gone and got engaged to the other bird after three weeks of knowing her! According to MacAh, he bought her a really expensive ring.'

Lucky girl. I've been with James for three years and he's hardly bought me dinner.

'What a tosser!' James shakes his head, then laughs, 'But as MacAh says, "A flopsy's for life, not just for Christmas"!'

We spend most of the holiday either bonking or playing on the kids' water slide (James tries to do them both at the same time, but it proves impossible). A few adults join us on the slide but most of them just watch disapprovingly. James bombs down head first, ignoring the 'Do not go head first' sign. I follow on behind as he loves watching the mixed expression of fear and excitement as I shoot out at the end, usually with a squeal loud enough to grab everyone's attention. On one occasion my bikini top pings open just as I am about to hit the water. James's deafening roars of laughter brought on by my misfortune lead him to swallow so much water he nearly drowns.

To add to the fun, gymnasium mats of some kind float on the surface of the water, much like lily pads, for kids to leap from. When we have a go our weight sends us flying into the water, splashing the sun worshippers who lounge by the pool in their Christian Dior sunglasses and DKNY swimwear while reading 'Artemis Fowl' by Eoin Colfer (I can't even read the title on the front cover, so not much point in me reading the book!).

The holiday flies past way too quickly and the reality of Hong Kong looms. James and I always get on famously on holiday. Oh, I wish it could be Christmas every day!

Chapter 6

February
Bottoms Up

Boy, oh boy, I'm suffering from terrible constipation these days. I used to live on fruit smoothies in London and they did the trick, but over here the rich food is taking its toll on my already sluggish digestive system. I'm the only person I know who can eat a tub of prunes or a bag of satsumas and remain constipated.

It's actually hereditary. My dad spends hours in the toilet trying to have a number two, without much success. Most families leave a couple of 'Hello' magazines in the toilet—we have 'War and Peace', 'The Complete Works of Shakespeare' and The Holy Bible in the original Latin. My mother blames my dad's potty problems for his permanent bad mood. My dad says our pipes (large intestines) are twisted (like his temperament), so we spend half our lifetime in the toilet squeezing out rabbit pellets that feel more like pineapples or small children. It's not much fun feeling bunged up. I'm so full I feel like it's going to come out of my mouth at some point. James jokes I'm full of shit, and I can't deny he's right in this respect.

In desperation I'm now trying a course of colonic irrigation. I feel like someone should be paying me to have a sizeable plastic straw stuck up my bottom followed by a reservoir of water, but no, it costs me a small fortune just to have a bloody crap. It's humiliating but thankfully doing the trick (although afterwards I do feel like it's all hanging out, if you know what I mean, which brings back memories of my poor childhood tabby cat, Jemima, who shat out her colon and died in agony on our dining room table).

I go to the 'Colon Hydrating Centre'(sounds so nice, you wouldn't know it's a poxy toilet in disguise), praying no one sees me come or go. The whole thing seems a bit kinky—some people pay good money to watch people poo! Maybe that would be the solution to my costly emptying of the bowels—getting some sick pervert to watch and pay for the privilege. Here, you get to watch your 'waste' through a transparent pipe—it truly makes me gag. Who on earth wants to see it? Interestingly for some perhaps, it can be pretty varied: big pellets, small pellets, logs, shades of brown, shades of orange, bloody, mucus-covered, bits and pieces, odds and sods, FELCH (ha, my favourite word of all, a delightful combination of poo, blood and cum!)—I half expect to see a bicycle, fridge-freezer and cuddly toy coming out next. I can hear dear old Larry Grayson's nasally voice commenting in the background, 'Hasn't she done well!'

Christ knows if it really does you any good. Sometimes the water temperature rises unexpectedly and it gets very hot up there. I may well die of a perforated rectum one of these days, a meaningless death to a meaningless life. I wish I were Angelina Jolie, lucky cow, a beautiful, rich and famous movie star and basically the new Mother Theresa. I bet she doesn't get bunged up. Instead of a saintly, transcendental existence, mine is rather more earth-bound and I nearly die of embarrassment today as when I am reluctantly paying up for my poo, Pippa comes in.

'Oh, I didn't know you came here!' she smiles.

Hmm, not something you really mention in conversation.

'I come here once a week and produce a big cow pat,' she enthuses. 'It's super! So good for detoxing.'

Oblivious to my reddening cheeks, she continues, 'Rupert, my husband, now comes and he's persuaded his friend Charlie to pop along today, too. Charlie's feeling a bit worse for it, though, and Rupert's trying to get him off the toilet.'

Imagine bringing a pal along! They must have gone to a boys' boarding school, as no normal bloke would ever go for a colonic, let alone bring a friend. Wouldn't hanging out in a bar in Lan Kwai Fong seeing who can guzzle the most beer be more appropriate?

'Charlie's a lovely chap,' Pippa informs me. 'I must introduce you. If I was single I'd go out with him!'

This is not the place to meet a 'lovely chap' ('How do you do? Sorry I smell of turd, but then it's not as bad as yours!'). Or maybe I should tell the girls that colonic irrigation centres have replaced the cucumbers section at the supermarket as the place to meet eligible blokes?

I hastily wave goodbye, saying, 'Must dash, Pippa, next time!' and leg it out of there, sharpish. How surreal!

Nice flat tummy for a little while. I read in the celebrity mags (so must be true) that all the Hollywood actresses (surely not Angelina?)—and no doubt actors, too—have a colonic just before the Oscars to lose a couple of pounds of poo stuck to their colons, resulting in the washboard-abs look. Personally I couldn't go through the ordeal just for vanity's sake. Plus you get bloody hungry afterwards, what with all vestige of food eliminated from your body (mmm, food... bad thoughts, bad, bad!). Do you think they're chewing their nails waiting to see if they've won the Best Actress Oscar? Nope, they're just ravenous from having such an empty stomach and turning to self-cannibalism during the twelve-hour ceremony, or however long it takes to say, 'You're wonderful, wonderful, wonderful, darling!'(air kiss, air kiss, air kiss) to each other. I look down at my nails—carnage. They look like they've been dissected by a group of fourteen year olds in double biology.

Colonic irrigation doesn't solve longer-term weight gain problems, however, and on my quest to burn the blubber I've been on the Atkin's Diet for the last few days. Cut out the carbohydrates and sugars, it says. Damn tough if you're a veggie living on carbs with a penchant (understatement of the century) for sugar. They don't even allow you healthy fruit, which seems very weird! Constipation seems inevitable (am I going full circle here?). I'm allowed to eat full-fat cheese and eggs, though (yippee?), butter, but no bread and no potatoes (what the fuck do I eat with the butter?). My breath is horrendous, smelling distinctly like a decaying furry animal. I sweat onions and let out eggie farts aplenty. James will leave me at this rate. I read that Kylie's been on this diet for years, well no wonder James Gooding kept sneaking off with other women—imagine what it must be like to kiss her! And Catherine Zeta Jones is on this diet, too (I wonder who she's trying not to kiss?). I can see why it has stopped Jen and Brad getting preggers—she doesn't have the energy to spread her legs!

I spend Day One feeling faint and lethargic, and have to loll about on the sofa all day long as I can't function at all. I cave into the carbs at midnight, demolishing three-quarters of a jar of strawberry jam (bad girl, bad girl!). Next day I spend half the day lolling in bed as I have so little energy I can hardly get up. Surely I'm close to death rather than just missing carbs? I give in at 10 p.m. and eat a family-size box of Frosties and a loaf of bread. Day Three and I'm on the verge of killing myself. I meet up with Pippa at 'Uncle Willie's Deli' and end up ordering a large hot chocolate with marshmallows and eating six white sugar lumps (free! and truly wonderful).

Pippa makes me laugh.

'I'll have the chocolate gateau,' she tells the waitress, 'and a coffee with skimmed milk—please make sure it's skimmed.'

Chicks and chocolate and diets! I now feel awake for the first time in three days. Damn this stupid diet, I feel a million times better on carbs and sugar.

What interesting emails await me today, I wonder. Have all my friends back home completely forgotten me? Yes.

```
From:     adriandukes@adsmart.com
To:       emilygreenhk@hotmail.com
Subject:  Problems with your Septic Tank.
```

Hmm, well Adrian, it's like this, you see, I live in an

apartment on the 34th floor and don't have a flipping septic tank! Why do they target me with this rubbish?

> From: Derek@hotbabes.net
> To: emilygreenhk@hotmail.com
> Subject: Let him break your walls with his massive Johnson...

Hmm, sounds terrific but not today, honey.

> From: Lianne@girlsgirlsgirls.com
> To: emilygreenhk@hotmail.com
> Subject: Hot girls waiting for your dick.

Sorry Lianne, they have a long wait in that case.

Oh the joy of SPAM. Why is it called SPAM? Why not SHIT? Although as kids we thought spam (bright pink meat from don't-ask-where served up for school dinners) tasted like shit, so there's the link, I guess.

I call home and catch my mother.

'I can't speak now, Emily, I've got Carol round.'

Christ, Carol is only the next-door-neighbour and she pops in pretty much every flipping day. My mother really doesn't want to know about me.

'Elizabeth's here, though,' she adds, calling, 'Elizabeth, do you want to speak to Emily?'

I can hear Elizabeth grunt 'no' in the background.

'She's on her way out, love. Dad's on the lawn mower—there will be no grass left at this rate. Call back another time.'

Hmm, good to speak to you, too, mother dearest. No wonder I don't miss my family. God, they drive me mad, and leave me sad.

James comes home late looking distraught.

'What's the matter?' I enquire, full of concern.

'Peter's leaving Hong Kong! He's given up looking for a new job. He's going back to Blighty next month!'

I'm half gutted, half pleased. As much as he's highly amusing he's changed James into such a lad.

'I can't believe he's off!' says James. 'He IS Hong Kong!'

He cracks open a beer, lies down on the sofa and plonks his feet (still wearing his dirty shoes) on the armrest. I can tell he's getting sulky so do my best to tempt him with some supper (although my cooking could never be described as 'tempting', more like 'diet inspiring!'). I boil up some spaghetti and make my own tomato sauce (Jamie Oliver, watch out, son!). Whoops! I tip in way too much chilli powder. 'Spaghetti Arrabiatta' it is then—good save!

So Peter's off—how will he survive without all the girlies jumping his bones? I doubt he'll find it easy to find one girl back home, let alone a different one every night. The gravy train has departed—Peter knows it and so do I. It's probably the best decision to leave and get his career back on track—maybe I should join him? Mine's looking decidedly lacking in prospects.

Desperate times call for desperate measures. Am I really totally unemployable? I meticulously scan the jobs section of the 'South China Morning Post' on an almost daily basis but there's absolutely nothing remotely suitable for me. Perhaps I could wing it trying something completely different? Hong Kong's certainly the place to give it a shot. After all, I'm bright(ish), hardworking (fifty percent of the day) and enthusiastic (about home time). Surely someone out there will give me a job?

Let's take a little look at today's measly offerings. Hmm, maybe, maybe not... yep maybe, baby.

'Wanted: Handbag Designer.'

Well, there you go, I own about forty flipping handbags so I do know a thing or two about them. Surely it can't be that difficult, I mean, a handbag looks like a handbag, doesn't it? I don't think I could go far wrong. Oh dear, they want five years' proven experience. Would fifteen years' ownership of hundreds of bags suffice? One potential obstacle, though: I have the drawing ability of a three year old. So although I could talk (or would I have to mime out here?) about my visions until the cows come home, my sketches would most certainly let me down. Perhaps I'll give that one a miss then.

Ah ha! 'Designer Label Laundry Supervisor.'

Probably testing designer gear in the wash to see if it shrinks. I've certainly done enough washing to put myself forward as an expert on the subject. Plus this would be simple. I'd always come up with the same conclusion as designer gear always falls apart in the wash. Then again, I don't know if I could bear to do even more washing. And I don't imagine it would pay me vast sums of money.

I wish there was a job for a 'Chocolate Taster'—I'd definitely be your gal! I worked behind the counter in Thorntons as a student so could claim I have extensive experience (I suspect during my time with them their annual profits plummeted while my weight escalated). But they don't exactly seem to be in demand.

Now, this is the ad for me: 'Western Fitting Model'. How hard can that be? Wow, and the pay is good. Money for standing around looking vacant (let's face it, that's all I'm doing all day anyway). I get a strange feeling it's no coincidence my body shape's ballooned, as I'm going to be much in demand by manufacturers targeting the buxom belles of the Deep South in the U.S. of A. I can hear it now: a fancy young French designer throwing his arms in the air exclaiming, 'You're Hong Kong's most sought after Western fitting model! Pleeeassse eat some more chocolate as you need to sustain your perfect outsize figure!' The job is practically already mine.

I trek into deepest, darkest Hong Kong to try out as a fitting model for several clothing manufacturers. Grim and grey industrial areas—think Sheffield but with monsoon weather and no street crime.

Turns out I'm good for nothing. Even my body is redundant. They measured up every last inch of me and told me I've got a peculiar body shape and am a bizarre mixture of sizes. My body starts off well, size 8 hips (yeah-hey!), but then sadly goes tits up. Waist: size 12, chest: size 10, and arms (wait for it): size bloody 14! I'm a freak of nature!

And the humiliation doesn't stop there. I've learnt why the crotch area always rides up my fanny and I can never find trousers to fit—my belly button to crotch measurement is abnormally long! I received a few 'oohs' and 'ahhs' and 'tut tuts' from the seamstresses measuring me. Maybe I'll end up as an exhibit in the Royal London Hospital just like the poor Elephant Man. People will point at me whispering, 'I've never seen anything like it. Such a long waist to crotch measurement!' For years I've tried on pair after pair of jeans, trousers and shorts, always cursing the store and complaining to shop assistants for making them too short in the crotch—and it turns out to be me at fault. I have the body of a freak! I AM A FREAK! I can't do anything right. I can't even sell my body for a living.

I should have ended the humiliation there, but I thought I'd try my luck as a bra-fitting model. The staff at Victoria's Secret were really terribly sweet about it, but turns out one boob is an A cup and the other a B cup, plus my neck to nipple length is abnormally short (must have got confused with my crotch). They kept gently cooing, 'Don't worry about it, Emily, quite a few people are made that way. But we need a standard size 34A or 34B for our fitting model work.' The more they said this, the more paranoid I got. They were being super friendly to me, like a teacher to a child who's just fallen over in the playground and grazed her knee. I realize lots of people don't have mismatched breasts like mine. Maybe I should join the circus? And the crowd could have a good laugh at my expense. Or maybe I should add my photo to the popular and awful 'Freaks' website.

Talking of freaks, Peter's shipped all his furniture back to the UK so has asked James and me if he can see out his last few days in Hong Kong kipping at our pad. Not a problem—until he brings a girl back one night. He's sleeping on a single blow-up mattress in our lounge for Christ's sake, how can he even think of bringing a girl back? He introduces a lanky Chinese girl with greasy hair.

'Hey,' she says in a quasi-American accent, 'I'm Swallow.'

James and I stifle a giggle. How flipping appropriate.

'Swallow Lay, would you believe?' Peter adds.

We can't help but laugh out loud.

'It's true!' he chuckles.

Swallow doesn't get the joke, silly cow. Peter yawns and

stretches his arms out with a twinkle in his eye.

'Well, I might have to give her a run of the lizard.'

James roars with laughter and Peter plays up to him.

'My gentleman, my sword, my goodly length!'

James thankfully cuts him off there. 'That's enough mate, I get the picture!'

James and I sleep fitfully due to the noise coming from the lounge—moans, groans, slapping, even the occasional squeaky scream from Swallow (as she swallows?). This goes on for ages, stops for a while, and starts up again. Peter's proving he's still at his sexual peak despite being thirty-nine not nineteen. Great.

I'm heavy with sleep when the alarm buzzes at 7.30. I stumble into the bathroom to find my toothbrush covered in remnants of toothpaste and brown particles. Yuck! Fucking Swallow has used my toothbrush! Aaarrggghhhh! This is the worst! I tell James, who shakes his head in horror. I'm furious. How dare that slapper use my toothbrush! I throw it in the bin and use James's, hoping Peter hasn't been using his. Just think of where they've both been!

Peter is slightly apologetic about the toothbrush incident but more concerned about his missing credit card. Turns out Swallow isn't as dim as she looked and had peered over Peter's shoulder when he was taking some money out of the cash-point yesterday evening. The little minx remembered the PIN number and took out a few thousand pounds the morning after their night of passion. Well, I'd want paying if I slept with Peter! But I am very sorry for him. He has no chance of doing anything about this, as he can't prove a thing. These girls, eh! A high price to pay for a quick (long, actually) shag! Peter leaves Hong Kong with his tail between his legs (and not erect for a change). Oh well, he's got being frisked at the airport to look forward to.

Chapter 7

July
Model Behaviour

Miraculously, despite my undisputedly odd-shaped body, I'm getting a few modelling jobs. They all seem to be very last minute (my gut tells me another model's actually dropped out and I'm the reserve). Today, would you believe, I'm doing a magazine shoot! I'm so excited! Move over Naomi Campbell (although granted, she earns in an eighth of a second what I get in four hours so she'd probably not want this particular job anyway). I'm sure Naomi would agree with me that the dress I'm to model is a little elderly—something my gran would pick out from the Co-op store in Hammersmith—and it uncannily resembles a big pink condom. But hey, I'm getting paid for smiling.

It is a truly awful dress. Actually, it's probably the worst dress I've ever tried on. In fact, it is the worst item of clothing I've ever worn. Can I disguise my identity, I wonder? I casually suggest to the wardrobe lady (perhaps with a mild touch of hysteria in my voice) that we add big dark sunglasses to the look, but she's not buying it.

'Hey, what if my hair is all over my face?' I try, 'You know, the sexy, windswept look, so "in" these days!'

But again she's not into it. Instead she pulls all my hair off my face and pins it into a plain tight bun, the sort favoured at the turn of the century by servants. Most attractive!

My apprehension over being discovered by my friends while modelling the worst item of clothing ever worn by a human being disappears, as the photographer tells me the photos are only for a trade journal, not Vogue or Marie Claire. Phewy! He starts clicking away.

'Relax, Green, relax!' he barks at me. 'Too stiff, too stiff!'

He should try looking like a giant condom and see how cool he feels about it. The wardrobe lady must realize the dress looks abysmal and tries to make it look shapelier by bunching the loose material behind my back and clipping it together with wooden clothes pegs. It looks slightly better but still ranks as the worst dress in the world ever.

The shoot lasts for two hours but I quite enjoy it, pretending to be Kate Moss and pouting coyly. All that smiling gives you jaw ache, though. Two months later I spot the trade magazine. I excitedly flick through it, hoping I still look vaguely pretty despite the comedy outfit. I'm right at the back. The hazy picture only shows my shoulders, nothing else. No face, no arms, no legs. I did want to stay anonymous in that dress but this is going a little too far! My shoulders look nice, though. I just hope it was the dress they wanted to cut out, not my freaky body.

James isn't impressed with my new line of work, even though he can now kind of tell his mates he's dating a model. Instead he's sullen, like I'm deliberately trying not to get a proper job and enjoying part-time stuff instead (he should try having pins stuck in him and see if he likes it!). Despite my efforts to convince him otherwise, he thinks I'm seriously slacking. I'm doing my best and regularly check the job adverts online as well as in the papers, but there's absolute zip to apply for.

There is one advert for a 'Cake Shop Manager' that gets my mouth watering. I could possibly blag my way into the role since I've certainly tried every type of cake under the sun. I surf the Net and read an article about chocolate making your skin pigmentation darker—what bollocks! With the amount of chocolate I consume I'd look like Whoopi Goldberg by now if that were true.

Talking of chocolate, my belly is really protruding these

days from too much of it. I make my way to the gym and spend half an hour half-heartedly hopping from one cardio machine to the other. What a good girl I am! That's five hundred calories burnt off! Shame about the box of Maltesers I ate this morning for elevenses. Pippa's advised me to beat my chocolate obsession by imagining it crawling with maggots—sadly the power of visualisation hasn't worked with me. Likewise, Deanna's informed me that all chocolate contains cockroaches, as they like to live amongst cocoa beans—and even that doesn't put me off. I just need my jaw wired.

Boy, oh boy, does exercise give you the appetite of a horse or what! I pad around the apartment like I haven't eaten for days and end up munching cheesy garlic bread. I bet Liz Hurley doesn't cave in to her hunger pangs. Apparently she can survive on watercress soup and toddler-sized portions eaten with a baby's first knife and fork set. The Pope should give her Sainthood for resisting temptation.

Astrid Fong from 'Top Models' calls me, panic-stricken (well she would be, I'm the absolute last resort after all).

'What are you doing tonight?' she demands.

'Err, erm, well err,' I wonder if I should say I'm already booked by Ralph? Calvin? or Donna? 'Err, nothing...?' My voice rises in anticipation of the embarrassing job on offer and I try to quickly figure out what excuse I can use to get out of it now she knows I'm free.

Turns out stuck-up pouty Pia (no surname, just Pia) pulled out of a PR modelling job just three hours before the event, and would I do it? Visions of me dressed as a bunny girl who's eaten too many cakes rather than too many carrots spring to mind.

'It's THE society party of the year!' Astrid wails. 'Emily, can you help me? Please can you help me? You won't have to bare much flesh. It's only three hours... and it's HK$1,500 per hour.'

Ah-huh, that does it then, over a hundred quid an hour, whoopee-do! I'll dress up as a bunny girl for that sort of money and even bare some of my odd-shaped flesh. Instead the theme is Tarzan and Jane.

I jump in the shower. Bugger—not enough time to wash my hair that is really greasy from the gym, so I'll don the wig I used at last New Year's Rocky Horror Show party. I hop on the scales, as I feel good (a hundred quid an hour makes me feel a million dollars!). Fuck no. Noooo way! Jesus I repent for eating so much crap and promise to eat brown rice and fruit from now on, just please let the scales go down by ten pounds!

How could I have put on this much weight? Christmas? But it's March now. Shite, shite, shite. Well I can't wear a skimpy outfit to THE society party of the year looking like this, can I! Maybe Tarzan bought Jane a baggy black dress, tummy-flattening knickers and thigh-shaping tights at some point after getting sick of seeing her in that flimsy strip of leopard skin day in, day out. Will I get away with this? Will they send me home saying Bette Midler looks more like a model than I do? The scales leave me with no option.

I catch the bus to the venue. I must be the only person in the world right now wearing an anti-SARS atypical pneumonia mask and a big plum-coloured wig. It's hard to fix the straps of the mask behind my ears—I must write and complain to the manufacturers as it's plain wiggist! Boy I'm heating up under all this fake hair (hopefully I'll sweat off some of the blubber from my face by the time I reach the venue, and end up with strikingly defined cheekbones like Linda Evangelista rather than flabby ones like a Basset Hound). I get some very strange stares from passengers on the bus and imagine they're thinking I'm Michael Jackson in drag. So what? A few stares for a hundred quid an hour—I'm having the last laugh here.

I arrive at the venue—a swish restaurant overlooking Repulse Bay. It's beautiful—a colonial-style building set on an immaculate lawn. I search for Cat, the party organiser, and find her powdering her nose in the ladies' toilets (which, incidentally, are about the size of my apartment). I try to act all cool.

'Hey Cat, yar, hiii there, I'm Emily, yar.'

No sign of recognition from Cat.

'...The, erm, model,' I continue, fast losing the little confidence I arrived with.

Cat's eyes widen in horror. I don't think she envisaged me when she booked a top model.

In desperation I add, 'Boy I've got soooo much work on at the moment. This was going to be my one night off but Astrid was let down by Pia so here I am!'

Cat doesn't look convinced but luckily decides to make the most of a bad situation.

'Where's your miniskirt and bra top?' she enquires.

'Oh Cat,' I appeal, 'I was only told about this job a couple of hours ago and this is the best I could do with so little notice.'

Once again she looks aghast. I grab the leopard skin boob tube she hands me (fake, thank God) and pull it around my waist as a belt.

'See, this looks sooo cool!' I exclaim with mock confidence.

The matching leg warmers are so tight they cut off my circulation, but for a hundred quid an hour I'll risk gangrene.

'This looks rather good!' I jolly Cat along and she seems OK(ish) with me (thank God!).

The other model arrives. She looks just like Grace Kelly and is twice as tall as me. Utterly stunning, a real live model. I've never felt so fat and ugly in my whole life.

'Hey, I'm Summer,' she twangs in an American accent. If she's a sizzling summer, then I'm a crappy winter. I can't take my eyes off her she's so gorgeous (hopefully the guests will feel the same way and won't even see me).

Summer and I make our way to the lawn as the guests are beginning to arrive. It's unbelievably posh. Everyone could have just walked off the cover of Vogue (and probably has!) whereas I look like something off the ghouls and freaks website. God knows what this bash is in aid of—perhaps simply guzzling champagne like there's no tomorrow and blessing their good fortune?

Summer seems to know everyone.

'Piers darling! I didn't expect to see you here!'... 'Jurgen, how's business?'...'Veronique, was that you in the latest Calvin ad?'

Bugger, all the wives and girlfriends look like supermodels, too! Tall as giraffes, slim as pencil lead and dressed for the Oscars. How ironic, I think, while posing (correction, attempting to strike a pose) for Hong Kong Tatler magazine (wowie?!). They're paying me to be a model tonight when the party's full of proper stunners!

I try to make small talk but it soon becomes obvious I'm nobody important, and as I don't have model looks to redeem myself I'm simply a waste of time to talk to. Suddenly the hundred quid an hour doesn't seem enough for mixing with these pompous twits. A couple of nice-looking guys ask me what I do for a living and when I say I'm here as part of the party PR they move away swiftly. A beautiful woman happens to be next to me and we get chatting. She laughs at my jokes and seems fun. She then suddenly takes on a horrified expression when she realizes she's talking to the hired help, departing mid-conversation.

It's strange how within half an hour I'm reduced to feeling invisible and worthless—my self-esteem consequently plunging to a new low. Have I really got so little to offer? Don't these people realize they're a pretty boring bunch without any manners? What does it matter what job I do, which school I went to, what my boyfriend does for a living? Three hours pass torturously slowly. I keep making small talk but it's such hard work with this lot. I want to disappear. My God, am I earning every cent of my money tonight!

Summer kindly suggests I share a cab home with her rather than take the bus. It turns out she lives in an exclusive apartment on the Peak with her Fund Manager boyfriend Sven. No wonder she knew everyone there; she already mixes in those circles. Summer says she hasn't any money on her so doesn't pay her share of the cab, air kisses me on both cheeks and waltzes off into her luxurious apartment block. No wonder the rich stay rich. I should have taken the bleeding bus. I make my way to my small but perfectly-formed flat. Oh well, HK$4,500 in the bag—exactly what my overdraft needed.

Astrid phones me early the next morning.

'Emily, I have some bad news for you,' she tells me. 'Cat has just called me and was most unhappy with you last night as you behaved more like a party guest having a good time than chatting with the guests. So she's only going to pay Summer's fee. I've apologised to Cat on your behalf. Humph, must go now, ciao.'

Life is truly shit.

That night James and I go to see the legendary Marcel Marceau perform at City Hall. I'm tired and really not in the mood for cultural stuff, as much as I've been looking forward to this, and James wasn't in the mood in the first place. There's a reason why mime isn't that common any more—it's shite! For an eighty-something, though, Marceau's got a surprisingly shapely bum and quite a packet on him so I find I am somewhat distracted by his tackle and don't pay much attention to his mime of someone waving their arms in the air.

James and I sneak off during the interval and go for a quick pizza.

'He had a big todger!' is all James can say about the performance.

'And a cute butt,' I add.

What plebby heathens we are!

The next day I go to a casting for rainwear. Turns out they want me to look ecstatically happy to be wearing a bright yellow poncho, complete with hood, that makes me look like Big Bird from Sesame Street. It's so ridiculous—surely no one would want to be seen dead in one of these? How on earth do they flog such monstrosities? Oh well, I suppose I can smile away as my mates won't be looking for yellow rain ponchos and see my photo on the wrapper.

Heidi Tam, a stout Chinese photographer with calves bigger than mine gushes, 'Emily you look so good in that! Will you do this job? I will call you later!'

I don't know whether I should feel elated to get the job or highly insulted—after all, the models who advertise items like this are usually in their sixties with blue rinses and jowls. I never hear from Heidi. Some other lucky bugger obviously got the job of my nightmares.

It's Saturday night and, for a change, I decide to join James on his weekend prowl. He's doing the Wanchai circuit tonight, like every weekend, with a few of his footy mates. They refer to themselves as the 'Wanchai Warriors' (I think 'Wanchai Wankers' is more apt). James is not particularly thrilled to have me there.

We begin our journey to oblivion by hopping from bar to bar, starting at a grotty pub called 'The Castle', then on to 'The White Stag', before moving next door to the 'Devil's Advocate' (full of middle-aged men and young girls), and getting tanked up. We end up in the infamous 'Carnegies'. It plays all the old favourites that everyone hates. Sing-along anthems with people belting out the words at the tops of their voices: 'We will, we will, rock you'; 'She is the dancing queen, ooh ooh'; 'Who the fuck is Alice?'; 'Come on Eileen, oh come on Eileen'. The bar is famous for its dancing—on top of the bar. I guess it's seen as your fifteen minutes of fame, or fifteen minutes of shame, either way, you've got to be extremely pissed to get up there. James drinks his beers like they're going out of fashion and looks up the skirts of the girls dancing on the bar. Everyone's on the hunt for sex. I'm on the hunt for aspirin.

Tonight we have a hen party larging it on the bar. James laughs, remarking bitterly, 'Girls hunting in packs, pissed!' Hmm. Of course it's acceptable for lads to behave like that. A Eurasian girl with pouting red lips is wearing a puffy white wedding dress with big angel wings sticking out the back. There's a sign fixed to her bum saying 'No entry'(does that mean no sex or just no anal sex?). Her buddies are all dressed as cheerleaders, brandishing huge silver streamer pompoms. Predictably they're going down a storm with the on-looking lads and granddads.

One of the girls with curly blonde hair is very tall and a bit on the chubby side. She looks rather embarrassed to be there. She half-heartedly waves her pompoms and wiggles her bottom at the crowd briefly before blushing big time. Another one of the girls, with long brown hair which reaches her butt, eludes confidence and runs through a series of sexy moves like a seasoned pro. She smiles broadly, lapping up all the male attention (maybe she should quit her day job in favour of lap dancing). A couple of guys can't resist her charms and clamber ungracefully up onto the bar to join her. One of them, surely old enough to be her great grandfather, is wearing a horrendous Hawaiian shirt, tight polyester trousers and white plimsolls, and he dances like he has a cucumber stuck up his arse. Two others sporting greying beards are wearing equally dodgy shirts, obviously with a penchant for busy patterns and mustard colours. Lucky girl, eh?

The giggling gaggle of girls jump to the floor as a buxom woman in a skin-tight black latex catsuit (seriously!) gets up and gets down to the funky beat.

'She's just known as "Catwoman",' James whispers. 'She's been doing this for donkey's years. Fanny the size of the Channel Tunnel by all accounts. A right old dog.'

No, she's definitely a cat. Catwoman is the real thing. She glides through her complicated moves with ease, her timing spot on (obviously been practising at home in front of the bathroom mirror). Her large bosom is on proud display and her male public look on with their tongues hanging out, openly drooling. Her big wobbling tits divert the attention from her wrinkled face, which reveals that she is getting on a bit. Her hair is worn in a tight ponytail that stretches the skin back across the face (otherwise known as the 'Croydon Facelift'). No one else dares join her on the bar as she'd put them to shame. The raucous singing also peters out as all eyes are transfixed by Catwoman's polished, sexy performance (and body-hugging latex!). It's strange what turns people on. I look at James with his drunken, pink-rimmed eyes and overpowering beer breath and think it's strange how he ever turned me on.

Sunday morning comes and goes. I wake up early afternoon with a shocking hangover. James is propped up on one elbow smiling down at me.

'What?' I croak.

'Look at you, pisshead!' he laughs.

'What's so funny?'

He pulls the sheet over his head and places wet kisses strategically along my inner thighs. I half feel like sex but feel too tired to move. I selfishly let James do all the work and close my eyes. I'm imagining my ideal man, General Maximus Decimus Meridius from Gladiator, doing the honours, rather than James with his halitosis breath and musty balls. I need a shower badly. James needs one even more, as I can see a tell-tale brown streak along his crack. He doesn't seem to mind my smelling like a fish counter at Billingsgate Market and fucks me with fervour. He roughly tries out a few new positions on me, making a very pleasant change. My pussy is so wet I can hear it squelching. James loves the sound and starts making loud 'ahh' noises. He slaps my arse hard and I exclaim, 'Ouch, stop it, bastard!' We're dirty in every sense of the word. James appropriately ends up my backdoor and cums inside me.

'God that was a lot of cum—a bucket load!' he laughs, shaking my arse cheeks. Mmm, what a lovely thought. I doze off again but James wakes me.

'Come on, sleepy head, let's do something,' he suggests.

'I thought we just did?' I reply playfully, but he wants to get going and drags me into the shower.

We decide to do what the tourists do and visit the Jade Market near Yau Ma Tei MTR. It's chock-a-block with tourists bustling to buy a hideous piece of jade for its luck factor. (Perhaps I should buy an outfit which covers me from head to toe in jade, seeing as I never have any bloody luck. I don't think a little pendant would do the trick.) We mooch along aisles and aisles of necklaces, bracelets and trinkets. Snot-green isn't my favourite colour, it has to be said, but I get into the spirit of things and try to buy a small pendant with my Chinese birth sign (a rat; James, naturally, is a cock).

'How much?' I ask the elderly lady sitting by her stall and slurping tea.

'One thousand,' she tells me.

What! Nearly a hundred quid for a poxy pendant the size of a penny? Forget it! James and I rubbish it and keep walking along the aisles. The lady runs after us.

'Five hundred dollar!' she shouts.

James laughs loudly, 'So it's half price now, is it? Surprise, surprise.'

Hmm, I reconsider but it's still way too much.

'Too expensive!' I tell her, starting to walk on again.

She grabs hold of my arm. 'How much you pay?'

I think for a moment and say, 'Fifty dollars.' James and I walk off but the woman runs up to us again.

'Hundred dollar,' she tries.

'Jesus!' says James under his breath. 'This lot will say anything!'

I stand firm. 'Fifty dollars.'

'OK, ahh,' she replies at last, pulling me by the arm back to her stall.

I'm rather pleased with my negotiating skills, even though James laughs, 'It's probably only worth 10p!' Oh well, I'd rather pay a fiver than a hundred quid in that case. We head towards the exit, stopping briefly to watch a huge American man buy a pendant for his wife. He doesn't bother negotiating the price down—two thousand dollars! James tuts incredulously.

'This lot are a bunch of thieves!'

I wear my pendant smugly (for about a week until, sadly, the catch breaks and I lose the bloody thing. So much for luck!). We head home to a bite of my usual haute cuisine—baked beans and veggie sausages on toast. I'm enjoying the meal tremendously until James flicks channels to watch 'Fear Factor'. The contestants, all resembling would-be models-cum-porn stars, are set the challenge of eating a bullock's penis within four minutes (in my opinion tofu's equally disgusting). It's so vile I start gagging and suddenly my veggie sausages become a challenge (and start to look very phallic). I'm obviously feeling worse than the contestants, who are probably well prepared because of their day jobs, and it certainly suppresses my appetite (which is no mean feat).

The next morning the alarm trills rudely, telling us it's 7.30 and time to make tracks. My head still feels heavy after Saturday night and I haven't yet caught up on my sleep. Monday, bloody Monday. I hate Mondays—and Tuesdays, Wednesdays and Thursdays, although Fridays are bearable. James, as always, is as bright as a button (annoying git), whistling 'We Will Rock You' in the shower.

Today I'm off to Dongguan in Mainland China to do a photo shoot for toys. I asked Anni Lo at 'Anni's Best Models' what kind of toys exactly (well, it could be kids' toys or sex toys!). She tells me children will be in the shoot so I assume it's kiddies'(but then again this is Asia, so we may well be lured into some kind of kinky sex toys with kids shoot).

The ferry to Dongguan bounces up and down turning me green, and I keep my mouth firmly shut to keep the puke down. I feel like I've already earned my money for today and my hourly rate hasn't even kicked in yet. Fun and games! Three American women are in our group of 'models', strangely all sporting the same colour hair (Clairol's blonde #3?) and they have brought their model kids along. Darleen has two urchins, Chanel and Armani (I kid you not), both obnoxious and hyperactive. Terri-Lou has one, Samantha-Jayne, a pretty little blonde thing (probably Clairol's blonde #3, too) who, despite being only five already knows she's pretty and has more womanly confidence than I do. Lastly, Betty has Keanu, a right little monster, intent on trying to get me to murder him. Anni told me the ferry crossing should take only half an hour. It is in fact nearly a two-hour journey. Mercifully, we finally arrive—to the stench of pollution and fumes.

It takes forever to get all the kids through the ferry terminal. They all need to pee and take ages wiping their little arses and picking their grubby noses (you can tell I'm really maternal). There's no sign of anyone meeting us and we don't have an address. Just wonderful. Fortunately, Darleen's mobile phone works here so she calls Anni, who says she'll call her back. Half an hour later Anni tells us to stay put as someone's coming to collect us.

I'm still not yet getting paid and it's already lunchtime. A girl on a motorbike screeches to a halt in front of us and beckons us over. She doesn't speak a word of English or

Cantonese but luckily Betty has done a course in Mandarin (courtesy of her husband's generous investment banking firm) and manages to convince the girl we can't all fit on her motorbike and will need to take taxis instead. The girl looks a little bewildered and tries to fit the eight of us into one cab. Good old Betty's having none of it and takes over coordinating two taxis—and she's not earning a dime for her efforts.

The girl (I don't have a hope in hell of finding out her name) whizzes off on her motorbike and our taxis follow in convoy. I'm wedged between navigator Betty, shouting instructions at the driver in her impressive Mandarin, and Keanu, who's giggling at how many farts he can do (not impressive unless you're six years old). We lose sight of the motorbike and Betty's freaking out. I've given up and just want to go home. Fuck knows what Keanu ate for breakfast, but I'd hazard a guess it contained lots of eggs. Little shit. Betty's managed to scare the driver into doubling back to try and find the girl on the motorbike. We end up sitting stationary in the fast lane of a dual carriageway, trying to catch a glimpse of our hostess. By some miracle she's also looking for us and figures the taxi doing the death-defying act is ours. I can see Darleen and Terri-Lou and their brats in a taxi following motorbike girl. They all make an illegal U-turn to come up behind us. We follow in convoy to a factory where it turns out the shoot will take place.

Motorbike girl expects us to pay for the privilege of riding in taxis on a death wish to a photographic shoot from hell. Betty's taking no shit and motorbike girl has to disappear into the factory to find some money (they don't seem to have much of it out here). She returns with a skinny man in shabby clothing who then pulls out an enormous wad of cash (I take it all back) and pays off the taxi drivers while scowling at us. Samantha-Jayne starts crying—she's so delicate she can't even take a scowl, bless her. Instead of telling her not to be such a wuss, Terri-Lou coos in her best Marilyn Monroe voice, 'Oh precious! Yes isn't he a nasty, nasty man. Ooh, my little darling!' If that had been my mother I'd have got a hard clout round the backside and been told to shut up or I'd get another one. Not that my mother would have taken me to a modelling shoot. She never took us anywhere, and my sisters and I spent the first thirteen years of life stuck in front of a TV screen (before we found boys!).

I'm exhausted. What would have happened to us without Betty? We'd be lost in Dongguan, never to be seen again! We walk into the factory in trepidation. I thought we were going to some nice photographic studio but instead we're in a cold damp building. We walk across the factory floor, which is full of badly dressed women sewing things. Every last one of them stops what she's doing and stares at our group like we've just landed from the planet Saturn. Jaws dropped, eyes fixated on us and audible gasps—the aliens have landed. It feels very strange having hundreds of people stare at you as though they've never seen the like before. I assume they've never seen Westerners, especially the blonde, blue-eyed, pale skinned types in our group. The skinny man screams something and they all get back to work, keeping their eyes firmly fixed on us. I can't decide whether I feel scared or like a famous movie star.

We're taken into a small room with a white backdrop at the rear of the factory. The photographer, whose camera looks as though it dates back to the 1930s, smiles excitedly at us, madly waving his arms in the air. We're then ushered into a tiny kitchen that doubles up as a changing room. It's rather a tight squeeze with all the kids and the hundreds of bloody toys which have materialised from nowhere, so I decide to act like a diva.

I ask for another room to get changed in. They seem in awe of my top model status and graciously meet my request. I'm escorted to a room with a big bed and a very dirty mattress. I don't even want to know what this is here for but I discover it's used by exhausted factory workers in need of forty winks before getting back to their twenty-four hour seven-day week shift.

The kids are running around wildly—quite why a dirty smelly factory is exciting I can't fathom. They charge into my room (sadly missing the star on the door), rolling over the bed to send my make-up bag flying, and screaming joyfully before bolting off again. Kids—why do people have them?

Betty walks in and says, 'Boy Emily, come see these outfits. I've never seen anything like them before!'

I dread to think what's in store for me and take a look at the long rack of clothing. It turns out I'm playing mum to all these brats (do I look old enough to have children of this age?), and, just to add insult to injury, I'm going to be in... maternity wear! I'm supposed to be pregnant, for crying out loud! I mime a bump to the photographer but he grins and points to my belly.

'They don't think you need the padding, Emily!' Terri-Lou titters.

Thanks for that observation, Terri-Lou, bimbo.

So I'm modelling maternity wear and they think my tummy's fat enough to look preggers just as it is. Fucking fantastic. Christ, is this what my life has come to? I'm never going to eat again.

The maternity clothing is amazingly awful. Charity shops would refuse it, it's that bad. My first outfit consists of stretchy white drainpipe trousers with a waistband high above my waist (even with my waist to crotch ratio!), and a big white T-shirt with (I kid you not) a rag doll attached to it, head lying between my boobs (lucky rag doll, eh?). Not only is it horrendous but it is downright weird. I flick through the other outfits hanging on the rail, and note that only the colours vary; the style is the same. Yuck!

Darleen, Terri-Lou and Betty roar with laughter when they clap eyes on my hideous ensemble. I'm sure Cindy Crawford never had to put up with this sort of entrance. Darleen's wiping tears from her eyes, she finds my get-up so hysterical. The skinny guy who seems to be running the show grins at me encouragingly, obviously liking what he sees (there's no accounting for taste). The photographer, too, seems really happy with the look, going so far as applauding. Boy, oh boy, have the Chinese got a fashion revolution heading their way or what!

The photographer arranges Samantha-Jayne and me in

a classical mother-daughter pose in which she presents me with a wilted plastic flower (in real life I used to present my mother with the finger and lots of verbal abuse). I have to bend down on one knee on the hard, cold concrete floor (as if a pregnant mother would be doing this!) and smile inanely, while Samantha-Jayne pulls a huge cheesy smile, displaying every single one of her tiny, dazzlingly white teeth. She sighs airily, 'Mommy, does this look nice?' while Terri-Lou coos back, 'You're sooo pretty. What a pretty girl! Who is that pretty girl?' Jesus, this showbiz mother would give Gipsy Rosie Lee a run for her money! I try to focus on fixing a smile on my face while Terri-Lou continues babbling, 'Keep smiling, pretty baby. No, don't move, that's right, you look like a princess.' She looks like a little twat to me, but then again, I'm not her 'mommy'.

Next, stinky Keanu has to sit on my knee. If he farts I swear I'll deck him one. He can't sit still for a minute—up and down, up and down, running around like a human racing car.

'Keanu, sit down now!' Betty screeches, injuring my ears. 'Right now, this minute, or I'll tell daddy!'

Keanu reluctantly sits down. Good for daddy. I hold him lovingly in a vice-like grip, plastering a cover-girl smile on my face while staring Keanu out to put the fear of God into him. Oh no, he's bolted—charging around knocking over the camera tripod. The photographer goes nuts in Mandarin. I'd love to know what he's saying about the little monster. Betty's running after her little angel, screaming blue murder. They certainly had a point about never working with children or animals.

Keanu's missed his chance of stardom. Instead Chanel and Armani take their turn. Chanel has a mass of golden curls, large blue eyes and a permanently stunned expression on her cherubic face (probably the shock of discovering she's named after a clothing label). Armani is also striking (good job, with a ridiculous name like that), with spiky blond hair, lovely blue eyes and long dark lashes. They certainly look the part, even if they are wearing kiddies' clothes that look like they could date back to the Victorian

Life is Pants

era. Despite their respective ages of nine and seven, they're clearly dab-hands at this modelling lark, and go through a succession of staged poses. Darleen's coaching behind the photographer.

'Look at me, Chanel, chin down slightly, lovely, left foot slightly forward, lovely. Armani, finger out of nose, thank you.'

Finally we really get cracking, with the photographer snapping away relentlessly. All the while Darleen puts her kids through their paces.

'Pose one, lovely. Pose nine, lovely!'

So they even have their poses pre-choreographed, and move like a couple of marionettes! Frightening!

A late lunch arrives. Rice and scrawny meat-cuts in ancient bowls, accompanied by a dirt-encrusted spoon. Hmm, I think I'll pass on the typhoid and hepatitis, thank you very much. The yanks all guzzle it down (rather them than me—hope they have good medical insurance). I'm knackered after three and a half hours of posing as a pregnant mother and I reaffirm my commitment to never have children (if I had ever needed persuading, a day with these brats would have done the trick). I sit in a comatose state as Keanu farts loudly before dashing off, leaving us trying to determine what smells worse—his guff or the lunch. This was supposed to be four hours' work but it feels like forever. And I have a stress headache for some reason.

Finally lunch is over and shooting resumes. I dress in yet another vile creation and fix the smile back on my face. Oh joy, Keanu again. Fortunately, he has burnt off some of his energy and is now tired (and grumpy), talking in a whiney voice.

'Mommy, I want to go home.'

You're not the only one, buddy.

'Mommy, mommy, when are we going home?' he witters on.

Betty screams back, 'Behave Keanu or I'll tell daddy!' which miraculously shuts him up.

I whisper in his ear, 'Stop farting or I'll tell your daddy.'

The next few photographs I'm sure will be lovely, with

me looking down at Keanu while holding his sticky hand (no doubt with a few bogies on it). He looks up at me with a sullen expression on his face while Betty shouts, 'Smile, Keanu, smile!' to no avail. The photographer starts flapping his arms about, then physically forces Keanu's mouth up at the edges to try to form a smile. I notice his hands are black with loads of dirt under his nails (gross!). I smile even harder to escape the same treatment.

I look at the time and see I'm over my four hours. Pia of the pouting lips had advised me never to go over the scheduled number of hours as they don't like to pay overtime. I've had about all I can take of this crap anyway. I step out of the shot and sit down on a chair by the wall. The skinny man comes running over to me, talking hurriedly in Mandarin.

'Betty, please tell him I've done my four hours and if they want me to do more they'll have to pay me for it,' I assert.

Betty's firm sure must have invested in her, as she gabbles on impressively in Mandarin.

'Emily, they said just ten more minutes,' she informs me.

'OK, but not a minute more,' I answer sternly. Now I must really sound like Naomi!

After twenty minutes, there's no sign of the shoot coming to an end. Once again I sit down. The skinny man runs over.

'He wants another ten minutes,' Betty translates.

'Tell him no,' I say, feeling utterly bushed. I get up to go and get changed. The skinny guy grabs my arm hard and pushes me onto the set again. I forcibly remove his hand and look daggers at him. As I walk towards my changing room he grabs my arm again. This time I position myself next to Betty and tell her to tell him to piss off. Good old Betty borrows Darleen's mobile to call Anni.

The phone gets passed to me and Anni pleads, 'Just ten more minutes!'

I've well and truly had enough and so refuse to back down. 'I've already done an extra twenty minutes,' I point out. 'You told me the ferry would be half an hour and it took almost two hours. I've already spent nearly seven hours on this job and will only get paid for four. Either they pay me overtime or I've finished for the day.'

Anni speaks to Betty who speaks to the skinny man who speaks to Betty who speaks to Anni who speaks to me.

'OK, he'll pay you one hour of overtime, but don't tell the mothers as we're not paying overtime for the children.'

Outrageous! But I'm tired and it's up to Betty, Darleen and Terri-Lou to fight their own battles.

'You've got me for forty minutes, that's all' I say as I move towards the set. And in those forty minutes I have about forty changes of disgusting T-shirt. I end up not caring who sees my bra or flabby abs.

I ask Betty to find out what time the next ferry to Hong Kong is. It turns out to be in twenty minutes, with the one after that leaving three hours later! Betty screams, 'Get your bags we're going NOW!' and we all dash about as if a typhoon is heading our way. The skinny man and grinning photographer (no longer grinning) are unhappy about this, and seem to think it's quite reasonable for us to wait over three hours for the next ferry. Even the kids behave, wanting to get the hell out of there. Only Samantha-Jayne is standing in front of the camera wanting more photos to be taken, smiling like bloody Miss World.

We end up crammed into one taxi; quite how we all fit in I will never know. Suffice to say I end up with Keanu's arse next to my face—a very dangerous position indeed without a gasmask. We hurtle towards the ferry terminal like the Dukes of Hazard, and manically pay for tickets. There are prams, bags of toys, and carrier bags of orange juice, apple juice and crisps strewn across the pavement. I leg it to the immigration queue—I'll be damned if I miss the ferry while waiting for Keanu to find his 'Scooby Doo and the Missing Donuts' LeapPad. Samantha-Jayne can't locate her 'Swan Lake Barbie' and is whimpering hysterically. I'm again reminded that the first thing I'm going to do when I get back to Hong Kong is see my doctor about getting sterilised. 'Whip the whole baby-making kit out!' I'll say. And it will be money well spent.

By some miracle we all make it onto the ferry, apart from 'Swan Lake Barbie' who's missing in action. This means we have to endure almost two hours of Samantha-Jayne crying in such a way you'd think she'd lost a limb rather than a plastic doll (although I did love my 'Tiny Tears', despite her literally being a complete wet). Terri-Lou looks terribly guilt-ridden, pleading with Samantha-Jayne to let her buy her another 'Swan Lake Barbie' plus a 'Mermaid Fantasy Barbie' by way of compensation for her tragic loss. Samantha-Jayne, however, doesn't want to strike a deal in the depths of her bereavement.

'Mommy, mommy, you lost her. I love her sooo much! I miss her!' Samantha-Jayne bawls, now rolling on the floor in agony. Chanel and Armani look across with distain, forever the professionals, while Keanu farts and chuckles.

Half an hour to go. Terri-Lou is still begging, 'Oh princess, I'll buy you "Swan Lake Barbie", "Mermaid Fantasy Barbie", "Groovy Girl Bindi", "Rainbow Horse and Sprinkles" and "Rock-a-bye Chou Chou Doll". What do you say, my pretty, pretty princess?'

I just want to grab Samantha-Jayne by the throat and shake her vigorously, telling her to take it, it's a very good deal indeed. Instead Samantha-Jayne thinks about it for a moment and then curls up on the floor, shedding more crocodile tears. I reach the point where I can't take it any more and am actually contemplating jumping overboard, when Samantha-Jayne hiccups, 'I want "Lottalittles Fairground Fun Bus", too!'

'Oh, princess!' says Terri-Lou, picking up the little thief and cuddling her, while smothering her face and head with loud kisses. I look directly at Samantha-Jayne who stares back with a twinkle in her eye. She knows exactly what she's doing, playing her mother like a fiddle. My mum would have given me the slipper and told me I was imbecilic for losing the doll in the first place. I wonder what Samantha-Jayne will be like when she grows up (if she ever does—she may end up like her dopey mother, cooing in a little girl voice). I pity the poor man she takes to the divorce courts!

It'll come as no surprise to learn that I'm the first off the ferry. I shout a cursory goodbye to Betty and the gang, and sprint off, leaving them collecting the hundreds of toys still strewn over the four corners of the ferry's floor. I can hear Betty shouting, 'Keanu, what have you done with "Shaker Maker Spiderman"?' and I have new determination to get my reproductive kit laid to rest in peace. This has been a ten-hour day for four hours' pay—just great. I don't think I've ever been so shattered in all my life and have a thumping headache. I jump into a taxi thinking, sod the bus, just get me home ('Mommy, mommy, I want to go home!').

The next day I have the squits. Big time. Every five minutes I charge to the toilet to release a symphony of sounds and half a tonne of runny orange poo. What did I do to deserve this? Perhaps it's a tummy bug as I have been incredibly farty the last few days, blowing particularly smelly pharps. Only last night James tried to snuggle up to me but moved away quickly, gagging and telling me, 'Phoar, you stink! God almighty, awh!' He ended up bolting to the bathroom, dramatically retching up a wee bit of spit (and they say romance is dead!). The only upside to diarrhoea is that you lose a bit of weight. I can also make a point of eating all my favourite naughty foods at times like this, knowing they'll be whooshing out of my body a minute later. (No one could ever accuse me of not trying to look on the bright side of life, could they?)

So far I've eaten three Mars bars, two tubs of Pringles and a large knob of Lurpak butter without any bread. I've truly overdone the gorging on fatty foods and now feel sick. Let's hope it puts me off eating crap for the next few months and gives me a craving for nutritious lentil broth and fruit salads instead (fat chance!).

Every ten minutes I go to the mirror and hold up my nightie to see if my abs' definition has improved. After eighteen visits to the potty I can see the slight outline of an abs muscle. Hey-ho, roll on the next urge to splurge! I'm sure I must have used a rainforest-the size-of-Peru's worth of toilet paper wiping my arse today. (That's a point—is toilet roll actually made from paper? Hmm, another clever question to put to Maurice McWerter. Christ knows my toilet paper feels so scratchy I could well be wiping my arse on a piece of bark wood.) Whoops, my anus is twitching again. Time to get rid of those Mars bars. Hooray!

Sarah Barclay, a great girl I stay in touch with from my old company in London, went to India recently on honeymoon and got a bout of the infamous 'Delhi Belly', losing over a stone in weight in just one week. Fabulous achievement! I suggested to her we start a business together offering the ultimate detox—tours to India—promising quick and drastic weight reduction while enjoying stunning sunsets at the beautiful Taj Mahal. Personally, I think it'd go down a storm. Sarah didn't see the funny side of it, though, lamenting how shit her honeymoon was (quite literally). But as my colonics prove, there's money to be made from shit.

I get a call from Anni of 'Anni's Best Models'.

'Emily, the factory in Dongguan will not pay you because you take so many outfits away with you.'

I don't quite get it. 'Excuse me, what?'

'They say you take many clothes home with you.'

I think this is quite possibly the angriest I've ever been. 'Anni!' I bark. 'They were the most disgusting clothes I've ever seen in my life. I would not want them if they were free!'

'But they say you take...' Anni argues, but I cut her off.

'No, it's untrue! And if you don't pay me I will take you to court and make sure your business gets shut down. I know many solicitors and journalists in Hong Kong and you won't stand a chance.' That should do it. 'I'll be round to your office tomorrow morning to collect my cheque.'

The next day I collect my cheque.

'Oh, they find the clothes,' Anni tells me meekly.

Hmm, she's a bloody thief and I vow never to work for her again. Later that day Anni calls me, offering a photographic job for a Hong Kong tours company. I take it.

I have no information about the job. I pack a small bag with my make-up kit and hairbrush—I do such cheap jobs that often hair and make-up is a DIY (Disaster-It-Yourself) job. In actual fact, their budget's always so low I keep expecting them to ask me to set up the camera on automatic mode and take the photos myself, simultaneously posing for the shots.

I take the MTR to Chai Wan. It's so different to the Tube and I still can't get over how cheap, clean and frequent it is, with helpful staff everywhere (OK, I know I'm going on a bit, but it's bloody wicked!). It costs me forty pence for a journey that would cost me four quid on the Tube—bargain! You don't even need to faffy around buying individual tickets with cash as you can buy an 'Octopus Card' that lasts a lifetime. You just keep adding value onto it to pay not only for trains but also buses—how hassle-free is that! It's ironic that some of my pals in London think I'm living in an uncivilized country. Here the trains arrive every one to two minutes on the dot without delays or pathetic excuses (there's no train driver available) or complications (there are leaves on the track), and it truly works like clockwork. I've spent half my life in London waiting for a Tube to turn up so this is just bloody marvellous!

In fact the MTR is so regular there's no such thing as people running for the train here like lunatics. They simply can't be arsed when the next one's just round the corner (in the tunnel). I think of my glorious rush-hour journeys in England, running down the escalator as fast as my legs would carry me, using all my strength to hold the automatic doors open before they closed shut. One body part usually did the trick: wedging your shoulder (ouch! but cheaper than the chiropractor), your foot (crunch! guaranteed limp), even your head (I assume the black rubber seal on the doors is there to stop you getting guillotined)—all preferable to sticking your handbag between the doors and risking getting it dirty or, worse, scratched. So I still can't get out of the habit of bolting for the train and the people standing on the downward escalator here with no sense of urgency amaze me. I want to shout 'Everyone, CHARGE!' (No wonder they never win the sprint event at the Olympics, although they do have a national talent for bashing your knees with their steel-capped bags and would get the gold medal for this every time if it were to become an Olympic event.)

I'm met outside Chai Wan MTR by 'Elvis', a young lad who appears to be mute, with dyed orange hair and big black sunglasses. I ask him what the advert is about and he totally ignores me, instead drawing deeply on his cigarette in an attempt to look cool (actually doing more an Asian Jimmy Dean than Elvis Presley), and just about getting away with it. I see a group of kids grinning from ear to ear and jumping up and down in excitement heading directly towards us. Oh God no, please, not kids! Give me animals! Even killer snakes and lethal spiders, anything in preference to grotty bogey-eating urchins!

Now, here's a surprise—I'm to play their goddamned mother! And one of them is a frigging teenager! How old do they think I look, for Christ's sake? I calculate I'd have to have given birth to the critter when I was twelve years old (must have gone to a comprehensive school, then, or been supplied birth control by my mother). A man old enough to be my dad strolls over and I'm told he's playing my husband... bloody paedophile! His name is Fred Parry (he is nearly as old as Fred Perry) but thankfully he turns out to be a real hoot.

We're all bundled into taxis and they try to fit us all into one. Here we go again. Another low-budget escapade. We actually have a make-up artist this time, though, called Forever (yes, I know!), and the photographer, Jokey (I won't even go there), is apparently quite well known in Hong Kong (for having a ridiculous name?).

It turns out the photos will depict tourists having fun in Hong Kong... ice-skating. Ice-skating! I haven't been skating since I was seven! I was crap at it and stopped altogether after falling over and lightly grazing my knee. I only liked going because I got to wear a sparkly little dress that I thought made me look like a fairy princess, rather than the twat I did in fact resemble. Holy shit! I have zero balance. I suddenly recall I got a little creative when it came to the Hobbies and Skills section in my 'model CV', and must have included ice-skating in amongst bare-back horse-riding, trapeze and sky-diving—well, what was the likelihood they'd call me up for all that? Time to start blagging it.

'Oh I used to skate all the time,' I say with mock confidence. 'A right little Jayne Torvill! Just not since coming to Hong Kong, so I'll be rusty for sure. Practice makes all the difference, you know. It'll be great to get back on the ice.'

Jokey gives me a small smile and Fred pipes up, 'I can't skate to save me life but I'll give it a go!'

'Excellent attitude, Fred!' remarks Jokey.

What? I wish Fred had revealed this earlier! They're now expecting bloody champion moves from me, when what they'll get is something akin to Charlie Chaplin on ice.

The skating rink is packed with people going round and round in circles (don't they ever get dizzy?). A girl wearing a sparkly dress who thinks she looks like a fairy princess but actually looks like a twat (well she is about forty!) does a little jump-turn and lands flat on her arse. Fred and I giggle. Naturally, we're paid back for this as soon as we get going as one of the little kids knocks into us, sending us sprawling ungracefully across the ice. Not a very convincing start.

'Ere, Jokey! 'ow about a photo in this position?' Fred quips, but Jokey's too intent on setting up his camera to notice.

Forever skates over to us with ease and redoes my hair (lots of backcombing that will destroy it for good) while everyone skates around us. Jokey takes an age to set up so Fred and I do a couple of circles around the rink, while holding onto the rail for grim life the whole time. I attempt a few rail-free strides, only to nearly lose my balance, toppling forwards or backwards, and muttering, 'Fuck!' rather too loudly. Fred thankfully doesn't comment on how incredibly rusty I am. Instead he's shouting 'Little buggers!' at the kids who whizz past us in the manner of professional speed-skaters.

After nearly forty minutes of setting up (hopefully we're heading for some overtime pay!) Jokey is ready to shoot. Fred cleverly holds onto one of our four kids' waists (four!

You mean I've mated four times with Fred? Hell!) and I in turn hold onto Fred to form a chain. Jokey is rather impressed with it and shoots an entire film with us like this holding onto each other. I fake a smile when all the while really I'm gritting my teeth and clinging on tightly to avoid going splat. Fred pulls the daftest faces, eye popping and mouth gaping, and I can't believe Jokey allows it. I can only imagine what the photos will come out like: Fred looking totally demented and me looking at him in abject horror. Come to think of it, my parents always look just like that in family photos.

Every few minutes, the kids bomb off around the rink, burning off all that boundless energy. They're fearless and don't seem to mind crashing headfirst into the barrier or grazing body parts on the ice. Fred and I, in stark contrast, hold our poses for fear of falling over. I wonder whether Jokey has caught onto me being a phoney.

Luckily, I survive the ordeal. Jokey seems very happy with us, and even suggests more work for our 'family' on the horizon. Fred and I leave the kids zooming around the rink, where no doubt they'll stay until closing time. We can't get out of there fast enough. All in a day's work!

I get a call from Anni the following afternoon. I'm ready to scream at her if she tells me they're not paying me because I took the pair of ice-skates home or something, but instead she's happy with me.

'Ahh, Emily, they like you so much! They want you to do lots of adverts. But can't pay you much, ahh.' There's always a sting in the tail, isn't there?

I don't hear from Anni again for over six months.

This modelling malarkey is really awful. I average ten million castings to get one job, not good odds. I'm backwards and forwards on the MTR, dashing this way and that for castings that more often than not I'm totally unsuitable for. I'm sure the MTR's profits have increased drastically since I joined this line of work.

Chirlee from 'Model Shots' has kindly sent me to an industrial slum in the middle of nowhere. It's for a famous brand of ladieswear who are looking for an in-house model to parade around in front of their designers, displaying their new season's range of clothing. Chirlee sounds confident.

'You're the body they look for, Emily!'

I double-check she's got the right sizes for me and she immediately replies, 'Yeez, yeez, they want to see you, hurry ahh.'

It's taken me over an hour to get here and reconfirmed my suspicions that I have no idea how to read a map. Finally I arrive and am ushered into a small room surrounded by clothes hanging on makeshift rails, over doors, chairs and piled up high on the floor. There's a very thin lady dressed in a trendy black tailored suit and wearing bright red lipstick, and a thin man, who for some reason is dressed in Joseph's multi-coloured coat (so that's who nicked it!). He has a little goatee beard and Elvis Costello-style thickset, black-rimmed glasses (doesn't the word 'rimmed' send shivers down your spine? yum mmm). He looks a complete arse, or like he's perhaps just stepped off the set of 'Sex and the City' (someone please tell me how those girls can afford those designer wardrobes on their salaries!!).

'And who are you?' the woman asks.

I give her my most dazzling smile and answer, 'Emily from Model Shots.'

The man's jaw drops. Christ, what now? The lady butts in.

'We asked for a US size 6 and you're at least a size 8 if not more!'

Joseph and his wanky-coloured coat joins in. 'What was Chirlee doing?'

'I even checked she had my current measurements,' I respond meekly. 'It's taken me over an hour to get here.'

'She's wasted your time,' Joseph chimes in. 'We don't ever use anyone your size.'

I prepare to go as the bitch with the blood-stained lips adds, 'We don't often see models your size. They are normally size 6 or less.'

Well, at least I don't look like Count Dracula sucking blood, I want to shout back at her.

I leave and immediately get on the mobile to Chirlee, on the verge of blowing a gasket.

'Model Shots, this is Chirlee speaking.'

'Chirlee, it's Emily. I'm at the casting and they say I'm the wrong size and that they asked you for a US 6.'

'Oh really?' Chirlee seems nonplussed. 'Do you know any models that size I can call?'

I can feel the heat rising in my cheeks. 'Chirlee, it's taken me over an hour to get here, it will take me the same again to get back home and I've spent forty bucks!'

'I call you soon and get you something else,' is all I get from stupid Chirlee (who can't even bloody spell her fucking name right) before she hangs up on me. Life sucks!

To top it all there's another leaving party tonight. It feels like all the expats are vacating Hong Kong. I don't blame them, though, as this town is tough to survive in. Matt and his Filipino wife Apple (of his eye? or cock?) are off to sleepy Saunton Sands in Devon. I fear Apple will experience rather a lot of ribbing for her fruity name and imagine she'll be like a fish out of water there, poor girl.

Matt's selected the 'Groovy Mule' in Wanchai as his party venue. An odd choice since it's a table-dancing bar, but I guess he'll miss that sort of thing in somewhat tame Devon. The bar has modelled itself on the movie 'Coyote Ugly'. James suggests this is 'because it's full of ugly dogs', which gains him a laugh from his mates and a frosty stare from one of the barmaids. These poor women not only have to serve drinks to a large crowd but also leap up onto the bar every ten minutes to belt out a song and dance wildly. They must get totally knackered.

A pretty girl gets up and sings Cher's 'If I Could Turn Back Time'. It's rather grating on the eardrums (if only I could turn her off!) but she shimmies her pert breasts nicely. Next up is a girl rather on the large size who's squeezed into a skimpy handkerchief-style top and hipster jeans. Everyone's too busy commenting on how fat she looks to notice she's got a cracking voice. She hits an amazingly high note and her top pings open to reveal her bare breasts. The crowd suddenly starts to appreciate her talents and starts clapping. The poor lass doesn't know where to put herself, so hides behind the bar to refasten her top. And like a real trooper she starts the song again, this time to shouts of, 'Get yer top off! Off, off, off!' Well they do say you have to suffer for your art.

James takes a last swig of his beer. 'Let's get out of here!' he suggests and we jump into a taxi to Central. His mobile rings ('...Yeah, mate. Yeah, mate. Yeah, mate...') and he leans forward to the taxi driver, 'Wyndham Street m-goi.' Then he turns to me.

'Emily, you lucky girl, I've just got us down on the guest list at Dragon-i, so try to look awake.'

Dragon-i is a swanky new bar where all the beautiful people hang out—quite why we're going I don't know. It's owned by a well-connected socialite and I've heard on the grapevine it's good for ponce-watching, correction, 'people-watching'. As expected, it's full of guys and gals who might just have stepped off the cover of Vogue, sipping cocktails gracefully as though starring in 'Tia Maria' TV adverts—not slurping them down ten to the dozen like me or downing beers like they're in fact not extortionately priced, like James. We don't give a monkey's arse about looking cool.

I clock the girls eyeing up every other girl who walks through the entrance, comparing looks before assessing whether the man on her arm is loaded. (Pu-lease!) James and I have a bit of a bop while the models look on in distain. They don't dance through fear of a hair falling out of place.

Somehow James knows the crowd in the VIP area, and the bouncer reluctantly lets us in. Am I supposed to feel privileged and special, hanging out with a bunch of posing tossers? Fortunately, James is equally unimpressed and we go home for nice cuddles.

Sleepy Sunday. Time to clear out my inbox.

From: katiets@abbotts-dury.com
To: emilygreenhk@hotmail.com
Subject: Sunday Pub Lunch

Dear all,

Timothy and I cordially invite you and your better halves (or new halves or even temporary halves if recent tittle-tattle is correct) to our lovely new home in Locks Bottom from 11am this Sunday for some housewarming drinks.

Children are also invited but please bear in mind that the intention is to move on to The Wheat Sheaf pub for Sunday roast at 1pm, followed by a short post-lunch tour round the village golf course (it may keep the children amused for a while).

RSVP.

Katie & Timothy

PS—The carpets have just gone down so, true to form and in keeping with recent social gatherings, shoes should be removed at the door with socks becoming the pressure fashion statement.

PPS—Alistair—please send your Mrs on a training course in Drink Management prior to this event.

Bloody hell! Katie's sounding all grown up! How flipping civilized—and tedious?

From: James1969@yahoo.com
To: emilygreenhk@hotmail.com
Subject: Wedding nite!

Newlyweds turned up at a hotel and asked for a honeymoon suite.

'Do you have reservations?' asked the hotel desk clerk.

'Only one,' replied the groom, 'She won't take it up the arse.'

Yeeesss... no doubt James found this one hilarious.

From: janeheffer@yahoo.com
To: emilygreenhk@hotmail.com
Subject: my news...

Hi Emily

I've had a really busy week.

I moved to Cockfosters on Sunday, and drove to Birmingham and back the following day to collect a sofa that I don't like the colour of. (It's supposed to be cream but looks really white—a white elephant!) But I had a week off work to recover which was nice.

Tuesday night—Mexican meal with the girls, good laugh but onions do funny things to my bottom! Thursday—my birthday, so Stewart took me for a curry after buying me diamond earrings! They're from Argos though.

Friday night—my leaving bash at Max Club. Do you remember the policeman I dated in April who suddenly ran away from me? He spotted me dancing and sent a text message to my old mobile (which Stewart now has!) saying how gorgeous I looked and how about a fuck in the toilets, and to text him back straight away! Didn't go down too well with Stewart I can tell you! However, Stewart still hasn't left his wife, so I did text the policeman back and he took me out on Saturday night. We had a really fun evening, ending up back at his place in Brentford for a kebab and you can guess the rest! He explained he felt I wasn't over my ex, ex, Paul, when he dated me back in April, hence why he texted me at the time to say it wouldn't work. Plus he was just about to start a custody battle for his 4 kids. Anyway, his name is Wayne Scoggins and he used to be in the Mounted Police so can horse-ride! 27 years old and has his own horse, Willy (although he may lose it to his ex-wife). Sadly he's gone right off the idea of marriage after his recent messy divorce and just wants to start dating again to get his confidence back. So we have agreed not to be too serious and just have fun (lots of sex!). Sounds good to me!

I'm still seeing Stewart though, who I do actually love, but can't sit at home sobbing over him. So I will go on the occasional fun date with Wayne too—why not!

Oh, last but certainly not least, I now have 3 cats, Blackie, Snowball and Marmalade (I prefer their company to all these stupid men!).

Miss you!

Take care

Jane

Well sounds like Jane's getting lots of sex, lucky cow. Which is more than can be said for me. James is dashing off to play football up by the border. Ninety minutes of football, nine hours of drinking! I, on the other hand, am entertaining Mandy's cousin, Jenny, who's passing through Hong Kong on her way to Oz.

I opt to take her to see the Big Buddah on Lantau Island, since this is something I've always meant to do but could never be arsed on my own. We take the ferry across to the island and then catch a bus. It's all up hill and the bus struggles at about one mile per hour. At one point we're chugging along so slowly a bunch of walkers overtake us! I have no patience during journeys and it takes us nearly three flipping hours door to door.

I get to know Jenny. She lives in a small town just outside Dorking with her third husband and five children (hmm, sounds delightful!). Jenny says, 'I only have to look at a man and I get pregnant!' Apparently so, although you'd think her looks would be a form of contraception for any man. I ask Jenny whether she works and my eyes nearly drop out of my head at her response.

'Yeah, I work in a laboratory, actually, doing product testing on animals.'

Bloody hell! As a strict veggie and staunch animal rights supporter, my impulse is to beat her to a pulp and stick shampoo in her eyes. I refrain, as Jenny happily chatters on.

'Oh yeah, lots of people hate us for what we do,' (you don't say!) 'but someone's got to do it.' (Have they?) 'That's why God put them on earth.' (Erm, right.)

I attempt to change the subject by asking, 'What are your plans for Oz?' but strangely, Jenny wants to talk shop.

'Yeah, we have monkeys, mice, rats. I don't like doing it on the dogs most of all, but hey-ho.'

Hey-ho indeed. My blood is boiling and my jaw clenched in anger, but I think of my friendship with Mandy and try to exercise some self-control while I sit next to this mass murderer. We continue the journey in silence.

The Big Buddah looms before us. It's big (name's a bit of a giveaway) and covered in gold (bollocks, I should have brought a chisel with me!). I wonder what Buddah, a fellow right-on veggie, would think of Jenny's job? He'd probably put a curse on her. Then again, she's not that easy on the eye (makes Ann Widdecombe look like a babe), so maybe she's had her share of bad luck.

You have to walk up hundreds of stone steps to reach the top of the statue. Jenny gives up after about eight and says she's going to grab a bite to eat from one of the roadside food stalls. I would normally warn her not to eat from these places as they're not the most hygienic, but I think of all the poor wee monkeys with bloodshot eyes from all her product testing and leave her to it. I walk up and down and then we catch the bus back. A wonderful six-hour journey for twenty minutes' sightseeing! Jenny talks non-stop about her kids and their behavioural issues at school—they all sound like right tearaways and should be donated to animal testing.

James returns home after only seven hours of hard boozing with his footy lads. After these drinking sessions he often tells me in a drunken voice he's the only one of his gang of merry men not to be struck down with 'yellow fever' (when only tan-skinned Asian girls will do), and says it like he wants a pat on the back or a medal of achievement. While he laments how his mates are saddled with economic refugees who are just after their money and Western passport, I get the impression underneath he's gagging to sow his seed throughout the whole of Asia.

When he gets really stormingly drunk he returns home converted to the belief that the grass is greener. He then proceeds to tell me how boring, fat and ugly I am. I'm embarrassed to admit he's got into the habit of pushing me around and slapping me across the face when he's had one too many. Recently he's come home in terrible drunken rages and tried to strangle me—very out of character so I cut him some slack, even if he doesn't deserve it. I've been recalling of late the good old days when we used to go out for dinner with friends and I would enjoy nothing more than sitting back listening to him dominate the conversation and laugh at all his jokes.

Nowadays, though, I feel relaxed enough to contribute to the conversation and realize he hogs it and won't let anyone get a word in edgewise. I try to tell a joke and he cuts in with his own. I could scream. I used to lap up his every word rather than silently comment 'wanker' after everything he said. These days I sit next to him thinking if he doesn't shut up I'm going to embed an axe into his head (in court I would plead I'd found my sanity). I hear the song 'He Had It Comin'' from 'Chicago' relentlessly going round and round in my head and it frightens me that I feel like this about someone I once adored and wished would ask me to marry him.

So I'm boring, am I? It brings stinging tears to my eyes. I listen to him recite the football scores and player transfers over and over again until I know them off by heart, but still, I'm the boring one. I hear him rattle on about Mrs Thatcher's achievements (I know, you wouldn't think it would last long but he somehow stretches it out for hours). Only his opinion matters. Only he is right. Only he knows everything. Everything I say is wrong. In the end you stop saying anything... yes, maybe I have become boring.

Mothers love their sons, though. In their eyes they can do no wrong. Snort (all my) coke, swallow ecstasy pills like they're M&Ms, hit the girlfriend when drunk—but, well, boys will be boys, dear! James's mother lovingly posted him a coaster and matching placemat last week. She labelled the envelope 'To the best son in the world', and the tacky tableware says '"James" means "hero" in Latin' (rather than "total wanker"). Sickening stuff. Even more sickening is that, like a little child, James now insists on having supper served to him on his personalised placemat and is using a coaster for the first time in his adult life. I must buy a dog so I can say it ate them, although I'm sure mummy would come to the rescue and send another set. I'm sad he's changed into someone I don't like.

I go on a three-week visit to the UK and James phones me almost daily, sometimes twice a day. For someone who thought the break would do us good he's not giving me much of one. The fact I pay the phone bill doesn't feel right either. I'm paying for the privilege of him wittering on for hours.

I return home to Hong Kong late at night to be greeted by heavy monsoon rains. The heavens have opened and the incessant downfall sums up my heavy heart. As the lift doors open I see James has hung a 'Welcome Home' banner on the front door. Very strange indeed considering his recent bad behaviour, but lovely all the same. He's almost euphoric I'm home—I assume he's been up to no good and his guilty conscience has got the better of him. He keeps hugging me tight and smiling broadly. Sadly, his loving attitude lasts exactly two days—my fault, though, for spoiling the moment...

I come home to a broken washing machine and three weeks' worth of his washing (festering football kit and the like) to add to my bulging suitcase of three weeks' dirty washing. Greeaaatttt to be back! Apparently, during my first week away he was being a good boy putting on a wash when the washing machine conked out mid-cycle. Rather than phone the repair service hotline to get it mended he thought he'd wait until I got back. Most thoughtful, James. So now we have a dirty, smelly laundry mountain taking up most of the apartment.

It takes the repairman four days to get his butt here and another five to order a million parts. I'm doing something I've never done before and wearing my knickers two days in a row. James seems completely unfazed by this, and proudly confides that he used to wear his boxer shorts five days running at Uni. That makes me feel so much better. Turns out James forgot to take out his shirt collar stiffeners and they destroyed the motor (which costs about the same as a new machine to replace). Oh, and the guarantee ran out while I was away, so labour charges on top. All at my expense, of course. Yes, welcome home indeed!

It doesn't stop there. He dropped the microwave oven's glass plate and I need to order a new one. The microwave is covered in sticky tomato goo as he had an accident cooking baked beans on too high a setting and didn't think to clean it up. I spend nearly an hour scrubbing the encrusted mess until my nails are filed down to the quick. No clean cutlery to be found as washing up is piled ceiling-high in the kitchen sink. No food in the vicinity. Fridge empty. Cupboards bare. I do what I rarely do—flip out at him. I'm jet-lagged and actually tired of three intensive weeks of catching up with family and friends and telling my Hong Kong life story to the world and his wife. So the 'welcome back' mood turns to mutual hatred.

The icing on the cake arrives one week later when the phone bill (which I always pay) reveals he's forgotten to use our four-digit prefix for economy international calls. So what should be a reasonably cheap bill now amounts to the equivalent of a deposit on a Porsche Boxster. I'm fuming. He says he'll pay it, but that's not the point. I can't leave him for three weeks without coming back to a disaster area!

I chat to my beautician Louise (or 'Nail Technician' as she insists on being called) at 'Body Beautiful', the salon I use occasionally. She tells me she's now teaching English on the side, despite failing her GCSE English when she was sixteen. (Blooming marvellous! It's no wonder the locals' English is so poor!)

'It beats waxing gay men's backs, cracks and sacks which is now all the rage!' Louise confides.

Yuck, you'd have to give me danger money to do that job! Perhaps I'm not doing too badly after all (although my mean side does rather like the idea of making men scream in agony).

My nails now look vaguely like they should, shapely and polished rather than the chewed corned-beef look I went in with.

I meet Pippa for a quick lunch at the Mandarin Oriental Café (her choice, not mine—it's sooo expensive!). I look at the menu and realize a main course will set me back about a week's wages. I order an appetiser instead, feigning to be not particularly hungry, a glass of iced tap water and a basket of assorted breads (free!). Pippa tells me her friend

Life is Pants

Janey is fervently looking for a husband as she'll be turning forty in a few months' time.

'She's dating a different man every night of the week to find someone remotely suitable. But all the ones she likes run a mile. They come up with lame excuses why they can't see her again—like their mother's got terminal cancer or some such rubbish! You see, they can smell the desperation and it sends fear coursing through their veins. It's a real problem for sorry desperate Janey,' says Pippa earnestly.

I nod sympathetically.

'These career women suddenly realize they're going to be old and alone and make a last ditch effort to find a husband. They despair at not having a husband. What they don't realize is that they're lucky never to have had one! In fact, they're very welcome to mine.' Pippa pauses and adds in a low voice, 'Although they probably have had him! Cheating toad.' She's clearly on a roll. 'When I met Rupert I wanted to have a child—not marry one! It's all hunky dory for a couple of years then suddenly they turn into complete babies.' She puts on a whiney voice, '"Pippa, where are the towels?", "Pip, where's the toilet roll?", "Where's the Frosties?"... I get more sense out of my three year old! Like they say, "It begins when you sink in their arms and ends up with your arms in the sink!" Bloody Rupert!'

At least he pays for her nice Mandarin Oriental Café lunches. Not a bad consolation prize.

As if I'm not depressed enough, I get the results of my family tree back. They're impressively bound in an elaborate folder with neat calligraphy and a shiny navy blue ribbon. That's about as impressive as it gets. Turns out I should have listened to my dad after all (for a change) as ironically enough, he was spot on. I'm very disappointed to have found absolutely no links to royal blood. Nor to the upper classes. Not the middle classes either. Not even the working classes. Nope, my stock is well and truly a bunch of paupers. And I was so sure I was either Marie Antoinette's or Anastasia's secret surviving family. In fact, scullery maids and footmen are the successful few in our family tree (the majority of relatives were committed to the workhouse or madhouse)—the rest couldn't even write down their livelihood or sign their names in the registry book. Fabulous. Once a serf always a serf! Maybe I should become an Amah since I come from such a long line of domestic serving staff.

James is out for the evening. These days he doesn't tell me where he's going and is secretive and sulky. I have a sinking feeling that he's seeing someone else, but prefer not to think about it. I listlessly watch TV—nothing but tripe on. I order a pizza demanding, 'Give me the greasiest one you've got!' (not really). I over-tip the delivery boy in error and he looks very happy indeed. It's all right for some.

The pizza is suitably smothered in cheese and large enough to give me great pleasure and plenty of guilt. I tuck into my fabulous feast and watch the news headlines. A man in Germany is under arrest for cannibalism. As if that's not weird enough, the victim volunteered to be sacrificed! It wasn't even someone with a crappy life like mine, but a successful 'intelligent' man in the IT business. I'm still chewing my pizza as the newsreader, with an openly shocked expression on her face, describes how the men cut off the volunteer's penis and ate it together with a red wine sauce. Gross! I've stopped eating altogether by this point, my appetite well and truly gone. In fact I feel like I'm going to vomit.

In desperation I turn to the sports channel, ESPN, but the image of sautéed cock won't leave my mind. They're showing some kind of dog Olympics—ten or so dogs fighting it out in the great outdoors, competing in events like the long jump, catch the Frisbee, swimming lengths in a lake (doggie paddle?)—stuff even I could do. They have names like Wally, Kiki and Jerry. Jerry, a black Labrador, even has his own fan club with him, a bunch of porkers wearing 'Team Jerry' T-shirts and chanting for him. Only in America—land of the nutcases, I mean 'the free'. Then again, I get quite into it, routing for a Golden Retriever called Lulu. Come on, Lulu, come on, Lulu! It's actually as good as the Olympics—if not marginally better.

The local news comes on with the disastrous presenter

with the overactive eyebrows. A crocodile has been spotted in Yuen Long and there's media frenzy over its capture. Unbeknown to the croc, he's reached celebrity status in only a few days. Even an Ozzie croc trapper (sadly not that funny Ozzie twit Steve Urwin) has flown to Hong Kong to hunt down the poor thing, but the clever croc is still on the run (or on the swim). (Incidentally, there's another reptile on the run—James, who is still out, God knows where!) That's Hong Kong's only piece of news. China's launching its first astronaut soon—strange when people are starving for a bowl of rice there. I guess this extravagant stunt means they no longer need the $18 billion in aid they receive? I turn to the Net for a bit of company.

From: claire_adair@btinternet.com
To: emilygreenhk@hotmail.com
Subject: All men are pants

Hi Emily

Men are pants as usual.

Keith still hasn't got a job. And I'm going to have to start weaning him off my credit cards! Fun and games.

My dad wants to move in with me because his lady friend has told him to bugger off. She told him widowed men only try it on with her as they want someone to cook their meals and do their washing. So now he wants me to do it instead!

Boys.

Take care sweetie!

Clare : (

From: mary1972@hotmail.com
To: emilygreenhk@hotmail.com
Subject: Hiya Emily!

Hiya girlie

Bit short on news and gossip for you.

It's mostly been minor annoyances i.e.

Washing machine was noisy, called in the engineers—it's a write-off!

Pulled out the fridge-freezer to clean it and there's something leaking down the back. First engineer says it's water and so I turn down the thermostat—sounds well dodgy. Then the fridge isn't cold. Called them back out again—you guessed it, a write-off!

Saturday—a rare bit of sunshine. So I thought I'd go to Southend-on-Sea for some fresh air. Get to Southend, pull up at some red lights—bang! Black VW Polo up me arse (so to speak). So taking the car for a quote for the repairs tomorrow—just hoping it's not the third write-off! I'll cry if I lose my little car.

Other than that, work, home, work, home, and not much else. Hold on a minute, there was something...

Bloke named Harvey comes by the office a couple of weeks back when I was on reception. After he leaves he calls me up and invites me out for dinner. I accept—he seemed alright, friendly, not too ugly etc. Anyway, we go out for a drink and meal at an Indian restaurant in Waterloo. Turns out he lives on the other side of my estate (he doesn't know this and I don't let on). So I've got me car with me and offer to drop him off. He's giving me directions and I'm innocently taking them—tee hee! Go in for a coffee (yes only coffee) and have the bare-faced cheek to ask if my car will be alright parked on the estate. When I leave I wave, get into the car and drive out... into the next estate entrance and into my garage—he could have spotted me from his living room window! I'm totally pissing myself with laughter. Especially when I next see him and he asks me where I live. 'Suffice to say I'm local,' I reply! Haven't seen him again yet. He sent me a few text messages asking me to go out with him but I'm not that bothered. Men mean one thing—trouble.

Well that's the best I can do for now.

Hope this reaches you well and happy.

Love

Mare :)

From:	sila@members.com
To:	emilygreenhk@hotmail.com
Subject:	Does size matter?

Well, Silas, not when it comes to penises, yes when it comes to chocolate bars.

From:	Ronaldo@xxx.com
To:	emilygreenhk@hotmail.com
Subject:	Are you lonely?

Yes, Ronaldo, I am. Thanks for reminding me.

From:	James1969@yahoo.com
To:	emilygreenhk@hotmail.com
Subject:	Joke

A woman standing nude looks at herself in the bedroom mirror and says to her husband, 'I look fat, ugly and horrible—can you please pay me a compliment?'

Her husband replies, 'Well your eyesight's fucking spot on!'

James

The phone goes. It's Louise from the beauty salon shouting into her mobile.

'I'm at Joe Bananas—come and 'ave a drink wiv us. Loads of gorgeous blokes in 'ere!'

That does it. I put on my cowboy jeans (too tight!) and a black T-shirt with sparkly diamond lettering saying 'Cutie' ('Fatty' would be more apt) and head out.

'Joe Bananas' is a Hong Kong institution—quite why, I don't know. It's nothing to look at, plays crap music and is full of horny, ugly blokes. I see Louise looking a bit worse for wear at the bar. Her mascara's smudged and her off-the-shoulder top is almost off the hip.

'Hey doll! Thanks for coming!' she says, giving me a big wet kiss on the cheek which leaves a bright red imprint of her lipstick. She then turns to the barman and yells, 'Oi, gimme a Slow Comfortable Screw, you!' and bursts out laughing. 'What do you want, doll?' she asks me.

I decide to get into the spirit of things. 'I'll have a Screaming Orgasm, please.' I can't help giggling either.

A man old enough to be my grandfather moves closer saying, 'I can help you out there, love.'

Yuck!

Considering it's a school night it's packed in here. There are way more blokes than girls, but I have yet to see one gorgeous guy. Mainly they're Australian, burly, beefy types. Louise has her flatmate Heather with her. Heather looks a bit vacant, on the dumpy side with strange red and black streaked hair. She tells me she teaches English to children and hates her job (I can understand that). She and Louise live together with three other Brits in a house on Lamma, one of the outlying islands. It's a favourite hang-out with hippy-oriented expats (mainly stoned English teachers). Every month they have mad beach parties; there wouldn't be enough police sniffer dogs in the world to cope with the free flow of devil's dandruff and happy pills there (mainly expats misbehaving as the law-abiding locals seem high on life itself). The expat inhabitants are collectively referred to as 'The Lamma Losers'.

Louise chats away excitedly. 'It's Cafae Pacific's flight staff night, so these guys are all pilots!'

Hmm, is that a good thing or a bad thing? They've probably got a girl in every port (airport!)—but at least they'd be out of your hair most of the time and you could just spend their nice fat pay cheque (what good is it to them in the skies?).

'Oi, Eunice!' hollers Louise to a skinny local girl with bandy legs and tiny eyes set too close together. 'Meet my mate Emily.'

We say 'hi' and she seems friendly enough.

'Eunice met three American sailors here last week,' Louise cackles, 'and she and her mate shagged them—all at the same time!'

Eunice smiles and nods nonchalantly. 'They were very good all night long. Nice big cocks.'

Wowzers, no wonder she walks like that!

A good-looking guy with black hair and bright blue eyes

walks over to us. He's a bit short, though—I guess he needs to be if he's sitting in a cockpit all day and night.

'Hello ladies,' he starts in a think Aussie accent. 'How's it going with you?'

'How's it hanging?' Louise replies excitedly. Christ, she's pissed.

'I'm Bruce.'

Louise howls with laughter. 'And I'm Sheila!'

'Really?' he says.

And I thought pilots were supposed to be intelligent?

I leave Louise gushing inanely to Bruce and locate the peaceful sanctuary of the ladies' bogs. There's a beautiful blonde girl in there, grating her hips wildly against a podgy old Western man. Yuck! What's she doing with an old timer like that? She's absolutely stunning—like Cameron Diaz without the zits. She's wearing a tight-fitting hot pink dress that shimmers and has a figure to die for. Her taste in blokes is very dubious, though. I take a pee and start eavesdropping. Ahh, now I get it. She's talking money, in a thick Russian accent. Three hundred quid for a shag! Count me in! Boy, it's tempting. He's so pissed it would all be over in seconds.

As I stumble across the dance floor I suddenly feel more aware of the surroundings. There are several gorgeous blonde Eastern European-looking girls hanging around, touting for work, and a dodgy guy wearing a black beret keeping a watchful eye over them. I feel really lucky to have been born in Blighty and to have options. At least I can choose to shag (or not to shag, that is the question) some sorry case for three hundred quid (actually, not really much of a choice with my current job prospects! Crikey, I can't believe I'm seriously contemplating joining the oldest profession on earth! Time to go home methinks!). I make my excuses and leave Louise to it; she doesn't have to be at work until midday. I wonder if she and Eunice will invite Bruce home for a ham sandwich? Would he pay for the privilege?

I catch a light bus home. It breaks the world speed record, taking just two minutes from Wanchai to Mid-Levels. The driver whizzes along at such high speed he doesn't even stop for passengers. (Maybe he's just pulled off a bank heist and is on the run? Then again, this is Hong Kong not Hackney.) One passenger is nearly thrown through the windscreen as he brakes sharply.

I manoeuvre myself, with great difficulty, onto the back seat next to the rear emergency exit, figuring if he takes the next bend at the same speed as the last one we'll fly off the mountain's edge and I can throw myself clear out the back. All the passengers are ducking down into their seats, bracing themselves for a crash. I'm half pleased to be getting home so quickly and half terrified for my life. And I don't know what's worse—this death-defying driving or the corny Canto pop videos playing loudly on the TV screen fixed up above the driver's head. Watching the feeble efforts of Twins, Gigi, Karen Mok and Faye Wong (so-called pop singers) is enough to make you want to end it all. I block out the dross by humming the Duke's of Hazard theme tune, praying to make it home alive. If I ever get round to taking Cantonese lessons the first phrases I intend to learn are 'Pull over, you lunatic!' and 'Stop the fucking bus!'

The next day on my walk to work I pass the Clarins salon and notice a colourful poster advertising an evening of beauty talk and makeovers with wine, cakes and free gifts. Mmm, cakes. (Why is it that if they're free then it doesn't count as naughty but a bargain? To hell with the calories!) I hand over my HK$100 (hey, I thought it was going to be free!) and congratulate myself on organising some me-time. That night I arrive and help myself to the assortment of cakes (only miniature-sized ones which means I can have one of each type—eight in total... whoops!). I'm not the only one making the most of it, although the other ladies look like they need feeding up, unlike me.

It dawns on me that I'm only one of two Westerners. Adrienne from Hertfordshire is elegantly dressed and immaculately made-up. She looks slightly middle-Eastern, with striking big green eyes and long lashes. And she's wearing white lipstick! How can olive skin wear white lipstick without looking like something out of Dr Who? Beats me, but she looks fabulous. She, of course, doesn't touch the cakes, making me feel incredibly guilty about eating for a family of four (not even Africans but four fat Yanks). I really don't look my best—actually I look worse than my worst. I have dark circles under my eyes, a mayonnaise stain on my shirt, onion breath (a salad for lunch may be healthy but boy does it give you rotten breath!), hair desperately in need of a wash, and not a scrap of make-up left (well, I did put it on over twelve hours ago). Looking around at the swanky, immaculate crowd I realize I'm the only genuine candidate for a makeover.

I spend the next two hours listening to the benefits of Clarins products in Cantonese. The beauty therapist giving the talk, Utah, smiles encouragingly at me, as though I'll suddenly find myself fluent in Cantonese (no such luck). Despite not understanding a word of what is being said, however, I know most of the products (I hadn't realized I'd bought absolutely everything they make!) and so pretty much get the gist. Adrienne and I roll our eyes at each other but hang on in there for the free gifts.

We're all instructed by squeaky-voiced Winnie, wearing a year's supply of lip gloss tonight, to pick a sock out of a wicker basket (bizarre but at least they look clean) and are told there's going to be a prize draw—the owner of the matching sock is the winner. Mine's very odd-looking—pale blue with yellow polka dots, like the ones I wanted to wear to school when I was nine but my mother wouldn't let me, choosing for me instead military-style plain navy blue (since her wardrobe only consisted of navy blue, mine had to as well). Adrienne and I wait with baited breath. Please God, let me win! I've never won a raffle before (unless you count my primary school raffle when I won a half-size tin of potato toppers beans that on opening were blue and mouldy).

I get the feeling the draw is rigged as the ladies who win all the prizes are obviously, judging by the beauty therapists fawning around them, top regular customers. Or else it's a phenomenal coincidence. Adrienne looks devastated and even starts eyeing up the remaining few cakes to ease her misery. What a waste of two hours! But just when all seems lost we're saved by the goody bags. They contain a very generous medley of sample-sized products I'll never use (result!). It doesn't stop there. As a commiseration prize I get a free makeover. Perhaps the make-up artist, a girl called Winner, singled me out as the easiest candidate for a dramatic 'before and laughter'.

After what seems like an eternity (tell me who has twenty minutes spare to put on make-up every morning?) I'm given a mirror and see Catherine Zeta Jones staring back at me—sure, on one of her bad days, but still looking lovely. Who said green eye-shadow is out of date? Although I'm not normally one for candy colours, preferring instead the natural look (the just-got-out-of-bed-and-slapped-on-a-bit-of-the-first-item-I-laid-my-hands-on-while-keeping-one-eye-on-the-clock-before-charging-out-to-work effect), I must admit the make-up artist (staying true to her name where I'm concerned) has performed nothing short of a small miracle. Move over, Jesus Christ turning fish into fish-fingers. I think this Alice Cooper-into-Catherine Zeta Jones transformation is just as impressive.

I'm so knocked out I buy half a tonne of make-up and book myself a personalised make-up lesson on Saturday morning. I'm clearly a late developer in this area and should have gone through this phase at seventeen. Oh well, it's nice to get so excited about the joys of a bit of slap! Maybe I'll start wearing high heels on a daily basis next to complete my new sophisticated get-up (hmm, one step at a time). Adrienne (who's also there for a lesson—not that she needs it) and I go home happy. She takes my business card and says we simply must meet for a coffee the following week but I never hear from her.

A couple of days later I dash into Marks & Sparks to contemplate purchasing shoes with a heel. Well, it certainly ain't Manolo Blahnik or Jimmy Choo, but my salary doesn't extend as far as those girls on 'Sex and the City' (no one's yet told me how lowly-paid journalist Carrie Bradshaw can afford that extensive designer wardrobe and exclusive pad!). Marks & Sparks has a range of shoes suitable for my grandmother. I single out a pair of caramel-coloured sling-back kitten heels (sounds swanky! Much better than my Clarks pumps!) which kind of fit and are kind of comfortable (borderline kind of don't fit and kind of uncomfortable). But then sophistication comes at a price—sore ankles and pinched toes—and I pay HK$550 for the privilege of having my feet ripped to shreds. I'm beginning to shuffle along as though I have a limp, praying to God to consider bringing me back as a man in my next life. They get away with not making any effort at all!

The following Saturday I don't feel too well but my new found passion brings me to Winner and her winning ways (sorry, I can't resist it), caking me in magnificent make-up. What a difference it makes! If only Winner could now come and live with me she'd be able to replace my Hammer Horror looks with Hollywood movie star glamour every day! I buy another tonne of make-up and realize I now need a separate bathroom to accommodate it all as, alas, my make-up bag is far too small. I chuck out old bits and pieces to make room (wow, have I really had that cherry-flavoured lip-gloss since I was fourteen? And that Lancome tester lipstick must be at least ten years old—not quite my colour but it would be a shame not to make the most of a freebie). The realisation that I could set up a make-up museum with what I had makes me feel better about spending my life's savings on a bag of new Clarins products. Anyway, I look so good I don't want to take my make-up off—ever.

Right then, all I need to do now is shed a stone of fat to complete the look! No chance. My desire for junk food is all-consuming. Healthy eating leaves me hungry. Yet I decide to complete my financial ruin and splurge on a nutritional makeover. Pollyanna McGaffy is really thin—but I guess that's what she's selling. Clad in a floaty Indian-style smock revealing plenty of flesh (not that she has much), tanned and toned biceps and calves (remember—next stop the gym, Emily!). She looks at my food diary from the past month and keeps tutting, 'Hmm, heart attack on a plate!'

She's asked me to write down my favourite foods—comprising pizza, chips, cheese, crisps, chocolate of all kinds (Mars, Snickers, Marks & Spencer's Belgian Chocolate Peanuts, Lindt Milk Chocolate, Toblerone, Flake, Marble, Minstrels, Maltesers, Chocolate Buttons, Time Out... shall I go on?). I'm banished to the yucky, I mean 'healthy' food aisles forever. I realize I don't have the willpower to sacrifice the best things in life, but agree to compromise and try to eat healthily during the week and allow myself something(s) naughty over the weekend. To think, when I met James I was a size 8 and could take or leave food (and mostly left it). Now I'm a size 12, heading towards a size 14, and can't leave food alone. I'll follow Pollyanna's advice from next week, as diets should always start on a Monday (and if you so happen to miss Monday then they start the following Monday and so on).

I suppose I should get my fat arse down to the gym this weekend, but a combination of my flawless make-up and sore heels says it ain't going to happen. Maybe I need a personal trainer? Maybe I need a personal chef? Maybe I need the food police? Maybe I should marry a rich oil baron to pay for all this? Maybe I should stop dreaming? I resist the temptation to please my sweet tooth on the way home and feel very proud of myself.

James and I are off to someone's leaving drinks tonight so I plan to wear my new second-hand (does that make any sense to you?) designer (can't spell or pronounce the label) dress. I'm feeling good about myself until I go to zip up the back of the dress and find, to my horror, that it no longer fits. I can't blame it on shrinkage from the washing machine or dry-cleaners as it's the first time I've worn it. I only bought it a few months ago, for Christ's sake! What's going on with my body? I feel my butt cheeks and admit they are rather voluptuous, rather Jo-Lo (I read recently she could set up her own bar and serve drinks off her bottom). It's as though I haven't looked in the mirror for several months and have suddenly really seen myself.

My cellulite looks terrible, covering my thighs, butt and stomach, and I generally look flabby and in the mid-term of pregnancy. Maybe that's it! Perhaps I'm in the same boat

Life is Pants

as one of those teenage girls from Sheffield you read about who don't realize they're pregnant and end up giving birth while having a poo or taking a bath! Come to think of it, that must be the most relaxed way to give birth and if I ever had to then I'd like it to happen that way. I could just hear James asking, 'What did you do today at work, Emily?' 'Oh,' I'd reply, 'I just went to the ladies and instead of a turd had a healthy, bouncing baby boy! I've called him Lou.' 'How appropriate!' he'd say. I decide to take a pregnancy test—but, alas(?) the bump is just fat.

The leaving do is in Lan Kwai Fong (as always), at 'Stormy Weather'. Jennifer is getting highly emotional, crying dramatically and telling everyone she loves them. Her hubby Steve, on the other hand, is slagging off Hong Kong, vowing never to return as long as he lives (something he ends up regretting since he's back after only five months, saying Hong Kong is the best place on earth compared to his hometown of Newcastle).

There are about twenty leaving dos a week at the moment and it's getting boring. Usually you get an earful of mud-slinging about Hong Kong and it's very tedious for those of us who like it here just fine. I feel like saying, 'Well don't hang around, just fuck off then!' but don't. Instead we endure this broken record of broken dreams over and over and over and over and... you get the picture.

The most common reason for leaving is Australia. Brits apply for residency to Oz thinking it's paradise on earth and have a time-limit to make the move there. People give up their high-flying well-paid (often undeserved) jobs to become very ordinary people in Oz, where, contrary to popular belief, there are lots of truly bright people. But then you can't tell people what to do. I'm not sad to see Jennifer go. I learnt the hard way that if you tell her something in confidence you may as well announce it on Radio Hong Kong. She's truly the cheapest form of advertising and lives for tittle-tattle—a professional gossip, a total pain in the neck. So adiós, Jennifer, go natter on some other island. I bet the Ozzies feed her to the sharks.

Walking home up The Escalator, James is a little sullen

for some reason. He's commented on my make-up ('God you look really good—so different!') but doesn't notice the heels until I get one of them stuck in a drain. The force of removing it nearly wrenches my ankle off. (These heels find every nook and cranny and I never realized before how full of tiny potholes and uneven the streets are.) James thinks it's funny.

'You idiot!' he laughs, but I'm not amused.

The shoe feels strange afterwards and makes a tapping sound. I realize when we get home that the whole heel has come right off and the tapping noise was in fact the nail in the shoe. Bollocks! More money to shell out on re-heeling, and I've only just got them! I think I generally wore flatties for a reason: I used to be sensible.

I ask James what's up but get no response. I feel randy and try to get him in the mood but he's not interested. I attempt to give him a blowjob but he pushes me away. For all the make-up he doesn't even see me.

It's Sunday morning and I'm restless. Last week our latest Amah, Joyce (OK, I know I said Jeabey had put me off maids for life, but James's pants drove me to it) told me she doesn't like cleaning. Who does? Isn't that what I'm paying her for anyway? Dippy cow. She forcefully announces that from now on she'll only do the ironing—oh joy, oh Joyce! Consequently, the apartment is filthy and muggings here has got to spend her precious relaxing Sunday morning with her head down the bog before scrubbing the bath clean of its resilient scum marks.

Only I could hire a cleaner who won't clean. James has no intention of helping. He doesn't thank me for my sparkling efforts, and promptly leaves poo skids all over my nice clean toilet bowl. I ask him nicely to wipe off the skids and he rants and raves that he always does—hmm, we must have an invisible man (well, it wouldn't be a woman, would it?) lurking here with visible poo skids! James rushes off to football in a huff, shouting, 'Nagging bitch!' as he slams the front door behind him.

I'm beginning to think life is simply one big conspiracy. We girls are brainwashed at junior school into believing marriage is the absolute be-all and end-all, and spend our teenage years in angst, deliberating over choosing a sleek and sophisticated wedding dress or a huge puffball meringue creation covered in lace, frills, sequins and fake pearls for that special day. To make matters even more complex, the church venue became a dull option when Caribbean beaches and Las Vegas weddings suddenly came into fashion—and we had to spend heaps more time planning the event. No one warned us, 'Kiss your freedom goodbye, girls!' or 'You'll be better off becoming a professional maid instead, as at least you'll get paid for it and there's less verbal abuse'. (By happy coincidence there's no wedding ring on my finger yet and as far as I'm concerned it's staying that way. The man of my dreams would have to be fucking amazing. I'd consider Prince William, but he looks a bit horsy for my liking and we'd certainly argue about his hunting hobby.)

Since James is out all day and I've got nothing to do apart from three hours' cleaning, I decide to colour my hair and restore its pre-sun-exposure richness. I've coloured my hair a zillion times before, mostly with success. This time, I've gone for a warm medium brown and I set about the task of applying it. I only realize I don't own a comb when reading I need to comb the solution through my hair. Instead I use my gloved fingers and focus on applying it evenly all over.

I sit and flick through a trashy local magazine while I wait, reading about some obscure Canto pop star and his penchant for poodles. Crikey, what's happened to the romantic personal ads? All the men want men and the women want women! The few men who do still want women are seeking 'afternoon play things' or are 'married but looking for extra curricular activities'. Then there are a huge number (OK, three) of swingers seeking new shagging couples. All in all, it makes very depressing reading. Whatever happened to love and marriage? I guess the same thing as the horse and carriage—remnants of a bygone era.

I glance at the clock and realize I've had the solution on for ten minutes longer than the instructions suggested. I quickly hose down my head and wait until the water runs clear before towel-drying. I turn and look in the mirror and involuntarily gasp aloud. 'Fucking hell that's dark!' I exclaim in shock. And indeed it is dark... dark as the blackest night. I blow-dry my hair, hoping it will lighten up but it is truly the blackest of blacks. I can hear my mother tutting, 'Emily, you look like the Wicked Witch of the North!' and on this occasion I couldn't agree with her more. I feel panicky and pace around the flat saying, 'Shit, shit, shit!' (words elude me, I look such a fright). I wash my hair again and again until it feels like straw. I dry it for a second time and it looks... jet black. 'Oh my God!' I wail, but no doubt He's got more important things to be worrying about than my hair (albeit a genuine natural disaster).

I dare not leave the apartment all day so sulk, watch 'The Bold & The Beautiful' and see that I'm not the only one with bizarre hair colouring. James returns late that night greeting me with, 'All right, Mystic Meg?' before dumping his enormous sports bag in the middle of the lounge. Inside are sixteen sweaty football shirts, sixteen sweaty football shorts and thirty-one sweaty football socks (there's always one missing).

I bravely volunteer to stick the festering contents of his bag into the washing machine. James casually says, 'OK,' and not, 'Oh darling, you're the most wonderful girlfriend a man could wish for.' As I open the bag, steam rises and the stench nearly knocks me out. I perform the task, cursing myself for being so obliging to Little Lord Fauntleroy, but realize I only have myself to blame for behaving like a doormat.

James asks where his new jeans are.

'In your wardrobe!' I respond.

'Don't snap!' he snaps back.

'What's up with you?' I ask him tentatively.

'You are!' he shouts, launching into a passionate speech about how strange it is that in a town of beautiful skinny women I've gone up two dress sizes and look my worst ever. 'It's not the best way to compete, it is, duh?! You wonder why I don't want to touch you any more.'

I get all Oprah Winfrey on him and argue the merits of loving someone for who they are not what they look like, but he's having none of it.

'You're not the girl I met!' he yells, leaving the apartment—presumably for yet another drinking session with the lads—and shouting, 'Bloater!' as he goes.

For a moment I feel like jumping out of the window of our 34th floor apartment... then I think, bugger him, I'll have a nice aromatherapy shower instead (sadly our bath is well and truly like sitting in the kitchen sink, allowing soakage of only five percent of your bits). As I wash my crotch I feel terrible that James no longer fancies me, that he no longer wants to touch me or make love to me. According to Cosmopolitan I'm at my sexual peak—yet I'm not having any sex! How tragic! Unless you count my occasional quick self-pleasuring frotter over a picture of Bill Clinton smoking a fat cigar (I know, I'm too old for him!). I feel I really look after James, running after him and falling over him—all for nothing. He is a different person to when I met him. Why has 'Mr Right' turned into 'Mr So Awfully Wrong'? I switch on the TV and half watch a B-movie about a hotel resort hit by an avalanche. The moral of the story is that surviving an avalanche brings people who aren't getting on closer together. Maybe I should suggest a skiing holiday to James?

I numbly surf the Net. I have one email in my inbox.

From: Laurie@Heavenknows.com
To: emilygreenhk@hotmail.com
Subject: Emily...

How would you like to slash your bills?

I'd like to slash my wrists! Is that OK instead? I snuggle into bed feeling really depressed. When did things change? When did romance turn to rubbish?

I'm woken up at 5.30 by the sound of the front door crashing open. I hear James kick my inflatable fit ball across the lounge, then stumble heavily (probably taking his shoes or trousers off) and swear loudly. I pretend to be asleep as he barges into our bedroom, slamming the door shut. I keep my eyes tightly closed and lie there, motionless. I hear a strange sound of water trickling and open my eyes to see James peeing into the corner of the room. It's flowing all over the floor.

'James!' I shout. 'Stop it!'

But he just looks at me with puffy pink eyes, and starts to pee into my pot plant. He's peeing the longest pee in the history of mankind. It's even spraying over our duvet (dry-clean only, too!). I jump out of bed, quickly put on my slippers and physically push him towards the bathroom.

'Get off!' he mumbles and slaps me hard round the face, leaving my cheek smarting. He pushes me forcefully against the wall then turns his back on me, his endless pee continuing in the toilet and all down its sides. I'm beside myself with rage and fatigue. He hurt me and the bedroom is a disgusting mess. My slippers are wet through and my feet are covered in his piss. They certainly don't call alcohol 'idiot juice' for nothing. I clean up his mess in the bedroom, hallway and bathroom. I chuck my slippers in the bin and go back to bed, knackered. James is snoring loudly with his mouth wide open, reeking of beer. He smells awful—it's like sleeping with some wino tramp.

In the morning he doesn't apologise for his behaviour or thank me for mopping up after him, and instead refuses to talk to me. He's in a horrendous sulk and I can't get through to him as much as I try. I end up apologising to him—I don't know why—perhaps just to keep the peace. The irony is he has loads of girls eagerly lined up waiting to replace me. I see the spark in their eyes when they look at his handsome face and manly physique and laugh at his boyish jokes and antics. Sometimes I feel I should warn them about him. Maybe I should place an advert in HK Magazine, something along the lines of: 'If you like little boys, heavy-duty cleaning, being bullied, and bad breath, then James is the man for you. Granted, he does have a big cock, but his lack of personal hygiene diminishes this sole plus point.'

Chapter 8

September
Breathe Easy

I phone James with a heavy heart.

'James,' I say, 'I don't want it to be like this. May I make a suggestion?'

'What?' he replies in a sullen voice.

'Pippa mentioned trying couples counselling...'

'You've told Pippa about our relationship problems?' He sounds angry.

'No. Yes. Look, we need to do something about us!' I plead.

'Yeah, maybe it's time to call it a day,' James retorts coldly.

'Please just try it once, James. For us. For me.'

No response.

'James?'

'OK,' he sighs. 'But you make all the arrangements. I don't have time for this shit!'

I locate the number Pippa gave me for a Relate-style centre and book an appointment for the next evening with a counsellor called Graham.

James and I meet outside Central MTR and walk in silence to the centre. I can tell this is going to be a complete waste of time. You'd think I was leading him to the guillotine by the way he hangs his head. We don't say a word. I'm feeling nervous but have high hopes for Graham and his counselling skills.

He turns out to be a middle-aged man from Cardiff with an unruly mop of curly grey hair and John Lennon glasses. At least he's not wearing brown open-toed sandals, which is a good sign; I was dreading a hippie type. Graham lets it slip he's new to the job, having just given up his career as an accountant. Then he corrects himself.

'Actually, I lost my job and felt it was a good time to try something different.'

Great, we've got ourselves a flipping rookie. As we all sit in silence in a small room with jolly red sofas it's instantly clear Graham is out of his depth.

'Come on,' I pray, 'please help us!'

Thankfully, after a few minutes Graham breaks the intolerable silence.

'Now then, breathe.'

Oh God no.

'Breathe deeply, it really helps.' Graham's nostrils flare to illustrate his point.

Is that the best you can come up with, mate?

'I want to see you both breathe. Yes, yes, that's right. Take a deep breath. I do this whenever I'm anxious.'

I'm now terribly anxious—how's breathing going to help our relationship, unless it's toxic gas, which might indeed solve our problems! I take matters into my own hands and give him our relationship history in a nutshell, a bit like the Reduced Shakespeare Company who perform Shakespeare's entire works in two hours.

Graham looks worried—maybe he should take a fucking deep breath! 'Hmm,' is all he has to say about my woes. The silence returns.

James starts to fidget with his cufflinks and huff and puff. This is terrible! The exact opposite of what I'd hoped for. He intervenes.

'Graham, we're just wanting some advice. Please tell us what you think.'

'I'm not here to tell you what to do,' Graham says anxiously.

Silence again. Why is Graham here? I'm currently paying him good money to just sit there looking startled.

'Graham,' says James, 'this seems pretty pointless. Emily and I know what's wrong but we're here for some advice on how to put it right.'

This puts Graham on the defensive.

'I'm not here to tell you what to do!' he informs us.

James sighs and reveals how he feels about our relationship. He pours out his heart and my eyes pour out tears. I'm proud of him. I know how difficult it is for him to expose himself in this way to a complete stranger, a real weirdo at that.

Silence. Oh come on, Graham!

Finally, Graham says slowly, 'I want you both to breathe.'

'We are!' I snap back. 'This really isn't helping us!'

Graham's face is etched with concentration as he responds slowly, 'I've listened to you both now.' He looks pointedly at me. 'Emily, you obviously love James.' He twists in his seat to look at James. 'James, you obviously love Emily.' He looks at me again. 'Emily, you don't know whether the relationship is working.'

Let me guess what's next.

'James, you don't know whether the relationship is working. Emily, you don't know what to do.'

I can't resist helping him out. 'James, you don't know what to do!'

James looks utterly exasperated when suddenly Graham appears much more alert, like he's had a flash of inspiration.

'Your relationship is going round in circles!' he enlightens us.

And?

'It's going round in circles. Round in circles.'

The only thing that's going round in circles is this poxy appointment. Graham continues to share his wisdom.

'Round in circles, round and round in circles. It's going round in circles.'

Got it, Graham. You're about as useful as a chocolate teapot. I turn to James.

'Shall we go now? This is of no help whatsoever.'
James nods.
Graham interjects, 'I'm not here to tell you what to do.'
'Let's make tracks, Emily,' says James, ignoring him.
I pay Graham his fee. If I weren't so emotionally exhausted I'd kick up a fuss and refuse to pay on principle. This couldn't have been more of a disaster. After he'd listened to me pouring out my heart and witnessed me getting upset I'd much rather he'd just turned to James and said, 'Dump her!' At least there'd have been some closure!
James loops his arm through mine.

'What a nutter!' he says good-naturedly. We then both laugh hard. It feels so good to laugh together again as we walk home arm in arm.

There's a loud bang. We look up to the sky and see fireworks. They often have firework displays down on the harbour front, celebrating one of the many Chinese festivals. We watch, awe-stuck, as we travel up The Escalator. As usual, the fireworks are all patriotic red—not terribly interesting.

'Yeah, we know,' laments James, 'we're part of China now.'

Oh, how PRC! He's so clever, James. I thought they just couldn't afford more than the one colour.

James and I snuggle up in bed and watch the late night news together, which is so bad it's terribly good. The annoying jingle is complemented by the horrendous newsreaders, who, rather entertainingly, fumble their words with a stunned rabbit expression permanently slapped on their faces. Christ, how difficult can it be to read an autocue? Unsurprisingly, there's a high turnover of staff but they all have one thing in common—they're completely useless. Apparent requisites for the job: hyperactive eyebrows, cross-eyed gaze, lisp, trout pout, unconcealed zits and bizarre dress sense. I keep thinking I should apply. If I couldn't improve on their performance I could at least match it.

All we hear about day in, day out on the news is SARS, SARS, SARS and it's getting incredibly boring. What pisses me off most is that SARS has put the kybosh on modelling work as clients are staying well away from Hong Kong. It's totally paranoid behaviour since flu kills many more people every year but then I guess it gives the media a good story. The whole country has gone crazy, disinfecting everything and anything—the stench of Dettol hits your nostrils like a brick wall. In lifts no one is prepared to press the bloody button in fear of catching the deadly virus. I deliberately push the buttons and lick my finger to wind these idiots up.

I hear stories on the grapevine of fitting models having to leave Hong Kong because of SARS after years of trying on the latest grisly fashions and having pins stuck in them for a living. The ones that are sitting it out are metamorphosing from outsize models to skinny models, as they can't afford to eat.

I get a rare call from Venice of 'Missy Models', which forces me to eat my words.

'Emily, Emily, ahh.'

'Yes?'

'You got job today to fit bras. Good money, ahh!'

Ahh, those magic words!

I arrive at the Intercontinental Hotel in Tsim Sha Tsui not knowing what to expect. For all I know I'm meeting Mr Kipper (Mr Shark Fin over here!). I stick my breasts out and tap on the door of Room 374. I should have told James where I was going, although I don't think he particularly gives a shit about my personal safety. In fact, he'd be glad if I went missing and wouldn't bother to inform the authorities. Weeks later they'd find my mutilated remains shoved in the mini-bar.

The door swings open and all I can see, praise the Lord, is bras. There are about half a million of them hung on every available doorknob and shelf. Unless this client has a fetish for bras then I think this is a genuine job.

It turns out to be a German bras manufacturer. A dashing silver-haired man smoking a fat cigar beckons me in. He looks like one of Hitler's youth (but no longer youthful), with chiselled features, an aquiline nose and piercing blue eyes. I'm just seething about Sophie from 'Sophie's Choice' and about to cry dramatically, 'Ich bin eine Jewess' when he tells me I have the perfect German figure. What a very, very nice man! Come to think of it, though, aren't German ladies built like brick shithouses? All the German women I've ever come across resemble Olympic shot-put throwers. Oh well, this little number is exceptionally well paid, so who am I to complain.

I never get to find out his name, or that of the Chinese lady who manages the factory that makes his bras. I try on three plain flesh-coloured bras (very heavy duty ones!) imagining I'm Frau Green, a country milkmaid yodelling high up in the Alps in need of a new functional support bra just like these monstrosities. The man seems very happy with my German-like breasts and thanks me profusely for my time. He tells me I can leave already. Wow, I'm being paid for two hours' work at a top rate and have only done ten minutes! I calculate that this is my highest hourly wage to date by a long way and am starting to relate to Naomi Campbell more and more. I walk out, proud of my fantastic Germanic figure. 'Heil milkmaids!'

I feel flush with my earnings and can't resist having a mooch around a curious little shop selling new age stuff—incense, crystals, angel ornaments. It also boasts an in-house psychic at a hundred quid an hour. I'm clearly in the wrong job! (Can I still use that expression after my bra-fitting work this morning?) I'm so confused at the moment about James that I reluctantly part with my hard-earned (can I say that, too?) cash to meet Betty 'Dhevantrahini-la-la' Pike, originally from Scunthorpe. Betty's wearing lots of pretty crystal necklaces and thick-set NHS style (i.e. no style) glasses. Her hair is tightly permed, just like Kenny G. She's a bit on the chubby side with swollen purple ankles protruding beneath her diaphanous floaty apricot-coloured kaftan. She smells of Johnson's Baby Lotion and Talc, which is strangely comforting. (Perhaps I should barter for her services and offer a free makeover?)

Considering I've paid Betty my month's earnings she doesn't have an awful lot to say about me.

'Your life is at a crossroads.'

Duh! I wouldn't be here if it wasn't!

'You will either stay in Hong Kong or leave it.'

How flipping extraordinarily perceptive.

'Your boyfriend wants to have his cake and to eat it.'

Now we're talking.

'He bursts your bubbles.' She looks me straight in the eye, her voice quivering slightly. 'Never let anyone burst your lovely bubbles, dear.'

Sure thing, Betty.

'You have a child waiting.'

That will be James back home. Better not forget to take the pill, though. A baby is the last thing James and I need right now.

'Eventually, when you have the courage to leave him you will meet a lovely man who will be your life partner.'

My ears prick up. 'Can you be more specific, Betty?' I plead.

Betty closes her eyes and takes a deep breath. 'All I can tell you, dear, is he's from a country beginning with the letter "A". I cannot say any more than that.'

Well that narrows it down! Knowing my luck, he'll be from Afghanistan. A Taliban zealot who locks me in our manure hut where I'm covered head to toe in a black veil (without even any holes to see out of). He'll harshly instruct me to cook all day long for the in-laws who'll beat me day and night.

Where else begins with 'A'? Angola. Crikey Moses. Armenia, Algeria—my heart sinks. Austria, Australia, America—my heart sinks. But I want a nice Brit! Like Hugh Grant or Greg Rudeski. Does this mean I must give every man I come across who isn't from a country beginning with 'A' the heave-ho? How can I live like this?

Thankfully, another modelling job saves the day and brings me back into the black. A famous chain of American department stores is in town to see its latest range and needs me to model for it. Turns out they've taken over virtually the entire floor of rooms in a posh hotel in Sheung Wan. Ironically, while in Asia I'm a fat outsize model, in America I'm the perfect 'teen', the size of a typical twelve-year-old

Yank—worrying, maybe, but my ego feels greeaaatt! I feel super slim and youthful, like a teenager no less! The designers are ever so nice and keep offering me food (I'll end up modelling outsize for them at this rate). There are huge bowls of mini chocolate bars everywhere which, lined up, would probably break any currently standing records for biggest chocolate bar in the world. I consume a tonne of them and feel a bit sick.

The clothes are gross—cheap and cheerleader-ish: jeans with tassels all over them, see-through blouses with big bra tops, baseball jackets in gold lamé—pure tackiness. I'm considering offering my services to come up with a trendy range of teenage clothing for their label, when a designer with masses of curly blonde hair and a Texan twang tells me they're the most successful department store in the States. I guess there really is no accounting for taste. There's not a single item I like, but hey, they're paying me good money so I tell them what they want to hear: 'Oh, this is sooo darn cute!' and 'This outfit is awesome!' rather than a more honest, 'Do American teenagers really buy crappy stuff like this? I wouldn't have been seen dead in this in my teens!' or 'I guess Jerry Springer's audience shops in your stores?' Who cares about integrity? The job pays.

Chapter 9

October
Back Passage to India

As a last ditch effort to save 'us', I suggest to James we take a spur-of-the-moment holiday. Some quality time together, away from the hustle and bustle, stresses and strains, of Hong Kong life. He half-heartedly agrees.

'Well you organise it and pay for it and I'll go.'

Great, I know, but if that's what it takes to put us back on track I'll do it.

I rack my brains (believe me, a great effort) to conjure up a once-in-a-lifetime holiday, one we'll always remember. Somewhere richly romantic. And there is it: India! The land of beautiful sunsets (most conducive to kissing!) and palaces (lots of king-size beds to get worked up over!).

At school I was (vaguely) interested in the history of the Taj Mahal, built out of love by a King for his dead Queen (how romantic is that!) and those sexy Maharajas covered in loads of jewellery (just like Puff Daddy and other modern-day rappers, jammy!). (To tell you the truth, I was more interested in Toby Smurfitt, the school heart-throb in the year above me, and his cute tight butt.) I wonder wistfully, could there be anywhere in the world more romantic than the Taj Mahal? And, by lucky coincidence, it's yet another one of the Seven Modern Wonders of the World so I could tick that off my 'to do' list as well! Marvellous, I think. We can kill two birds with one stone. In reality, we nearly kill each other.

It takes five and a half hours to fly to Delhi from Hong Kong and about the same amount of time to clear Indian immigration. James and I play our favourite airport game—putting airline stickers on each other's backs without the other's realising it. I sneakily save a classic one and wait excitedly for seven hours to have some proper fun with it. A nice pat on the back and the childish deed is done. Unfortunately, I have only had about an hour's pleasure from this when a spoilsport passenger in the queue stupidly ends my fun by telling James he has a 'Handle With Care' sticker on the back of his shirt. James looks at me as I look away innocently and we both crack up laughing.

Mercifully, we are met at the airport by our driver and guide Rajeev. He's to ferry us around from sumptuous city to sumptuous city. Christ, it's fucking freezing! Strange, as I thought India was always baking hot. James and I look at each other in horror, realising we have suitcases full of totally inappropriate flimsy summer clothing. Oh well, we'll just have to get creative and use our hotel bedroom's quilt as a shawl (and thus blend in with the paupers).

By the time we reach our hotel (supposedly five-star but you have to wonder how it surpassed two) our teeth are chattering and James is moaning, 'Why didn't you pick the Maldives, you berk?'

I spit back, 'Well you should have helped me organise this holiday, rather than leaving everything to me as usual. Lend a hand next time!'

'There won't be a next time,' he mutters.

Hmm, everything going to plan then. Not.

Rajeev gives us an hour to freshen up before taking us on a sightseeing trip around Old Delhi and New Delhi. (Little did we know we weren't going to get to really freshen up until we were back in Hong Kong two weeks later!) James and I had braced ourselves for the sorry sights of poverty, but nothing can quite prepare you for the mayhem and utter misery and sadness here. Dust and dirt cover you from head to toe, travelling up your nostrils and into your ears. The stench of rotting rubbish strewn all over the place makes you want to gag. To give you some kind of idea just how bad it is, James's breaking wind at every opportunity (making the most of being able to blend in with the surroundings) actually smells pleasant in comparison. There are sorry looking adults, sorry looking children and sorry looking animals hanging around everywhere. James has an annoying habit of patting the wildest and most neglected dogs—clearly the thought of rabies doesn't scare him.

'Careful, James, they may have rabies,' I say to him as though he's a child.

'These fellas are fine,' James coos in a baby voice, patting a greasy mutt who's bearing its lethal set of yellowed gnashers, a thick glob of saliva dripping from its chin. The dog barks fiercely, snapping its teeth, and James jumps back. 'Easy, fella!' he squeals. I leg it. What an arsehole.

Delhi's streets are not only home to countless people (all shoeless) and dogs, but also to dancing cobras, bears, monkeys and cows (although the cows don't dance, just swagger). Zillions of cows, in fact. Every road we go down has them, blocking the traffic and taking up every inch of space on the pavements.

'Emily!' James shouts. 'Bet you didn't think you'd meet your ancestors here!' He roars with laughter.

Hmm. His mother's the biggest cow I've ever met, but I won't start another war by telling him that.

'Government take thirty-seven thousand cows away out of Delhi to countryside,' Rajeev pipes up.

Is he kidding? Christ, it's bad enough now! And why do all the people look like they're starving when they could be eating lean steak every day of the week for the rest of their lives? Instead, everything on four legs is tucking into the rubbish.

'There's one thing to look forward to about this holiday,' smirks James.

'The Taj Mahal?' I nod encouragingly.

'Nope, curry every night for a fortnight. Hoorah!'

Bugger, not every night! Once a month is OK but any more than that and I'll be on the lavvy the whole time (cheaper than a colonic, admittedly).

We decide to live dangerously and eat in the hotel restaurant that evening. I suddenly become aware I'm an invisible guest. Only James has his chair pulled out for him, only James is given a menu, only James is asked what he'd like to drink. I anticipate a long night ahead.

I'm right. The service is so slow the meal becomes a three-hour affair. We argue about what not to eat. I recite the motto 'If it's not baked, boiled or peeled, don't eat it'. James rolls his eyes and shrugs nonchalantly, tucking into everything placed in front of him, while I pick at what looks well cooked.

'When in India, do as the Indians do,' says James authoritatively.

Eat rubbish and shit on the streets?

'Or,' he sniggers getting carried away, 'if it moves, shag it, don't eat it!' He finds this hilarious. I guess he's trying to be witty.

'Tourists always make a big mistake by not eating what the locals eat,' James goes on. 'How else can you really experience a country?'

Here we go. He's about to launch into a story I've heard a million times over.

'When I travelled through Cambodia with Peter's scouse mate, Bob, every goddamned place we went to all he ever ordered was bloody peppered steak—even in wood huts in the middle of bloody nowhere where they'd never heard of peppered bloody steak! Bob would always get upset they didn't do it and say...'

I can't resist and cut James off, putting on a whiney Liverpudlian accent, 'Faaackin' 'ell, this is shite. It's total gobshite!'

James shuts up and continues eating.

We can hardly get out of the restaurant because of the huge numbers of waiters wanting their tips, miraculously popping up from nowhere when it's time for us to pay the bill. 'Tip, tip!' they all whisper. It's heartbreaking and uncomfortable.

In the lift James lets out a loud, smelly burp and an

even louder and smellier fart, ending our meal together in that most romantic of ways. It seems he's lived in Hong Kong for too long. After holding my breath for what must surely be a record-breaking length of time (risking brain damage), we finally get back to our drab room and James immediately christens the toilet with a burning, hot curried poo. The smell is unreal, rivalling the streets of Delhi. That's it! Curry has to be held responsible for the overpowering stench everywhere. Funnily enough, I don't fancy a roll in the hay tonight, and would rather suffocate myself with a pillow to get away from the overwhelming smell of curried shit.

Our bedside telephone buzzes at the crack of dawn (10 a.m.) and Rajeev tells us it's time to head on to Agra. We bolt down breakfast, an uninspiring buffet of rock hard croissants, bland chocolate muffins and curry. (Jesus, curry for breakfast? My butt ring can't take it! These people are gluttons for punishment!) Rajeev speeds us away from our 'luxury' hotel, dodging the ensuing traffic: dilapidated cars, motorbikes, auto-rickshaws and bicycles. Strangely, their hooters and horns—incidentally in non-stop use—sound more like quacking ducks. It's comical in a this-will-drive-me-crazy-before-too-long, kind of way. No one seems to know how to steer a car here and this is somewhat worrying, especially as overtaking on bends at high speed appears to feature in their 'Highway Code'.

I expect to see stunning countryside as we head out of the city, but all I actually see are people so poor they are semi-naked (clad in rags of rags), people shitting in full view on the pavements (couldn't they find a department store or McDonalds to pop into instead?), semi-wild packs of dogs running around with their pink tongues hanging out (reminding me of the girlies in Wanchai), litter (worse than on the streets of London, would you believe) and piles of rubble (why don't they put it to good use and build themselves houses?). The further away we drive from Delhi the madder the dogs get—they try with all their might to chase our car, and casualties of this behaviour are splattered blood red across the road.

In the middle of nowhere, a massive McDonalds drive-through looms and spookily, although the road is deserted, its car park is chock-a-block. People just can't seem to stay away from junk food in this crazy world of ours! Normally, James would insist on having a 'snack' there, i.e. double cheeseburger with large fries, large coke and (!) a strawberry milkshake plus an apple pie, but for once the greedy bugger with an enviable metabolism stays quiet. I glance at him suspiciously and note he looks unnaturally pale and clammy.

'Are you OK?' I enquire, concerned.

'No!' he snaps irritably. 'My tummy feels really dodgy.'

He looks to me for sympathy with pleading, puppy dog eyes and I find it hard to feel any—there's a price to pay for being so gung-ho about what you eat in frigging India of all places. But I feel bad for being so uncaring and give him a big hug to make up for it. It's not unlike hugging a radiator his temperature is so high.

We pass a giant Pizza Hut and I'm torn between being scathing of America spreading heart disease around the globe and gorging on a deep-pan pizza laden with cheese and veggies. Mmm, my mouth is literally watering thinking about it! Ooh, garlic bread smothered with cheese, and a rich chocolate fudge brownie cake to finish would be nice, ecstasy in fact. Fortunately for my scales back home, our car speeds past and we shortly arrive at our hotel. Granted, it would have been 'five-star' and quite lovely in the 1970s—but now a refurb is, at a conservative guess, at least twenty years overdue. The wallpaper is peeling and the carpets threadbare and patchy.

As we settle into our room, James dramatically flops on the bed, clutching his stomach and groaning. I hit the shower as I feel so grubby but it proves to be temperamental—a choice of either scalding hot (first-degree burns hot) or freezing cold (North Pole cold). So I switch between the two, muttering 'ouch!' a lot. The water is an inviting yellowy brown (yuck!), the towels grey and thin (probably in use since the hotel opened), and the built-in hairdryer so feeble that at this rate it will dry my hair in around eight months. I aim the nozzle closer to my head to cut the drying time down to four, and it viciously sucks up a big chunk of my hair.

'Ouch!' I scream.

James darts in and sees me with the hairdryer nozzle fixed to my scalp. He roars with laughter, runs out to get his camera and proceeds to take photos of me not looking nearly so amused. I attempt to pull my hair out of the nozzle but it's tangled up. James gets my nail scissors and takes great pleasure in cutting my hair free—he looks as though he wants to cut my throat while he's at it.

I'm now missing a clump of my lovely long hair. (Bloody marvellous—it only took me fifteen years to grow it!) I wrap my head in the bathmat as, disgracefully, there are no hair towels. Despite almost being scalped alive by the hairdryer and all my smoothing efforts on the remaining strands, my hair is a complete frizz-ball.

'You look like one of the Jackson Five!' James laughs, gleefully singing, '"A, B, C, easy as 1, 2, 3!"' For someone feeling so unwell he's full of beans (or could that be 'dog steak' after last night's dinner?).

I run a bath for James (it looks more like a mud bath, but, on the bright side, people pay good money for these) and help him wash himself (willies bobbing in water are endless hours of fun, aren't they? Absolutely fascinating!). I help him into his PJs (not easy when he doesn't help at all, so it takes about half an hour to complete the task and I end up flushed and sweaty), then tuck him into bed and organise for a doctor to check in on him (Florence Nightingale is now, fittingly, my middle name, treating my man with tender loving care). The jovial doctor (no doubt the bill keeps him happy) gives him a jab and half a million tablets (has he got food poisoning or AIDS, for crying out loud?!).

What a day. I undress for bed, feeling knackered. James mutters, 'Christ you're fat these days, Emily. Stay off the fucking chocolate, would you, for the love of God!' I feel my heart sink as he adds for good measure, 'Hurry up and put something on, will you? I feel sick enough as it is.' Tears now prick my eyes. Why is he being so awful and totally hateful? I put my heart and soul into looking after him and this is all the thanks I get. I know I've put on some weight recently—but is a size 12-14 really so obese? At times like this I crave chocolate even more. I duck under the bedclothes, pulling them up to my neck. I know he's a stupid, irritable shit—but he still makes me cry.

Despite my protestations, James manages to pig out at breakfast. We enjoy toasted stale bread, melted, rancid butter, strawberry jam with ants in it, and, you've guessed it, curry. I chew half-heartedly on my toast, watching the bored-looking chef making omelettes in front of us while picking his nose then using his fingers to mix the eggs. Yuck. My stomach heaves violently and I put down my toast. Dear God, get me home! But home will have to wait as today's the big day—visiting the Taj Mahal!

We work our way through the crowds of beggars who are pleading for money, while numerous stumps are waved in our faces. Sadly, it's a well-rehearsed performance, guaranteed to get the waterworks going. Our guide tells us in a very matter of fact manner that many parents select one of their healthy and able-bodied children to cut off a limb or two in order to enter the begging 'profession'. Apparently, this is also regarded as a ticket to heaven (and the paraplegic Olympics!). I feel like throwing up, it's so outrageous, gruesome and tragic. Words simply cannot describe the overwhelming poverty here and I wonder if a trip to see the Taj Mahal is worth witnessing all this harassment and sorrow.

Kind of... yes, definitely. It's much smaller than the pictures you see (well bigger than the actual pictures, but smaller than the—oh, you get what I mean!). But it is spectacularly beautiful, and it makes you feel as though you're entering the gates of heaven (no, not Godiva!). I expect an old bloke with silver hair and striking blue eyes to greet us playing a wee golden harp.

I catch what our guide is saying. Wow, even better! Bill Clinton was here a few weeks ago. (He plays the saxophone not the harp, but close enough!) Our guide tells us how lucky we are that Bill came just before us, as they cleaned the entire Taj Mahal especially for him. Hmm, so they don't bother doing it for their thousands of fee-paying tourists, just for someone famous who no doubt gets the trip as a freebie? To wind me up further the guide adds, 'They only turn the fountains on for the VIPs.' I now feel entitled to a refund and might just write a letter of complaint. The Taj Majal is only seen in its full glory by a famous few. Scandalous.

The most popular area here is the seat where Princess Diana sat looking as though she was sucking on lemons. I have my photograph taken sitting on her seat trying to mimic her miserable expression, but can't help smiling—I'm at the bloody Taj Mahal, how amazing is that! I wish I could have told Diana that old floppy ears truly wasn't worth the tears and better left to the Rottweiler. I turn to my own Prince Charmless—poor James looks more out of it than usual, still feverish and needing the toilet every five minutes. So, annoyingly, we cut our tour short and head off to the Red Fort to finish up.

It's stunning. A red fort as the name suggests (fortunate coincidence, that) with magical green parrots flying all around. It's such a shame, though, to see how ill-kept it is. I'm appalled to note that graffiti defaces every wall (I'm probably starting to sound like a right granny!) but the weird thing about graffiti is that even if you don't approve you can't help but read it. It's most distracting but debatably more interesting than our guide who is giving us the history of the fort in mind-numbing detail (personally, I prefer the colourful videos—the all-singing, all-dancing history for kids). There are, sadly, plenty of Western culprits tarnishing the walls—'Shannon 4 Micky' (must be American), 'Chandra for Tray' (American again), 'I love Imran Khan' (Jemima? Jesus, didn't all that expensive private school education teach her anything?). I glance at James and consider etching, 'James is an arsehole' but as I don't agree with graffiti, think it's perhaps unprincipled to do so.

I'm discovering that women in India are treated as second-class citizens, correction, fifteenth-class citizens. The guide runs through his blurb, speaking to James, totally ignoring me. He hasn't made eye contact with me once! No wonder I can't concentrate; he's totally alienating me. I deliberately huff and puff to signal my dissatisfaction. He darts his eyes at mine a couple of times and asks stiffly, 'Any questions?' I dumbly answer, 'Do the parrots talk?' to annoy the shit out of him. It does, and he doesn't merit it an answer, marching on to the next bloody area of disinterest. We meet Rajeev in the car park and get to watch a dog having a humongous shit up close—it's so hot it's steaming (guess the dog was also on the curry last night). It's a relief to get back to the hotel and I'm grateful James's illness has depleted his energy levels.

The next day we travel to Jaipur. On the long and tedious journey, James and I set the world record for eating the most bags of crisps in a day. Bored to tears, we wind each other up relentlessly.

'Emily, pull my finger,' says James.

Like a mug I pull it and he farts loudly. The smell really takes your mind off the journey and on to how to lose your boyfriend while driving in a car a hundred miles per hour. The journey goes on and on. James snuggles up.

'Kiss me,' he whispers.

I lean in close and kiss him as he lets rip another huge fart. He's laughing hysterically and the driver nods his head and smiles encouragingly. I look away from the pair of idiots and spot another huge Pizza Hut ahead of us—they really should rename 'The Golden Triangle' tour 'The Pizza Hut Triangle'.

Thankfully, it's much warmer in Jaipur and we can take the quilt off that we pinched from our first hotel. This hotel is Spartan, with not even a mini-bar (good time to detox methinks). No bloody kettle for a cup-a-soup either. James phones room service.

'A kettle and two cups, please.'

Ten minutes later we're brought two samosas.

'I asked for a kettle and two cups!' James says to the swarthy waiter.

'Samosas?' he replies in earnest.

'Forget it,' James sighs. 'We don't want samosas.'

The waiter appears confused. 'No samosas?'

James looks ready to physically throw him out and the waiter scampers.

'Emily, where do you want to eat tonight?' James asks.

'Pizza Hut!' I perk up.

'You must be joking! I'm not going to fucking Pizza Hut when we're on holiday in India!'

'OK,' I huff. 'You asked me where I wanted to eat and I told you.'

'We're not going to bloody Pizza Hut!' James fumes. 'Fucking hell, Emily!'

I shrug, seething. 'Whatever. If you want dog curry again, go for it.'

'We'll eat in the hotel,' he decides, flopping on the bed dejectedly. Why are we arguing over a poxy meal?

This hotel has clearly been recently refurbished and its restaurant is particularly run-of-the-mill, thank God! Mercifully, it also has an extensive menu of both Western and Indian food. James takes hours making his selection. I need a decent feed and am sick of crisps.

James orders. 'I'll have the vegetable lasagne and chips, please.'

'You must be kidding!' I stutter. 'We can't go to Pizza Hut because it's not Indian enough and you're ordering lasagne and chips?'

'I just fancied it, that's all,' he shrugs.

Someone strangle him for me!

I order through gritted teeth. 'I'll have the same, thanks.' As the waiter leaves, I whisper, 'You'd have liked Pizza Hut's food much better.'

James ignites, 'Oh leave off flaming Pizza Hut, Emily!' and we sit in angry silence until our meal arrives.

On the one hand, it's always nice to be able to say, 'I told you so'. On the other, I'm really hungry and looking forward to eating supper. The chips are cold and undercooked. The lasagne is the size of a postage stamp and doesn't appear to have any vegetables in it, just runny white sauce—not at all inspiring. James picks at his food then calls the waiter over.

'This is inedible. There's no point giving your customers a nice menu if your chef has no idea how to cook it. Very, very disappointing indeed. Come on, Emily, let's go.'

'Where to?' I ask in a small voice.

'Pizza Hut,' James simply says.

We jump in an auto rickshaw with no lights. It's pitch dark tonight and we're driving with no lights—fabulous. The driver acts like he's pissed, veering along in a zig-zag, and we lurch about in the back of his 'vehicle' (in most countries it wouldn't pass as one). I hold onto James's arm, believing the end to be nigh. Fortunately, we live another day to savour the delectable delight that is stuffed crust pizza. We order so much food the waitress no doubt thinks three of the kids in the play area are ours. Total pig out—sublime.

'That's actually the best pizza I've ever eaten,' remarks James.

I could quite happily throttle him.

On our return to the hotel the concierge kindly offers us a free shoe-shine service. James and I cheekily give them every pair of shoes we've brought with us on holiday.

'Let's hope they don't go missing,' says James, padding around in his Bart Simpson socks, 'or we're in trouble. We'll end up walking around barefoot local style!'

'Well, you do always go on about doing what the locals do!' I point out. (Word of warning: never take up the complimentary shoe-shine offer in India. Ours were returned looking dirtier than when we'd handed them over and James's brown loafers are now black.)

Despite being finally well fed, we have a sleepless night. We discover some tosspot thinks it's all right to harness his herd of camels right outside our hotel, and all night long the camels grunt noisily at one another (probably discussing legging it out of India). There's also the continuous clinking of bottles, and it turns out the locals scavenge for such finds in the hotel's bins. Marvellous! The alarm clock rudely sounds, although we were already awake.

'Shit a brick!' James groans. 'Whose bloody stupid idea

was it to take a relaxing holiday in flaming India!'

Guilty as charged, milord.

At least we have the elephant ride to look forward to today. We queue for ages with a lot of fat Western tourists (the blonde plaits on the top of their heads suggest Croats). The poor elephants probably weep inside when they spot the size of some of their arses (who should be giving who the ride?!). It's jolly good fun once you're hoisted up, even if you do feel like you're going to fall off at any minute and break your neck. James and I share an elephant—the oldest, most decrepit one there, bless the poor bugger. During the short journey to yet another palace, about thirty more nimble and energetic elephants overtake us.

'Come on, Nelly!' James gees it up. 'You're letting us get thrashed!'

I just hope we make it sometime today.

The elephant 'driver' uses two lethal-looking stakes to push down on poor Nelly's head to speed her up but to zero effect. Every couple of seconds he turns around to us, smiling a toothy grin, and asks if we'd like to buy a set of elephant stakes. Why on earth would we? What the hell would you use them for, apart from as dust collectors?

'No thanks, mate,' James chuckles. 'I'd be too tempted to use them on the Mrs.'

Funny, I was just thinking of ramming them into his head, too.

The driver doesn't give up and produces eight different sets of stakes until it's time to dismount. We eagerly get off the poor beast, who gives us a defiant glare which says, 'Fuck you, cheapskates!'

'Stand next to the elephant, Emily,' James instructs while getting the camera out.

I fix a smile, aware the elephant has two massive gleaming white tusks right behind me, and a bad attitude.

James laughs loudly. 'Spot the elephant!'

Ha-dee-fucking-ha-ha.

The elephant takes a steamy dump just as the camera clicks. Nice one. It will make the album.

Before we buy our tickets, we're mobbed by hawkers

and urchins trying to sell us souvenirs (another word for tat)—grubby-looking chess sets and gaudy jewellery that even my undiscerning sisters would turn their noses up at.

A skinny girl pleads, 'Buy, buy. You like my ring?' James chuckles, picking out a disgusting massive one.

'Hmm, nice ring. Hey, Emily, will you marry me?' he says sarcastically, hurriedly adding, 'That's as close as you'll ever get to me proposing to you!'

What a complete dildo he is. As if I'd ever marry him! Well, I would, but why?! All that bloody brainwashing at junior school has a lot to answer for.

James marches off ahead of me, clearly not wanting company. God only knows why he's now in such a foul mood. I finish looking around the beautiful palace and wonder if I could afford to buy it. Not that I'd really want to live there, just hypothetically speaking, since everything's as cheap as chips here. I catch sight of James vigorously rubbing the underbelly of a manky old dog. In fact, he's surrounded by dogs of all shapes and sizes. I just watch as other tourists stare at him like he's either amazingly brave or incredibly stupid. I know which one it is. Two of the dogs start rutting.

'Oi, James,' I shout, 'are you working your magic honey? You've turned them on.'

'Well they turn me on more than you do!' he retorts.

We won't even go there.

We amble down the hill back towards the car. James is chewing his nails and rubbing his eyes—and after touching all those dirty dogs! Does he never learn? He's asking to get ill. Despite knowing where he's been, I try to hold James's hand but he's having none of it, instead pushing me away from him so hard I fall over. He looks at me coldly, bows his head, and continues to walk on. I feel like crying. What's got into him? He can be so mean at times. As we reach the car, a man whips a cobra out of nowhere and starts playing his flute.

'Money, please, money!' he says out of the side of his mouth, still playing. Even the cobra looks fed up.

As we check out I sarcastically pipe up to the receptionist, 'Nothing from the mini-bar!'

Meanwhile James is diligently filling out the hotel's customer feedback questionnaire. Since when did he start completing these forms with such enthusiasm at every hotel we stop at?

'Come on, James, let's get going,' I suggest. 'Long drive ahead...'

'Will you let me finish!' James admonishes. He's a strange fish.

Boy, oh boy, another endless journey, this time to Jodphur. Hundreds of people are riding around on ancient motorbikes—often the husband driving with wife and three kids hanging onto the back of him. You'd think they were out to prove just how very many people you can fit on a bike. Scary. Even scarier is that cars and lorries seem to ignore all motorbikes entirely and constantly crash into them—I dread to think what the death rate is. Perhaps with the largest population in the world it's viewed as culling. James and I are behaving like two irritable kids in the back of the car. Squabbling, pinching, Chinese burns—that sort of behaviour.

'Pull my finger,' James giggles.

'No way, it's stuffy enough,' I tell him.

He lets rip regardless—a monstrous guff. Rajeev nods and smiles. Weirdo. The car flashes past kids openly pooing by the roadside, dogs shamelessly rutting in full view of all passers-by. The sight inside the car is worse, with Rajeev digging into his nose big time and eating chunky globs of snot. I close my eyes, which seems to intensify the strong smell of James's fart.

After hours of sitting cramped up in the car, James and I are relieved to note our Jodphur hotel has a fitness centre. We put on our shorts, T-shirts and trainers and hurry down for a good old run on the treadmill or an exercise bike ride to stretch our stiff legs.

The 'fitness centre' turns out to be the oldest in modern history, with early examples of cardiovascular machines that have come a hell of a long way since their invention.

(My parents' exercise bike would blend in well here.) Our faces drop and we reluctantly abort mission and head back to our room, opening a tub of Pringles.

'This is the worst holiday of my life!' James states dramatically.

Mine too. There's a reason India is described as a 'once in a lifetime experience'.

James lolls on the squishy bed while I dig into my three hundredth bag of crisps followed by a bar of chocolate. Why does the Cadbury's chocolate here taste like shit? Not worth thinking about. For the first time in my life I don't finish the bar and toss it into the bin. James digs it out and finishes it up. 'Tastes like shit!' he says. Maybe I should write them a letter of complaint and see if they'll give me a complimentary year's supply as a gesture of goodwill (must be made in the UK, though). Well there's a thought.

I pad into the bathroom to line up my array of lotions and potions along the side of the bath. I notice the hairdryer has no plug, just wires sticking out of the end of the lead. I must encourage James to use it. He'll hopefully do me a favour and electrocute himself.

'Do you think their beauty parlour is worth a shot?' James sighs.

'How should I know!' I snap back.

'Well, we may as well give it a go,' he says.

The salon is dirty, but dirt is never a deterrent for James. I scrunch my nose up but he's already making our appointments for an Indian Head Massage followed by a Full Body Massage. (The head massage is so oily it takes me about three months to restore my hair to its former condition—I won't say glory. It also gives me a dandruff problem for the next six months.) The body massage is OK, but the girl has long nails that dig into me. I wonder whether James is enjoying his. We exit our treatment rooms simultaneously. James looks tight-lipped as we take the lift back to our room.

'What's up?' I ask him.

'He was a bloody gay boy,' he says. 'He kept brushing against my balls for ages and then asked me if I wanted a hand-job!'

Hmm, since we haven't had sex for weeks I'd imagine James literally rose to the occasion.

I bought some sexy new red Calvin Klein lingerie especially for this holiday. I quickly change in the bathroom, then shimmy out to James who's reading a book on George Best (a fellow alcoholic).

'Hey, sexy boy!' I call.

James looks up at me then back at his book.

'Hey, big boy! My pussy needs a good seeing to!' I try.

James reluctantly looks up again and stares at me. His expression says it all—he's not in the slightest bit turned on, and is looking down his nose at me.

'Emily, you look chubby in that outfit,' he tells me.

I run back into the bathroom and cry. James doesn't come to check on me, bloody bastard. It's his flaming midnight munchies that made me put on weight in the first place! He's always stuffing his face with Cornettos and crisps late at night, testing my willpower against temptation to the absolute limit. He doesn't want to make love to me any more. I remember Pippa's wise saying: 'Those who mind don't matter and those who matter don't mind', but it doesn't really make me feel any better.

Our last city on this tour from hell is Udaipur, a beautiful place with a stunning lake, in the middle of which lies a palace (one way to keep the paparazzi away!). Westerners with dreadlocks and tie-dyed clothing ride by on motorbikes—probably spoilt rich kids on their year off (from what?) before Uni. By now, James and I are barely on speaking terms. He's all tight-lipped and not really with me. We've got another bloody temple to visit today. I can't be arsed, and refuse to take my socks off to go inside. James freaks out at me ('We're missing the best temple just because you won't take your fucking socks off!'). Christ, we're not joined at the hip! Why doesn't he just go in on his own? I've had enough sightseeing to last me a lifetime. It's strictly beach bum holidays for me for the next decade to recover from this ordeal.

If James burps or beefs one more time on this holiday

I will seriously strangle him, even if we are now finally moving through the queue at Delhi Airport immigration. I cannot wait to leave. I know that James has stuck a 'Fragile' airline sticker on my back and I don't care—I do feel extremely fragile. The only thing James says to me on the flight back is that he could be with the rugby lads in Bali right now rather than on this crappy holiday with me.

We learn the next morning that six of his rugby mates have been caught in a bomb blast in Bali. For some unfathomable reason George Bush's war has moved from sandy Iraq to sunny Indonesia's Sari Club and Paddy's Bar. Instead of trained soldiers, now party-goers are killed—utterly senseless. A bunch of young people disappears forever. They had absolutely nothing to do with this fucking war. They were just having an innocent drink and a laugh. How scary is that? Terrible, terrifying, tragic. And I'm to believe God exists! James is obviously devastated. In fact the whole of the Hong Kong Football Club is in shock. Grief falls like a cloak. So many people are touched—someone had a brother there, someone else a fiancé, someone else a best friend. Tears are spilt whether you knew the victims or not. Surely the world will never be the same again. Sickening to think James could well have been there. Certainly only the good die young.

Chapter 10

November
Rock n Roll

I'm feeling constantly under the weather these days. I can't put my finger on exactly what's wrong. Sometimes I have a headache that never goes away, stomach cramps or semi-squits. I decide it's time to investigate and book an appointment with John Braun, a renowned homeopath. I prefer the alternative route as I don't like all the chemical drugs doctors give you—in fact, the only drugs I like are the class A variety! Unfortunately, you have to wait for weeks for an appointment with John Braun. Fortunately, he's had a cancellation so I jump at the chance to see him and go there straight away.

He has a team of therapists in his clinic—from the conventional physiotherapist to the weird and wacky sound therapist. Pippa tried the sound therapy last week and said she was made to sing 'Happy Birthday'—apparently it recalls happy memories and sends positive energy around the body. Not for Pippa, though, as she'd just had (can't use the word 'celebrated' in this instance) her fortieth and started crying.

Anyway, John's running behind schedule so I sit and observe the other poor souls seeking good health. There's a boy of about eight dressed in a posh school uniform and daft straw hat, whose mother moans on and on to the receptionist in a whiney tone.

'Ambrose is such a sick boy. I spend all my time in clinics.'

Ambrose is running around the reception area, looking a picture of good health.

'He never wants to drink any fluids,' she continues.

I look at him again racing up and down the room and think it can't be doing him any harm.

'And he will not stop chewing the top of his lead pencil!'

I can sympathise with the poor wee mite. Pencil kits taste good! As a kid I used to love eating the erasers that smelt of exotic fruits—mmm, yummy memories! I also loved to drink the water we washed our paintbrushes in. (Is it any wonder I've turned out to have so many illnesses in adulthood?)

John Braun doesn't find anything wrong with me but still prescribes over a hundred quid's worth of vitamins. This little lot will last me for the rest of my life. I hate taking vitamins. I already have enough unused tablets to open my own pharmacy and now I've got more. What an utter waste of money!

John also imparts some pearls of wisdom as I leave his palatial office.

'Perhaps you just need to have some fun in your life.'

Hmm, thanks for that gold nugget. Well worth the thousand-buck fee for your time.

I hear rumours that Prince is coming to town for one night (by the way, when did he change back from Symbol to Prince?!). Only in Hong Kong could the concert event of the decade, if not the country's entire history, arrive with so little publicity! It turns out he's playing in two days' time—two days! I rush to buy a ticket, heeding John Braun's advice, and find I have the choice of the whole stadium. When I lived in London events like this would be sold out within minutes—I'd always telephone just as the booking lines opened, hold for half an hour (costing little under the price of the ticket itself), only to be told the gig was totally sold out. What is it with this town? Why can't they organise a piss-up in a brewery? At least when the Brits were here they knew how to run things! Good old British.

Poor old Prince comes out of hiding to perform a concert to 4,960 empty seats and forty people lucky enough to have heard the Chinese whispers that he's playing in Hong Kong. And boy, did those 4,960 people miss out! Prince is totally sensational and I now understand what the word 'charisma' truly means. He may be pint-sized but his aura fills the stadium. I manage to join the scrum at the front of the stage. Not only am I loving every minute of it but am also burning loads of calories from dancing like a loony! I even get to see the clear outline of Prince's tackle (glad I brought the binoculars) when he comes out dressed as a pixie in white tights. Some bloke shouts out, 'Oi, Prince is in his pyjamas!' which the crowd cracks up at. I'm sure Prince hears and I wholeheartedly commend him for not pissing himself, too.

So there I am, singing 'Purple Rain' louder than Prince with his mic, when someone knocks into me, nearly sending me sprawling to the floor. I'm just about to give her a massive push back when I realize it's Shona, the travel agent James and I book all our flights through. Lucky I stop to look who it is before retaliating or I'd have lost my twenty percent discount!

I miss my chance to join Prince on stage as about ten people are chosen from the front row to boogie with none other than the Prince of pop himself. I bottle going up as it involves hauling yourself onto the stage and, to be honest, the thought of the crowd seeing my mini skirt ride up to reveal my horrible cellulite (far worse than Donatella Versace's!) and fat arse (J-Lo eat your heart out!) puts me off. James's calling me a 'big bloater' the other day didn't inspire me either. But I'd have liked to have been up on stage giving it some and dreaming of Prince asking me to be in his dance troupe from now on (there's enough flesh on me alone to count as a troupe so it could have been just me and him!). Instead I watch the medley of wannabes showing off to the world that they can't dance for toffee and that you should never wear a scarf bigger than you or white sports socks with black work shoes.

Prince finishes to great applause, with everyone clapping extra hard to make up for the 4,960 people missing. I stomp my feet and yell for more but he's having none of it—I don't press him further as it's clear he takes his beauty sleep very seriously. After all, he looks younger now than in his heyday twenty years ago (I wonder what his secret is or who's his plastic surgeon). As the stadium quietens I leave walking on air, having lost my hearing through all-night too-close proximity to the loud speakers and having lost my voice from singing as loudly as my larynx let me.

I hadn't been too bothered about see the Rolling Stones, having had my mother drum into me from an early age that the Beatles were far superior and the only band in history worth listening to. Such was her devotion that she was attracted to my father simply because he vaguely resembled Paul McCartney (little did she know he had the personality of Sid Vicious). Therefore, I'd never really paid much attention to the Rolling Stones, apart from reading in 'Hello' magazine about Mick Jagger siring yet another child in one of the four corners of the world (he obviously took advice from my mother).

I buy their latest album '40 Licks' (and the bloody rest, with the amount of testosterone in that band) to find I love their music! By the night of the concert I am totally excited. James loves them and puts everyone else to shame with his word-perfect renditions of all the songs—much to the aggravation of the people standing close to us, as, understandably, they have come to hear Jagger sing and not James, who has a tendency to shout off key. Consequently, I angle my body slightly away from him to pretend we're not actually together.

We're dancing like we have ants in our pants while the people behind us want to stay seated. A pasty blonde doing her bit by wearing tight black leather trousers and red pixie boots taps James on the shoulder and asks him to sit down. Not a good idea.

'We're at a fucking Rolling Stones concert, not Charlotte Church!' James shouts back. 'I'm not bloody sitting down!'

Luckily the fat bloke next to him joins in, 'Go and buy the video instead and watch it on the telly at home!'

Just our luck, the next song, 'Angie', is a slow one that we'd normally sit down to, but we still dance in protest despite the cries of, 'At least sit down for this one!'

As I watch Jagger strutting his stuff I realize that despite being built like a whippet he's really rather sexy. Ronnie Wood's sexy, too, strumming his electric guitar between his legs like he's wanking off an enormous erection (sorry for any offence, but they're the only words I can use to describe him). Keith Richard's such a dude, chain-smoking while giving his guitar a right old pasting; he even makes choking on a ciggie look cool. And Charlie Watts, erm, well, not sexy perhaps, but nicely toned arms from all that drumming. I wouldn't say no to a gang bang with them!

I feel so overwhelmed by their blatant sexuality I have the urge to whip my knickers off and throw them on stage. On second thoughts, I don't think Mick would be overly impressed with my girdle-control Marks & Sparks' knickers. Not very 'Agent Provocateur', nor 'Victoria's Secret' nor 'Fredericks of Hollywood'. As the screen reveals a camera panning out to the faces of the crowd I'm overcome with the desire to show my breasts. I mention this to James who laughs loudly, 'Mick would need binoculars to see them!' So what, I don't have the body of a groupie but by gum I can dance (well, in my opinion).

Chinese whispers have gone round the stadium saying Bill Clinton's in the crowd. I keep hoping he'll join the band playing his saxophone, sexy bugger. I bet he wishes he'd chosen to be a rock 'n' roll star rather than President of the United States—he could have bedded thousands of women and would have looked every inch the rocker. Instead he had to play the role of a paragon of virtue and act like the Pope, which can't be much fun. Alas, I don't catch a glimpse of Bill. I'd have asked him if he had a cigar on him, as I find them, too, very sexy!

Goddamn it, why did I wear these frigging high-heeled boots? They may look kinky but my toes must be like raw beefburgers by now. Ouch! I can hardly walk in them, let alone dance. Hope Mick bloody appreciates them.

The Rolling Stones prove sensational. The next day the

BBC World website asks for comments from the crowd and I email a highly literate response to them:

> To: info@BBCworld.com
> From: emilygreenhk@hotmail.com
>
> I know it's only rock n roll but I like it! They're so fabulous—I want all their babies!
>
> Emily, Hong Kong

I feel so elated I spontaneously book another ticket to their concert which is taking place two days later. I justify the expense to myself figuring I didn't really get to hear Mick sing the other night, just James. Hmm, a perfect reason for blowing another week's wages. I then phone my mother to wind her up and let her know I've renounced the Beatles in favour of the Rolling Stones.

'Say hi to Keith for me if you see him,' she casually responds. 'We used to hang out together when he did gigs at the "Purple Onion" in Middlesbrough.'

What?!

'Yes, I saw them many times before they made it big. It took a long time for them to get it right, but I always knew they'd be huge in the end.'

'Why didn't you try and shag one of them, mother?' I cry. 'At least I'd have got a decent dad out of it rather than some demented Paul McCartney look-alike!'

'Well, Keith was a love and Mick always tried it on with me, but he was going after everything else that moved.'

Christ, she was even in with a shout! Bugger, I wouldn't have an overdraft problem right now if she'd done a bit of forward thinking.

My mother never ceases to amaze me. She had very wealthy parents and went to a top boarding and finishing school, met loads of famous minted people but wasn't impressed by any of it. No, instead she was dreaming of a constipated hermit who looked a bit like Paul McCartney (while Paul McCartney was dreaming of a blonde, blue-eyed, horsy, animal lover - just like my mother is!). I could be hanging out with Jade and Stella right now instead of modelling cheap plastic 'Big Bird' raincoats. Don't you just love it?

The Harbour Fest has come to a close. After seven concerts of wild dancing I'm knackered but haven't lost a blooming pound. I'm going to book myself in for drums and electric guitar lessons (perhaps not at the same time, that's a little too ambitious). I'm sure my life wasn't really supposed to be this dull and that, unbeknown to me, inside is a natural rock 'n' roll star waiting to get out. I can see it now. I'll pick up the guitar and immediately be able to faultlessly play 'London's Burning'. Without any practice, I'll launch into a Carlos Santana-style piece with highly complicated and original chords. Obviously, my tutor will be astonished, proclaiming me a natural-born legend. Yikes, I just hope I don't have to cut my nails short. But then it's a small price to pay for fame and adulation.

OK, that scenario's very unlikely. But drums, how difficult can they be? Just banging on the beat with a stick! Hmm, thinking about it, I'm more likely to take to the drums instantly. Well, if that one-armed geezer from Def Leopard can do it then so can I!

I scour 'HK Magazine' and 'Dollarsaver' for lessons. After a couple of calls I'm all signed up for a course at 'Perfect Pitch' in Happy Valley. I have a skip in my step on Saturday morning as I enter the crowded shop. It's swarming with little kids—I guess not many people take up an instrument at my age. There are all sorts of instruments on sale. As a kid they seemed really expensive but as you grow into an adult (something James has yet to do) they become cheap as chips.

Take, for instance, this fetching bright blue child's violin (not like in my day when they were all bog standard boring brown). It's only about thirty quid—such a bargain I'm almost tempted to buy it. Wowzers, I see even recorders now come in sophisticated colours (I like the pale green one in particular—hmm, shall I, shan't I?). Then I get totally distracted by a super-duper drums kit in vivid yellow—sadly not thirty quid but closer to three hundred. I guess I could stretch to that, perhaps as a Christmas present to myself?

Rocky is to be my teacher for the next six weeks. Unlike most Chinese men he's huge, in all directions, with everything pierceable pierced. He has a long black ponytail and a T-shirt with the name of a well-regarded local rock group, 'Lam Ki', emblazed across it. He looks a bit scary, but then drums are a macho instrument. He leads me down a narrow corridor with small rehearsal rooms leading off it and I see mums and dads waiting patiently for their kids—little Vincent on the violin, little Priscilla on the piano and little Teddy on his trumpet. They all look at me with curiosity, clearly finding my walking into the drums room highly amusing. The room is soundproofed in thick black rubber wallpaper, S&M parlour-style. Sexy!

In the middle of the room is a flashy drums kit, fortunately adult-sized and not the Fisher-Price kiddies' drum kit I was dreading. Rocky does a bit of showing off to prove he is in fact a drums teacher, before handing me the drumsticks (I keep thinking of chicken legs). I feel a bit of a chicken when he tells me to beat the snare drum (whoohoo!) in a steady fashion. I'm a bit self-conscious at first and tap timidly, creating a tinny sound. Rocky immediately shouts, 'Harder, harder, Emily!' (reminding me of James when I wank him off) and, what the hell, I go for it. Well, that sounds much better!

I didn't realize there'd be quite so much to it—I don't hit the drum or cymbal properly, don't hold the drumsticks properly and don't sit properly. I start to get disheartened, wondering if I'm not a natural after all. I look at my watch. I've only been here twenty minutes and have already given up. I'm pathetic, I admit. So I persevere, remembering 'practice makes perfect' (the exception being making love to your boyfriend when 'practice makes monotony').

Three quarters of the way through the lesson and I'm using three drums and one cymbal. I'm encouraged by Rocky's enthusiasm (hopefully about my drumming skills rather than my being a chick. He must get sick of teaching snotty schoolboys day in, day out. Hmm, maybe I should suggest to Teets that she re-train to be a drums teacher. She likes her men young). Rocky tells me I've already reached lesson three level. Ringo Starr move over! Charlie Watts get off my cloud! I'm in seventh heaven. So a little perseverance does pay off! Rocky sells me some drumsticks before the end of the lesson and I choose the most expensive pair (nice purple ones with pink stripes). I sign up for twice a week instead of once, and leave skipping.

I feel euphoric for days afterwards. Motivated. Inspired. Alive. I wake up singing, 'Oh What a Beautiful Moooorning' (well, that's not exactly true as I just groan when the alarm goes off and can't speak until mid-morning as my body's generally in shock). And I think to myself, it's a wonderful, wonderful world (I'm still singing—in my head). This lovely mood stops abruptly when James gets so blottoed on Saturday night he does the unthinkable. He comes home at six in the morning, jumps on the bed and shakes me vigorously. I'm sound asleep and none too happy with this.

'Shhhello, sshhdarling,' he drawls. 'Shhwake up, wake up!'

I eye him angrily through half-closed lids.

'ShhEmily, I had a fucking great time. Sit up!'

He tries to pull me upwards and I elbow him away, groaning and still half asleep.

'Piss off, James, I'm asleep!' I moan.

'Oh you're so fucking boring, you fat bitch!' he shouts. 'I should throw you out of my fucking flat!' He roughly grabs hold of one of my legs and tries to pull me off the bed. I hold onto the headboard. 'In fact, I'm going to throw you out the window instead, you fucking waste of space bitch.'

He is ranting and raging, totally fuming. He tries to open the window but is so drunkenly uncoordinated he fails.

'Shhbugger, I'm throwing you out the window. I hate you.' He pulls both my legs forcefully and I hold onto the bed for dear life. I'm petrified. In fact, I've never ever been so scared. After all, we are on the 34th floor and this would send me to my death. He's pulling and pulling at my legs and I'm frozen with fear. He could easily overcome me—he's twice my size—and our windows are so big he could throw me out without my being able to do much about it.

Thankfully he's so drunk he gives up and leaves the

bedroom, slamming the door shut. I can't even cry I'm so shocked. I lie on the bed in a ball with my heart palpitating madly. I don't think to call the police—all I can think is how I used to love that sod with all my heart, how we used to have a fantastic time together, and how I can't believe this is what it's become. He's gone from being tender and fun to becoming a potential murderer. The saddest thing is I still love him. But I know I can't stay with him after this.

The next day I do something I usually avoid—I confront him.

'Do you realize what you did last night?' My voice feels raw.

'I don't remember anything. What?' he responds lightly.

'James!' I scream. 'You tried to throw me out of the window!'

'I can't remember,' he replies, showing no emotion.

I'm incredulous. 'Well I do, I remember feeling scared out of my wits and thinking I was going to die!'

'I don't remember anything,' is all he can say, no apology, no remorse.

'Oh, well that's alright then!' I whisper.

'Look, I don't remember!' he insists heatedly.

'But I do,' I respond sadly.

'Look,' he shouts back, 'why don't you just piss off for good!'

My mouth droops in anguish.

'I don't love you any more, Emily. You're not the girl I met.'

I'm horrified. He continues.

'I'm seeing other people. I want you to move out ASAP.'

I'm completely mortified. Seeing other people? Plural?

'What do you mean?' I whisper.

'Do you really want to know, Emily? OK, if you want the full details, I've been dating three Chinese girls. Will you leave now?'

Not one, not two, but three! He sees my eyes well up with tears.

'But I've only been having sex with two of them,' he adds quietly.

That makes me feel a whole lot better! At this moment I could quite happily stab him to death, plunging a kitchen knife into him at least fifty times. I'm exaggerating perhaps (forty should do it), but the anger is bubbling up inside me.

The day passes in a blur of tears. My eyes are puffy and red from so much crying. That night I don't sleep a wink and lie rigid in bed staring glassily at the ceiling. I fantasize about ways of getting him back, and for endless hours plot how to hurt him. Perhaps doing a 'Bobbit' on his pride and joy, his manhood. Or cutting out the crotch of his favourite 'Armani' jeans. Wishing on him unbelievably itchy genital crabs (although his new dates may have already seen to this). Hoping he gets a fatal disease and dies a slow, agonising death. Dear God, I don't want to be thinking all these horrible things. I hate him! I love him. I... I... I need some chocolate!

It dawns on me that while James has been shagging around he's also been shagging me, both pussy and bareback—without condoms. He obviously cared for and respected me so little he thought nothing of putting me at risk. In this day and age he's put my life in danger! It makes me feel sick to my stomach. Bastard with a capital 'B'! How dare he treat me like this? I'm seeing red. In the heat of the moment I pierce a needle through his extensive array of condoms (including his favourite glow-in-the-dark ones and my favourite banana flavoured ones). My heart is beating so loudly my ears can hear nothing else. I relish the thought of him getting some silly twit of a slag pregnant (preferably a really ugly one who can't speak a word of English) and ending up having to be the family man he's tried so hard to avoid becoming. Or of him catching something nasty (that nearly, but not quite, ends his deceitful, low life, and puts him off sex forever).

It feels good to be bad and I feel it's payback time. A little voice inside my head reasons with me that 'Two wrongs don't make a right' and I tell it to 'bugger off!' What if he finds out? I may face the electric chair, or community service! Oh, James is as blind as a bat, I remind myself, he won't see—especially if he's as horny as hell and just about to rut a slutty minx. If he does find out, my actions may make the tabloids—I can see the headline: 'Hell Hath No Fury Like a Woman Scorned—Psycho Girlfriend Emily Green Proves the Point.' Again I need chocolate.

Breaking up is so hard to do. In fact it's tragic. I feel like I've had open-heart surgery without the general anaesthetic. Utterly unwanted, and alone in the world. All our good times instantly forgotten, only the three other women (hussies!) remembered. Shall I end it now? Stick my head in a gas oven, step out in front of a speeding bus or jump off a tall building? Perhaps overdose on sleeping pills? No one would give two hoots. Several months would probably pass before the authorities were alerted to a bad smell coming from my apartment only to find my badly decomposing body and a neighbour's Chihuahua called Camilla heartily gnawing on my ulna bone. I just want to be with 'Mr Right', whoever the hell he is. Preferably 'Mr I-Know-How-To-Operate-A-Washing-Machine'. But actually 'Mr OK' would suffice. I'm really not that fussy.

I recall the saying, 'Jesus loves you—everyone else thinks you're an arsehole'. Wise words indeed, except I believe in Santa Claus and the Tooth Fairy more than Jesus Christ. Perhaps I should become a nun and be done with it? No more worrying about being crap with men and jobs... or about what to wear. Would it matter that I'm an atheist? Probably not, the House of God seems to shelter anything—closet gays, paedophiles... A broken-hearted cynical atheist will be the least of their problems. Oh God, I feel so alone. I must dig out my 'Sex and the City' DVDs for a bit of female comradeship (will I still be allowed to watch them in the nunnery?).

I consider digging my heels in and staying put until James comes to his senses, but in my heart I know he doesn't have any sense. So, I leave him nearly five years to the day I met him. Pippa's encouraged me to book a room at 'The Edith Wardle Watkins' as a temporary solution before finding my own pad. It's a residential home for women (i.e. refuge for dumped ones) that's well located and at a reasonable all-inclusive monthly rent. James, in his eagerness to free up his shag-pad, helps me with my suitcases. I can feel scorching hot tears running down my face and hug him to me, clinging to him not to let me go. He's all hot and sweaty and his shirt is scratchy against my cheek—I know I'll never forget this hug as long as I live. I also know we're well and truly over. He can't wait to extract himself from me and looks stony-faced.

Chapter 11

January
Dump

The Edith Wardle Watkins is one of Hong Kong's oldest colonial buildings and, judging by the ancient furnishings, not much has changed since it was erected. Whoever decorated certainly liked chintz—it's Laura Ashley on acid! There's a musty smell of moth-balls (or ladies who've lost the will to wash their private parts!).

I sit in reception with my cheque-book at the ready and watch two forty-something women weeping opposite me. A distinguished-looking lady clad from head to toe in 'Country Casuals' runs past me, sobbing, 'Don't leave me, Roger!' All right, that's a bit of a fabrication which I owe to an overactive imagination. I am in fact sitting there alone with only 'Homes & Gardens' to keep me company (an odd choice of magazine since people here don't have either a home or a garden, just a measly, solitary room).

While the good news is James didn't manage to throw me out of the window to my death, the bad news is I'm beginning to wish he'd succeeded, as I have to share a bathroom with twelve other women! A Victorian bathroom to boot! Complete with yellowed tiles and greying lino flooring. I'm shown to my room. The word 'Spartan' instantly springs to mind (I'm sure nuns are allocated rooms more luxurious than this!). I start blubbering like a kid who's been left at boarding school for the first time (although with parents like mine the tears would have been of joy).

If you're not depressed on arrival at this joint then it's surely only a matter of time. I decide not to let it get the better of me, however, and take my shoes off to try to relax. I pad around my matchbox in my socks, unpacking as quickly as possible.

'Ouch! Jesus!' I shout as a splinter the size of a small tree embeds itself in my foot. I squint at the bare boards and notice they're unvarnished with bits of wood sticking up.

'Great!' I lament, starting to sob loudly and feeling extremely sorry for myself.

I spend the whole day lying in bed crying, believing it quite likely that I'll never get up again now that no one wants me. There's a soft tap on my door and the cleaner enters before I have the chance to shout, 'Bugger off, leave me alone!' (although I'm not usually that rude). She sees me and bolts out—do I look that bad? I prop myself up on one elbow and peer at my reflection in the mirror that's facing the bed. Jeez, my eyes are bright pink and really puffy—they look like small vaginas. No wonder I scared her—I scare myself.

She comes back and hands me an orange. She seems to think a piece of fruit will make everything all right. Sweet, but delusional. I've just found out my boyfriend of five years is bonking three other women (OK, two of the three but it may as well be three bloody hundred), that he hates me so much these days he wants to kill me, and once again I'm a Jinxster! It will take more than an orange to make me feel better, let me tell you, missy! Surprisingly, though, it seems the orange does stop me crying, and my anguish evidently hasn't extinguished my appetite (more's the pity). To the contrary.

I finish the orange and order some food to my room from the restaurant downstairs. They have an unexpectedly extensive menu, with a rather pleasing dessert section.

'I'll have a chocolate cake, please. And a chocolate brownie, too,' I request.

'Anything to drink, Miss?'

I should drink something, get some fluids down me.

'Hmm, a hot chocolate then, please.' Start as you mean to go on.

After my little binge (total pig-out) I don't feel like crying—just being sick from the chocolate overdose. I switch on the little TV and watch the fuzzy screen for a while—it reminds me of our TV in the 1970s that my dad still insists on watching in his toy railway room. A cheesy lovey-dovey movie is showing which depresses me even more.

I surf the channels. The music station is playing Canto pop album clips, like Hacken Lee's 'I Don't Know How to Sing' (rather an ironic choice of song title). In between programmes there's always a series of Hong Kong Government advertisements trying to bring a little wisdom to the populace—themes like 'How to wash your hands' (no wonder SARS came about), 'How to poop scoop and help the dog poo collection squad' (my fantasy job), 'Don't throw your old TV or washing machine out of your high-rise apartment window as you may well hit someone on the head with it by accident' (unless it's James below, then just go right ahead and throw away), and 'Don't carry balloons onto public transport as they may burst' (party poopers). Government adverts say a lot about a nation (no further comment).

It's now pitch dark outside and I need to sleep. I reach over to turn off my overhead lamp and involuntarily yelp in pain. I hadn't noticed that the bulb is exposed and red hot. I only grazed my wrist across it for a moment but now have a big red welt forming. I can hear James's voice clearly in my head saying, 'You idiot!' and I wholeheartedly agree with him. I start to cry. I miss the old devil. I miss our little apartment, where I know where everything is, where we don't have dangerous flooring or naked light bulbs. I run my arm under a cold tap (I do at least get a sink in my room even if it only has the 'icy cold' water option).

'Bloody hell!' I mutter dejectedly. I'm not having much frigging luck! My arm's really sore—the skin has actually broken and is bleeding steadily. I'm probably going to have a flipping scar for life! I lie in bed with my foot stinging from the splinter and my wrist throbbing from the burn.

So much for someone looking down on me—I guess I must have done something really, really bad in a previous life. I feel hot tears streaming down my face. I bet Bastardface is out shagging and having the time of his life. Thankfully, sleep has to come eventually.

I'm woken up by my bladder advising me, 'If you don't go for a pee this very second you're going to wet the bed and that will really add to your depression.' Bugger, I'm half asleep and the poxy bathroom (incidentally a perfect setting for 'Psycho') is about two bloody miles away. I can't be arsed to risk bumping into Norman Bates. Hmm, time to be creative—what are sinks for anyway? If the chefs can do it in China Town restaurants then so can I. It's at times like this that having a penis would prove very useful indeed. Instead, I make a botched job of it and end up with pee all down my legs. Sod it—it's only water (or hot chocolate). I use a tissue to wipe myself dry, and hope the cleaner doesn't catch on to me from the giveaway stench of urine.

When I wake up, I'm still crying. I can't wait to get up and leave this asylum. I walk aimlessly round the shops, not wanting to go back to Mrs Bates' house. What I need is one of those self-help books the magazines always recommend for dark times. I check out the extensive range in 'Page One' bookshop, looking for titles like 'Why All Men Are Wankers', 'How to Legally Marry Your Vibrator', 'He's Just Not That Into You Coz He's a Cunt' and 'Vengeance—101 Ways to Get Away with Murder'.

Sadly, it appears no one has written these helpful books. Instead, there's a miserable selection including 'After His Affair—How to Love and Trust Again' (I don't fucking think so! The bastard can rot in hell for all I care!). I spot 'Why Men Can't Commit' (I think his behaviour shows he should be committed... to prison!) and 'Stand by Your Man' (only with a loaded gun pointed at him!). What a pathetic choice. Maybe there's a market for me to write 'Women are from Heaven, Men are from Hell' or 'The Girls' Handbook on How to Spot and Exterminate a Bastard'. I can't be fagged, though, and leave the bookshop in disgust at their paltry selection.

The weather's turned grey and miserable. How fitting. I return to the Edith Wardle Watkins with dread. I have to ring an ancient doorbell to get in. 'Miss Haversham, are you there?' I want to call out, standing there in the eerie, dimly lit foyer. I've been desperate for a plop for the last twenty-four hours so reluctantly enter the communal bathroom. As I open the door, a middle-aged woman with a greying frizzy perm, stodgy bum and red-rimmed eyes screams, literally jumping in fright. This makes me jump, too. Bloody hell, I can't live like this! I try to take a dump but am aware that someone's having a shower and someone else is loading the washing machine. The cubicle's walls are paper-thin and every sound can be heard distinctly. My plops recede back into my stomach and I give up. Nothing makes me rattier than constipation (apart from thoughts of James).

I wash my hands in the icy cold water. There's no soap to be seen. Christ, I'll end up with Legionnaires Disease in this place! I'll be the one suffering a long and painful death while James is merrily shagging for England. I can't be fagged to have a shower—although I'm acutely conscious it's been two days! (I haven't gone this long without washing since my early teens when I tried to get away with just once a week, until my father would comment on how 'fresh' I smelt and ask if I'd care to take a bath. The good old Elizabethans did it once a month, so what's a week?) As I walk along the dingy corridor back to my cell I see someone's dropped an item of washing. At first I think it's a white T-shirt, but it turns out to be a pair of huge knickers. Gross! Once white, they are now grey and yellowed and crusty around the edges—someone's clearly not getting laid! This place certainly has bad karma. A home for Jinxsters no less.

I order some food—lentil and vegetable soup followed by scrambled eggs on whole wheat toast—in the hope it will kick-start my bowels and remind them that pooing is a normal bodily function. It's not the greatest food on earth, the sort of fare I imagine is served up in prison camps, so I down it quickly. Unfortunately this gives me indigestion and I feel terribly queasy, with something like the onset of food poisoning. I decide I'm not up for much this evening and turn in for an early night. But my armpits smell so bad and feel so wet and sticky I reluctantly grab my wash kit to take a shower.

A couple of days without shaving and I've turned into Neanderthal man. I'll need to hire the services of a sheep shearer at this rate! I see an elderly woman with white hair walking toward me as I move deftly along the hallway. She's probably lived here since the place opened over a hundred years ago. As I approach her, she jumps and gasps in fright. Jesus, what is it around here? Why is everyone so flipping jumpy?

I turn the shower on and—no water! Not a drop comes out. I say loudly, 'Give me a fucking break! I just want a shower!' thinking I am alone, but an Irish voice pipes up, 'That'll be the washing machine, always affects the water. You'll have to wait until the cycle's finished.' I pull my dressing gown on quickly, and peep my head around the shower cubicle door. A dumpy lady in her fifties is loading up the dryer. She looks like the owner of the passion-killer knickers, but then so do all the other residents here. She's wearing brown polyester trousers and a hideous bright orange T-shirt, which does little to hide her buxom bosom lolling in all directions.

'I'm Bridie,' she nods sternly.

'I'm Emily,' I respond softly.

'Try the shower again,' Bridie suggests. 'It should come on now.'

True to her word, it does. So there is a God! I jump in and wash myself quickly, thinking the water may stop at any moment with me covered in lather.

I hear someone else come into the bathroom who asks, 'Has your money come through yet, Bridie?'

Bridie laughs bitterly. 'No, the fucker's digging his heels in. He'd rather spend his money wooing those silly air hostesses he's always chasing than look after the wife who's dedicated nearly forty years of her life to him!'

Boy, oh boy, welcome to the house of fun.

'I just want the fucker dead,' adds Bridie.

And I know exactly how she feels.

The hot water feels wonderful and I linger under its none too powerful spray. There's a strange little patterned-glass window which looks onto the shower, and Bridie appears in plain view in front of me hanging out her smalls (big smalls!). I know she must be able to see me as naked as the day I was born—Jesus, is there no privacy in this place? Apparently not, as whoever Bridie is talking to is clearly taking a dump. I hear a couple of staccato farts, a long windy one, and then the splash of a sizeable turd hitting the toilet bowl. I can't bear this! My 'relaxing' aromatherapy body wash can't perform miracles! I abruptly finish my shower, wrap a towel round me and leg it back to the safety of my room.

That night I can't sleep. I'm all itchy and put it down to bed bugs. There I was wishing herpes on James and I'm the one scratching away like a chimpanzee! I hear every sound—women walking along the corridor to go to the bathroom, my sink tap dripping slightly, the cleaner brushing the steps to the entrance directly beneath my window, a car blasting its horn and the skid of tyres. In fact there's no end to it.

I lie awake for what seems like an eternity until I hear someone shuffling past my door and then turning the handle. I'm frozen rigid. I look again and definitely see the handle being turned, not in the manner of someone who's mistaken the room for their own but of someone trying to get in quietly and deliberately, without being heard. I think of calling James for help, but the image of him in bed with other women stops me. I feel my heart pounding and hope this is a bad dream. Whoever it is shuffles away but I realize I've really got to get out of here.

I feel like I'm being eaten up inside. Here I am, trembling and blubbering like an idiot, while James is off gallivanting, without a care in the world, shagging anything and everything that moves and having a whale of a time. I'd like to teach him a thing or two. As much as I'd like to move on, the anger doesn't subside. Maybe he should get a reality check. I pour it all out in an email and click 'Send'

Life is Pants   247

before I have a chance to reconsider.

> From: emilygreenhk@hotmail.com
> To: James1969@yahoo.com
> Subject: The Truth Hurts
>
> James
>
> You can shag Daphne 'Hairy Pie' Wong and whoever else you want—I don't feel jealous at all. They'll find out like I did that you're pretty on the outside and ugly on the inside. I stopped having sex with you when I got to know you—a devious, smarmy, smug, disrespectful, deceitful tosser. I rarely think this of anyone, but you are truly a BAD person. You chipped away at my confidence to the point where I was frozen to the spot, a dithering wreck no longer able to function and make decisions. I feel like I was under a spell and now that I've stepped away it's a relief to be out of your destructive clutches. Quite simply, you have an inflated ego and a shallow soul—and are not worth loving.
>
> I never want to see or hear of you again. DO NOT BOTHER TO RESPOND WITH YOUR MEAN AND CUTTING WORDS AS I AM NOT GOING TO OPEN ANY OF YOUR EMAILS FROM NOW ON.
>
> Thank God I am free of you. God help the next sucker.
>
> You sad wanker.
>
> Emily

I can hear Pippa in my head saying, 'That sounds about right', and can visualise her nodding encouragingly. I'm quite within my rights to let him know he's not as perfect as he thinks and how cruel he's been to me. Despite what the books say about not lowering yourself to that level, it feels great to give him a piece of my mind for a change! And it doesn't stop there. I'm seething with anger and whack out a letter (of complaint, I mean 'compassion') to his parents.

Dear Kaye and Derek,

This is Emily. As someone who loved and deeply cared

for your son James, I'm writing this letter to both of you. As much as you may try to forget your marriage and ignore the existence of each other, you made a son together and your son needs you to help him.

I put 100% into my relationship with James, but I learnt the hard way that he's so badly damaged by your divorce that it rules his love life, and all his relationships are doomed from the start. It's taken five years for me to give up on him.

James has always been cynical and scathing about love and marriage, but I thought the strength of my love and total devotion would prove him wrong. Naively I thought I'd be able to change him.

I now understand that James has absolutely no respect for women. He thinks that every woman is after his money and will then run off and leave him. Consequently, I've discovered his philosophy is to beat them to it—so he treats women very badly until they stop loving (or liking) him. He wants to prove to himself that all women are out to swindle him. I have tried with all my might to persuade him that your failed marriage and bitter divorce doesn't mean he'll have the same experience in his life. I've even tried to get him professional help to deal with his issues, organising for him to go for counselling and hypnosis—but he refuses to help himself and instead sees it as the cross he has to bear. I can't understand his stubbornness since I, too, have childhood issues, but I have made the choice to leave them where they belong—in the past—and to not let them affect my life negatively.

I ran around James, pampering him and doting on him. I really looked after him and always had his best interests at heart. Sadly, the more I gave to him the less he gave back. He's on the road to self-destruction. He now drinks so heavily I'm utterly convinced he's an alcoholic, and his recreational drug-taking has become much more regular. He's become terribly argumentative, aggressive and impossible to be with. I realize he can't cope with a nice, normal relationship, and does everything he can to destroy it. He used to tell me about the many sexual flings and affairs he had while dating his ex's Kirsten and Shelley, and he feels no guilt whatsoever over this. Stupidly, I didn't think he'd ever do this to me (despite not telling me he had a girlfriend, Shelley, when I first met him!). But I recently discovered that he's been screwing around, and know of three women he slept with during our relationship—God only knows how many others there were.

He ended up verbally abusing me and chipping away at my self-confidence, then wanting to pick fights and lashing out physically. I put up with the slaps, which progressed to hitting, and then the strangling—to the point where a couple of my friends noticed the bruises and marks and wanted to report him to the police. Recently, he tried to throw me out of our 34th floor window and I feared for my life like never before—and that's what made me finally leave him. He scared me so much I decided to leave Hong Kong too, despite enjoying it and building a life there.

I didn't deserve what James did to me. I understand why he did it, but he really hurt me, mentally and physically. Ultimately his betrayal was the worst thing of all to cope with—it made me question whether any of our time together was real and meant anything. I feel like he ruined every happy memory. Funnily enough, a couple of his mates have since contacted me to say how they disapprove of James's womanizing ways and bad attitude towards women, and how lucky I am to be free of him as he'll never change.

I'm unbelievably relieved to be free of him, and should have left him a long, long time ago. Thankfully, I still believe in love and happiness—that is something he hasn't taken from me. And despite everything, I genuinely do want him to be happy—but that's down to him and, I think, both of you. I feel that you have both leaned heavily on James and now it's his turn to lean on you. It's time to act like adults and parents and combine efforts to help your son.

Perhaps if you hear James's version of your divorce—and I'm writing it as he has told it to me on many an occasion (his version, not mine!)—then you'll be able to understand why he behaves as he does, and try to help him move on.

One day James and Derek came home to find Kaye had left them for Geoff, and taken a lot of furniture and the car. It then came to light that she'd been unhappy for a long time in the seemingly happy marriage, and had been planning to leave Derek for years. Kaye had even been siphoning money from Derek to fund her leaving him. Derek has since said to James that Geoff was probably not Kaye's first affair. Kaye divorced Derek and lied to her solicitor, saying she was beaten up and abused by Derek, in order to get a bigger settlement. Kaye tried to take every penny away from Derek. Derek became suicidal and depressed, and went on anti-depressants which he's been addicted to for many years but is trying to stay off them now. Derek said if he ever gets a terminal illness the first thing he'll do is murder Kaye. Derek has told James many times how awful women are, how they can't be trusted, and to never marry as it's nothing but trouble and inevitably ends in divorce. Kaye, too, says marriage ends in divorce so why bother. Kaye continues to have failed relationships, as no man will put up with her constant whining and sponging money off them. Kaye is always looking for the sympathy vote, and talks about her years of living in fear in an abusive relationship with Derek. Kaye is always scrounging money off James, even asking him to pay off her mortgage, despite her being able to afford two properties. Kaye regularly calls James, crying and telling him how miserable she is. James says he can't cope with his Dad's hatred of Kaye, and the ease with which Kaye begs James for money and relies on him as an emotional crutch. James says he's left the UK to get away from this. James says he couldn't marry, as Derek and Kaye would try to kill each other at the wedding. He doesn't want children as Kaye would want to move in to look after them. James says he loves Derek, who is a little distant now he's married to Maureen and devoted to her, but love/hates Kaye. James vows never to be exposed to his parents' type of relationship.

I know that not many women will put up with James's behaviour like I did. I also know he won't find many women who genuinely love him for him, as he's so twisted and ungiving. I know that he will never be happy in a relationship, as deep down he hates women.

Shockingly, I'd never be surprised to hear of James dying from a drug overdose or AIDS—but I'd truly much rather hear he ends up leading a happy life with a committed and loving partner.

The truth hurts.

With very best wishes and love to you both, Kaye and Derek,

Emily

Well that gets things off my chest! I print off the letter twice, neatly address the envelopes to Kaye's and Derek's respective addresses (ironically within a stone's throw of each other, but they've successfully avoided bumping into each other for the past ten years). Feeling decidedly revitalised, I check the rest of my emails.

From: deano@btinternet.com
To: emilygreenhk@hotmail.com
Subject: God Loves Blondes

A blonde is in trouble as her business has just gone bust and she's now in serious financial difficulties. In desperation she prays to God for help, 'God, please help me! I've lost my business and if I don't get some money soon, I'm going to lose my house, too! Make me win the lottery!'

The lottery night comes and somebody else wins it. Devastated she prays, 'God, please hear my prayers and let me win the lottery! I've lost my business, my house and I'm going to lose my car as well.' On the next lottery night she still has no luck.

Once again, she prays, 'My God, why have you forsaken me? I've lost my business, my house and my car. My children are hungry. I haven't asked for your help before and I'm a good person, please let me win so I can get my life back.'

Suddenly there is a blinding flash of light as the heavens open and the blonde is confronted by the voice of God saying, 'Sweetie, work with me on this—buy a lottery ticket!'

DeanO

From: mary1972@hotmail.com
To: emilygreenhk@hotmail.com
Subject: Five tips for every woman…

1. It is important that a man has a job and helps you around the house.

2. It is important that a man makes you laugh.

3. It is important to find a man you can count on and who doesn't lie to you.

4. It is important that a man loves you and spoils you.

5. It is important that these four men don't know each other.

Hee, hee!

Mare :)

Well, that would be about right. I'll put it to the test, eh?

From: katiets@abbotts-dury.com
To: emilygreenhk@hotmail.com
Subject: Forget him!

Dearest Emily,

You are always so good to men on a personal basis. In your romantic relationships you give so much. But in a funny way that's what you should need to do the least. If someone loves you or even likes you a great deal, they should not need to have it proven to them all the time. A gesture of love—the little precious things in life like a smile or the grasp of the hand, or getting something they especially like to eat ready for them, shows volumes of real feeling. You don't need to do and show everything to a partner. Peel back the layers of yourself one by one, as though you have a secret at the kernel of your heart. They will find you much more mysterious—and a woman should always be that in some way if she can.

Thinking of you during this tough time.

Love

Katie

Wow, I never knew Katie was such a psychiatrist, or a poet. No wonder Timothy's so besotted with her if she's so bloody mysterious. I must start to imagine I'm an onion henceforth! I do have onion breath right now—does that count as a step in the right direction?

> From: fernrocks@yahoo.com
> To: emilygreenhk@hotmail.com
> Subject: AN AMERICAN WOMAN'S PERFECT BREAKFAST

* She's sitting at the table with her gourmet coffee.

* Her son is on the cover of Business Week.

* Her daughter is on the cover of the Wheaties box.

* Her boyfriend is on the cover of Playgirl.

* And her husband is on the back of the milk carton.

Q: What do you call an intelligent, good looking and sensitive man?

A: A rumour!

Fern

That's the spirit! I'm feeling better by the minute! In fact, I'm going to move out of this flaming dump and start having some serious fun—footloose and fancy-free (whatever that means!).

Since Hong Kong's economy has been having a tough time for a while now, many of the middle- to low-end hotels have begun letting out some of their rooms as rentals. I check out a couple of hotels and end up taking a room in the ageing 'Pacific Hotel' near Admiralty. Anything to get me out of the old-aged folks' home!

> From: emilygreenhk@hotmail.com
> To: hicks16@hotmail.com, katiets@abbottsdury.com, janeheffer@yahoo.com, sandiebeech@yahoo.com, fernrocks@yahoo.com, deano@btinternet.com, mandyandandy@yahoo.com, teets@hotmail.com, mary1979@hotmail.com, clare_adair@btinternet.com
> Subject: Living in 'Freaks Hotel'

Howdy all,

Living in a hotel is very strange indeed! I get all my meals included in my rent so feel I have to make the most of it (three courses, seconds, desserts galore etc). I can either sit opposite the help-yourself-to-ice-cream tubs (seriously bad news!) or the help-yourself-to-cakes section (seriously bad news!). My diet has become a healthy combination of potato wedges and sour cream, creamy mashed potato, chips, chocolate ice-cream with 'hundreds and thousands' (millions in my case), or chocolate cake and a sneaky slice of cheese cake... I'll end up booking a double seat on flights at this rate! I feel quite sick, but compelled to get what's due to me as part of my rent.

Apart from the creepy crawlies in my bed (no, not what you're thinking!) the other disturbing thing is that I've never been so chatted up in all my life. Sadly, they're not even remotely half decent (apart from the New Zealand Air Force fighter-pilot, obviously married). There's one chap in particular who, honest to God, is the ugliest man I've ever clapped eyes on. He keeps wanting to join me at breakfast and dinner. The first time he came up to me he tapped my shoulder from behind and I turned around and, really and truly, let out a scream. Bizarrely, this did not deter him from sitting down next to me and drivelling on about his wife in Perth, girlfriend in Russia and girlfriend in Hong Kong (yawn, yawn, so hookers find you attractive?). It's very depressing his thinking he's in with a shout. I now bolt past him when I see him and he scowls. I'm going to send his photo to Stephen King to inspire his next horror novel.

A friend of a friend here took me to a swanky fashion show last night. She's a well-known TV presenter and model so I got to meet a lot of poncey show-offs. Not my thang. She commented, 'Agnes B is so Marks & Spencer,' and there I was dressed head to foot in dear old Marks & Sparks (they make the best undies in the world after all!). I could never afford Agnes B! She, on the other hand, is clearly labels-crazy and boasted that her frock cost over three hundred quid—a lot of money to look like Coco the Clown! Colourful it certainly was, nice it certainly wasn't. I kept wanting to ask her what time the Punch and Judy show was going to start, but figured as a model she'd be too thick to get the joke (miaow!). Emily's trendy fashion tip: to get this look, simply pillage a local primary school's dressing-up box. I know I'm being bitchy, but her crowd of preeners took themselves so seriously. Any joke I made they didn't get. I met a glitzy couple and chatted for a while—she said to me in all seriousness, 'Just don't talk to my husband about thinning hair.' He chuckles (ahh-hah, a trace of a sense of humour!) so I respond, tongue in cheek, 'What about baldness?'—and they didn't get the flaming joke! Hard work or what?

Severely regretted my recent dessert binges—being three times the size of any other chick there. I think I made up for it with a bit of crazy dancing when the DJ came on at the end, as MTV had their camera on me for a while (hopefully not to publicly ridicule me). I came back to the hotel rather drunk and disorderly—according to one of the staff the next day. I tell you, the hotel staff know my every move, exactly what I do and don't eat, what knickers I wear, that I'm not getting any sex at the moment etc.—it's scary!

Must dash, I'm trying to socialise big time as everyone

> keeps telling me I should be doing so! I'm actually better at it than I imagined—I guess five years with 'Mr Life and Soul of the Party' has rubbed off!
>
> Stay in touch!
>
> Love
>
> Emily x

It dawns on me that I really must move on. I must make a huge effort to put James behind me. Onward and upward, tally-ho! On to the next victim! After all, 'There are plenty more bastards in the sea'! I must find a date—anyone! I surf a couple of dating websites that have been popping up in my junk mailbox (thank God for SPAM!), as well as recalling a few websites James kept on his 'Favourites' list. There's a hell of a lot of 'Men Seeking Women', even more 'Women Seeking Men', and an unbelievable amount of 'Men Seeking Men'.

Where does one start? How can you wheedle out the psychos, the guys who'd rather sever off your limbs with a chainsaw than kiss you? I don't think I'm ready for this yet. I still miss James too much. I want to date someone who is him but a nice version.

I surf a couple of dirty, I mean 'adult' websites, just for good measure. I take solace in the fact the website tells me there are 83,401 other sad cases looking for lady love (or a quick shag), so at least I'm not alone in stooping this low. After a day of diligently reading a million profiles and flagging up my interest in a date from hell (using the 'winks' and 'nudges' buttons), I go to bed feeling incredibly depressed.

I wake up feeling incredibly happy—I've had forty-two responses for dates overnight! Not a bad start, if I say so myself. Someone wants me! I feel in total control of my love life. I call the shots now... or do I? On second thoughts, maybe I'm not ready to date yet.

> From: emilygreenhk@hotmail.com
> To: hicks16@hotmail.com, katiets@abbotts-dury.com, janeheffer@yahoo.com, sandie-

beech@yahoo.com, fernrocks@yahoo.com, deano@btinternet.com, mandyandandy@yahoo.com, teets@hotmail.com, mary1979@hotmail.com, clare_adair@btinternet.com
Subject: Living in 'Sons of Freaks Hotel'

Me again.

Been stood up tonight by a pal of 'Bastardface' who was going to take me out on the town in sympathy. Hmm. A let-down just like his pal!

Oh well. I thought I'd have a relaxing supper in the hotel but ended up dodging 'The World's Ugliest Man' and getting the hell out of there. I'm now sick of hotel food. Chips, chips, chips, desserts, desserts and more desserts. I watch how people select their desserts, generally starting by putting a little something on their plate, then gaining confidence, adding more and more, until they have one of each pudding piled high on the plate. Frightening stuff. The Asians tend to be rake-thin but eat just as much crap as the rest of us (lucky sons of bitches!) while the whiteys are porky. I'm sure I give some of the wobblers a look which says, 'Do you really need all that, pigsy?'

I nearly passed out in fright earlier in the week, as I thought I was seeing double. Terrifyingly ugly man has a frigging brother! I kid you not! Who looks just like him, but a tad younger! There are two of them, for Christ's sake! What was their mother thinking? You'd have thought she'd have done the world a favour after having her first ugly critter and got her tubes tied for all eternity. So now I'm ducking and diving both of them as, strangely, they think I want them to join me at breakfast, and lunch, and supper... Good for my diet, though, as I'm ending up skipping meals. How long are they staying in the hotel for? I hope to God they're not here long-term like me! I can't face moving again right now.

I'm still besotted with the self-service ice-cream tubs, though, and am developing a very strong right arm from all the vigorous activity of scooping the hard ice-cream into a ball. The staff here must think 'hundreds and thousands' are my staple diet, as I'm suddenly addicted to them in vast quantities. Oh well, it will keep the dentist busy.

I've hardly slept since I got here. Once a week the fire alarm goes off by accident at about 4am—I wonder if it's my aromatherapy oil burner?

I suppose things can only get better!

Funnily enough I miss old Bastardface immensely—why? Answers on a postcard please!

Over and out.

Love

Emily x

I do miss James desperately. The slapping, the hateful words and the attempt to kill me seem strangely forgotten. It's like I've got amnesia and can't remember the bad stuff. I sorely miss our cuddles at night, our running and jumping on the bed and bouncing up and down, trying to whack our heads on the ceiling, tickling each other to death and roaring with laughter, even his pull-my-finger farts. The jokes, snuggles, waving goodbye and hugging hello. I miss the old devil. Every street I walk down there are memories of us—every restaurant we've eaten in, every cinema we've been to (particularly the ones I gave him blowjobs in). I feel haunted.

I phone home. Dad answers.

'Hello, love. What did you do at the weekend?' he asks casually.

'All I do is sleep, cry and eat,' I respond despondently.

Dad brushes over this. 'Did you watch any of those violent Tarantino movies you like so much?'

'Dad, I stopped watching violent films when I no longer wanted to murder my parents.'

Dad laughs. 'Well, must press on, Emily. There are chores to do here. I can't expect your mother to help. She's usually too busy talking rubbish on the phone to her friends. I must attend to my duties.'

Someone confirm I'm adopted! Please reveal I'm the

lovechild Julie Andrews gave up to protect her squeaky clean public persona!

> From: mary1972@hotmail.com
> To: emilygreenhk@hotmail.com
> Subject: Hiya Emily!

Hiya Girlie!

Chin up, mate! He's not worth it. Go and buy yourself some chocolate and a rampant rabbit vibrator and enjoy your freedom. Anyway, this will cheer you up!

DON'T MESS WITH A WOMAN...

The CIA had a vacancy for an assassin. After all the interviews, tests and background checks were completed, there were three finalists left in the running—two men and a woman.

For the final test, the CIA agents took one of the men to a large metal door and handed him a gun. 'We need to ascertain that you will follow our instructions no matter what the circumstances. Inside this room, you will find your wife sitting in a chair—kill her!' 'You cannot be serious!' the man cried in disbelief, 'I can't shoot my wife!' The CIA agent responded, 'Then you're not the right man for this job. Take your wife and go home.'

The second man was given exactly the same instructions. He took the gun and went into the room. All was quiet for about five minutes, until he ran out crying loudly. 'I tried, but I can't kill my wife!' The CIA agent told him, 'I'm afraid you don't have what it takes. Take your wife and go home.'

Finally, it was the woman's turn. She was given the same instructions to kill her husband. She took the gun and went into the room. Shots were heard, one shot after another. They heard screaming, crashing, and banging on the walls. After just a few minutes all went quiet. The door opened slowly and there stood the woman. She wiped the sweat from her brow... 'This gun is loaded with blanks,' she said exasperated, 'I had to beat him to death with the chair instead.'

Nice one!

Chin up girlie!

Mare :)

From: mary1972@hotmail.com
To: emilygreenhk@hotmail.com
Subject: ...and another one to make you smile!

Emily—this will make you giggle too!

A couple is in bed together. He says, 'Since I clapped eyes on you I've wanted to make love to you really badly!'

She responds, 'Well, you've succeeded.' Undeterred he continues, 'I'm going to make you the happiest woman in the world!' She retorts, 'I'll miss you.'

Mare :)

I invite Pippa round for an afternoon of lounging by the hotel's swimming pool. It's small, worn out and grubby, with rust at the edges and loose tiles—not very trust-inspiring.

'I'll warn you now, Pippa,' I say, 'I saw the hairiest man alive by the pool yesterday. He had so much chest hair he actually looked like he was wearing a black mohair sweater!'

Pippa giggles. We turn our faces towards the sun—fuck the sun protection cream.

'Did you see the brand name of the cleansing cream in the changing room?' asks Pippa.

'Nope,' I reply.

'"Pimpless"!' she tells me. 'Who thought up that name for God's sake? Quite ridiculous!' I giggle.

It's a very humid day and before long we're both looking very sweaty.

'God it's hot!' exclaims Pippa, perspiration running down the sides of her sunnies. 'I don't care how uninviting that pool looks, it's going to cool me down. Are you coming in?'

I look at the grimy pool and shake my head. 'A pleasure deferred.'

Pippa sleekly dives in (well she would—Rupert's probably been forking out for diving lessons on top of the tennis, art and pottery). With unbelievably great timing, Mr Mohair Sweater walks along wearing nothing but skimpy purple speedos and an awful lot of black hair. I look at Pippa who starts to laugh uncontrollably, and I can see her choking on the water and ducking under several times. The young pool attendant has headphones on and so doesn't look up, his head in a magazine—what a job he has!

Pippa ungracefully clambers out of the pool, spluttering but still smiling. I glance sideways at Mr Mohair Sweater and am relieved to see he's reading 'The Economist', thus hopefully failing to realize he's become a laughing stock.

'You'd think he'd get waxed!' Pippa whispers.

'Yeah, a Brazilian with a few extras,' I suggest dryly. 'The beautician would be able to retire on his custom alone!'

A pool boy comes over and asks us whether we'd like to order anything. We're peckish and take a look at the menu.

'Mmm,' I jibe, 'The pig's stomach soup sounds appetising!'

'Yuck! And by the pool, too!' adds Pippa. 'Although I do love Durian Mooncake.'

I order a piña colada and Pippa asks for a gin and tonic and Durian Mooncake. An hour later our order arrives. Pippa grimaces the moment she bites into her delicacy.

'This is dreadful!' she says, screwing up her face. 'It tastes like a sweet pork pie flavoured with cat's wee!'

'That doesn't sound too good!' I chuckle.

Pippa and I talk about anything and everything, in no logical order, gassing away, putting the world to rights. Chicks certainly know how to talk—we have so much more in common than we do with bloody men!

Pippa states, for no apparent reason, 'Sanitary towels are sooo expensive!'

Mr Mohair Sweater looks up at us for a moment, then

passes out again, undoubtedly from the intolerable heat his body hair is generating.

'And bloody uncomfortable!' I pipe up.

'Ha, bloody!' laughs Pippa. 'Yes, they are, quite literally! Why are they called "sanitary towels" anyway?'

'They should be called a "Bloody Nuisance" instead!' I suggest. 'Or how about "Blood Suckers"? That's a good one!'

Pippa changes the subject for the umpteenth time. 'My friend Jill recently had her baby, Attica, in a taxi in a hospital car park! She was very pissed off as she still had to pay HK$30,000 in hospital fees, even though she only got to use their car park! Seems rather excessive, don't you think?'

I'd say so, although parking fees are hefty here.

'Did you know that Catherine Zeta Jones and Michael Douglas share the same birthday?' Pippa enthuses.

'Just not the same century!' I joke. 'Still, it's my dream to marry a handsome sex addict billionaire too!'

'And now with Viagra it doesn't matter how old they are, they're still up for it!' Pippa laughs, sitting up on the lounger. 'Listen to this,' she continues, 'apparently men who take Viagra keep their erection even after they die! Their body may be dead but their penis is up and ready for action!'

I'm feeling so horny at the moment maybe I should go raid a morgue.

Thus our girlie banter continues without us pausing for breath for the next three hours.

Undeterred by the ancient pool and disappointing food, Pippa and I risk booking a massage in the hotel's beauty salon. It seems I've been allocated their top masseuse, Bobo, but I don't take her title too seriously. And with good reason. Bobo rather unimpressively pokes her fingers deep into my ears to massage my eardrums, and rather too intimately massages my groin area and beyond (Brad Pitt—yep, golden oldie with black teeth and arthritic hands—nope). Pippa complains the massage oil smells dodgy, and asks whether it's from the hotel's kitchen rather than France. I can't stop sneezing for some reason.

'Ooh, you must have an allergy, Emily!' Pippa exclaims with concern. 'I know a great place to get you tested.'

The sneezing continues and I reluctantly take the telephone number she gives me.

> From: emilygreenhk@hotmail.com
> To: hicks16@hotmail.com, katiets@abbottsdury.com, janeheffer@yahoo.com, sandiebeech@yahoo.com, fernrocks@yahoo.com, deano@btinternet.com, mandyandandy@yahoo.com, teets@hotmail.com, mary1979@hotmail.com, clare_adair@btinternet.com
> Subject: I'm allergic!
>
> Hallo there!
>
> I'm reeling from shock—I've just been allergy tested and am apparently allergic to chocolate! How can this be? It's my staple diet! I'm manically depressed. I'm also allergic to cat fur and feathers, so tried to get the doctor to compromise by saying I'd give up eating cat fur and feathers but not chocolate.
>
> Well that's my big news for today, folks. Drop me a line to let me know what's up your end!
>
> Must dash, off to get my chocolate fix!
>
> Love
>
> Emily x

You'd have thought this experience would put me off taking Pippa's advice again, but it hasn't. She phoned me this morning to say there's a famous psychic in town and it would do me good to see her. I feel I'm clutching at straws seeking out a stranger to tell me that everything's going to be all right. To hell with it, I'm desperate. Pippa kindly offers to join me.

We mooch around a shop called 'New Age Corner' looking for divine inspiration. The shop's well known for bringing famous psychics, clairvoyants and healers into town. It sells an array of weird and wonderful things—Tarot cards, Tibetan singing bowls, white witches' wands, pendulums,

Indian incense, aromatherapy candles, birthstones, trinkets—you name it. Pippa points at a box giggling, 'This is for you, Emily—a spell kit to turn ex-boyfriends into toads!' I buy it without hesitation—it's worth a shot. Even though James is already well and truly a rat!

Annie Lomas has been flown in all the way from London. She certainly looks the part with pale skin, luminous green cat-like eyes, ginger hair and a colourful outfit. She begins by telling me I've just left a man who burst my bubbles and who would keep going round and round in circles for the rest of his life (sounds like a promising start). She tells me to avoid a man with black hair and blue eyes (Hugh Grant? Pierce Brosnan? Mel Gibson? Hugh Jackman? Endless possibilities!). Apparently I will marry between the ages of thirty-five and thirty-eight (what! That's light years away!) and have four children (now hang on a minute! My life's going to be a total nightmare!). I'm even more depressed for seeing her. Four kids?! That's a warning if ever I heard one and realize I must be extra vigilant with regards to contraception from now on. I leave her musty consultation room quite deflated. Some life!

I clap eyes on a rather striking man with bright blue eyes (his hair is grey not black so I don't need to avoid him). He stares at me with such intensity I feel he's penetrating my soul. He introduces himself as David and tells me he's a Canadian Energy Healer doing some work in Hong Kong for the next week or so. Pippa smiles and moves briskly towards the pet aromatherapy section (money to burn! I want to come back as a rich lady's pet pooch!). David's eyes bore into mine.

'I know you from a past life,' he says in all seriousness.

'Oh really?' I say, stifling a giggle. 'Are you sure it's not from the supermarket?'

He smiles confidently. 'Meditate on it, my dear, and remember me. We were lovers many lives over.'

'Ho-kay!' I chirp in a silly, girlie voice, suddenly taking an interest in pet aromatherapy and joining Pippa.

Herbal remedies to cure dogs' dandruff aren't in actual fact particularly interesting and when it feels safe I sidle along to the section on tantric sex instead. I'm just taking a peek at what Sting and Trudi apparently get up to when he's up, when David moves up close behind me.

'My guides are giving me some important advice,' he tells me, rather disconcertingly placing his hand on his head, closing his eyes and nodding. 'Yes. Yes. OK. Yes.'

I can't wait to hear what his guides are telling him.

'They say you need me to give you twenty-four hours of unconditional love. I can make time for you as they're adamant you need it.'

I feel my jaw drop in horror.

'What does that involve exactly?' I barely dare to ask.

'Well, we'd do everything that a loving couple does.'

Hmm, I assume he means shag like rabbits.

'Like what?' I shouldn't be asking but am intrigued by this stranger with the magnetic eyes.

'I'd start by giving you a massage, then I'd brush your teeth and give you a bubble bath, scrub your body and wash your hair and...'

'Erm,' I cut him off, 'I know how to brush my teeth, thanks. My mother taught me well. I won't be needing it. Thanks all the same.'

As I walk off he calls out, 'I'm your destiny!'

Hmm, not in this bloody lifetime, buddy.

Pippa thinks it's hysterical. I think it's downright scary. Why, oh why is it so easy to attract the guys that you find repellent? The short ones, the ginger ones, the old ones, the weird ones. The one you want never gives a shite.

Pippa kindly lends me a book called 'What Men Want From Their Women' written by four 'regular' guys (I don't think I've ever met one of those). I can, however, already summarise their best-selling three hundred-page self-help book in one sentence: they want it all their own way. We learn that the ideal woman who is viewed as potential wife material allows her man to (1) hang out with the lads while ogling women and talking lewdly about the female anatomy; (2) go to strip bars; and (3) cheat occasionally (they let on that all men are programmed that way. It's about variety, not emotions, apparently, and that makes it OK).

In addition, as ideal woman she will make the bed in the morning and clean up after her man. And these 'qualities', my friend, according to four lovely, regular guys, are what makes a chick 'nice' and 'cool' (personally, I think 'doormat' or 'maid' would more aptly define her). That's really all a girl has to do to get a ring on her finger. I ask myself, is it any wonder I'm still single in my thirties with no sign of marriage on the horizon?

Chapter 12

March
The 'Colourful' World of Internet Dating (or How Low Can You Go?)

I'm discovering Internet dating is great—you don't have to change the bed sheets, it involves no wet patch, no unwanted pregnancies, no STDs—it's quite simply perfect.

I finally dare to take the plunge and stick a personal character profile up on a couple of websites, presenting myself, one might argue, as a little too good to be true (well, I am!). 'Beautiful' (it's in the eye of the beholder after all, and my eyes see me as totally gorgeous), 'Intelligent' (despite what my A-Level results indicate), 'Independent' (except when it comes to men and chocolate) and 'With a great sense of humour' (I'm Internet dating, ergo, I must have a SOH. I'm already suffering from hysteria at the prospect of dating a knife-wielding dwarf). So, with brains and beauty (and a tight wet pussy), what more could Prince Charming ask for, for crying out loud?

I didn't in my wildest (dirtiest) dreams expect over four hundred hits on my profile in just twelve days! It appears the entire male population of Hong Kong has responded and it becomes a full-time job managing the replies (maybe I'll employ a PA to handle them and arrange my diary...?). I feel quite exhilarated as a mad whirlwind of blind dates begins, averaging three or four 'hot' dates a week (totally exhausting!). I try my best to rise above the whole James saga and my unfeeling heart, and simply see this as a necessary part of the moving on process. So the games begin.

I insist that each one emails me a photograph before I go ahead and organise a date (admittedly for shallow rather than security reasons) but I don't give one in return. Why the hell should I? Judging by some of their graphic responses they are quite capable of using their imagination. After receiving a couple of photos of cocks, just cocks, I reply to one, 'Very nice, but is it attached to a body and head by any chance?' So I learn to specify 'Head and shoulders shot, please' at the outset, as I don't particularly relish the idea of asking these idiots to pull down their trousers in a coffee shop in order to identify them. (How bizarre that some of these guys think a photo of their less-than-attractive manhood—some are bright red with purple veins popping out, yuck!—will secure a date with a nice girl like me?)

While seeing the guys' faces allows me to separate the wheat from the chaff, so to speak, disappointingly I find myself more often than not opening their JPEG attachments gasping, 'Dear God, no!' in abject horror. It beats me how these short, fat, pot-bellied losers have the gall to put themselves forward as potential candidates in the tall, athletic and handsome category. A particularly offensive mug-shot, all yellow teeth and wrinkles, accompanied by the words 'I'll make you shudder with pleasure' certainly makes me shudder!

What's also bizarre is how many guys in their forties and fifties believe they can get away with the 28-35 age range I've specified, and that so many Asian guys think they can fit the bill of 'Caucasian with blue eyes'. The non-English-speaking ones are often a giggle, though, coming up with replies such as 'You have a desire to carcass a man? You have suddenly surge to do it. Here I'm am!!!' or 'I have gery-green eye and black hairs.' Then on a more romantic note, 'I look a bit like Shrek', 'I have all my own hair, Andre Agassi style, and teeth', 'I look like Christopher Reeve from Superman but don't wear my undies outside my trousers—unless you want me to' and 'Tell me about yourself, better still, let's meet up and get it over with'.

There is also no shortage of potential lesbian liaisons, threesomes and orgies (twenty couples! Boy, you'd be showing your cellulite to all and sundry!) and one woman asks me whether I'd volunteer as her husband's birthday present (whatever happened to a nice tie and cufflinks?). Sadly, a lot of married men are on the prowl, all looking for the sympathy vote with 'I'm stuck in an unhappy marriage' (who's making it unhappy, buster?) or 'My wife no longer wants sex' (with you, matey!), and the classic 'Considering divorce' (I'm considering sky-diving but does that mean I'm going to go through with it?). Sadly, despite all the initial excitement, several of my encounters turn out to range from mildly depressing to the stuff of horror stories.

Picture the scene of a typical blind date in its early stages: I'm walking to the coffee bar dressed up to the nines and teetering on my heels, trying to create the impression that I always make this amount of effort. I spot a gorgeous, fit Matt Damon look-alike and think, 'Oh, yes! I am in luck tonight! Come to mummy, Mattieboy!' when I clock his plain, mousey girlfriend who he then smiles at adoringly. I wait for my date with my fourth frothy sugar-laden hot chocolate of the week, already feeling despondent. I wonder if all I'm going to get from this blind dating crap is a couple of pounds of fat around my midriff and diabetes. Then a man with a big reddish beard and chubby white calves walks past me. 'Please God, don't let it be him!' I silently pray. (I've detected a sly pattern with these guys—they fake their photos, sending a male model's shot, when in reality they look like Robin Cook.) A man in khaki shorts, long white socks and brown open-toed sandals makes prolonged eye contact with me as he slowly passes—jeez, pleeaaase, don't let it be him either! I can feel my heart palpitating and feel sick.

And this, my friends, pretty much encapsulates the build-up to all my blind dates. By the time the actual date arrives I'm a nervous wreck and just happy to see he's mediocre-looking rather than a hobo hillbilly. My victims (no,

I'm the victim here!) so far include:

'Energy Boy' Kris from Norway—chose to meet me in a bar so dark I could barely make out his features. In fact, I wouldn't recognize him in daylight if I were to meet him again. I learnt that Norway has a lot of oil, shipping and salmon—kind of interesting, kind of not. He smoothly plied me with Cosmopolitans and we shared a taxi to our respective homes. On drawing up at my place he whispered in my ear, 'Let's go to bed now, baby.' I agreed I was sleepy, too, and pecked him on the cheek saying, 'Good night.' He pulled me to him and kissed me on the mouth, then accidentally burped—gross! I never heard from him again. Maybe he was married? Maybe he thought if I wasn't up for a one-night stand I was frigid? Who gives a flying fuck.

'Loverboy' Dave from Oz—kicked off our date warning me he had verbal diarrhoea. What he neglected to add was that he was the most boring conversationalist on the face of the planet. He was at least ten years older and twenty pounds heavier than in the photo he'd sent (the second photo, that is. The first one was headless, with just him in his tight, white y-fronts—probably with a big woolly sock shoved down the front—and a six-pack, believe me, long gone). If he ever gets married I'll buy his wife a wedding gift—a lifetime's supply of earplugs. Lessons learnt: never go out with a guy who admits to verbal diarrhoea, and the camera does lie.

'Junior' from Washington—itched and scratched throughout our date, reminding me of Tom Hanks in 'Philadelphia'. Shirt open to the waist revealing picked red zits. I learnt that he loves hunting and fishing and sucking toes. Certainly won't be mine.

'Doctor Denver' Kevin from, you guessed it, Denver—told me he'd be wearing green pants to the coffee bar (Christ, is he really going to turn up just in his undies? I panicked. And green isn't a particularly promising colour, is it?) Turns out the doctor needed a check-up from the neck up.

'Dr Love' Klaus from Austria—a heart surgeon without a heart (he wasn't at all interested in me!). He made me feel a bit thick (now I know how my sisters must feel all the time). He told me he liked to collect human skulls—I ran. Enough of this skulduggery, it's giving me a headache.

'Peter Piper' Patrick from New York—freaked me out telling me four times that he'd like to put me in a warm bath back in his hotel room. Definitely something out of a B-movie where I end up knifed twenty times in the tub, with the water turning ketchup red. I told him I'd just bathed and left quickly.

'Don Juan' Donnie from New Zealand—Adonis! His movie-star looks took my breath away. Definitely the most handsome guy on earth (and I'm serious). I couldn't wait to get my hands on him... only to discover he's hung like a sparrow. Just my bloody luck.

'Jack the Lad' Jack from Scuddersfield—certainly not a lad! Paint him green and you'd have Shrek. Honest to God, spitting image. Super guy—would treat me like a princess, but I just can't go there, even with the bedroom lights off.

'Scarface' Spencer from North London—I met while utterly sozzled and thought he looked just like Tom Cruise. Woke up in bed with him the next morning and realized he actually looked like Freddie Mercury. After having pretty hot sex, the cheeky git turned his snake-like yellow eyes to me and said, 'Oi, darling, you're a bit chubby and pasty, aren't you,' and I retorted, 'That's rich coming from you—you're no oil painting!' He popped Viagra like Tic-Tacs and we stayed in bed all day having mild to medium hot sex eight times. He still had an erection as he dressed to leave. 'Sorry darling, you're binned,' he half jested as he prepared to run for the hills. 'Whatever...' I responded sadly. For some strange reason I warmed to this little monkey. Lessons learnt: excessive alcohol consumption distorts reality; Viagra is great if you need to make up for a shag famine; little ugly guys can be just as mean to you as tall handsome guys.

'Ladykiller' Benny from Holland—whose code name (and name for that matter) were somewhat bloody frightening, sending out extremely strong warning signals. But (thank you, God!) he turned out to be a total fox! Handsome, charming, successful, supremely confident, intelligent, fun, funny—simply too good to be true. A dreamboat, crumpet, hottie, tip-top, the nuts, the dog's dangleys. A sure-fire candidate for the position of Mr Rebound Man.

Suddenly schlepping my wares through humiliating and depressing blind dates has all become worthwhile. I've hit the jackpot (g-spot next I hope!). Benny and I start dating immediately and I'm back to being a starry-eyed gal. 'Benny'—it has a certain exotic uniqueness to it, doesn't it? (I'm kidding myself, I really keep thinking of that retard in 'Crossroads'.) 'Benny Ringenssen'—it has a certain ring to it, doesn't it?

Silly name or not, big Benny certainly knows a thing or five hundred about using his tool. He has a magnificent manhood and is phenomenal with it! He deftly moves me into positions I didn't know my body was capable of achieving (I'm discovering I'd be good at advanced Yoga). Our chemistry is so strong we experience hot sex like something straight out of a porno movie (a good one without a white sports sock in sight). Every cell in my body responds to him and my skin burns for his touch. I love him fucking me. I'll do anything he asks, he turns me on so much. He makes me feel sexy and wonderful. And in between our wanton sex sessions Benny treats me to dinners and makes me laugh. If I bump into James I'll say, 'Honey, you're a novice in the bedroom compared to Benny,' (maybe I'd miss out the 'Benny' part), 'You may have A-Levels in the subject but Benny has a Masters.'

Ah! There's nothing like the mystery and excitement of getting to know a new man to put your ex out of your mind! Benny's unbelievably good looking (black hair and blue eyes), funny (for a Dutch man), intelligent (compared to me), successful (he can afford to pay his rent on time), and fantastic in bed (don't get me started again)—could he be the perfect man?! Benny well and truly gets me back in the saddle (and saddle sore!).

It's great to take pride in myself again—shedding a few pounds (sexercise certainly beats going to the gym) and limiting my chocolate binges to every other day rather than twice a day (on a good day), buying trendy new clothes and sexy underwear, wearing cute high-heeled shoes (otherwise known as 'fuck me shoes' as when you walk in them you go,

'Ouch, ouch, ouch, fuck me! These shoes fucking kill my feet!'). I feel alive again, such a girlie girl. We spend blissful dates together (mainly in bed) and I rarely think of James (the bastard). Benny is indeed heaven sent.

Benny and I go out for long expensive dinners, spend time relaxing by the pool and kiss in the Jacuzzi (and more). We talk about anything and everything and wear the bed out. I'm having an absolutely lovely time with him and am convinced he is indeed the perfect rebound man, perhaps even the perfect man. He asks me to get a Brazilian wax (actually he said 'That's an order!' Mmm). I'm not so keen on looking like a three year old, but since it's the current fashion and I really, really like him, I do it anyway.

Had I known how bloody painful having every last pubic hair ripped away from my poor pussy was going to be I'd have told Benny, 'You first, buddy!' In fact, had I even considered what a Brazilian wax involved I would have run a mile. They should at least put you under general anaesthetic and give you painkillers for a week afterwards. My poor little beaver glows red raw for days—not very attractive. I end up having to make love to Benny in semi-darkness, but the sex is still amazing (as always, ha ha, got you foaming at the mouth in jealousy yet?).

We spend the whole day and night together on the best date I've ever been on in my life (they do say with the Rebound Man you get rather too enthusiastic, but it was a truly fab day!)—chilled out, plenty of laughter and giggles, great sex, good food. Wow, there is a God looking down on me and making up for James's meanness (bastard!).

Chapter 13

May
Unlucky!

My story ends at Chapter 13, which is quite appropriate, as it seems I'm destined to be unlucky.

After three months of glorious dating (venue: his bedroom) full of excitement, fun and laughter, Benny calls me to say what a great time he's had with me (yippee!), that he's not up for a relationship (what? Did I hear him right?) and that he doesn't want to see me any more (oh!). I'm too shocked to speak. How can he do this after we had the best date ever together? He doesn't respond to my subsequent phone calls, texts, emails or my banging on his front door late at night—and I get the message. I'm gutted.

I want to ask the usual hysterical twenty questions: Why? What's wrong with me? Why can't you love me? Do you realize how much you've hurt me? Don't you realize I'm heartbroken? etc. I really, really liked him. Perhaps, I loved him a little already as I feel like a bit of my heart's been chipped away (three months' worth). The most terrible thing of all is that I'll have to go back to blind dating! I cry my eyes out (over both Benny and that miserable prospect). How can I be this emotional over a man I've only known for a few months? Why am I always crying over a man? I cannot continue to live my life like this. It's breaking my heart.

So, Mr Too Good To Be True turns out to be Mr Too Bad

To Be True. I try to take solace in 'There are plenty more bastards in the sea' (my favourite saying and one I return to quite often, as you know). Benny even left his boxer shorts and toothbrush at my place—I'd mistakenly read this as a very good sign, great progress in fact, like he was putting down roots. I end up hugging his boxer shorts in bed (even if they are a bit fruity), blubbering for what might have been.

I try my hand (mind?) at telepathy, asking him to realize he's being a total idiot, a sad wanker, and that he wants me back. It doesn't work. The most gutting thing of all is I had all my flaming pubes painfully whipped off especially for him and then he immediately went and dumped me! My pussy looks like a plucked chicken and is a constant reminder of him, sexy Benny. It's almost a movie theme: the perfect man always gets his conquests to get a Brazilian wax and then dumps them immediately afterwards. He's clearly psychologically damaged!

And that's another thing—I've never been dumped, not really (James doesn't count because I would have gone anyway). My untarnished record is now broken. Dumped! Bugger! I guess there's a first time for everything. I will now be able to truly empathise with my girlfriends when they get the heave-ho from their scumfriends, I mean 'boyfriends'. Oh my God! That psychic, Annie Thingumajiggy, told me to avoid a man with black hair and blue eyes—it was Benny! Fucking Benny! Wowzers, she was right! I just wish I'd remembered her advice at the time. I must start doing crosswords to improve my memory.

I cry, feeling extraordinarily sorry for myself. I miss James. He always had a tender hug and a wink for me, even when we were on the rocks. Suddenly, in a moment of madness, I'm convinced I want him back.

```
From:     emilygreenhk@hotmail.com
To:       James1969@yahoo.com
Subject:  Big Bear
```

Darling Big Bear,

Well, you certainly live and learn. You know it's

either all or nothing with me—I've been on a gruelling dating spree using your close friend, the Internet. And you know what? Sex with someone new is absolutely fantastic to the point where I'm wanting it far too much (just like our early days!) and am up for anything. But one thing I've learned from Dave from Oz, Kris from Norway, Benny from Holland, and Peter Piper from fuck knows where, is that while sex can be red-hot, wanton, insatiable stuff, it's the other things that matter the most by far—like larking, tickling, shrieking with laughter, airport stickers secretly stuck on backs, Frank Drebbin, Blackadder, Ricky Gervais, night time cuddles, running jokes, you correcting my mixed metaphors, snuggling up close, Big Bear & Little Bear, waggling your floppy ears, Babyface & Squeaker, stocking up on your favourite Magnums and Cornettos. Just having something in common to talk about (house prices in London, your mate Tony Blair) and with someone intelligent (opposites attract). The little things are the big things.

And what else have I learnt? That I felt inhibited and rejected when you complained about sex becoming samey, and it then became a chore rather than just great fun. And I actually enjoy a good party! I've been to a lot of fab parties and BBQs with a fun, intelligent and talkative expat bunch, without an air-headed gold-digging girlfriend in sight—and realize most of your buddies are plain old boring, just wanting hardcore drinking with the Wanchai whores and nothing else (no wonder I didn't want to go out with them!). And that I spent too many hours doing your laundry (including soaking your pants in 'Vanish') instead of talking to you. And that your exasperation at how long I took in the bathroom (even though you liked the end result) meant I didn't spend as much time on myself as I would have liked. And that when you

> find someone you love, you forego some social events to spend time just with them.
>
> I know for certain you will not meet anyone quite like me again, or have someone who cares about you so much. This will hit you in a year or two when the shagging around starts to feel empty and samey. It's a tragic shame you're on the path to self-destruction and that you won't value 'us' until it's too late.
>
> And lastly, love never dies, no matter how hard you try to deny it.
>
> Love
>
> Emily xxxxxxxxxxxxxxxxxxxxxxxxxxxxxxxxxxxxxxxx xxxx

James doesn't respond. I wonder if the letter I sent to his parents has blown my chances of a reconciliation. I take a peek at the letter again—Jaysus, Mary, Joseph and a little donkey! I haven't looked at it since I sent it and nearly puke my heart up. While it is an honest account (that's my feeble defence) it is harsh (honest but very harsh). I imagine Kaye immediately faxed it to James and then phoned him (reverse charges) to sob hysterically and tell him how hurt she is, and can he pay off her mortgage to make her feel better. I imagine Derek felt remorse at how he'd shaped his son's view of women pre-Maureen. Maureen would be happy at all the horrible things said about Kaye, and secretly happy that Derek has neglected his son for her. James would feel—punched in the gut? Thinking murderous thoughts towards me? In mega deep shit with his parents for the rest of his natural life? I don't know what really happened, but certainly he won't be a happy bunny with me. And then there's the small issue of the pierced condoms. Did he find out? For his sake I hope so; for mine I hope not. He'd definitely want to hunt me down and murder me. He'd make it his life's mission.

Surely I'm not the only woman who has committed a crime of passion? Think of Britain's very own Ruth Ellis (who was hanged for her payback method). At least I didn't murder James—I just fantasized about it and surely that doesn't count. So I'm not so bad after all—am I? I recently read in a women's magazine about a housewife who found out her husband was cheating on her. She prepared a delicious meal for him—a crusty potato-topped pie, with an attractive parsley garnish, sautéed onions, mince meat fried in a little extra virgin olive oil, and a huge log of dog shit! He ate up every last scrap and commented on how unusual but tasty it was. A few days later the wife told him she knew about his affair but did he know he'd eaten a dog poo pie the other evening? She'll probably end up getting her own cookery TV series (perhaps called 'Pies for Every Occasion').

Apparently vengeance is sweet, but it feels bitter to me. Will he ever forgive me? Will I ever forgive myself? If the saying 'What goes around comes around' is true, then I'm in big fucking trouble. If karma is true, then I'm coming back as plankton. I do still love the naughty monkey deep down. In fact, I miss him desperately.

From: emilygreenhk@hotmail.com
To: james1969@yahoo.com
Subject: Let's forgive and forget...

Dearest James,

I totally and utterly understand the feelings of anger and dismay you must have felt over the letter I sent your folks. I re-read the letter for the first time the other day and nearly puked up my heart. While it was genuinely written out of care for you and is an honest account (I really wanted your parents to take some responsibility for your actions), I felt desperately for you all the same.

I wrote it when I was incredibly angry and very upset. I left the UK with a fabulous man I was convinced I was going to marry and have children with, only for him to change, and for it all to fall horribly to pieces. I felt robbed of my dream. We had the most brilliant start and the most terrible end. We came a long way in a short time, and a long way apart in a short time.

You hurt me. I hurt you back. But I have learnt that two wrongs don't make a right and feel bad. I would like us to understand this, accept it, forgive and move on. I'm not asking to come back to you (would you want this?) or to become great friends (although you are and always will be a friend), but would like to stay in touch and acknowledge we had a meaningful relationship.

Yes, of course I have a rebound man (it's honestly the only way I can cope and move on). He's been great fun for me and yes, sadly, if I'd met him a little sooner then I'd have felt no need to do the things I did. But also remember that you're not whiter than white in all this, and that your actions led me to this. We're equal now, we're quits, we're still us.

There is no going back, but we can go forward salvaging the good memories, forgiving the bad.

Yours

Emily x

From: James1969@yahoo.com
To: emilygreenhk@hotmail.com
Subject: RE: Let's forgive and forget...

Emily, those five years together ceased to count the moment you sent that letter to my parents. It wasn't very clever, was it! What did it achieve—momentary self-satisfaction? I hope so, because it achieved nothing else apart from hurt and pain for everyone else. However, what it did achieve for me was TOTAL CLOSURE ON YOU.

I assume you are now willing to 'forgive and forget' because you have found someone new. Enjoy him and move on PLEASE.

I have no hate for you. I feel nothing any more.

James

My howling sobs can be heard all the way across the harbour in Kowloon.

The thought of bumping into my beloved 'Bastardface'

every which way I turn means I leave (flee is a more appropriate word) Hong Kong. I leave a country I've grown to love because of one silly man. My disastrous track record with men means that at this rate I'll be working my way around the globe (one way to see the world, I guess). By the time I'm forty I'll have run out of countries to escape to and have to become an astronaut to reach Space, the final frontier and only option left for me (I don't think my maths is good enough, though, and I can just about spell 'physics'). Bloody men.

Before I leave, I do all my favourite things in Hong Kong—mainly gorging on food. Curing my addiction to the Mandarin Oriental Cake Shop's raspberry-filled doughnuts is a good enough reason to leave the country. (I've read that Britney Spears went through a similar obsession recently and we both have the zits to prove it.)

It feels like Hong Kong is telling me it's time to go. I go to my favourite beauty salon to find my wonderful therapist Louise has quit and instead I'm allocated a dopey girl who over-zealously massages my butt crack. This is followed by a supposedly relaxing dry-water float, but the bloody thing punctures and rather than leaving me warm and sleepy I feel cold and wet. The horrendous spa experience is finished off with a St. Tropez tan but the spray machine doesn't want to work. Marvellous.

I go to my favourite hairdressers and my usual guy is on holiday (again? We must be giving him too many tips!) and the guy I'm allocated burns my neck with hot tongs, saying to me in a drippy voice, 'Ahh, you've got sensitive skin', (tell me who isn't sensitive to first degree burns!). To top it all, there are posters stuck up all over town advertising children's clothing modelled by none other than that stinky little critter Keanu. He smiles smugly, little snitch, making my blood boil and veins of unsuppressed fury pop up all over my face—if only I had a spray can on me, I'd desecrate the ads, writing 'WORM' and 'MAGGOT' all over them. Hong Kong is definitely sending me a message: 'GO!'

Bugger, I just want a nice man (he must be very handsome, incredibly funny, highly intelligent and amazingly successful, though). I want to get married and be done with all this dating malarkey. I've had enough of it. I want a silly OTT meringue white wedding dress, gigantic chocolate wedding cake topped with millions of 'hundreds and thousands', cheesy 'His' and 'Hers' towels (to sit unused in the airing cupboard for many years until the cat sleeps and pees on them), a Wedgwood dinner set (that reminds me, I must learn to cook) and a gravy boat (to keep loose change and hairy elastic bands in). I want to be a housewife and watch daytime TV all day, nibbling on chocolate digestives and not caring about the size of my thighs.

No I bloody don't! What do I want? Life is pants.

My mobile goes off as I'm waiting to board my plane at the airport. It's Benny.

'Hey Emily,' he says. 'I haven't heard from you for ages, sexy!'

I can't believe my ears. Surely when you dump someone you don't expect to hear from them?

'Look, gorgeous girl,' he goes on, 'I'd love to take you out for dinner—are you free tonight?'

The man must be suffering from amnesia! He dumped me in a heartless thirty-second phone call and now acts like nothing's happened!

'Benny, you're an idiot,' I snap. 'Plus you have a ridiculous name!' I add for good measure, hanging up. I feel a whole lot better about myself.

Life does have its moments.

The End?!

ISBN 141205570-9

Printed in Great Britain
by Amazon